PHILIP COLLINS

The Men From the Boys

HarperCollins*Publishers*

HarperCollins*Publishers*
77–85 Fulham Palace Road,
Hammersmith, London W6 8JB

www.fireandwater.com

This paperback edition 2003
1 3 5 7 9 8 6 4 2

A catalogue record for this book
is available from the British Library

ISBN 0 00 712682 4

Printed and bound in Great Britain by
Clays Ltd, St Ives plc

This novel is entirely a work of fiction.
The names, characters and incidents portrayed in it
are the work of the author's imagination. Any resemblance
to actual persons, living or dead, events or localities
is entirely coincidental.

To my parents

Acknowledgements

For a solitary exercise, writing a novel generates a lot of debt. The sharp and cogent reviews of David Farr, Sarah Fitzpatrick, Richard Kelly and Matthew Wheeler all improved the text a good deal. Joanne Wilson skilfully retrieved the last section when it was eaten by a malicious computer. The vicious attack restored my faith that computers are unlikely to catch on in the longer term. This important issue will have to wait for another book. Geeta Guru-Murthy has shone light on the last days of preparation.

I am enormously grateful for the support and acute critique of my editor, Susan Watt at HarperCollins. The way in which Susan managed to deliver devastating criticism disguised as praise was an object lesson. Thanks go also, for the same reason, to Antonia Loudon.

To my agent Tif Loehnis I owe the largest debt of all. There have been times when her presence in this book has been so strong that it might have been quicker if she had written it herself. I am sure all the words are now right although, as Eric Morecambe once said, they may not necessarily be in the right order.

My family have been a constant source of support and pride. To Min, Jonathan, Elizabeth, David and my wonderful nephews Benjamin and Dominic, thank you. Finally, I dedicate this book to my parents whose personal sacrifices ensured that I have lived my life on the right side of the chasm it describes.

part one: *Blood Brothers*

Just Chips and Gravy

'Where are you going? Come back, you stiff.'

'No chance.'

With Kevin McDermott in close pursuit, Adam Matthews sprinted past the mill in which their grandparents had worked. He blasted into the dark tunnels under the railway bridge where the bats flew at night. As his plastic soles wobbled on the treacherous oil that clung to the stones, sure-footed Kevin McDermott leapt onto him from the back and wrestled him down.

Kevin pressed Adam's newly washed, newly combed brown hair into the rancid moss that gathered on the cobbles in the dirty puddles. If Adam had moved six inches to his left he would have rubbed up against a squashed rat. Two boys unknown to them skidded by on Grifters, their wheels parting the puddles which splashed over Adam's face. Kevin pinned Adam's puny biceps to the floor under the weight of scabby, freckled knees.

'Just . . . just don't. Aaaargghh, that crebs! Stop it!'

'This is your birthday present.'

'Do you surrender?'

'Surrender.'

'Don't trick me again. Right?'

'I won't. I promise.'

'Are you coming then?'

'I don't want to.'

Kevin took Adam's arm and twisted it behind his back. The

effort of trying not to shake with fear was making Adam shake. Adam begged even louder.

'Just stop it will you? I said "surrender".'

Kevin rocked back and forth, taunting his easy prey. He feigned to pull back his fist but, just as his mock punch was about to land, felt an adult hand lift him under the socket of the arm.

'What the bloody hell? Get off, you bloody hooligan.'

Bob Matthews walked through the tunnels late every afternoon on his way home from work.

'Get up out of that filth, Adam.'

Bob pulled Adam up with his spare hand. Adam rubbed the knots in his stringy muscles and tried not to look humiliated as the three of them emerged at the top of the incline into the grey light of the main Bolton road. Adam snivelled through the streets. Even at walking pace the hissing roar of his own alarmed breath seemed to play at an overwhelming volume.

'Dad, we were only play-fighting.'

'It didn't look like that to me.'

Ten minutes beforehand Adam had been swapping football stickers with his best friend in their den, enthralling Kevin with his ability to retrieve the names of exotic foreign teams from memory. But then Kevin had finally realised, by saying it out loud for the first time, that the reason nobody had an Ivan Olegs sticker was that Ivan Olegs was Adam's invention rather than Dynamo Kiev's centre forward.

'I wasn't really after him, Mr Matthews. Honest.'

'We'll see what your father has to say about it shall we?'

Suspended from Bob's grip, Kevin's feet floated six inches above the cracked pavement for the five-minute journey back home. Kevin McDermott lived on the Harwood estate in Brandlesholme where the streets were littered with cheap debris and the walls were adorned with parochial, usually misspelled, graffitti: 'Brangy born and bread'. Every house was the same: semi-detached with a wild, overgrown lawn at the front and a stone yard at the back. As Bob pulled Kevin up the garden path, the trellis door flapped insistently in the wind, a noisy reminder of the inattentive landlord.

Bob rapped on the regulation grey door which opened straight onto a dark living room in which the loose window frames reverberated to the wind and the television shouted unheard in the corner. Kevin's sisters, Irene, Maria and Tina, fought for a space by the heater as Sammy McDermott warmed up for one of his legendary rants.

'I'm not having no darkies in this family.'

'You're an ignorant bastard, you are,' spat back his eldest daughter, Irene.

'At least I'm not a slag who drops her keks for the first nig-nog who comes calling.'

'I hate you. Tell him, Mum.'

Wendy McDermott put down the pan she was wielding and went to the door. Irene threw a cup of tea at her father who responded by chasing her upstairs. Armed with prejudice, Sammy battered his pregnant daughter down. He wanted her to have an abortion because of hatred that was a long time in the learning.

Sammy McDermott came downstairs in violent steps. Kevin's dad had a way of moving which meant that even everyday actions, like changing the television channel, seemed to contain a threat. He had angry skin, in which pinched features bubbled and disappeared, and a large red nose that looked set to burst. His wide face sat on thick shoulders with no visible support from a neck. He lifted his hooded eyes at the sight of Bob holding Kevin by the back of his neck.

'Take your fucking hands off that lad, Matthews.'

'You can tell where he gets his manners from.'

'Take your fucking hands off him.'

'Or else what exactly?'

'Or else I'll be doing more than holding you by the scruff of the fucking neck.'

'You want to get a grip of him.'

'Don't tell me how to deal with my own kidda. It's not to do with you.'

'It is when he's beating up my lad.'

'We were only play-fighting,' pleaded Kevin.

'You want to teach your lad not to be such a queer shite and he might not need his fucking pa to run to the fucking rescue.'

Bob had nothing more he wished to say. Sammy did not warrant it. Instead, he raised his hand imperiously as if to say that there was no honour in further questions. Sammy snarled at Bob who did not flinch. Wendy jumped between the two Brangy warriors and tried, not for the first time that day, to repel her husband. Maria and Tina hung onto their father's backside and Wendy to his front as Sammy stomped at Bob.

'You're so fucking high and mighty, you Matthewses.'

Sammy burst through his wife's defences and ran straight into a forearm from Bob. By the time that Sammy had recovered his senses Bob had fled through the front door, back to the other side of the wooden fence that separated their two houses.

When the intrusive audience had departed Sammy pushed Kevin across the room into the decrepit gas fire.

'See what you've fucking done now, you little bastard? Get up them fucking stairs.'

Sammy's arm flashed through the air and the large gold face on his wedding ring broke the skin under Kevin's left eye. Irene, Maria and Tina shrieked as Wendy ran to her son's defence. Kevin swore at his father, ran up the stairs and slammed his bedroom door.

The iron law of gender decreed that Kevin had a room of his own while Irene and Maria had to listen to the cough that ripped the insides off their younger sister's chest. The iron law of poverty meant that there was nothing in Kevin's bedroom except Kevin, a bed and a football kit. And the cold, which announced itself daily. Kevin sobbed gently as he sat staring at the wall, tending his cheek, looking at his own breath.

Adam Matthews lived fifty yards away from Kevin McDermott. Adam's house backed onto Kevin's house. Their yards were joined. But the Matthews house had a lovingly tended garden at the front and a punctiliously swept yard at the back. It had a bold navy-blue door and central heating which Bob Matthews rarely used despite the gnawing pains in his joints that threatened his proud boast never to have taken a day off work in his life. The pavements had to be freezing outside before Bob's radiators came on all over the house. June Matthews, who felt the cold more keenly, had learnt over the years to wear at least two cardigans in winter.

Over fish fingers, chips and beans Bob asked Adam for an explanation.

'So what is it between you and Kevin then?'

'Dad, we were only messing. It was your stupid fault anyway.'

'Don't talk to me in that way, Adam. How could it be my fault?'

'You made Ivan Olegs up. I just pretended to Kevin that he was real. And he started asking everyone at school if they had an Ivan Olegs sticker, and when he worked it out today that I'd made him up he started battering me.'

'You want to be more careful who you trick in future.'

'Kev's a right tapper.'

'What on earth is a tapper, Adam?' asked June, whose slang was out of date.

'It's a nutter, a loony bin.'

'Will you please use proper words, Adam. What have we taught you?'

'In any case, Kevin's not such a bad lad, considering.'

After tea, as soon as Adam had convinced Bob and June that Mrs Rudd had set no homework, he crept down the McDermotts' path as if he was playing furtive in an especially crucial game of hide-and-seek. He tip-toed round to the back, bending double so that Wendy would not see him pass as she washed the pots. Adam straightened up at the back of the house, took a small pebble from the gravel in the yard and cast it at Kevin's window. He was just about to try a larger, and positively risky stone when Kevin opened the window and clambered onto the drain-pipe. The pair of them bent double round the side of the house and ran off through the streets, racing the litter that the wind was raising on the Harwood estate as it swept off the West Pennine Moors.

Adam apologised for his trick and accepted Kevin's terms.

7

He had to do a dare of Kevin's choosing. Kevin led Adam to the Bolton road where he played reckless chicken with the traffic. Adam held back and waited for the little green man on the pelican crossing. With dusk settling, he followed Kevin down the wet slope towards the tunnels. He found his tormentor and best friend standing guard at the dark entrance, pointing ominously into the black.

'I dare you,' said Kevin, patronisingly.

'No.'

'It's a dare.'

Kevin flapped his arms by his sides and made chicken noises. A boy's prestige suffered by refusing a dare but Adam was absolutely not prepared to run through the tunnels under the railway at twilight, when the bats came out. Kevin teased Adam remorselessly for his squeamishness. But the stench of cat piss on abandoned mattresses, the gutter water washing down from the estate above, the luxuriant creepiness of plants that can only grow in the dark and the scuttling rodents emerging from behind half-bricks prevailed over the full embarrassment he felt.

Kevin increased the stakes.

'You can't be my best mate again if you don't do a dare. That's the rules.'

'I'll do one but I can't run through the tunnels in my new trainers.'

Adam offered to walk across the ledge on the outside of the railway bridge instead. This was not much less of a terrible prospect but he had to gain Kevin's respect somehow and at least there were no flying squirrels aimed at his head. Adam swung his leg up onto the top of the bridge while holding on precariously with the opposite hand. This movement produced a whisper of downward momentum so sickening that Adam balked.

'I don't want to do this now.'

'You've got to. You can do it. Go on. Just reach out.'

'Who do you think I am? Stretch Armstrong?'

Adam shuffled, in a slow and demented side-step, across the ledge, encouraged with every faltering foot by his huckleberry friend. At the other end of the bridge, Kevin helped Adam back onto *terra firma*.

'Are we best mates now?'

'You've got to do one more thing. You've got to come and look for the tramp.'

'We're not allowed.'

'You're a right stiff, you are. Come on, it's all reet.'

Kevin pronounced right as 'reet', in imitation of his uncle Bobby, who had assured him that the tramp definitely lived in the old mill by the River Irwell.

Kevin and Adam's grandparents, the Matthewses, the Greenhalghs, the McDermotts and the Powells, had spun Egyptian cotton in the mill. Now it was an exciting, dangerous ruin and Sammy and Bob both forbade visits. the *Bury Times* regularly carried stories about intrepid young boys who fell through the rotten floorboards to be splattered on the stone floor fifty feet below. Kevin and Adam were more fascinated by the tramp than they were frightened by the floorboards. The tramp in the mill was the equivalent of the bogeyman, a mysterious devil substitute. Excited Harwood children recycled the rumours that he had once been seen. He was reputed to be very tall, with a huge, unkempt ginger beard and a long, heavy overcoat, a cross between the children's Bible image of God and Ron Moody playing Fagin. The boys were obsessed by the tramp. It even seemed that Kevin wanted to *be* the tramp.

'I'm going to live in the mill when I grow up.'

'Eurrrgh, it'd be horrible.'

'No it wouldn't. It'd be brill. You could scare everyone off and you'd never have to have a bath.'

Adam already had loftier ambitions, for both of them.

'You're going to play for City anyway.'

'I bet I don't.'

''Course you will.'

'My dad says I won't. He says he used to be brilliant at football but he doesn't play for City.'

'That doesn't mean anything. My dad's not a football commentator but I am going to be.'

9

'How do you do that?'

'You have to go to London.'

'I wouldn't want to go to London. It's crap.'

'You've never been.'

'So? I don't want to.'

'I bet City scouts come to watch Brangy Warriors.'

'Do you reckon?'

'Yeah, course.'

'Oh, right.'

Kevin was the captain of Brangy Warriors under-twelve football team. He was already beginning to attract the local clubs and the attention had gone straight to Adam's head. Adam talked as if Kevin were already on the verge of the England squad.

'Could I play for Brangy Warriors?' Adam wondered.

'I might be able to get you in. You'll have to play better than normal, though.'

'I'm better now. Ivan Olegs has been coaching me in the back yard.'

Kevin suddenly grabbed Adam and rapped his knuckles.

'Aaaargh, that crebs, that does!'

'Beg for mercy, stick insect.'

'Mercy.'

Kevin let Adam go.

'Hey, Kevin. Do you know what a prostitute is?'

'Yeah.'

'What is it then?'

'It's when you have it off.'

'No it isn't.'

'What is it then?'

'It's a woman who's really ugly, like a woman tramp. And you can buy them.'

'I'm not getting married.'

'I'm not either.'

'Come on; let's go and find the tramp.'

At school the previous week, Terry Berry had confirmed that the tramp lived in the tower at the top of the mill. To reach the summit of the mill was an improbable and dangerous climb, to be attempted only by trained mountaineers, tramp super-beings and very determined eleven-year-old boys. Kevin led Adam into the line shafts and out onto the roof. They had both been this far many times but the tower was uncharted. A successful ascent of the tower would make Kevin and Adam the Edmund Hillary and John Hunt of the old mill by the river.

Kevin threw himself up the tower without a hint of fear, as if his very legs were crampons fastening themselves into the gaps in the crumbling brickwork. Adam made his way by stealth, checking every movement meticulously, carefully planning every next step. Close to the top, some loose masonry came away in Adam's hand, giving him a suggestion of mortality and the feeling that he was gasping through his stomach. It didn't help that Kevin, who had by now reached the gantry and was beginning to feel an isolated prey for the cannibal tramp, started to implore him to hurry up.

'Come on, slowcoach.'

'Shut it. I nearly fell then.'

Finally, Adam reached the top and rolled himself over the edge with inexpressible relief. Only the appalling descent to conduct now, if the tramp spared them. As Adam collapsed onto the firm roof Kevin rained down pebbles at his feet.

'Dance.'

Adam danced ridiculously to avoid the stones and used one of the rudest words he knew.

'Cut it out. I'm knackered.'

The top of the tower was a space of a hundred square feet which was empty except for one long-since abandoned old sack. Kevin held the sack up and let its contents fall. A festering collection of old clothes dropped to the floor. This irrefutable evidence that they had invaded the tramp's abode sent the fear of the Devil through Kevin and Adam.

'He's here. Leg it.'

They bolted for the edge. Propelled by gravity and adrenaline the descent was a good deal easier than the climb. On each floor the boys gave a cursory look to check they were not running into the tramp on his way back. They pelted back up the hill, the sludge in the tunnels washing their white trainers as they came to rest finally, safely, in their den on the disused railway line.

'Oh God, I thought he was going to get us. Irene Bradshaw says the tramp eats children if he catches them.'

'You fancy her, you do,' said Adam, meaning that *he* did.

'No I don't. You do.'

'I don't.'

'You do.'

Their den smelt of rotting damp flowers. The alignment of three bushes of weeds and brambles and a single overhanging birch made a perfect shelter, once Kevin had rooted out the dirt, the yellowing grass and the stinging nettles. The den was a fine vantage point for espionage, sitting as it did immediately above the tramp's Victorian palace. Further on, beyond the mill, the two consuls of the den looked out over the meeting point of the Rivers Irwell and Roach, and over Peel Tower atop Holcombe Hill.

'You can look at that when you don't know where you are.'

Adam's dad had told him that if he was ever lost he should look out for Peel Tower, which could guide him home. Adam explained how he used Peel Tower as a compass whenever his mum and dad took him on the bus up through Ramsbottom. Kevin was fascinated by the things that Adam knew about. Kevin had never been to Ramsbottom and it seemed a very long way away.

Kevin reached under the stone floor which had once been part of a coal bunker. A week before he had cleared the dirt out to make a secret storehouse for the cigarettes that his uncles bought for him. He pulled out a pornographic magazine grubby both to the touch and the eye and a rusty compass with a blunt point.

'Give us your arm.'

'What's that effort?'

'We've got to be blood brothers.'

Adam did want to be a blood brother but he wasn't sure about the ceremony. He gave his arm to Kevin as if he never expected it back. Kevin made a small and delicate lesion on

Adam's soft skin, just enough to draw blood. He then made a less careful incision into his own arm and pressed the two red trickles together.

'Blood brothers. That means we have to tell each other everything and we have to help each other and everything. And it lasts for always.'

The sun was going down over the Irwell valley and the blood brothers were sound in their den. Adam's first act of friendship was to read aloud from the copies of *Tiger* and *Scorcher* and *Roy of the Rovers* that Kevin had hidden under the stone floor. With Kevin's encouragement he distinguished between the different characters with funny voices. Adam learnt the joy and the pleasure of unrestrained laughter from Kevin in these moments in their den. He spoke formally and sensibly for Blackie Gray, comedy villain Spanish for Paco Diaz, a glamorous purr for the sexy Mervyn Wallace and an odd Kenneth Williams squeak for his favourite, Tubby Morton, the reserve goalkeeper.

Adam had already paid the wages of cowardice. Now Kevin really tried him.

'Let's sleep here tonight.'

'What about your mum and dad?'

'They won't know. Come on; it'll be brill.'

'I can't. I've got to revise.'

'What for?'

'For my Bury Grammar exam. So have you.'

'I don't care. I'm not doing it.'

'You've got to. Your mum's put you down for it.'

'It doesn't matter.'

'Anyway, we'll get caught. They'll know we're not back.'

'What's up with you? Are you chicken again? I thought we were blood brothers.'

Adam knew that his mother would worry and his father would smack him if he didn't come home. But Kevin was his blood brother. For always.

'What you scared of?'

'I'm not scared.'

'I'll buy you some chips.'

'Have you got any money?'

'My mum gave me some.'

'Brilliant. I'm starving.'

'I'll go and get them. You guard the den. Do you want chips and gravy?'

'Yeah. Thanks Kev.'

' 'S'all right.'

Kevin had enough money to buy one portion of chips and gravy in a tray which, with unheard of self-denial, he managed not to open until he rejoined Adam in their bivouac.

'What d'you get?'

'Just chips and gravy. I didn't have enough for a pudding.'

Adam ripped the newspaper off hungrily and the glorious smell wafted over the disused Heywood-to-Bolton railway line. If there was indeed a tramp in the mill he could scarcely fail to come and join in the feast of perfect chips coated in thick brown gravy from the Golden Moon, not just the finest chip shop in the world but the finest shop of any description. Adam plunged into the tray, dangled a chip into his mouth and licked the gravy off his index finger. To his great surprise, Kevin fumbled inside his parka and produced two plastic forks. *Plastic forks*, costing a penny each, rather than the useless wooden ones that were free.

'I got you one of these.'

'Hey, thanks.'

This was a special occasion for both boys and not only plastic forks made it so. This was the first time that Kevin and Adam had stayed the night in their den.

'It's better here than staying at home. I think my dad might be going away.'

'Where to?'

'I don't know. He said he might go back to Scotland.'

'What, for work?'

'No, to live. Him and my mum are always shouting. And now our Irene's having a kid and my dad says he's having none of it.'

'My mum and dad are always shouting as well.'

'But they're only joking, aren't they?'

'I don't know.'

'They are. They're only joking are your mum and dad.'

Adam rested his hand on Kevin's arm and, though he saw the tear that trickled out of his friend's eye, he had no idea what to say about it. He picked up a comic instead and read aloud from it for as long as the fading light allowed. As the scope of a whole night dawned on Kevin and Adam they rehearsed their repertoire of conversation about motorbikes, football and who might be Cock of the school when they went to Elton Moor.

'Hey, guess what?'

'What?'

'Guess.'

'You fancy Irene Bradshaw.'

'No, I'm gonna offer Terry Berry out.'

'You're mad; he's rock.'

'*I'm* rock. Rocker.'

'Yes, off your rocker,' Adam thought but dared not say. Terry Berry was the undisputed Cock of St Thomas's. He had won the title from the once invincible Wayne Nuttall in an impromptu scrap one Friday playtime. Terry Berry was untouchable. He was, it was universally agreed and Kevin was no dissenter, *an absolute tapper*. Adam let the topic pass in the hope that Kevin would come to his senses. He resumed his Tubby Morton impression, which at least managed to change the subject.

Without bed clothes or anything more comfortable to settle on than brambles, stone and dirt, sleep was impossible. Peel Tower disappeared into the dark and the moon came up in a perfect crescent. The descent of night brought out the demons.

'I hope the tramp doesn't come.'

'He won't. He won't be able to see.'

'He might have a torch.'

'Tramps can't afford torches,' said Adam confidently.

'What was that?'

Every rustling blade of grass in the wind was amplified by

the sensitivity of fear. Adam, no less apprehensive but sensing that he was suddenly in charge, tried to allay Kevin's concerns.

'It was just the wind.'

'It wasn't. Listen. There's someone coming.'

Kevin was right. They heard the sound of large boots moving frantically over dried grass, kicking pebbles and stumbling on muddy ruts. Kevin and Adam conjured up tramps in their own imaginations.

'He's coming. What we going to do?'

'Shhh. Don't talk.'

Kevin stopped talking and let his chattering teeth make all the noise. The tramp's big boots got closer and closer. Adam took his blood brother's hand. The tramp seemed magnetically trained on their den and the crunching of boots on broken branches was head-splitting. Kevin was all set to give himself up to his fate and allow himself to be cannibalised when the tramp shouted out from the dark.

'Adam!'

'That's your dad.'

'Shhhh.'

'Adam, is that you? Adam. Come on, son. Where are you? Stop being such a bloody fool.'

Bob never swore within earshot of his son. Adam gulped at the realisation that he must be very mad.

'We're in here,' said Kevin.

Bob hacked away the overhanging birch and swept up the black outlines of two children.

'I'm really sorry, Mr Matthews.'

'You bloody fool, Adam. What do you think me and your mother have been thinking?'

Kevin and Adam were delighted to have been rescued. The tramp was on his way even now, to be sure.

Bob marched the two little drifters back down the railway line and through the fence onto the Harwood estate. He took Kevin home, where his return did not stir much of a commotion, and then took hold of Adam.

'Get inside now, young man.'

Adam knew where he would spend the next few evenings and he knew what colour his backside would be. After Bob and June made him cry by expressing their disappointment that he should be so thoughtless, Adam was sent to his room where, he saw, June had taken away all his books as an extra punishment.

Cock of St Thomas's

The next morning, Adam came out of his front door just as Kevin was passing by on his way to school. Kevin did not even look up. He was away with a dream of the day to come. Today, Monday 11 April 1978, was the biggest day of Kevin McDermott's life. Today was the day on which he was going to challenge the mighty Terry Berry to defend his title of Cock of St Thomas's primary school.

'I'm going to offer Terry Berry out today.'

'What for?'

'I'm Cock. I want to have him.'

'He can have you though. He can have anyone.'

'He can't have Tez Satchel.'

Nobody could have Tez Satchel. Tez Satchel was the Cock of all Bury. Every part of town had its prevailing terrorists but the Cocks of all Bury were the family gang led out of Brandlesholme by Tez Satchel. Nobody really knew how many mad big brothers Tez Satchel actually had but everyone was sure there were plenty of them. There was Ray, who was in Strangeways for an unspecified crime of unspeakably frightening violence. There was Lewis, who rushed down from Middleton whenever trouble flared. There was Jermaine, who was entirely fictional as far as anyone knew. Jermaine was a synonym for viciousness. If Ray and Lewis were not threatening enough, the spectre of Jermaine was truly terrifying. The fact that nobody had ever actually clapped eyes on Jermaine only added to his lustre.

And then there was Tez himself. Adam had been surprised

when he had seen the fabled Tez Satchel for the first time. Tez was small and squat, even a bit fat, with a round, crumpled, jolly face. Tez looked more like a stand-up comic than a small-town madman. It didn't help that he was named after a girl's bag. Adam called him Tez Handbag but only when none of the Handbag brothers was actually present.

The attendants to Tez Satchel were more respectful because Tez was, in their own word, mental. Tez prowled the concrete precinct with cowed myrmidons, each one wearing a mask of viciousness, at either side. They walked by rocking back on their heels, their shoulders slightly stooped, their heads swaying ostentatiously, almost absurdly, from side to side. It was the work of a drunk or incompetent puppeteer. Kevin McDermott aspired to do the walk of the Cocks with the Cock of the walk. But it was unheard of to be a courtier to King Tez without reigning supreme in your own school. Kevin's membership of the gang was conditional on him displacing Terry Berry. The only trouble was that Terry Berry was really hard. Terry Berry had been Cock of St Thomas's for most of the fourth year and that was absolutely *ages*.

Kevin spent assembly going over tactics in his head and, by the first playtime, had convinced himself that Terry Berry could be vanquished. He went out to play football in the playground simmering gently, set to boil after school. Adam engineered himself onto the same team as Kevin and then risked Kevin's irritation by scoring an own goal to put the opposition, who were pretending to be Manchester United, a goal to the good. Kevin answered with a brilliant equaliser, an overhead kick that he called a Dennis Tueart, and a winner that was even better. Kevin McDermott was the best footballer at St Thomas's by some distance. He was captain of Bury Boys and had already drawn the attention of the scouts at Manchester City. Eleven-year-old boys in Bury distinguish themselves through football and fighting. As he was now about to call Terry Berry into the ring for the Cock fight, Kevin McDermott was as close as St Thomas's came to having an aristocratic pupil.

The game finished 2–1 to Manchester City. Mrs Rudd ended

playtime with a shrieking whistle and Class 8 lined up to be led back inside.

'Why do we have to line up, miss?' asked Adam.

'Because you do.'

'But why?'

'Why is it always "why" with you, Adam Matthews?' said Mrs Rudd with a smile.

Adam was still waiting for a satisfactory answer beyond the fact that Mrs Rudd said so, when Kevin muscled his way in behind him.

'Will you let us copy?'

'All right then.'

'Ace.'

'But don't copy all of them or else Speccy Four Eyes'll know. Just copy some.'

Every day after playtime Mrs Rudd treated Class 8 to half an hour of loopy handwriting practice and a multiplication test. On the classroom wall a vast chart mocked the least gifted, illuminated by the brilliant orange stars against the names of those who knew all twenty-four answers. Adam was the cynosure of mental arithmetic; his stars trailed across the page as on a beautiful clear night. Next to Kevin's name there was an unbroken expanse of black cloud. Mrs Rudd did not appreciate how much Kevin resented this reminder of his stupidity.

Alphabetical serendipity meant that Adam and Kevin sat next to one another in class. As Mrs Rudd rubbed the Romans off the board the boys shuffled their desks within easy sight of one another. Adam usually laid his head on his work to conceal it from Kevin on one side and from thick Shaun Masters on the other. Today he curled his right arm around his answers to protect them only from Shaun's prying eyes. Mrs Rudd went rat-a-tat-tat through the times tables, never pausing for breath as she chastised recalcitrant children.

'Eight sixes. I don't think you'll find eight sixes by looking out of the window, Irene Bradshaw. Nine sevens. Twelve elevens. Have we quite finished, Terry Berry? I don't suppose Paul Cornish knows the answer any more than you do, so we can stop whispering right now, thank you very much. Five eights. Put that chewing gum on my desk, Sandra McEwan. Six nines. Keep your eyes to yourself, Kevin McDermott.'

'I'm not copying, miss.'

'I'd better not find that you are. Right, Class 8, a hard one to end with. Thirteen sevens. Do your best, Shaun.'

Kevin wrote down a hundred and one a fraction of a second behind Adam and sat back in triumph as Mrs Rudd told Class 8 to put their pencils down and redistribute the scripts for marking. Kevin had never before reached double figures but he had a surprise for Mrs Rudd today, his day of days.

'Shaun Masters.'

'Seven, miss.'

'Well done, Shaun. That's getting better.'

'Adam Matthews.'

'Twenty-three, miss.'

'Twenty-three, Adam?'

'I got the last one wrong, miss. I put a hundred and one.'

'Oh dear. You're slipping. We'll have your father down here again if you don't pull your socks up.'

Adam knew that Mrs Rudd was joking. Mrs Rudd was always joking about sums with Adam.

'Kevin McDermott.'

'Twenty-three, miss.'

'Which one did you get wrong, Kevin?'

'The last one, miss.'

'See me at the bell, Kevin.'

The dinner bell sounded, promising quiche Lorraine and semolina that turned pink when mixed with jam. As Adam dallied around his desk, trying to convince himself that he wasn't really hungry, Kevin hung his head for Mrs Rudd's perfunctory ticking-off. When she had finished, Kevin initiated proceedings.

'Get everyone to come and watch the scrap. Tell Shaun Masters to find a place.'

Shaun Masters was seven out of twenty-four at multiplication but he was full marks at organising fights. Cock of the school was an important honorary position and a contest had to be

organised properly. Shaun earmarked a patch of grass behind
Class 1 that was large enough for a crowd but secluded enough
to escape the attention of any teachers who were staying late
after school. It was also vital to avoid Kevin's mum who cleaned
his classroom on the other side of the building.

Kevin wagged reading groups for the afternoon to seek last-
minute advice from his uncle Bobby, who had reached his own
zenith as Cock of St Thomas's fourteen years previously. Kevin
wrestled with Tyke, his uncle Greg's bulldog, as Bobby gave
him a lesson in Cock fighting. Meanwhile, Terry Berry got in
the mood by sitting in the doorway of the newsagents on the
parade, systematically dismantling three sherbert dips.

Adam took his job as fight lieutenant very seriously and
canvassed everyone in the fourth year to ascertain whether their
support could be guaranteed. The best thing about being Kevin's
agent was just being Kevin's agent. The second best thing about
it was that it gave him an excuse to talk to Irene Bradshaw. All
the boys at St Thomas's fancied Irene Bradshaw although few
of them would admit it to one another.

Amidst the pallor and crushed ugliness of the Harwood estate,
Irene Bradshaw was the one that got away. The joke about Irene
was that she had eaten too many black peas. This was a reference
to her skin, which she had inherited from Gypsy Joe of the fair,
the father she had never known. Irene's mother Dawn had briefly
joined the travelling fair, the peripatetic orphanage which came
through Bury in March and September of every year. Dawn
discouraged all mention of Gyspy Joe, muttering darkly about
his problems with drugs. But for all Dawn's efforts to erase the
great love of her life, her Irene was his living image. Irene's
natural ringlets hung down in jet black twirls over her deep tan
skin, threatening to droop over her eyes as purely coloured
as piano keys. Irene had a charming, girlish way of blowing
her hair up off her face. She had a little black mole over the
left-hand side of her upper lip and a smile that lit up the
Harwood estate.

Adam was at the age where the notion that girls were smelly
creatures who spent their days doing handstands against the

wall and showing their knickers was starting to give way to the idea that there might be more to it than that. Adam sunk his chin onto his collar bone as he approached a giggling gaggle of girls.

'Are you on Kevin's side in the scrap?'

'Deffo. He's easy going to win. He's rock, Kev.'

Adam borrowed one of Kevin's words to demonstrate that he too was rock.

'He's going to fucking batter him.'

Irene pulled her face at Adam's language. Irene never swore. She was the illegitimate daughter of an itinerant fair gypsy and a coarse Brangy woman but, all her life, Irene reserved profane language for severe provocation. Unless it was really important Irene Bradshaw *never* swore.

'Well . . . errr . . . see you, right?'

Adam became an idiot at once. Irene Bradshaw could take away his power of speech just by blowing her hair up off her face.

The speechless idiot continued his poll of allegiance until the bell rang for afternoon reading groups. Adam sat alone, having completed all the working exercises, reading an abridged version of *David Copperfield*. He had started calling his mother Betsey Trotwood, at which June smiled indulgently although, never having read Dickens, she did not know whether she should be pleased or not. But today Adam did not read a great deal more about the young David's adventure. He was nervous. He found it hard to concentrate. Terry Berry was *really rock*.

Ten minutes after the school bell sounded Adam assembled Kevin's supporters behind Class 1. The crowd of baying children is an integral part of the Cock fight. Their behaviour is ritualistic and always the same. They gather in a circle which slowly declines in diameter until one of the combatants lashes out at the compressing crowd, who veer backwards, like an excitable game of ring-a-ring o'roses. All the time they keep up the hypnotic cry.

'Barney, barney, barney, barney!'

This is the war-cry designed to bring others to the fray. As everyone knows about the fight in advance save the teachers it is a strangely pointless form of advertising.

The crowd was already getting restless but, with immense self-possession, Shaun Masters called for order. He brought the two candidates together into the centre of the circle and pushed the crowd back to give the fighters room enough to hurt one another.

'Right. No girl-fighting. No scratching; no pulling hair; no kicking. First to give in loses.'

'What if no one gives in?' asked Kevin, betraying his respect for his opponent's renowned endurance and pointing out that he would rather die than give way.

'Then it's a draw. And it's up to me to say when.'

A draw was no good. A draw was only ever a deferral while a rematch was arranged. During the *interregnum* the title of Cock was shared but this was unsatisfactory to all, including the two Cocks. Nobody wanted to be half-Cock.

Shaun Masters declared the barney on and Terry Berry and Kevin McDermott tore into each other like fighting cocks. Terry struck the first effective blow, knocking Kevin to the ground with a left hook out of nowhere. The two of them struggled on the wet floor, their dervish thrashings turning the green canvas into a mud bath. The crowd quickly divided into its respective camps and minor skirmishes broke out between the two sides. After a couple of minutes both pugilists had become unrecognisably caked in mud and Kevin was getting on top, literally, as he lay on Terry, suffocating him into submission. It was a slow maceration in mud. Kevin was weighed down by the mud clinging to the pockets of his Oxford bags and his yellow Adidas T-shirt turned a filthy brown.

Terry's legs twitched and jerked ferociously in the attempt to escape Kevin's enemy hug. Suddenly the demons sprung into life and Kevin unleashed volley after volley of blows onto Terry's muddied torso. With angry freckles and a grown-out skinhead escaping in the wind, Kevin looked like he was on fire. An eleven-year-old boy's pained yelp rang out across the football field as the crowd sung on its mantra anthem: 'Barney, barney, barney, barney!'

Kevin rained down punches onto Terry, to his body, then to his face. Terry took the punishment at first as a man, with spitting defiance, then as a boy, with tears. For a thankfully fleeting instant Terry lay motionless. And then, the concession. Terry held up his hand in a gesture of submission, to say no more, to say that you, Kevin McDermott, are from this moment on the undisputed Cock of St Thomas's primary school.

With skin as greasy as his diet, short red hair and pale blue eyes shining out from a desert of sandy freckles in sunken cheeks that were slowly acquiring poverty's hollow, Kevin was an unlikely Lothario. Mere appearance, though, was overwhelmed by grandeur. Irene Bradshaw came out of the crowd and placed a soft kiss on Kevin's lips which was all the more captivating for being so unexpected.

'I knew you'd be Cock. You can be my boyfriend now.'

And with that promise, Irene blew her hair fetchingly out of her eyes and disappeared back into the barney assembly, wiggling her bottom flirtatiously. Kevin watched her go, his mouth agape. As Irene wiggled out of sight the boys made the noise that boys make when they are embarrassed about girls.

Terry Berry picked himself up slowly, with honour and dignity intact. Kevin held out his hand magnanimously to Terry who took it. It had never been personal. The noise of primeval advertising gave way to cheers of recognition for the new champion. The Cock was dead. Long live the Cock. Kevin McDermott stood in triumph, raised his arms in the air and saluted his people. He was a boy at the top of his powers, Cock of the school.

But just as Kevin's hand was raised in salute Mrs Rudd appeared. She had been alerted by Mrs Greenhalgh, the scary cleaner of Class 1, that there was trouble brewing on the other side of school.

'Leg it!' cried a voice from the crowd.

In the chaos, Adam turned to flee, ran bang into Sandra McEwan and bore the full brunt of the collision. Sandra ran away with the rest but, by the time Adam had come round, Mrs Rudd was standing over him. The whole scene was otherwise deserted, seconds after the sighting of the teacher. The bushes were hiding a host of children hurting themselves trying not to giggle.

'Right then, Adam, you can tell me what's going on here.'

'Nothing, miss.'

'I wasn't born yesterday, Adam. Who was it?'

'I don't know, miss.'

'I want to know who was fighting. I'm not bothered by all those watching but I want to know who was fighting.'

Twenty yards away, Kevin McDermott and Terry Berry were wrapped together in a prickly bush. They could hear every word of this exchange.

'If you don't tell me, Adam, then you'll be the one in trouble. I don't suppose it was you who was doing the fighting, was it?'

'No, miss.'

'So who was it?'

'Don't know, miss.'

'I'm warning you, Adam. We might have to think again about you having the day off to go to the grammar school. Who was it?'

'Don't know, miss.'

'If you don't tell me who was fighting I'll be going straight down to see your mum and dad. Now you don't want your dad to know about this do you?'

'No, miss.'

'So get yourself out of trouble and tell me who was fighting.'

Adam said nothing. He was thinking, trying to work out which was the least terrible option. Twenty yards away the Cocks of now and then breathed as quietly as frightened children are able.

'Who was fighting, Adam? Was it Kevin McDermott?'

As soon as Adam heard Kevin's name he decided he would not be a tell-tale. He told his first functional lie and it felt fantastically good.

'No, miss. It wasn't Kevin.'

In a bush, with prickles in his hair, Kevin recognised a blood brother.

27

'So who was it if it wasn't Kevin?'

'I don't know, miss. I don't know who it was but it wasn't Kevin.'

Mrs Rudd called in on June Matthews to say that her son had started to tell lies. As soon as she had seen Mrs Rudd off with her thanks, June uttered the most frightening words in Adam's comprehension, words which promised the return of his father. But Adam knew he had done the right thing when he saw Kevin through the back room window. Kevin's smile and his thumbs raised to the sky were worth a white lie.

Bob Matthews prevailed at once where Mrs Rudd had failed. Adam was astonished at how easily his father detected lies. His dad was practically psychic at times.

'Why didn't you tell Mrs Rudd the truth?'

'Because.'

'Why, Adam?'

'Because.'

'Who do you think you are, the Wizard of Oz? Now you're already in trouble, young man. Don't make it worse for yourself. Why did you lie to Mrs Rudd?'

'Don't know.'

'Has Kevin been threatening you again?'

'I told you, Kevin's not really after me. He's just messing about.'

'So why didn't you tell the truth then?'

'Don't know.'

'Why not, Adam? I'm waiting for a proper answer.'

'He's my friend.'

'It's not five minutes since he had you pinned to the floor of the tunnel.'

'I told you about that. And, anyway, that was yonks ago.'

'You have got to start standing up to Kevin, Adam. Would you jump off a bridge if Kevin McDermott told you to?'

The truth was that Adam might not jump off a bridge but he was certainly prepared to shuffle along the outside ledge if that's what he was told to do.

'And you do not tell lies to Mrs Rudd, do you hear?'

Adam was finding the carpet suddenly fascinating. Bob turned the volume control all the way up.

'I said, do you hear?'

'Yes.'

'Now get up them stairs and don't come down till morning.'

Adam carried a trail of smoke up the stairs into his bedroom where he sat for two hours, looking at his own breath, half-reading the child's copy of *Great Expectations* that his parents had bought him when he was born.

Ally Ally Eeno

Adam was not allowed to play out for a week. He spent every day at school teaching Kevin how to copy unobtrusively but every evening he was condemned to watching the grand Harwood game of hide-and-seek from his bedroom window. Finally, on Saturday night, Adam was permitted to join in but even then Bob made a fool of him by calling him in before anyone else. Adam was regularly embarrassed by his father. Bob was notorious for telling the children of the Harwood estate to play outside their own houses and he objected whenever anyone trampled on his flowers. As Adam slouched towards home, a heavily pregnant Irene McDermott brought the game to a premature end.

'Ally ally eeno.'

These strange words bring everyone out of hiding. They mean that some rule of engagement has not been correctly observed. Ally ally eeno is never a hoax. Nobody ever calls ally ally eeno in jest.

'It's not fair.'

'Life's not fair.'

'Kevin's dad lets him stay out late.'

'Do I look like Kevin's dad?'

Adam's dad did not look remotely like Kevin's dad. Bob Matthews was five feet eight, wiry and slender. He had large, sad blue eyes that sat like bright shells in the rough skin that his son had not inherited. He had wisps of thin hair which flew out in the wind exposing the baldness that was too extensive to be described as a patch.

On the Sunday evening before taking the grammar school exam on the Monday, Adam was allowed a visitor.

'Hello there, Kevin. Ready for tomorrow?'

'Don't know really.'

'Adam's in the front room.'

Adam was lying on the floor in front of the fire snorting at *Songs of Praise* and working through a book of verbal reasoning. He saw both Kevin and an opportunity to impress his parents.

'High is to low what small is to what?'

'What you on about?'

Adam mimed his explanation as he spoke.

'High is the opposite of low isn't it? So it's about opposites. So what's the opposite of small?'

'Big.'

'No, it's large.'

'Why?'

'I don't know. It just is. Big is the opposite of little.'

'But large is the same as big. So why's large the opposite of small but big isn't?'

'I don't know. It just is.'

Kevin could be very obstreperous sometimes.

'I reckon it's big.'

'Look at the answers then.'

'No, you.'

The answer was 'large' but Adam had to admit that he didn't really know why. Apart from the fact that Mrs Rudd had told him, of course. And it said so in the book, which Adam had to concede was not an entirely satisfying reason.

'Come on; let's go out. This is boring. We have enough of skoo in the week.'

Kevin didn't really care about going to the grammar school. He just wanted to go to the same school as Adam. Kevin was only doing the exam because Adam had asked him to. Adam didn't want to go on his own and nobody else from St Thomas's had entered. Kevin reasoned that he might be able to copy because the examiners would not know what score to expect.

'Come on; put it down, you stiff.'

Kevin grabbed the book of sample Bury Grammar School entrance examination questions from Adam and suggested a game of football instead. Adam knew his parents well enough to save him the trouble of asking.

It was all Bob and June could do not to wrap Adam in a ball of wool for the night. For Bob and June tomorrow would be, in two senses, the day of reckoning. They had shuffled their finances night after night to enable them to afford the fees for Bury Grammar School. They had headed down the supermarket class scale from Tesco to Kwik Save. Bob and June were prepared to eat cheap, tasteless baked beans to ensure that Adam was educated, although Adam himself was less keen. They had limited themselves to one night a week in the Greenhill Working Men's Club and Bob had resigned from the committee. He had decided to put the kitchen refurbishment on hold, to spend less on the garden and to make Christmas presents rather than buy them. Whichever way they reckoned up, the sums always came to twelve out of twenty-four. But there was no question that Adam would not go to the grammar school if he passed.

'Do you think he'll pass, love?'

'He'd better. I'm not having him go to Elton Moor. He'll never get on that way. We'll move house if it comes to that.'

'Is it that bad?'

'It's bloody awful.'

'But flitting's a bit drastic isn't it? Can we afford it?'

'We'll cross that bridge when we come to it. We'll have to find some money one way or t'other.'

'It won't be so bad if he gets a bursary.'

'Aye, if them Labourites don't abolish 'em. Let's hope that bloody woman gets in and then that should be all right.'

At eight-fifteen the next morning Adam called for Kevin so they could walk together down to Bury Grammar School. They had the morning off school to go. Adam led the way out of the back of the Harwood estate, down through the smelly tunnels and up the dirt path towards the mill and then across the river.

It was an unfamiliar journey over familiar territory. Adam was nervous but excited. Kevin was thinking that he would rather go and climb in the mill or kick a football around.

Adam and Kevin seemed to be the only boys who arrived on foot. The front of Bury Grammar School was overrun by large silver cars and groomed little men clutching pencil cases. Every other boy was being kissed on the top of his head by a painted lady in a fur coat. Peel Tower was visible in the gap through the houses but Kevin was already lost. He wondered where all these weird people came from. It couldn't be Brangy because he had never seen anyone remotely like this in Brangy before.

They were swept inside with the pencil-case clutchers and into the large hall at the side of the school. There were so many boys sitting the exam that there were even desks arranged up on the stage. Kevin was surprised not to be sitting next to Adam as usual. That had been his main hope. But there were lots of boys between Matthews and McDermott all of a sudden. As they were separated, Kevin arranged to meet Adam in their den on the way back to St Thomas's.

A very tall, abnormally thin man with a large forehead and bulbous eyes introduced himself as the headmaster of Bury Grammar School. Mr Moore said that boys were free to leave after half an hour but that they should use all the time available as it was a very testing paper this year. He wished all the candidates the very best of luck and told them they could turn their papers over and begin. Adam sat back in his chair and looked around the room. It occurred to him for the first time that the room was full of boys. There were no Irene Bradshaws at this school. Adam thought briefly about getting some of the answers wrong on purpose but, when it came to it, he was far too competitive. He didn't want to be beaten by a bunch of stiffs with pencil cases.

Adam had just begun to puzzle over the section headed 'What is the next item in the sequence?' when he heard a chair scrape violently over the wooden floor and a desk crash to the ground. Two hundred and fifty small boy heads, ten large teacher heads and one headmaster looked up as one to see a boy leaving after thirty seconds. Kevin brushed off the intervention of the weedy invigilator and ran out of the school doors, pursued by the sixth-form Latin master. But Kevin was too quick for Mr Pittam and he was soon out of sight on his way back over the bridge towards his den on the railway line. Adam wondered if he should go after Kevin but he knew that he couldn't. His mum and dad would not understand at all if Adam had not passed for the grammar school because he had been chasing Kevin down the railway line.

And so he turned back to his paper and decided to do the arithmetic sections first. He fizzed through multiplication and long-division questions. Then he moved on to verbal reasoning and filled in synonyms, antonyms, similes and abbreviations. He did his best with a very difficult English comprehension and an impenetrable exercise in précis. With time running out, Adam's usually ornate handwriting was suffering badly as he scribbled two illegible pages on why Pip had been rude to Joe Gargery. Then he went back to some of the difficult mathematics questions that Mrs Rudd had taught him to leave until the end. Adam was struggling. He had spent most of his school days doing arithmetic and his knowledge of vectors and sets wasn't as good as it should have been. The novel experience of guessing several answers and leaving a handful blank meant that Adam closed his paper with an unsettled air. Really for the first time in his school career Adam had an inkling of what it must be like to fail. Sitting there in the sweaty, airless hall of Bury Grammar School, surrounded by assured boys packing 2H pencils back into cases, Adam felt his confidence evaporate. All these other boys were scribbling maniacally until the very last moment, with vectors and set geometry evidently printed on the insides of their eyelids.

A man who looked like Adam's mental picture of Uriah Heep placed a scaly hand on his paper and told him that he was now free to leave. Then, when all the papers had been collected, the other candidates broke into groups of friends. Adam was on his own. He did not know anyone else. He was the only boy from St Thomas's who was sitting for the grammar school. Adam's only friend in this room had upset his desk before a minute had elapsed.

Adam walked thoughtfully back to his den. On one side of the river bank there was Elton Moor comprehensive school and, on the other, Bury Grammar School. Adam knew how much his mum and dad wanted him to pass the exam. Bob and June had unwittingly increased the pressure and the price of failure now felt very high. Adam felt he would be letting his parents down very badly if he failed.

Adam called in to see his dad at work in the yard of Brown's Plumbers and Joiners, as he had promised to do. He was delighted that Bob was out on a job and he got away with leaving a lugubrious message with Joey Brown. Adam wandered out of the yard, past the mill, up through the tunnels and onto the railway line. He found Kevin in their den looking at a pornographic magazine.

'Are you all right?'

'Yeah.'

'Why did you run off like that?'

'I wanted to. I can't be bothered with all them sums and what have you.'

'You'll have to go to Elton Moor now.'

'So what? There's nowt down for skoo anyway.'

'Bury Grammar's different, my dad says.'

'You'll go really posh.'

'As if.'

'You will. You'll be a right snob.'

There was an edge of nastiness to Kevin's voice which hurt Adam, who couldn't believe that passing for the grammar school was a bad thing. He was assured enough in his relations with Kevin to answer back more forcefully than before.

'There's nothing wrong with Bury Grammar.'

'It's skoo for posh gets. You saw all them rich gets.'

'But you don't have to pay if you do well in the exam. Unless we get Labour in, my dad says.'

'What you on about?'

'I won't go posh.'

'You will. Anyway, I don't care. You don't need skoo when you're a footballer.'

Kevin had given up on school. Adam had convinced him that he was going to play for Manchester City and he didn't need to go to Bury Grammar School to achieve that.

'You should still try and get your exams.'

'It doesn't matter if you're a footballer.'

'Are you going back to skoo now?'

'Nah, let's go down the arcade.'

'I can't. I've got no cash. We should go back and tell Mrs Rudd how we got on.'

'She won't know. Come on; let's wag it. I know; let's go fishing on the res.'

There is a fine line, as a comedian once said, between fishing and just standing on the shore like an idiot. Adam thought fishing was very dull but there were few things he would not have done if Kevin McDermott had invited him. From behind them, from the railway line, a soft voice spoke.

'He's dead fit, your brother.'

'He's horrible.'

'Is he 'eck.'

Kevin startled Irene Bradshaw and his sister Maria by jumping out from his den.

'What you doing here?'

'We're wagging it.'

'So are we. Do you want to come up the res?'

'Might do.'

'We're going fishing.'

'All right then.'

'Tell you what, you can do us a favour. Can you go to the pet shop and get some bait?'

'All right. Do you want some maggots?'

The way Irene asked it was the most romantic question Kevin and Adam had ever heard. Suddenly standing on the shore like an idiot didn't seem such a bad idea.

The girls went to the pet shop and Adam went straight into battle.

'Is she your girlfriend still?'

'No. I chucked her.'

'I might ask her to go to the fair then.'

'*I* might.'

'You said you've chucked her.'

'Well? I might ask her out again.'

'Tell you what, we'll have a fishing competition and the winner's allowed to ask Irene Bradshaw out.'

'You're bob at fishing.'

'You should win then. I'll bet you that I can catch as many fish in one hour with my rod as you can with that great big effort of your dad's.'

'You haven't got a fishing rod.'

'I know; I'm going to make one.'

'All right then, I'll bet you.'

'But on one condition.'

'What?'

'If it's a draw, I win. And the winner gets to ask Irene Bradshaw out first.'

'All right.'

Kevin went to fetch his father's fishing rod while Adam ran back home again for a rapid Blue Peter session. He took his father's stop-watch from his parents' dressing table. He took a twenty-five-centimetre ruler and a ball of string from the bureau in the back room. Adam sellotaped the string to the ruler and set out with his brand new rod to prove that fishing was boring and to win the right to approach Irene Bradshaw.

Kevin was in his favourite spot on the far side of the yachting club when Adam arrived. Irene and Maria arrived a minute later and offered the boys a cigarette. Kevin accepted and Adam declined.

'You ought to jack those in. You can't be a footballer if you smoke.'

'You can.'

Undeterred, Kevin lit his fag and winced at the first drag.

'Did you get some maggots?'

'Yeah.'

'Must be love,' whispered Adam to make Kevin giggle.

Kevin did not look up as Adam sat down beside him, melo-dramatically starting the stop-watch which he lay down carefully on the bank. Adam took his Blue Peter rod out of his sports bag and could scarcely suppress a grin as Kevin saw what he was going to do.

'What's that effort?'

'It's a Matthews fishing rod. Brand new. Never been used.'

'You'll never catch owt with that thing.'

'That's not the point.'

Kevin never caught anything when he went fishing. What Kevin did shouldn't have been called fishing. It should have been called rod-in-watering. Adam had decided to hang on for 0–0. With only fifty-nine minutes and counting Adam had a sportsman's chance. Irene Bradshaw seemed to have missed the point, though.

'You've no chance, you haven't. You can't catch fish with a ruler.'

'I know you can't.'

'It's a joke,' said Maria, ensuring that the joke was rendered as unfunny as it could possibly be.

'Well I don't think it's funny,' said Irene, without any need, as the disdain on her face made that clear enough.

'I do,' said Maria without smiling or laughing.

The girls chattered on while Kevin and Adam sat in silence and the stop-watch ticked the hour inexorably by. With ten minutes remaining Kevin took out his most delicious maggots. He could testify to their tastiness because he regularly won bets by swallowing them. He fixed the bait to the end of the line and cast out. After five uneventful minutes Kevin felt the slightest of tugs on his line, so slight he thought it could be the movement of the water. And then again. This time the tug was unmistak-able. It was hard and tenacious, a monster pike, taking a bite.

'I've got one.'

'Yes, go on, Kevin,' exulted Irene, showing her allegiance.

Adam, who had kept his piece of string dangling insultingly in the water a foot away from the shore, looked out at the end of the line, which was bouncing violently. With a mental shrug he gave up the game as lost. He was frightened Irene Bradshaw would turn him down anyway and he wasn't sure his mum and dad would let him go to the fair on his own even if he won. With concentration and careful deliberation he showed for so little else, Kevin lifted his line, slowly, ceremonially, out of the water. There, hanging in the air, in unbearable agony, speared by a hook for want of a maggot, was a magnificent fat pike. Showing manual delicacy that surprised and briefly entranced Adam, Kevin began to reel the prize back home. But as the line came ashore the damnable creature slithered and wriggled to evade the hook which was killing it and fell, with a splash of finality, back into the muddy water. There were only three minutes left on the clock.

'There. I had one. You saw it. You saw it. I had one.'

'You *had* one. You don't now.'

A stickler for the letter of the law all of a sudden, Adam insisted that fish in the water didn't count.

'But you saw it.'

'The fish has to be in a box.'

'We never said that. We just said we had to catch one.'

'But you haven't caught one.'

'I have. You saw it.'

'Yeah, it was massive,' said Irene.

'So what?' said Maria.

Irene and Maria mirrored the argument that Kevin was having with Adam. In fact their dispute was so vehement that it began to look like a set-up, of which Adam felt without doubt the victim.

'I've won. I had a pike. I caught one.'

'So where is it now? Not very caught if it's swimming in the res, is it?'

'You're a cheater, you are.'

Kevin and Adam bickered until the stop-watch of time ran out and Adam declared the game a 0–0 draw, which granted him the right to ask Irene Bradshaw to go to the fair. Disgusted with the argument, though not aware of its implications and quite *why* it mattered so much, Irene and Maria declared that fishing was boring anyway. As they left, Kevin wrote off their lack of staying-power as evidence of being girls. Adam agreed with them and thought he might yet get along with Irene if she was prepared to go to the fair with him, which he had severe cause to doubt.

Adam pointed his rod disdainfully. He detached the string from the ruler and threw it into the water. Kevin sat quietly, with saintly fortitude, holding his fists.

'A famous 0–0 victory and the prize belongs to the one, the only, Adam Matthews. I told you I'd win.'

'Just shut it.'

'What a marvellous victory . . .'

Kevin slapped Adam across the face. It was not a hard blow; more of a warning to be quiet than a desire to cause pain, but it was enough to knock Adam off balance. He tottered comically for a second on one leg, trying desperately to save himself from toppling over into the grimy reservoir. His ruler slid through the surface of the water followed by a skinny arm. Then Adam's face hit the top and he bobbed under. Kevin laughed aloud, splashed Adam and immersed him fully under the freezing water. Kevin knew Adam was soft but he was surprised, all the same, at the fuss his scaredy-cat friend was making.

Kevin was now in the water up to his knees. He pushed Adam ten yards further from the shore and then gave him a huge final push, sending him out of his depth beyond the point where the reservoir shelf deepens. Then he ran for the shore, making as big a splash as he could manage.

'You've lost anyway. You just don't even know it.'

Kevin gathered up his fishing rod and his maggots and packed them away. It was only thirty seconds since he had left Adam in the water but he had a sense of anxiety in the silence. Whether it was the absence of returned badinage or none of the sounds of struggle Kevin did not know, but when he looked back at his friend in the water he was astonished to note that Adam was not there. Kevin blinked and looked again but it was incontrovertible. Adam was not there. Something inside Kevin called ally ally eeno and ally ally eeno was never called in jest.

He threw down his fishing rod and ran out into the shallow water. Kevin dived into the depths and held his breath as he ducked under the dirty surface. It was near impossible to keep his eyes open in the filth but, through one half-opened eye, he saw a human form sinking gently to the reservoir's deep muddy base. Kevin closed both eyes for a few seconds and swam in the direction of Adam's body which had drifted further from the shore. When he sensed that he was close, Kevin opened his eyes as wide as the stinging water would allow and grabbed hold of Adam by the midriff. Kevin was a strong and stocky boy but he had never shown greater strength than when he wrapped himself to Adam and pushed up off the floor of the reservoir for the air. The two boys broke through the surface, allowing Kevin to open his eyes and catch his breath. Adam was spark out. He was dead weight, unable to offer any support at all and he was slipping from Kevin's grasp. Fortunately Kevin only had to swim twenty yards to reach shallow waters where he could prop Adam up, sit down and have a rest. But, without the support of the water, and with the wetness adding weight to his clothes, Adam was too heavy to carry. Kevin did not have enough strength left to get him out of the water, never mind to carry him home. He needed help.

Kevin might not have been very good at multiplication but he struck the gold star for ingenuity. He laid Adam down carefully on his back, submerging him temporarily. Then he ran as fast as he could to the shore, picked up his fishing basket and ran back into the water. He picked Adam up, placed the basket into the small of his back and propped him up so that his head rested safely on the wire top. Kevin ran back to fetch his fishing rod which he completely ruined by forcing it into the muddy floor as if he were posting a flag. Positioned carefully between Adam's legs it prevented him slipping too far down off the fishing basket. Then Kevin ran for help, running like he had never run before.

By the time Kevin arrived at Brown's he was all but unable to speak. His breath, however, told a story.

'Kevin. What is it?'

'You've . . . You've . . . got to . . . come.'

'Where? Where, Kevin? What's happened? Is it our Adam? Where is he?'

'The res.'

Bob was out of the yard before Kevin had finished enunciating the word. The front gate oscillated like a saloon bar door in a bad western. As he left Kevin behind in a sprint that went back twenty-five years, Bob cursed himself for not having insisted that Adam conquer his fear of water and learn to swim.

Kevin caught up with Bob who was coughing and spluttering badly as they arrived. After wheezing to catch his breath, Bob waded into the water and picked his son up from the basket that was still holding him up. Adam had started to come round.

'It's all right, lad. We've got you now.'

Bob carried Adam to the safety of the side and cradled him like a baby in his arms for two minutes. As Adam came to, he began to sniffle and the tears of his son enticed a gulp from Bob who turned his face and wiped his eyes. Kevin approached gingerly, still panting from the sprint and frightened that he would take the blame for this escapade as he seemed to for every other.

Kevin hung his head in expectation of a telling-off as Bob beckoned him over. Bob told Kevin to lift his head and to look up. Then Bob ruffled Kevin's hair and offered him a handshake which he took with the immense pride that a boy should be shaking hands with somebody's dad.

'Well done, lad. You've done well there. Good lad.'

'Can we still be mates, Mr Matthews?'

'Aye, I suppose so. Proper little hero you are now.'

Kevin insisted on helping Adam home and, by the time they had arrived back, Adam was well enough to remind Kevin that he had won their bet. Now he was part of the fraternity of the fathers, Kevin borrowed a patronising tone from his own father.

'I wouldn't be so sure about that, sunshine.'

'What do you mean?'

'I've won already. I'm going to the fair with her on Tuesday.'

The stab of thwarted desire attacked Adam's heart for the first time. Kevin said goodbye to Mr Matthews and, with a smug grin all of his own, set off home. 1–0, 0–0, it really didn't matter. Kevin had won before they had even begun. He was a footballer and a fighter and that was what counted. And now he was a proper little hero. They were the things that girls liked. As Adam changed out of his soaking clothes and got into the bath, catching a glimpse in the mirror of his baby face, he wondered whether this ever changed.

Where is Latin Anyway?

When the letter finally arrived from the Local Education Authority it sat unopened on the mantelpiece for two days. Finally, drunk on Friday night, Wendy summoned up enough curiosity to rip it apart. The letter was addressed to her and Sammy and it told them that their son Kevin had been allocated a place at Elton Moor comprehensive school. Wendy put the letter behind a clock above the gas fire and made a mental note to tell her husband. Nobody told Kevin that he had been the subject of a letter. He found out by overhearing his parents arguing late at night, as he did most nights. Kevin sat on the stairs listening to grown-up arguments with grown-up words he had begun to use but did not wish to hear.

'Will you stop fucking fussing, woman? What's it fucking matter what school he goes to? There's nothing wrong with Elton Moor.'

'You must be joking. I went to Elton Moor, Sammy. I know what it's like.'

'That's bloody years ago.'

'It's not changed.'

'It's been all right for our Irene.'

'You're having me on, aren't you? Have you seen her mates? They're a right set of bloody scrubbers. And look at the state she got into.'

'Yeah, well that's over and done with now.'

Irene McDermott had stolen quietly in the night up to Jericho to give birth at Fairfield Hospital. Wendy, who found it difficult

45

to be angry at babies, no matter what colour they were, had gone with her. After a Caesarean, Irene had handed her son Nathan over to his proud paternal grandparents.

'You've got no choice anyway, so you might as well forget it.'

'You don't even care, do you? You'd never know it was your lad we were talking about.'

''Course I fucking care. I care about him getting on with his football. That's what he's good at. The sooner he can get out of school the better. He's got talent, has Kevin, but he's no brain box. You've got to stop pushing him into school work. That's not his thing.'

'All right, Sammy. We've been through all this.'

Wendy retreated. She went into the kitchen to make a cup of tea. Kevin hurried up the stairs when he heard her coming. He had expected all along that he would be going to Elton Moor so he didn't really understand the point of the argument. But Sammy didn't need a point. He only needed a pint and then he was ready to fight. Wendy had endured almost twenty years of volatility. Two years after he had arrived in Bury, Sammy had courted Wendy Powell, a Brangy girl ten years his junior. Wendy had lived all her life on the Harwood, the only daughter of the notorious Powell family that had governed the estate in the years between Elvis and The Beatles. In the absence of her father, Wendy had been reared by her beleaguered mother, Iris. Wendy had returned the service, with equal devotion, in her mother's declining years. Kevin's grandma had died a month after he was born, no longer knowing who she was.

Sammy shouted through from the living room, 'I've got plans for that lad anyway. And make us a cuppa, will you?'

Sammy planned to induct Kevin into his new trade. Sammy McDermott had come to Bury from Glasgow thirty years before to work in the paper mills. Sammy McDermott was a wounded man. The precipitous decline of the paper industry had ended his working life. With no trade or training, a history of causing trouble, and a foul temper, Sammy, at the age of fifty-four, had not worked for five years. He spent the morning in his armchair, dinner time in the pub, the long afternoon in Ladbroke's and the evening in the Greenhill Working Men's Club. And then he went out to work.

At five past two, Sammy woke Kevin and, without explanation, instructed him to get dressed. He led the way round to Wendy's old family house where Greg and Bobby Powell were sitting in their parkas in the living room, staring at the blank television screen. They both grunted hello to Kevin as he came in. Sammy sat in his armchair and issued the instructions.

'Right, this is what we'll do.'

'Where we going, Sam?'

'If you shut up, I'll tell you. Number 44. And no crap.'

'Front or back?' asked Greg.

'Back window. I've checked the trellis and it's bust.'

'Who's house is it?'

'Doesn't fucking matter.'

'Cornish.'

The Cornish twins, Scott and Paul, were in Kevin's class at St Thomas's. Their father was odd and it was rumoured that their mother was backward. Whether or not this was true nobody really knew but the Cornish boys certainly suffered at school on account of the weirdness of their parents.

Sammy broke the small back window pane with a pebble and put his hand inside to open the flap. It was just large enough for a small boy to clamber through.

'Come on, Kev; in you go.'

'And be careful.'

Kevin clung onto the net curtain to steady himself and upset the ornaments on the window sill.

'Clumsy get. For God's sake. Open the big window.'

The three adults stepped in through the window, taking care not to disturb any more of the brass pots that decorated the window sill.

'You stay there. Don't move,' said Sammy, scaring Kevin.

Sammy crept upstairs and rifled through the drawers. Knickers and bras seemed to spring out of every one. It was a pervert's paradise when Sammy left, empty-handed except for a piece of Wedgwood taken from the dressing table.

'Couldn't find the fucking jewellery anywhere,' he whispered to Bobby at the foot of the stairs.

Bobby had the television in his hands and Greg had swept up all the metal trinkets he could find downstairs. Kevin had obeyed his father literally. He hadn't moved a muscle.

'Grab hold of something, lad. Come on.'

Kevin lifted a large plastic globe from the living-room table and scuttled out of the back door after his father.

They went back to the Powell house to drink and to assess the haul. Sammy was pleased with the Wedgwood and the ornaments but the television was a disappointment. BBC1 was blurred and there was no picture at all on ITV. BBC2, however, was perfect.

'Who the fuck wants to watch bollocks BBC2?'

'And in fucking black and white.'

'Fucking Cornish. What a twat.'

'What did you get, lad?'

'I got that globe.'

'Good on you. That should fetch a quid or two. How's it feel to be in work, lad?'

Sammy, Bobby and Greg laughed. Kevin yawned and wished they would let him go back to bed.

Six hours later, on the other side of the fence, Bob Matthews examined a long brown envelope, straining his vision as if the bottom lens in his split glasses allowed him to see through the paper into the future. Bob was barely able to contain himself until June had come back from the Co-op. Even then she had to tell him to stay his hand.

'Let our Adam open it. It's his letter.'

'Where is he?'

'He went out with Kevin. They've gone down to see if they can get a tent.'

'What does he want with a bloody tent? He can't put it up in the yard.'

'He said something about going up Holcombe Hill tonight.'

'I don't know about that. He's a bit young yet. Where's he getting this tent from any road?'

'Down Castlecroft. Didn't you see the paper?'

The front page of the *Bury Times* that week had carried the story that the huge camping shop, imaginatively named Castle-croft Camping, had burned down. With the implicit consent of their parents, young boys from all over Bury had descended on Castlecroft Camping to steal away with tents, poles, gas fires, stainless-steel mugs, hiking boots and enormous kagoules that you could fold up into the pocket on the front.

Bob ran down through the tunnels and past the old mill where he met a four-legged canvas-and-poles monster, struggling back home.

'What's up, Dad?'

'You've got a letter. From the grammar school.'

'What's it say?'

'Your mum won't let me open it. So come on.'

'Have you brought it?'

'No, your mum wants to see you open it as well.'

'What am I going to do with this stuff?'

'Here. Give me some of it.'

Bob grabbed the camping equipment and strode out so quickly that Kevin and Adam had to trot to keep up, even though Bob was now carrying half the charred remains of Castle-croft Camping. Kevin made his excuses as they came out of the tunnels into the light. He relieved himself against a tree, happy to be freed from the dull conversation about school.

As soon as Adam came through the door June handed him the future in a long brown envelope. Adam was more nervous than he was letting on. June was more nervous than Adam, and Bob was twice as nervous as June. Bob threw the tent onto the kitchen floor, the sheer carelessness of which showed that this was a crucial moment.

'Come on, son; put us out of our misery.'

Adam struggled with the glue, opening the envelope as though it mattered that it not be ripped. He panned slowly across the paper, taking in the words, 'We are delighted to inform you' and going on to refer to his allocated house, named Derby after the local landowners.

'Well?' asked father.

'Well . . .' teased son.

'For Heaven's sake, Adam. What does it say?' demanded mother.

'It says I've got to get a uniform with a yellow badge for my house.'

'Oh, Adam.'

June squealed and hugged Adam while Bob ripped the paper out of his hand and read aloud, as if he were announcing the shortlist at an Oscar ceremony.

'. . . and we are delighted to inform you that you have been awarded a Local Education Authority bursary amounting to half the annual payment on account of your performance in the entrance examination.'

That was the bit that really turned the temperature up. June squealed again and went out to fetch the sparkling white wine which she had smuggled in from the Co-op. With a quivering lip, Bob offered Adam his worn, hardened hand because Adam had just won the right to keep his hands soft.

'Well done, son. Well done. We're both very proud of you. It's grand news, is that. Absolutely grand.'

Bob pulled Adam to his chest, slapped him on the back and swallowed very, very hard. Bob Matthews was five feet eight inches tall but he felt four feet four inches taller. His lad was going to the grammar school. This was what getting on really meant.

The Matthews family very proudly went to the big Co-op in town to buy a grammar school uniform. After Irene Bradshaw, his uniform became Adam's first love. Though sorry to be denied the more expensive barathea, Adam fell for his crimplene blazer. He adored the school insignia, a swan carefully sewn onto the breast pocket in yellow, the Derby colour. Through the long summer holidays Adam suffered Kevin's taunts for wearing his school uniform on the way to the swimming baths. This habit altogether killed off any chance he had with Irene Bradshaw. Irene did not want to be seen with a stiff in a crimplene blazer with a swan sewn onto his breast pocket.

During the watershed summer holiday Kevin and Adam did not mention their new schools. The subject promised a parting which neither welcomed. Instead, they carried on much as they ever had. They carried on looking for the tramp in the mill, continued playing football for the Harwood estate in its huge battles with the Brownvales estate and they planned a camping trip. Finally, on the Saturday before they were to go to their new schools, Bob and June relented and permitted Adam to go camping for a night without supervision, on the strict condition that he got back in time for Holy Communion on the Sunday morning.

Kevin and Adam headed for Peel Tower on Holcombe Hill. Adam packed the tent into one of the huge plastic bags that his dad brought home full of soil from the garden centre. When the 474 bus turned from Brandlesholme into Longsight Road, Peel Tower loomed straight ahead, a stone exclamation mark beckoning them on to an adventure without parents. They wanted to camp as close to Peel Tower as they could get. At Holcombe Brook, at the bottom of Holcombe Hill, they got off the bus.

'Where you going?' asked Adam as Kevin turned away from the forbidding hill.

Kevin skipped through the traffic to the off-licence across the road. Adam looked away, embarrassed, as Kevin gave a five-pound note to a stranger who came out, two minutes later, with a large bottle of cider. Kevin stuffed it under the canvas, nodded at Adam and headed off for Peel Tower.

To eleven-year-old boys carrying a heavy tent, Holcombe Hill is all but vertical. Adam resorted to laying the canvas down on the floor and trying to roll it up the hill as if he were playing a game in *It's a Knockout*. Kevin was stronger and full to the brim of hubris. As he ran up the steepest path on offer, a solitary pole slipped out of the pouch and slid, agonisingly just too quickly to catch, all the way back down the hill to the Hare and Hounds at the bottom.

'Shitting hell.'

'You idiot. What you doing that for?'

'It fell out. I couldn't help it.'

'You'll have to go and get it.'

'We can do without one of them. It doesn't matter.'

''Course it matters. You can't put a tent up with a pole missing. Go on. I'll wait here,' said Adam, glad of the rest.

Kevin lay down and rolled through the gorse and brambles to the foot of Holcombe Hill. He picked up the stray pole, took a stick of Spearmint and a large swig of Woodpecker cider and ran back up.

Eventually, the pair of them made it up the one-thousand one-hundred feet to the summit where they posed in front of Peel Tower. Then the exposure hit them.

'God, it's windy up here.'

'It's freezing.'

Neither Kevin nor Adam wanted to draw the obvious conclusion. Camping *was* a good idea. It had taken Adam far too long to persuade his parents to let him come to decide so readily that it was awful. But it really was extremely windy.

'We'll never put the tent up in this.'

''Course we will,' said Kevin, who knew very well that Adam's 'we' was royal.

'Have you ever put a tent up before?'

'Sometimes.'

'So, no then.'

'No, I have.'

'When?'

'I can't remember.'

'Brilliant.'

'Come on; let's get it up.'

As soon as Kevin unwrapped the canvas it became a kite. The tent took off and flew in the general direction of Ramsbottom. The military personnel on *The Krypton Factor*'s obstacle race stopped their assault on the course and gazed up at two little boys chasing a tent over the West Pennine Moors. Adam twisted his ankle in a trough in the grass but Kevin kept up the chase. He wasn't going to be beaten in a race with a stolen tent. Just as he had caught the runaway canvas, a counter gust of wind blew up and the tent turned and attacked him. Adam picked himself up, moaned to nobody in particular, and arrived to find Kevin very much the victor, albeit one hidden under an exhausted tent.

'Told you,' said Adam, not at all necessarily.

'What we going to do?'

'There's a massive ditch on the other side of Peel Tower. My dad showed me last time we were here. We can go in there and it'll be sheltered.'

'Now he tells me.'

'Soz, I forgot.'

Kevin dragged the tent back towards Peel Tower and down into the crater. He lay it on the floor and Adam spread it out in the correct fashion while Kevin assembled the frame. Adam stared in admiration at Kevin's ability to insert the right end of the right pole into the right hole. Very quickly, the frame took shape. Unfortunately, not the same shape as the tent. That day in Castlecroft Camping Adam had taken a full canvas and an outer sheet which folded into a small porch. At the same time Kevin had been pilfering a whole, complete, brand-new frame. For a different tent altogether. No matter how dextrously Adam folded the canvas, and he became a proper origami scholar in the attempt, there was no way it was going to fit onto Kevin's frame. It was demonstrably for a different tent altogether.

'We'll have to go home,' said Adam, realistically.

'No, we won't,' replied Kevin with no regard for the weight of evidence.

'The tent doesn't fit, Kev. Look at it. It doesn't reach the floor.'

The tent looked like an old man wearing half-mast trousers and showing an inch of flesh above his socks.

'I reckon I can fix it.'

Kevin's solution lost in practicality what little it gained in ingenuity.

'Take that one out and it should be all right.'

'You're joking.'

Kevin unscrewed one of the poles only to find that he was left with two holes that he needed to fit together. Undeterred when he ought to have been, he took the chewing gum out of his mouth and strapped the two poles loosely together. The frame toppled over onto one side to form an apologetically sagging triangle at the top. It looked like a not-quite-full tent, which was exactly what it was. This is what tent frames look like after a bottle of Woodpecker cider. To Adam's consternation the canvas almost fitted the drunken shape. He felt fastidious complaining that the new frame had no use for the porch and that surely suggested something fundamentally amiss with the structure. He concentrated on chewing his gum very hard and very noisily which was an extremely cool thing to do.

'It won't stay up.'

'It will. There's no wind in here.'

It was a good job there was no wind. It would only have taken one of them to breathe out sharply and their tent was in peril.

'Come on; let's get in.'

The tent was up and in one piece, albeit in a shape in which no tent has ever been, before or since. But Adam and Kevin couldn't see how odd it looked from the inside. It was a den from the inside. And there they were, after all, on the top of Holcombe Hill, underneath Peel Tower. In sympathy with their tent Kevin and Adam were soon sagging themselves, both seeing stars of their own making.

'I love cider,' Kevin lied.

'So do I,' said Adam, joining in.

'Have you seen *Carry on Camping?*'

Adam took the cue to do his Kenneth Williams impression and his Sid James laugh which, on the umpteenth repetition, Kevin still found hilarious.

'Do you remember that bit in the field?'

'It's brilliant, isn't it?'

When Kevin and Adam had seen Barbara Windsor doing

aerobics they had lost themselves in the sheer rudeness of it all. The memory stirred Kevin, who had drunk most of the Woodpecker, into jumping up and upsetting the precarious tent as he went. Adam followed by habit as Kevin ran at Peel Tower and bounced off it. Adam did the same and the pair of them lay on the gorse laughing hysterically. Kevin got up and put his arms round Peel Tower as if he were hugging it.

'Come on; give us a hand.'

'What you doing?'

'I'm pulling up Peel Tower. I'm nicking it. It'll look great on our mantelpiece.'

'You'll never get away with it. The cops'll notice it's gone. We'll never get it home.'

'We'll take it on the bus.'

Kevin and Adam pulled and pulled on Peel Tower but Peel Tower stayed where it was. After ten minutes of giggling and pulling, Kevin declared that he didn't really want to steal Peel Tower anyway. Ten minutes in the wind was enough so they slid back down the sides of the ditch to their drunken tent. If they hadn't both been a little tipsy themselves both Kevin and Adam would have sworn that the tent had tipped over to the left in their absence. As it was, they snuggled into their sleeping bags with no clouds in their minds. Apart, of course, from the fact that they were both lying on sloping, stony ground on the windy West Pennine Moor.

Kevin finished the last of the cider and offered Adam the final stick of chewing gum. Adam was ever so slightly afraid of chewing gum, even allowing for the fact that chewing it made him feel so tough.

'Have you been swallowing yours?'

''Course.'

'You're not meant to. It can stick in your windpipe.'

'What's your windpipe?'

'It's in your mouth.'

'No it can't. I always swallow it.'

'It goes hard in your tummy and then they have to cut it out.'

'As if.'

'Have you heard that crap song about chewing gum?'

'What song?'

'I don't know. My dad has it on the radio on Sunday mornings before church. It's really bobbins.'

Excepting his love of hymns, Bob Matthews had some dubious musical tastes. Adam did rather a good impression although it was lost on Kevin.

'Does your chewing gum lose its flavour on the bedpost overnight?'

' 'Course it doesn't.'

'Doesn't what?'

'Chewing gum gets its flavour back if you leave it out. If you leave it when you go to sleep it tastes better when you wake up.'

'No it doesn't.'

'It does. You should try it. Leave it out now and see what it's like in the morning.'

Adam was sceptical but he could see no harm in trying. It would be a fabulous discovery if it turned out to be true. He placed his ball of tasteless gum on his plastic pillow, said good night to Kevin and rolled over onto a new stone.

As the night passed the tent started to sag seriously. Kevin woke up three times and, on each occasion, the roof was a few inches closer to his head. Adam was woken by a desperate desire for the toilet, which the cold outside prevented him from satisfying. Somehow, in anaemic sleeping bags, the pair of them managed three hours of uninterrupted sleep before dawn.

They woke at four to discover the roof on top of their heads and their shoes floating past their ears. The advantage of camping in a ditch was shelter from the wind. The disadvantage was that they were pitched in a lake. The repetitive drumming of rain on canvas woke Adam with a start. He opened his eyes, startled, not knowing where he was. He was dismayed to discover that he was at the bottom of a flooded ditch at the top of Holcombe Hill in a leaky tent held together by chewing gum. He knew that one of the other lumps under the canvas was Kevin, but it wasn't obvious which. Kevin emerged from between two broken zips and stood up stark naked, trusting that nobody would be out walking on a rainy Sunday dawn on Holcombe Hill.

'This is crap. Let's go home.'

They didn't bother packing up the tent. Kevin and Adam would not carry on camping. Kevin was wet, cold and suddenly aware that this marked the end of the last long holiday before he started at Elton Moor and Adam started at Bury Grammar.

'It's skoo on Monday.'

'I know.'

'I don't want to go.'

'Neither do I . . .'

'I'm sick of skoo.'

'So am I.'

Adam had been looking forward to starting at his new school but Kevin's melancholy tone upset him. In sopping socks and shoes Adam groped carefully down the sodden hill with the only thought in his head the hope that the buses ran this early from Ramsbottom to Brandlesholme. He couldn't have been any more miserable even if he had noticed that he had been rolling in chewing gum all night and that his hair was dotted with sticky Spearmint.

Kevin noticed at the bus stop. As they waited for an hour and a half there was little else to look at. He amused himself quietly by not mentioning the disaster to Adam. If he could somehow nurse Adam all the way through to the church service with his chewing gum intact, Kevin would be providing comic genius for the other choir boys.

At his father's suggestion Adam had badgered Kevin to join the church choir. Kevin had no interest in religion, sang like he was having his teeth pulled and misbehaved in choir practice. He could not resist pointing out that Arthur, the choir master, had a head like a golf ball: bald and pimpled. Arthur tried to instil the beauty of church music into the boys but none of them was there for religion. The choir boys received sixty pence for each service and they were all there for Mammon. Kevin was even prepared to put up with the fancy dress. The long red cassock was basically a dress, the surplice was a bed sheet with four holes and the neck ruff made the boys look like they were being choked to death by a paper doily. But sixty pence was a lot of money.

There was nobody on the first bus out of Ramsbottom until, at the next stop, a choleric old crone stepped aboard and announced her madness by sitting immediately behind Kevin and Adam even though the bus was empty. She then proceeded to mutter audible invective about punk rockers being a disgrace and the state of kids these days when Adam started swearing about church.

'I don't want to go to shit church. I hate carrying the wine up.'

'How come you're doing that?'

'It's my gran's anniversary.'

'You've got to go then. You definitely can't get out of that, can you?'

Adam gave Kevin a funny look but thought no more of it.

As soon as Adam walked in through the front door his mother screamed.

'What the bloody hell have you been doing? That's it, young man. That's the last time you stay out on your own.'

June marched Adam to the mirror in the living room where junior Johnny Rotten stared back at him. June had warned Adam not to chew gum in bed and now he realised why.

'Look at what he's done, Bob. He's meant to be taking the wine up today.'

Adam's dad looked up from the newspaper and contorted his face to suppress a laugh. Adam noted the buried grin and smiled back, to his mother's annoyance.

'It's not funny. You look a right sight. What would your grandma say?'

Hilda Greenhalgh, June's mother, had been the verger at St Paul's, Jericho, and then at St Thomas's, Brandelsholme. She had died on this day five years before and her name had been entered in florid calligraphy in the Book of Remembrance which sat in a frame by the font, discreetly hidden behind drawn scarlet curtains. Adam had only an infant recollection of his grandparents who, in another age, another place, would have left town to seek their fortune. That had never been an option for Hilda and Jimmy Greenhalgh. Jimmy had worked instead in the cotton mills until he decided to become a business tycoon by starting a window-cleaning round at Fairfield Hospital. He was soon doing all the churches in Jericho and became adept at bringing out the vivid colours of the stained glass. June Matthews was now the verger of St Thomas's in the Church of England, like her mother before her. June arranged the flowers, ensured the altar wore the vestments appropriate to the Church calendar and polished the sanctuary lamp. June spent every Saturday afternoon stretching her tiny limbs to polish the sanctuary lamp that hung over the altar. The sanctuary lamp is the lamp of everlasting light, the lamp that never goes out. It frightened Adam who thought it was going to fall on his head as he went up to Communion to be blessed. On this Sunday of every year the Matthews family took the Communion sacraments from the back of church up to the altar. There was absolutely no prospect, on this of all days, that Adam could be excused church.

'I can't go like this.'

'You're dead right you can't, you daft apath. Come on; I'll give you a quick trim.'

Adam recoiled. For all his many virtues, Bob Matthews was no barber. Bob left the room and came back with the kitchen scissors.

'You can't use them. You've just been cutting sausages with them.'

'I've given them a good wash.'

'Jimmy doesn't make his breakfast with his scissors, Dad. You need proper barber's scissors.'

Jimmy owned the barber's on the Bolton road. Jimmy was the perfect barber for people who, like Adam, hated having their hair cut, even when it was full of chewing gum. Jimmy loved hair like it was his own and usually it was. He was known as the Hair Bear Bunch because Jimmy had massive hair. It wasn't especially long but it was very, very big. He had a beard larger than Solomon Grundy's and, three buttons down, a pubic jungle. That is how barbers *should* look and Jimmy's hair had earned Adam's trust. Bob's thin wasps gave him no such confidence.

'Sit still, lad. Come on; we've got to get to church.'

'I'm not going to church.'

'You are, sunshine, and you can change that tone of voice this minute.'

'I'm not going.'

Adam pulled a strange contortion which involved retracting his chin and pushing his jowls down to rest on the top of his neck.

'Can you please take that silly look off your face, Adam?' said June. June said that a lot.

June did not realise that she had just been in receipt of an insult. June had been known in her youth as Olive Oyl, due to an unfortunate absence in the chin area. But, over the years, the pasties and the chips had taken their toll and June was now the only person in the world who had no chin but had two of them.

'If the wind changes . . .' impersonated Adam.

'Sit still and stop being so lippy. I don't know what's got into you these days.'

'You'll not be let out of our sight again, young man. That's for certain.'

Bob started attacking the chewing gum. This was his first error. He allowed himself to be distracted by chewing gum which had become so ingrained in Adam's hair that no sensible cut in the foreseeable future could entirely dispense with it. Then everything flowed from Bob's second error which was to cut one side slightly too high above the ears. In seeking to repair the essential balance of the cut, he made the same error on the other side. Adam was already on the threshold of lunacy when Bob returned to the first side, now with an inch and a half of virgin flesh exposed. His passion for symmetry now sated, Bob started on the top.

'You're meant to run it through your fingers and cut off the ends. That's what Jimmy does.'

Disdaining Jimmy's technique, Bob hacked away at random. He took a huge clump out from the middle of Adam's scalp, then took the uncut strands from the front and draped them apologetically over the patch like old men do when they are trying to pretend that they are not bald. When Bob held up the mirror, in undeserved imitation of a real barber, Adam saw that Johnny Rotten had been transformed into a hair-brained lunatic. He took one look in the mirror and called ally ally eeno on his haircut.

'Hey, I haven't finished.'

'Dad, you've cut all my hair off.'

'It's not that bad. It's your fault for chewing that gum stuff.'

'I'm definitely not going to church now. I look a right idiot.'

'You've got to go, love,' June said gently. 'It's your grandma's day today. We're taking the wine up.'

'I can't go like this.'

'Just do it for your grandma.'

'You don't have to go in the choir today. Just sit in the pews with me. I suppose you do look a bit silly, love,' said June, breaking ranks.

When his parents' smirks broke into hysterical laughter, Adam stormed upstairs to his bedroom. He had never heard unrestrained laughter from his parents before and it sounded peculiar, especially as he was its victim.

Adam turned his father's wardrobe upside down looking for a hat. Bob's flat cap looked even sillier than his haircut, so, when Kevin called for him to go to church, Adam sulked down the stairs wearing a big kagoule with the hood up. He forestalled any inquiry.

'I've got really bad earache but my dad says I've got to go.'

'Did you get it last night?'

'Must have done. It was freezing.'

Adam was just warming to the sympathy when the elements took over. A ferocious blast of wind ripped his kagoule helmet from his head and revealed Bob's concoction beneath. Kevin seized on it at once.

'Wow, look at that. That is absolutely ace. Bobby Charlton.'

'Shut up, you. Shut up.'

'Earache. Oh yeah. Chinny. *Reckon.*'

Kevin pushed his tongue to the front of his mouth and made a lump on his chin which he stroked, by looping his arm under his raised leg. Kevin found it hard to conceive of anything funnier than a rubbish haircut and this one was a gift from above.

'Right, that's it. I'm not going in.'

Adam broke away from Kevin's attempt to pull him back. He was in tears.

'Come back.'

'Piss off.'

'Come on; I didn't mean it. Come on; you've got to go in.'

Kevin paused, for timing.

'Come on, Bobby.'

'Get lost. I'm not going in.'

Kevin held Adam to prevent him from escaping. He seemed to gain years as he spoke.

'Adam, you have to go. It's for your gran.'

The existence of Adam's hair under his kagoule hood made the Eucharist service less dull than usual, for both of them. Adam lined up with his mother and father and took the sacraments up to Communion in memory of his grandmother. There was *one* choir boy who was not pointing at Adam's kagoule but Kevin soon directed him to do so. The Reverend Truman indulged himself with twenty minutes on loving thy neighbour while Bob sighed far too loudly, impatiently checking his watch. Adam spent the sermon dreaming of being picked to play for Brangy Warriors, frightened that everybody was looking at him.

Adam looked so miserable in the front pew that Kevin decided to cheer him up. He caught Adam's attention from his position in the choir stalls and mouthed the words 'watch this' Adam knew what he meant. Kevin threatened to do this whenever he carried the cross. The art of the server, who carries the cross and leads the procession at the end of the Anglican service, is to ensure the choir disappears into the vestry *during* the final chorus of the hymn. The choir had barely started the second verse of 'Guide Me o Thy Great Redeemer' when Kevin picked up his cross and walked. There was no way the procession could stretch to two further verses even if Kevin had walked at funeral pace. As it was, he set off like Bob Beamon heading for the long-jump pit. The choir boys bolted for the narthex, sprinting after Kevin, who was already turning the corner at the bottom of the knave and heading for the vestry. Meanwhile, the adult choristers rebelled. 'Cwm Rhondda' was Bob's favourite tune and he stood stock-still to treat the congregation to his huge bass rendition of 'give to thee' during the final verse. As the organ subsided and the glorious final notes hung in the air, Bob led the choir out of the stalls and back into the vestry, the only sound breaking the silence the drag of their soles on the stone floor.

Kevin was enjoying himself too much. In the vestry he lost his composure altogether. If his only crime had been anticipating the end of a hymn, he would have survived. But that was not all. By the time the choir and the vicar had arrived back in the vestry, Kevin had flashed his willy at Jane Truman, the vicar's daughter, who was allowed into the vestry every Sunday as a special treat. Jane was in one corner, screaming that she had never seen anything so terrible. Kevin was in the other corner, panting after shattering the all-comers' record for the cross-carrying sprint, surrounded by choir boys convulsed in hysterical laughter at the brilliant comic antics of their crazy mate.

Kevin was expelled from St Thomas's at once. The Reverend Truman marched him personally to the stiff oak door and out of the church to which he would return only twice more in over a decade. As he reached the door, Kevin looked round at Bob Matthews who, as hard as he tried, could not suppress a grin that reached from ear to ear.

Worried about his hair, Adam slept very badly on his last night before Bury Grammar School. June packed his new protractor and compass into his new briefcase and made sure all his uniform was washed and pressed. He woke up far too early, refused breakfast and was ready to call for Kevin an hour before he was expected.

'I thought we were going to take you.'

'You've got to go to work.'

'It's only round the corner.'

'I said I'd walk down with Kevin. No one goes with their mum and dad.'

Bob protested briefly but he realised his own benefit was at stake more than his son's. Adam was still half an hour early when he could wait no longer. Kevin hadn't even got up, so he had to wait anyway. Even worse, he had to talk to Irene, Maria and Tina as they threw Rice Crispies on the floor. Wendy called Kevin again and he came downstairs slowly, loosely clad in clothes bearing a family resemblance to a school uniform. Adam had a briefcase full of pens and complex mathematical equipment. Kevin took a pound from his mum's purse for his dinner and headed out for his new adventure with both hands in his pockets.

Adam was full of the day to come but Kevin was uninterested and surly.

'My school's got a brilliant library. It's got everything. And they've got loads of science laboratories and a massive sports hall. It's got loads more than Elton Moor.'

'So what? Who wants a library?'

'The brochure says that we do Latin.'

'What's that?'

'It's a language. I've learnt some. Listen: *Amo, amas, amat, amamus, amatis, amant*.'

'Who speaks that?'

'No one now.'

'So why do you have to do it then?'

'I don't know. You just do.'

Kevin thought for a moment and then produced a killer question: 'Where is Latin anyway?'

Adam knew where Latin was but he didn't tell Kevin. Kevin didn't really care where Latin was. Kevin set out on that journey, the Cock of St Thomas's. By the time he arrived at Elton Moor he had been made painfully aware that everything had changed.

Adam and Kevin were approaching the river when they were stopped by a boy with a thirty-year-old face on top of a twelve-year-old body. Mark O'Reilly had been the Cock of St Joseph's primary school and he wanted to establish his ascendancy at Elton Moor at once.

'Are you Kevin McDermott?'

'Might be. Who wants to know?'

Mark O'Reilly already knew enough to attack. Within a minute he had ripped Kevin's jumble-sale jumper and bloodied his face. Mark O'Reilly was so hard that even Tez Satchel was reputed to be wary of him. Fortunately, he was easily satisfied and he left Kevin with his pride more bruised than his skin.

Adam and Kevin parted at the walls of their schools. Elton Moor comprehensive school and Bury Grammar School were four hundred yards apart on either bank of the River Irwell. And, as Adam crossed the bridge and they said goodbye, neither of them had a sense of quite how much it mattered. Adam Matthews and Kevin McDermott were blood brothers. For always.

part two: *Brangy Warriors*

Teenage Kicks

Teenage Kicks were born on 10 April 1983, Adam's sixteenth birthday. Bob and June tried to disguise his cheap bass guitar with clever wrapping but it looked only like a badly wrapped guitar. Adam had no talent for the bass guitar and no desire to play one. He resented taking up both his birthday and his Christmas present allocation on a bass guitar he didn't even want. But he had formed a band with Sacha Bland, his friend from school, on the express understanding that he would fill the vacant bass player's slot as well as taking on the far more glamorous lead vocals.

Teenage Kicks were inspired less by dreams of pop-star glory than by the availability of equipment and rehearsal space. Sacha's father owned a second-hand electronic bric-à-brac business in Cheetham Hill which meant both that they had a warehouse to rehearse in and that Sacha was never short of temperamental toys to play with. Sacha had a Scooby Doo sandwich of a stereo system and a vast, immobile Marshall amplifier that sounded like it was exploding whenever Sacha strummed his Fender Stratocaster. It was only when Adam plugged in his sixteenth-birthday present that Sacha even considered that it might be a bass amplifier. Sacha also had an old drum kit that his uncle had given him. Sacha's uncle Jacob claimed to have been the drummer in a band called The Hollies. Adam listened to a song about him not being heavy, him being his brother, and confidently declared that The Hollies were rubbish. Then he read in *New Musical Express* that Paul Weller liked them, so he changed his mind.

Adam and Sacha had a seven-year plan for world domination which they had been sketching in their rough books for months. They would start by supporting The Style Council and then move on to a British tour of their own. Ambition and plans they had aplenty. Only musical talent stood between Teenage Kicks, fame and fortune. From the way that Adam and Sacha dreamed together at the back of Latin lessons, one would have thought that Teenage Kicks actually existed. In fact, they had a guitarist with a guitar and an inappropriate amplifier, a vocalist and reluctant bassist with a cheap bass and a drum kit but no drummer.

Teenage Kicks only ever became more than rough-book fantasy because of Trevor West. Trevor was in the year below and played the piano in the school orchestra. He wore National Health spectacles in the days before Morrissey turned them into the eyewear of choice for people in advertising agencies. He had a helmet haircut out of the Bob Matthews style book and preferred classical music to pop.

'It's shit. There's no words.'

'Well, I like it.'

'It's shit,' repeated Adam, feeling that his case simply needed asserting again, more vehemently.

'You'd have to get your hair cut, Trevor,' added Sacha, thinking ahead.

'I don't know if my mum will let me,' said Trevor, not showing much of a rock-and-roll sensibility.

'And you'll have to change your name as well,' said Adam, looking for Trevor's exit strategy.

'Why? What's wrong with Trevor?'

'Pop stars are not called Trevor.'

'What about Trevor Horn?' asked Sacha.

'Yeah, and look at him.'

Adam put on a squeaky voice that could make any song in the world sound stupid.

'Video killed the radio star. Crap. Anyway Buggle, what can you play?'

'Piano, flute, trumpet . . .'

'No, I meant what songs?'

'I can play anything, really.'

Adam auditioned Trevor by humming the piano riff at the beginning of *Oliver's Army* and challenging Trevor to reproduce it, which he did, perfectly.

'God, that's amazing.'

'Do you want to be in a band?' said Sacha, seizing his chance.

'All right.'

Adam had relented. He had been overpowered by Trevor's piano prowess.

'You're in. But we'll have to give you a new name. Trevor's hopeless. Let's call you Look North. Look North-West.'

'I don't want to be called Look North-West. My name is Trevor.'

'Sorry, Look North; that's your name.'

Look North-West was the early evening local news round-up, starring Stuart Hall on his day off from *It's a Knockout*. Stuart wore shirts with a different coloured collar and a necklace underneath his tie but outside his shirt. Adam had a sudden vision of a gimmick for Trevor that would turn him into a weird pop star, like the scary one in Sparks, rather than a classical music nerd.

Look North-West made Teenage Kicks possible. Now they were short only of someone to hit The Hollies' drum kit. When Sacha suggested his friend Howard from Manchester Grammar, Adam leapt in at once.

'I've got a mate who'll do it.'

'Is he a drummer?'

'Not yet, no.'

'Has he *ever* played drums, Adam?'

'Oh yeah, he used to. He's just a bit out of practice.'

As far as Adam knew, Kevin had never so much as tapped on his school desk with a pair of plastic rulers. But he wanted Kevin to share his Teenage Kicks.

Adam walked up Kevin's path with some trepidation. They had seen less of each other recently. Adam had his O levels looming and Bob was keeping a tight rein on his extra-curricular activity. Kevin, for his part, was on schoolboy terms at Bury and playing regularly for the youth team. When he wasn't concentrating on his football Kevin was terrorising Bury precinct with Tez Satchel. But, for all that, Kevin and Adam were still Brangy Warriors together. Kevin was the captain and Adam was an irregular in the team but they trained hard together. Brangy Warriors were at their peak, just one game away from the Lancashire Youth Cup final. Every Thursday evening Kevin and Adam wandered down the hill to the sloppy patch of grass where Brangy Warriors trained.

Adam was shown in by Wendy and was discouraged to hear Genesis bleating out 'Turn it on Again' from Kevin's bedroom. Adam slammed open the door and knocked Kevin's record player off the table onto the floor.

'Fucking hell. Watch it.'

'It's a stupid place to put it, right behind the door.'

'The plug doesn't reach any further.'

'Where did you get this effort from anyway?'

Kevin's record player was hardly Sacha Bland state-of-the-art. It had an arm like Popeye and a stylus like a chisel which didn't so much slot into the groove of the vinyl as make a new one.

'I got it from the skoo fête. It was only a quid.'

'What you listening to?' Adam said, without hiding his scorn.

'It's not mine. My uncle Greg lent it us.'

'I'll lend you some stuff. Some Motown or something, not that old bloke's crap.'

'All right.'

'Do you want to be in a band?'

'What sort of band?'

'We're mods. Well, me and Sacha are.'

'Is there a girl in it?'

'No, Sacha's a lad.'

'He's got a girl's name.'

'Sacha's a boy's name. What about Sacha Distel? He shags for France.'

72

'Who else is in it?'

'This kid called Trevor. But we call him Look North.'

'Why?'

'Because his surname's West. Look North-West.'

'Oh, I see. Is he from your skoo as well?'

'Yes, he plays piano. And he's got one. I got a bass for my birthday and Sacha's got a guitar and a drum kit but we need someone to play drums and I thought you could do it.'

Kevin thought about being a drummer for a second and then smiled.

'Go on then.'

'We're going to have a rehearsal on Saturday.'

'All right. Do you want to go to Rebecca's after?'

'I'll never get in.'

'Tez Satchel's brother works on the door. I can get us in.'

'Can you get Sacha and Look North in as well?'

'Yeah, probably. If I have to.'

Adam retreated to his bedroom to write lyrics. Sacha had insisted that they would never amount to anything unless they wrote their own songs and Teenage Kicks had a clear division of labour. Adam had been given a week to come up with a full lyric for three original songs. In the meantime Sacha would collaborate with Look North-West to write some music. It never occurred to Adam or Sacha that the words and music had to fit together.

Adam had read an interview in which Paul Weller had told him to write about what he knew. That didn't seem to leave him much to go on. Adam decided he would write about the content of his O level History and French courses. 'The Jumble Sale' was a searing indictment of nuclear proliferation which compared world leaders conducting an arms race to old women grabbing jumpers off the stalls. 'The Stranger' told the tale of a man who killed someone because the sun came out and 'Biscuits in History' was a study in modern nationalism. Adam soon abandoned his projected song about Bismarck when he failed to find anything that rhymed with *kulturkampf*. If Paul Weller was

Adam's inspiration as a vocalist and a fashion icon, it was AJP Taylor who lurked behind most of his words.

Adam unveiled his work at the first full Teenage Kicks rehearsal. Sacha was impressed and Look North-West was uninterested. Kevin, however, was very clear.

'You what? Say that again.'

'He loses control.'

'What, because it's sunny? What sort of excuse is that? Sorry, constable, but the weather's turned out nice again so I stabbed the bastard.'

'It's more complicated than that, Kevin.'

'Why? What's the weather got to do with it? You're more likely to do it while it's raining anyway.'

'Ah, so you admit that the weather does have something to do with it,' said Sacha snottily.

'That's not what I was saying.'

'It's a silly song anyway,' said Look North-West.

'Some people are very sensitive to the world, Kevin,' said Sacha.

'Fucking hell,' said Kevin, suddenly. 'What the fuck's that?'

He held out his drum sticks which he had rubbed against the wall and which were now covered in thick navy blue paint.

'I forgot to mention that. My dad painted this morning. It should dry soon.'

'It's no wonder it stinks in here.'

'Oh do stop moaning, Kevin.'

Kevin disliked Sacha's habit of using his name at the end of the sentence. From Adam's description Kevin had assumed that he wouldn't like Sacha very much. As soon as they were introduced, he realised he had been quite wrong. He hated him.

'Look at my top. It's covered in shit.'

'It is shit.'

'You what?'

'You'll have to change your dress sense if you want to be in this band.'

'Why? What's up with my clothes?'

'They're so . . . so towny. Can't you tuck your shirt in? It looks ridiculous.'

'It doesn't. Everyone does this.'

'And you can't wear Farahs. What jumble sale did you drag those out of?'

'Have you heard my song called "The Jumble Sale"?' asked Adam in a spirit of diplomacy.

'There's no need to take the piss. I'll wear what I fucking want. All right, *Sacha*?'

When Sacha popped out to go to the Kentucky Fried Chicken for some thin chips, Kevin confided in Adam.

'He's a right dick, him, isn't he?'

'He's all right.'

'Why's he got a crap beard?'

'He reckons he's Jimi Hendrix.'

'Looks more like Jimmy the barber. It's all bum fluff.'

'He's all right when you get to know him. And he might have a point about your keks.'

'There's nothing wrong with my keks.'

'They're not exactly cool, are they?'

'Nobody can see your keks anyway when you're sat behind the bloody drums.'

'What about the pictures? You can't wear Farahs. They're really stiffy.'

'Right then, you give us the money and I'll get some new keks.'

'I might do.'

'Fucking hell. I didn't know that drummers had to wear special keks. Jesus, I feel faint in here. These fumes are fucking awful.'

'Oh do stop moaning, Kevin.'

'Shut it, you, or else I'll have you.'

Kevin and Adam play-fought, with drumsticks as swords, while Look North-West sat in a corner and juggled the words and the music until their jagged edges touched. When he had finished he devised an elementary bass line which did not require Adam to stray from the top string. He taught Sacha the relevant chord order and spent ten minutes with Kevin tapping out the rhythm of the track. Kevin looked at Trevor blankly, not knowing what he was talking about.

Teenage Kicks were almost ready to play. They tuned up for half an hour, making the most grotesque cacophony until Look North-West took each instrument in turn and set them to a common register. The very first song that Teenage Kicks attempted was the Matthews/Bland/West composition, 'The Stranger'. Adam moved his hand up and down the top string in approximate time to the music. Kevin slapped the skins violently, left-handed, because that was the way he had seen the drummer from Genesis play. It was obvious at once to the other three band members, though not to the drummer himself, that Kevin was, in fact, right-handed. Adam and Kevin parted company as soon as Adam mouthed the first words:

There once was a man who lived by the sea,
But he was very different to you and me;
He went to the beach but he had no fun,
Because he hadn't banked on the power of the sun,
He's a stranger, a stranger, a strange, strange, strange,
    strange stranger.

As soon as he became the lead singer Adam forgot that he was also the bassist. As a rhythm section, Adam and Kevin were as tight as a tent hitched to the wrong frame. Meanwhile, Sacha strummed hard, savouring the echo of chords he was inventing as he went. And then, above it all spiralled Look North-West with his flowery classical keyboards. Suddenly it mattered a lot less that Adam could only manage one bass string at a time or that Sacha Bland played the guitar like he was wearing oven gloves. As long as Look North-West was painting pictures on the piano it didn't matter. In the early days Teenage Kicks were more of a piano concerto than a band. 'White Riot' sounded odd with the piano to the forefront, with no bass and irrelevant drums. When Adam shouted down the microphone, 'white riot, I wanna riot, white riot, I riot on my own' he turned to look at Trevor West on the piano and couldn't help but feel that they didn't look or sound a lot like The Clash. Teenage Kicks were on their way all the same.

After an hour of noise Teenage Kicks were overpowered by paint fumes.

'Right. I've had enough of this. I can hardly breathe in here,' said Kevin.

'We can't stop yet; we've only just started,' objected Sacha.

Look North-West intervened. 'I agree with Kevin. This is hopeless. We sound awful and we can't breathe properly.'

'We can't stop yet; we've got a gig already,' revealed Adam.

'You what?' asked Sacha.

'I asked my mum if we could play the church hall. And the vicar said yes, whenever we're ready.'

'That'll be never,' said Look North-West, with the authority of his musical pedigree.

'Are you having us on?' said the unprepared drummer.

'No, honest. They said we can play there.'

'So we've got a gig already?'

'I think that's been established already,' said Look North-West, more testily than usual.

'He's from Barcelona,' said Sacha, patting Kevin on the head. Sacha loved quoting comedy programmes, convinced that his delivery added something to the original.

'What you on about, you dick?' demanded Kevin.

'Just joking. Can't you take a joke?'

'You'll be laughing on the other side of your face if you don't watch it.'

'All right; that'll do. Come on; we've got a gig to prepare for and we're not exactly ready. So let's try that one called "Start". Adam, have you got that bass line yet do you think?'

'I think so.'

'Right, away we go then.'

Teenage Kicks lumbered on, held together by Look North-West. They chugged through a gruesomely slow version of The Jam's 'Start!' It was supposed to be a quick version but Adam could not manage the stolen bass line at the required speed and kept being left behind by the rest of the band. At the third attempt they gave up and played it at the only pace he could manage. Look North-West took over lead vocal and, unencumbered by the need to do a Paul Weller impersonation, sang the melody in tune and in time with the music. By seven o'clock Teenage Kicks were starting to believe that St Thomas's church hall would witness a triumph and they packed up the equipment in good heart.

Kevin then insisted they celebrated at Rebecca's where he had arranged to meet Irene Bradshaw, his girlfriend. Ray Satchel let them all in, as promised, much to the chagrin of Look North-West. Trevor had never been into a night-club before and he was immediately entranced. It was all so much *chrome*.

'Look at all those plants. Amazing.'

Look North-West decided to get drunk to see what it was like. Slowly, Look North-West was becoming a pop star. Kevin felt at home in Rebecca's. His clothes worked here and he had a pretty girlfriend to prove it. It was Adam and Sacha who were incongruous in their cardigans and Hush Puppies. With the first note of Edwin Starr's 'Contact' Kevin dragged Irene Bradshaw and the rest of Teenage Kicks onto the dance floor.

Look North-West scuttled back and forth between the bar and the dance floor where he found his feet but lost his mind. Kevin, Adam and Sacha jogged up and down in imitation of good dancers. Reckless females revolved in and out of their charmless circle. A pretty girl called Maxine lingered to dance with Adam who, with his dimples, his smooth skin, his symmetry and his neatly brushed brown hair was a choirboy dressed as a soul boy. Maxine was known to be Tez Satchel's moll. Maxine regularly protested, to no avail, that she wasn't going out with Tez and had no desire to do so. She never had a boyfriend because all the boys knew that Tez fancied her. Apart from off-limits Maxine, Adam danced with Kevin who danced with Sacha who danced with Adam. They were all beginning to tire of miming at each other when Sacha spotted a miracle.

'Jesus.'

'I thought you didn't believe in him.'

'I do now. Look at that.'

Sacha pointed through the plastic jungle to a red leather sofa in the corner on which Look North-West was grappling with a girl like she was a blow-up doll with a puncture. When Look North-West allowed his girl briefly to come up for air he found that they had three new grinning companions.

'Bloody hell, Look-North. What are you doing?'

'You said you were called Trevor.'

'I am.'

'That's my uncle Trevor's name.'

'Is it? I thought he was called Barry,' intervened Sacha.

'Who?'

'Your uncle Trevor.'

'There's no need to be so sarky.'

'Yes, shut up, Sacha. Just shut up.'

Trevor West had never told anyone to shut up before. He felt the drink talking and the glow of showing off in front of a girl.

'These are the other people in my band. Gentlemen, this is Gwen.'

'Hello, Gwen.'

'Trevor says you're all punks.'

'Mods.'

'Gwen likes Mozart. That's what we got talking about.'

Trevor and Gwen collected their coats and, having both located the other unlikely person in the club, left the three Teenage Kicks to return to the dance floor. Adam attracted a lot of attention but was too shy to follow up on it, except when he used Kevin as his mouthpiece. Adam danced and looked cute while Kevin walked up to the prettiest girls.

'You see that lad over there. He fancies you.'

'Who, Adam Matthews?'

'Yeah.'

'He's fit, he is.'

Adam took a fluttering girl called Lucy into a corner where he told her he just wanted to talk. Kevin and Irene sat next to them. Kevin interrupted Adam's monologue by tapping him on the arm. He pointed to Sacha Bland who was standing in the queue for the coats on his own. As Sacha left in a huff, Kevin and Adam grinned at each other.

Marauders

On the last day of term, breaking up for Easter and for ever, Kevin observed the leavers' tradition. Every year on this day the fifth year of Elton Moor comprehensive stormed Bury Grammar School. There was notoriety to be won in being the boy who penetrated deepest into hostile territory and honour for bringing back the finest souvenir.

Kevin's army made their way across the bridge, climbed over the small wall at the back of Bury Grammar School, and moved menacingly past the rifle range. The Elton Moor boys expected the Grammar School boys to roll over, as they did annually. The Battle of Leaving Day was always a walk-over. But as they wrapped round the corner like a snake, they were met by thirty boys in khakis, carrying rifles.

'Fucking hell. They've got guns.'

The Combined Cadet Force was rehearsing its drill in preparation for Founder's Day. The guns were all empty and the soldiers were all little boys. Indeed, the Combined Cadet Force scattered in all directions at the first sight of the Elton Moor marauders, leaving behind only the third former who carried the huge bass drum and was therefore unable to run. Mark O'Reilly put his foot through the big bass drum while his infantrymen moved on towards the cricket pitch.

'To the white grass!' shouted Kevin.

Elton Moor's small fields did not include white grass. Their cricket pitch had been sold years before any of these boys were out of primary school. The Elton Moor army moved on towards

81

the sports hall and the arts and crafts block where they were met, on the far side of the cricket wicket, by the Bury Grammar prefects. Hidden in the crowd was Adam. Kevin looked right through his friend as the Elton Moor marauders charged on.

'Snob attack. Charge.'

Kevin ran at Sacha Bland, aimed for his straggly beard, and landed him a heavy blow on his guitar-strumming hand. The Elton Moor boys brushed aside the weak defence of the prefects. They were more interested in souvenirs than violence. In all the annals of Elton Moor legend nobody had ever managed to walk away with all three layers of a gymnastics box. Kevin ran for the newly built gymnasium.

As they arrived at the door of the new block, the Elton Moor boys were met by Mr Malcolm who, despite wearing rouge and owning a collection of florescent neckerchiefs, caused all manner of speculation about whether it were actually possible for a teacher to be homosexual. Mr Malcolm was a broad and hard man and it took four Elton Moor boys to hold him down which, he reflected later, he had rather enjoyed.

Ten of the Elton Moor crew ran into the art room and emerged with four large pictures of apples and pears, an easel, three papier mâché models of the Queen's head and a box full of charcoal. Ten others raided the craft room and came out with a wonky bird box, six metal pendants with squiggles burnt on, a yellow screwdriver and a brand-new wood planer.

Kevin led ten more of his gang through into the sports hall where they interrupted a first-year PE lesson by tripping up the teacher, Mr Ross, and sitting on his head. Thirty twelve-year-olds in identikit white vests and white underpants ran for cover into the storeroom where they hid behind rows and rows of expensive basketballs. While one of his apaches tried his level best to fart on Mr Ross's head, Kevin supervised the theft of a gymnastics box. On their way back out, Elton Moor again met the defending ranks of the Bury Grammar School prefects who gave a better account of themselves against opponents carrying the wooden layers and the felt top of a gymnastics box.

The two half-Cocks of the school, Kevin and Mark O'Reilly,

ran ahead. They had never fought each other to work out who was the champion. Kevin refused to jeopardise his longed-for apprenticeship at Bury Football Club by risking injury at Mark's hands. But, in exuberant mood at the end of five years of boredom, he forgot all risk and ran headlong at the Bury Grammar School prefecture. His school friends laid down their boxes and joined a full-scale fight which spilled back onto the white grass.

Led by Kevin and Mark, Elton Moor fought their way through with all layers of box intact. A group of teachers in tweed jackets stroked their arm patches, fascinated and appalled and absolutely not wanting to intervene. What did they care for the odd gymnastics box in any case? Mr Ross would make a terrible fuss but a wealthy parent could always be prevailed upon to replace the lost items. The groundsman, though, was close to tears when he saw the scuffs on his beloved pitch.

As they made their way back to base camp the Elton Moor invaders encountered no more boys on sentry duty. They found instead a scruffy boy with a big curly Afro and a straggly beard, and a slender boy with neatly combed hair and smoothly scrubbed skin. Adam and Sacha had been behind the rifle range for a cigarette though Adam had been strictly a voyeur. As the two of them came out from behind the rifle range, wary of teachers who refused to respect the truce for legal smoking, they were met instead by the returning conquerors and their dismantled Trojan Horse.

Mark O'Reilly suddenly had the idea of taking a hostage back to Elton Moor. He grabbed Sacha Bland and, cottoning on very quickly, one of the O'Reilly sycophants took care of Adam.

'Right, how much cash have you got?'

'What?'

'One of you can go. But you have to pay. The one who pays the most can go.'

'But I haven't got any money.'

'What about you, beardy weirdy?'

Sacha took a leather wallet from his inside pocket and offered Mark a crisp five-pound note.

'Will that do?'

'Very nice. Go on then; piss off.'

'What about me?'

'You're going on a trip, you are. Unless you can beat a fiver.'

'Sacha, you can't leave me here . . .'

Sacha had paid the price of freedom and was already heading off for lunch. At that point Adam saw Kevin peeking out from behind a bit of wooden box.

'Kevin,' he implored.

'Don't,' whispered Kevin in return.

Mark O'Reilly and Kevin frog-marched Adam over the bridge between the two schools. They dragged him through the corridors of Elton Moor which seemed so dreary and musty after the new-lick-of-paint smell of Bury Grammar. Adam trusted that round every corner there would be a teacher to rescue him but they walked on and on without sight of authority. Kevin hung back, out of sight of Adam. Eventually Mark led the gang into a tiny, empty, dark room.

'Get on the floor.'

Adam did as he was told.

'On your front. And roll your legs up.'

Mark took the first layer of the box and laid it over Adam's scrunched form. He rebuilt the whole box, placed the felt on top and jumped over it for good measure. As he did so he exerted pressure on Adam underneath and there was a muffled cry from within the box.

'Go on; everyone has to have a go.'

The Elton Moor boys each took a turn to jump over the box and hear Adam squeal.

'Go on, Kev.'

'Nah, you're all right.'

'Go on, Kevin. Jump over the box,' said Mark.

'I can't be bothered.'

'Jump over the fucking box, Kevin. What you scared of? Just jump over the box.'

Kevin ran at the box and tried to hurdle it without exerting any pressure on the top. He misjudged his approach slightly and knocked the top hard. The bottom layer of the box was lifted from the floor and pressed down onto Adam's coiled legs.

'Oh what was that, I wonder?'

'Sounded like a posh get in the box. Oh, what a shame.'

The Elton Moor gang trooped off to show their booty to the girls and the younger boys.

'Right, a new rule. Every time you go past that room you have to go in and jump over that box. See if the posh get squeaks.'

Mark O'Reilly inspected the plunder and declared that this had been the most legendary raid in the distinguished tradition of Elton Moor stealing objects from Bury Grammar School. He strode off to find Irene Bradshaw whom he had resolved to woo with a large picture of some apples and pears and a squashed papier-mâché model of the Queen's head.

Kevin broke off from the crowd with an excuse about football and made his way back to the small room in which Adam lay underneath a poorly reconstructed gymnastics box. Kevin lifted the top off and peered down through the hole. The look of fright on Adam's face startled him but not nearly as much as he had startled Adam.

'Soz, mate. You know how it is.'

'I could have broken my leg then. It creased when you jumped over it. The whole box was on my leg. I might have missed the semi.'

Kevin and Adam had arranged to meet after school for the semi-final of the Lancashire Youth Cup. But loyalty to a Brangy Warrior was superseded by the fact of attending a different school.

'You're all right though, aren't you?'

'Just.'

'Go on; leg it.'

'Can't you come with me?'

'I can't. Go on; leg it before anyone comes back. See you round the front of your skoo at fourish.'

Adam ran through Elton Moor's unfamiliar corridors, out of the back door and across the bridge. He jumped over the wall into the safety of a parade-ground full of little boys practising military drill just in case a Dad's Army should ever again be required.

Adam stretched his leg obsessively through double Chemistry, searching for an injury and, on not finding anything, stroking his thigh because it was more interesting than listening to Mr Hyde's speech about the degree to which the elements reacted with water.

'Kate's navel can't magnify all zinc ferrets,' said Mr Hyde.

Adam groped himself.

'Adam Matthews. What did I just say?'

There wasn't much chance of guessing. Adam stalled.

'Err, you were talking about putting things in water and what happens.'

'Kate's navel can't magnify all zinc ferrets. That is what I said. Now have you the first idea why I said that?'

'Errr . . . no.'

'Potassium, Sodium, Calcium, Magnesium, Aluminium, Zinc, Iron. I guarantee, Adam Matthews, you will never forget this sentence now as long as you live which, as long as you keep Kate out of the water, I trust will be a long time.'

This was Mr Hyde's Chemistry joke. He chuckled to himself at the thought that, next lesson, he would make the class sing the periodic table.

Adam was delighted to hear the bell. He collected his sports bag from his form room and ran out to meet Kevin.

'Your leg all right?'

'Yeah, should be.'

Adam had secretly hoped to be injured. Brangy Warriors were playing a team from Skelmersdale, the very prospect of which he found frightening. When Adam had asked his mum where Skelmersdale was she had replied, 'Skem? It's near Liverpool,' with such scorn that she might well have said that it was near Hell. The nearer people came to being from Liverpool the more Adam, as a general rule, was frightened of them. Adam's unreasoning views that people from Liverpool were all Catholics and that all Catholics were hard and good at football even survived his father pointing out that not *every* Pope had been good at football. Skem Marauders promised to be both good and hard.

Kevin and Adam walked through Brandlesholme to the foot of the hill where dilapidated houses gathered apologetically around the green hole that was once Bury's largest cotton mill. They chatted about football as they passed by the remaining outbuildings, the abandoned seraglios of yesteryear's prosperity.

'I don't know if I'm going to be in the team,' said Adam, asking for reassurance.

''Course you will. I told Terry he's got to keep you in.'

'Do you think we'll win?'

Kevin stopped as they crossed Bury Bridge, at the bottom of the Bolton road. He took Adam by the shoulders and held him still to steady the nerves.

''Course we will. Marauders are bobbins. And we're both going to score.'

This was the first time that Brangy Warriors had reached the semi-finals of the Lancashire Youth Cup. They had achieved it principally due to the brilliance of their captain and midfield impresario, Kevin McDermott, who was the top scorer in the competition.

Kevin and Adam arrived at the pitch on the flat mud-land in the shadow of the shell of the mill. Their team was known, appropriately enough, as the Warriors. And Brandlesholme was known to all the locals as Brangy. It was a prestigious team to play for, champions of Bury, and the boys were proud to be Brangy Warriors.

Adam greeted Terry Mackie, the milkman-turned-manager, who told him he would be starting on the left wing. The boys went into the dressing room to get changed. As they rubbed cooking oil into their legs and pulled on boots softened by dubbin, the crowd assembled outside. Ten of the Brangy Warriors' fathers were there. Sammy McDermott was elsewhere, busy washing down his tea. One hundred Brangy folk: mums and dads, nannas and pappas, brothers and sisters, aunts and uncles, even cats and dogs, lined the sides of the pitch.

This was a Brangy crowd. It was made up of people who were, variously, proud, virtuous, fractious, honourable, ebullient, funny, truculent and kind-hearted. Their lives were a battle and they fought their way on, remaining spiky and entertaining throughout. They were the Brangy warriors of life.

As the game kicked off the crowd was so close to the line that any Marauder taking a throw-in had to push a Brangy granny out of the way, with the promise of terrible retribution. The temper of the crowd worsened when the opposition took an early lead with a goal of genuine brilliance by a splenetic young man who would one day make a name for himself as an international footballer. Barry Mawdsley, the Brangy Warriors' goalkeeper who had a lazy eye, was helplessly rooted to his spot.

But, roared on by the bellicose Brangy warriors on the side, and with Kevin leading by example, the Warriors launched themselves at the Marauders. The poor referee tried manfully to maintain control in the flurry. Kevin coaxed his blood brother into the game. Adam pushed the ball outside his brutal full-back and stretched into his superior stride. Having been taught by his manager that the first tackle should always be vicious, the Marauder chopped him with studs to the calf. As Adam fell he kicked out in retaliation, giving his guilty opponent a pretext for righteous indignation. The Marauder was drawing back his foot to kick the prostrate Adam into the River Irwell when he was smothered from behind by Kevin McDermott.

'You cropping bastard.'

Kevin grabbed the Marauder by the throat before the referee could intervene. He pushed his opponent away and bent down to tend to Adam.

'I told you. You can stuff him every time.'

'Mmm,' said Adam, not convinced.

Adam feared for his skinny legs and so retreated into the periphery on the left wing despite his father's prompting from the side. The game was frantic and the players were still beset by nerves. After half an hour of disjointed sparring, Kevin emerged from the mass with a truly majestic swivel to make the score 1–1 at half-time.

The second half was bad-tempered but uneventful until, with two minutes remaining, Kevin picked the ball up on the half-way line. A range of possibilities shot through his head and, with intuitive precision, he classified them and chose the best option in an instant. He slid the ball elegantly between a pair of Marauders to Adam who was hurtling down the left wing. Kevin set off like wind flowing through a tunnel and made the penalty spot when Adam, without so much as glancing up, hammered the ball across. As if trained by a magnet towards his steel head, the ball made Kevin McDermott a hero. Taking off with no care for safety, Kevin guided the ball unerringly into the bottom corner of the net past a flailing Marauder goalkeeper.

Kevin ran to the crowd like a conquering monarch, like a Brangy warrior. He punched the air repeatedly, a coiled mixture of deep belonging and brimming anger. His pale-blue eyes seemed to surge out of freckles on a canvas of pale white skin. Kevin McDermott was the true hero of the hour, the toast of the cheering Brangy warriors.

The game meandered to its end until, with seconds left, a Marauder received the ball on the left-hand side of the penalty area. He immediately came under intense pressure from a cavalcade of Brangy Warriors and his hurried shot carried no conviction. The ball was drifting definitely wide of the right-hand post, slowly but surely. Barry Mawdsley had judged the ball well with his one good eye. At just this moment, Tyke, the bulldog owned by Kevin's uncle Greg, wandered onto the field. The ball seemed suddenly trapped in slow motion as it freeze-framed its way onto Tyke's backside and flicked agonisingly into the net to send the lucky Marauders wild with delight. According to the rules of football, which make no mention of dogs, this had to stand as a goal.

For another mournful minute, the ferocity of the Brangy warriors quivered like strained elastic. As the final whistle sounded, it snapped. The field exploded into a conflagration of irate relatives and muddy schoolboys, arguing about the rules, berating the referee, intimidating the Marauders, punching their parents. This outbreak of Brangy war, which ended only with the arrival of the police, was a collective burst of vengeance against malign fortune, come down to mock in the form of Uncle Greg's bulldog who had unwittingly scored the equaliser for the Marauders.

The captain of Brangy Warriors trooped away, alone but not unremarked, his virtuoso performance spoiled by a bulldog.

'Never mind, son. You did all you could.'

'Thanks, Mr Matthews.'

Kevin bore the eleventh-hour draw with good grace. That was because, as Adam curled his arm around his huckleberry friend, Kevin was already looking forward to greater things. He had the grandest dreams of them all and Kevin McDermott was going to make it all the way to glory. Everyone knew that because Kevin McDermott was just about to sign schoolboy forms at Bury. Everyone knew that because Kevin McDermott was the finest footballer ever to grace Brangy fields.

Musical Differences

On the day that Adam received his O level results, Kevin's talent was subjected to a cruel annual ritual. At the start of every new football season Mickey Bell, the youth team coach at Bury FC, called the schoolboys into his office and broke the news about whether or not they were to be offered an apprenticeship. Kevin was captain of the youth team but his form in the latter half of the previous season had been poor. He had been celebrating real life, lager and cigarettes a little too enthusiastically. Like Adam had felt five years before when the fact of sitting the Bury Grammar School examination had suddenly made him equal with his inferiors, Kevin had a glimpse of failure.

Mickey nodded to a chair as Kevin entered his spartan office. Mickey rocked back on the hind legs of his chair and nibbled a biro with which he had been doodling on Bury FC notepaper. Kevin fixed his stare on the pictures on the wall as Mickey trotted perfunctorily through the preliminaries. The stars of Bury FC past looked down on him. The biggest pictures were the Bury teams from 1900 and 1903 who had won the FA Cup at Wembley. The 1903 team were legendary. They had not conceded a goal throughout the competition and had beaten Derby County in the final 6–0, the largest ever margin, then and still.

But after 1903 all the stars had been forced to leave Bury to make their true fortune. There was a portrait of Eddie Quigley and Eddie Gleadall in their days at Sheffield Wednesday, of Alec

Lindsay in his Liverpool kit, of Eddie Colquhoun in his Sheffield United colours and John McGrath in the black-and-white stripes of Newcastle United. Kevin knew all of these players. Mickey Bell used them as examples for motivation. 'Do well here and you can leave,' he used to joke. Only Kevin knew he wasn't joking.

Kevin wanted to play for Manchester City, so the real hero on the wall was Mickey's cousin, Colin Bell, who had gone to Maine Road and had played for England at Wembley. Colin Bell played in Kevin's position, in the middle of midfield, in the middle of everything, and he was the best player Bury had ever produced.

'So, how do you think you've done lately, Kevin?' said Mickey, finally getting to the point.

'I know I've not played as good as I can but I've been injured. My foot's not right and . . .'

Mickey raised an eyebrow which was enough to stop Kevin's flow. Mickey took the biro out of his mouth and a subtle grin emerged out of his expressionless face.

'Sign here, sunshine. You've been our best man this year. You'll do for me.'

Mickey offered the pen. Stunned, Kevin did not take it.

'What's up? Don't you want to sign? Have Man United got you first?'

'I wouldn't play for them in a month of Sundays.'

'So go on, then. We've a contract here.'

Kevin scribbled illegibly on the paper without looking at it.

'Aren't you going to even read it? Your dad can have a look if you want.'

'Nah, it's all right. I don't care what it says as long as I'm in.'

'Can I ask you a question, Kevin?'

'Yeah.'

'What's your ambition, son?'

'I want to play for Man City and play for England.'

'So you're thinking of leaving us already are you?'

'No, I didn't mean . . .'

'It's all right. I know what you mean. You're right to want that. There's something of our Colin about you, lad. If you don't get waylaid you could make it. I hope you do.'

'Yeah,' said Kevin, most of the way into wonderland.

'I mean it though, Kevin, about not getting waylaid. You've got to be very careful. I've said this before to lads with all your talent and more and they've thrown it away. You're only starting out now and we'll see how much you want it. You know what separated our Colin from me?'

'No.'

'You don't realise that I was a great footballer, do you?'

'You're not bad.'

'No, I wasn't bad. I was brilliant. I was better than you are at your age. I was better than our Colin as well. But he wanted it more than me. I was like Georgie Best, I was, on and off the pitch. I was a young lad and I enjoyed myself and that was all right but I haven't played at Wembley and I haven't got forty-eight England caps. Our Colin's got all that and that's why I sit in an office with a big picture of him looking at me. It's not just about talent, Kevin. You've got to try hard. You've got to give up a lot if you really want to make it.'

'I will.'

'I hope you do. If I were you I'd settle down as soon as you can. You've got a very nice young lady and I hope she can keep you out of trouble.'

'Yeah.'

'You're in this band, aren't you?'

'Yeah.'

'There's nothing in it for you, Kevin. You can't be a pop star and a footballer. Just jack it in. You can be Colin Bell or Georgie Fame but you can't be both.'

'Who's Georgie Fame?'

'Never mind who Georgie Fame is. The point is that you should give up your rock band and concentrate on your football.'

'All right. I will.'

'Good.'

'But we've got a gig tonight. I'll have to do that; then I'll jack it in.'

'Good lad. Where is this gig by the way? I might come along.'

'St Thomas's church hall.'

There was a dramatic pause.

'I think you've made the right career decision, Kevin. Go on, go and tell your folks.'

Kevin went round to see Adam and gave away his news to Bob with the width of his smile.

'Well done, son. Well done. It's a good day all round then.'

'Why?'

'I'd better let our Adam tell you.'

Bob went over to the bookshelves and took out an envelope from between two gardening manuals. He stroked it and placed it back, with great care. Puzzled by this behaviour, Kevin ran upstairs where he found Adam playing cricket with dice, a game he had invented himself.

'Guess what?'

Adam didn't need to.

'You guess what as well.'

'What?'

'I got all ten.'

'All ten what?'

'O levels, you spacker.'

'Oh right. Yeah, great.'

'I'm staying on. I'm doing History, French and Latin. Did you get your results?'

'You're mad. You could get a right good job with all them exams.'

'I want to get some A levels and go to university.'

Kevin looked at Adam as though he had said that he had shot someone because the sun had come out.

'So are you definitely in at Bury?'

'Definitely. I'm an apprentice. I've signed up this after.'

'That's ace. I knew you'd be all right. I knew you'd get in.'

'I know. I thought I would but you never know.'

'So when do you reckon you'll get in the first team?'

'Pretty soon, I reckon. They'll put me in the reserves first and then I should be in the firsts pretty soon.'

'They're shit in midfield. They're way too old.'

'I know. That's what I told Mickey Bell. He told me not to be so cheeky but I reckon he thinks that as well.'

'What's your dad say?'

'Don't know. I haven't told him yet. I'd better had.'

'Come and call for us after and we'll have a practice before tonight.'

'Oh God, I'm bobbing it, me.'

'I know. It'll be all right though. Trevor'll sort it out.'

Kevin met his father at the gate of their house. Sammy rocked back when he saw his son. He burped and steadied himself by leaning on the low wall.

'I'm in, Dad.'

Sammy grunted. He stifled a second burp and began three physical gestures. He started to give Kevin his hand, raised his arm to pat his son's back, then lurched gently into a proffered hug. He completed none of them and shrunk instead into resting his head on his collar bone and murmuring, barely audibly, 'Good on yer, lad. I'm ... well, you know ... I'm ... Have you told your mum?'

'No, I've only just got back.'

'Come on; let's tell your mum.'

Wendy was so proud that she would not stop saying so. She assembled the three sisters to make the announcement that their brother was going to be a famous football star. His eldest sister Irene told her son, Nathan, who had come to visit without his grandfather's knowledge, that he could play for Bury too when he was grown up. Maria presented Kevin with a small teddy bear in a Bury kit which he christened Colin. Tina was so delighted that she decided to iron Kevin's best trousers for his gig.

That did not mean that they met with the approval of Sacha Bland.

'You can't wear those efforts.'

'Why not?'

'We're meant to be a mod band. Mods don't wear keks with pockets on the side.'

'There's always something up with my keks. Anyone'd think I pissed in 'em. No one can see my keks anyway. I'm the fucking drummer, if you remember.'

'Is that what you call it?'

'If you don't want me to do it I don't have to. I'm not going to be a pop star anyway. I've got a job already.'

'Kevin's got in at Bury.'

Sacha gave a *'so what?'* look and Look North-West concentrated on tuning the guitars.

'Here, Trevor. Put this on.'

Adam produced a rusting St Christopher on a thin silver chain.

'I'm not wearing that.'

'You've got to. It's your image.'

Adam placed the chain over Look North-West's head, under his tie and outside the white collar of his blue shirt.

Out at the front, an audience trickled into St Thomas's church hall as the inadequate loud speaker struggled with 'All Mod Cons'. At the back of the hall stood June Matthews and the rest of the St Thomas's Mothers' Union, watching guard over tressel tables loaded with sandwich triangles and sausage rolls. It wasn't rock and roll by any stretch of the imagination. Suddenly the lights went off. Not down but off, at the flick of a switch from Adam's mum. Meanwhile, twenty teenagers stood spaced evenly so that they could have stretched their arms out had they wished. The last notes of 'Down in the Tube Station at Midnight' faded away and a weedy, boyish voice declared:

'Ladies and gentlemen, please welcome for the first time, Bury's finest, Teenage Kicks.'

There was a ripple of applause, of the sort which would greet a slightly fortuitous boundary in a village cricket match on the green. The fab four bounded onto the stage and Adam went over to the microphone.

'Good evening, St Thomas's.'

The crowd said 'Good evening' back. There were so few of them that Adam managed to distinguish quite a few individual voices. He gathered from this that the hall was not brimming. It was hard to see because the unsophisticated lighting rig was trained in his eyes. From what he could actually see, he might have been the headline act at Madison Square Gardens.

'This is for Irene. It's called "Love Will Tear us Apart".'

Before a static crowd of twenty, who stood with their arms folded, Teenage Kicks huffed, puffed, collapsed and died. At the striking of the first chord, the Mothers' Union, as one, put their fingers in their ears. Teenage Kicks didn't need love to tear them apart. They did it all by themselves.

'This one's called "Biscuits in History". It's about Garibaldi and how his dreams were shattered, like a biscuit in history,' said Adam, immensely pleased with himself.

Teenage Kicks chugged through their Small Faces and Kinks standards. Even their audience, which was not versed in such esoteric choices, could work out that Teenage Kicks were a pale copy of a cover-version tribute band of The Jam's tone-deaf younger brothers.

The only high spot was a version of 'Anarchy in the UK' for piano and vocal. It wasn't supposed to be for piano and vocal but Adam and Sacha forgot their parts and Kevin stopped as soon as he could no longer take his cue from the bass. Their version lost nothing as a result. The gig then ended with the loudest whimper the poor mothers of St Thomas's had ever had the misfortune to suffer. Teenage Kicks played their signature tune with Adam chasing Feargal Sharkey up the vocal scale, with Sacha fluffing the guitar line which was most of the song, with Kevin in a time of his own and with Look North-West dreaming of the North Manchester Youth Orchestra.

There was no call for an encore. There was more chance of someone shouting 'less' than 'more'. The audience filed out in silence past the tressel tables still as loaded with sandwich triangles. The Mothers' Union nibbled on their handiwork and tipped most of it into the large steel bins that stood outside the front door.

Behind the scenes, Sacha had started the recriminations.

'You are the worst drummer I've ever heard. You were all over the place.'

'You're not exactly brilliant yourself. You think you are but you're not. You're just a dickhead and a loser.'

'Oh I'm a loser, am I? How many exams did you get, Kevin?'

'I don't need any exams. I've been signed on at Bury so you can stick your exams up your arse and you can stick your group up your arse as well.'

'Being a footballer's no guarantee of anything. You could be injured just like that.'

Sacha did a wholly inappropriate Tommy Cooper impression, at which Kevin punched him on the bridge of the nose. Trevor West, showing physical courage that nobody, not even he knew he had, jumped up between them.

'Come on, Kev; let's leave it,' said Adam.

'I can't be mithered with any of this. And I'm not hanging out with that idiot.'

'If you think you can stay in the band after you've punched me . . .'

'Weren't you listening? I don't want to stay in your stupid band.'

'Don't be like that, Kev. You don't have to decide now.'

'I've decided. The music's shit; we are shit; it's all shit.'

'We're not shit. Some of our own stuff is good.'

'No, it's not. It's total bollocks.'

'It's not. "The Prisoner" is a good song.'

'It's shit. What do you know about being in prison anyway?'

'It's not about just being in prison. It's about being in prison and not wanting to get out.'

'Why wouldn't you want to get out? That's just stupid. Anyway, I don't care that the words are crap, because you can't hear 'em anyway. The tune's total shite as well.'

'You just don't understand music,' chipped in Sacha. 'You like Whitesnake, for example.'

'I think we should split up. I think that's best for everyone.'

Trevor West spoke calmly and authoritatively. He managed

to make the others shut up with maturity of tone. 'I don't think there's any other way, is there?'

'We can get better. There's no need to overreact.'

'It's a nice idea, Adam, but it's not true. We all have different ideas of what this group is for.'

Teenage Kicks split up over musical differences. The difference was that Look North-West was musical and the others weren't.

Virtus Vera Nobilitas est

Adam knew that Kevin was wrong about school when he saw glossy pictures glistening with old colleges and new opportunities. Adam spoke to his Latin teacher, Mr Pittam, who promised to have a word with the Classics tutor at Trinity. Adam had to return to the glossy book in the library to find out whether Trinity was at Oxford or at Cambridge. He found out it was at both.

Adam wrote to Cambridge for details of the courses. He applied to four other places as well but he had already lost himself on a picture of Clare bridge. The hefty brown packages came back by return and for a long time Adam felt that the best thing about applying to university was that he suddenly got a lot of post. Adam read the prospectus keenly but far less so than Bob and June who really wore the words out. As Adam filled out the application form one Saturday morning in September, his parents consumed everything that Trinity College could send.

'*Virtus vera nobilitas est.* What's that mean?' asked Bob.

'It's *virtus vera*, with a "w".'

'It's not, it's a "v".'

'You say it with a "w".'

'Well, whatever. What's it mean?'

'I don't know. What is it?'

'It's the motto of the college. *Virtus vera*, with a "w", *nobilitas est.* Look it up, Adam. Go and get your dictionary.'

Adam flicked through the Collins Gem Latin Dictionary his parents had put in his Christmas stocking two years before.

'I know *vera* is "true".'

'I know a young woman called Vera. I'll let her know.'

'Shut up, Mum.'

'Yes. Shut up, June.'

'And *est* is "is".'

'So, "true is".'

'*Nobilitas* . . . *nobilitas* . . . yes, I thought so, "nobility".'

'It's easy, is this. You can guess half of them.'

'So what does *virtus* mean then?'

'I don't know. "Virtually", probably. "Nobility is virtually true".'

'*Virtus* . . . "virtue". So does "virtue" agree with *vera* or with *nobilitas*?'

'You what?'

'That's how you do it. It's not in the same order as English. You have to work out which one goes with which.'

'Bloody hell. No wonder it didn't catch on.'

'"True virtue is nobility." Or it might be "true nobility is virtue". It's one of them two.'

'Well they both sound grand to me. Whatever it is.'

There was a knock at the door which Adam opened on Irene Bradshaw.

'You coming to the match?'

That afternoon Kevin was making his debut for the Bury first team. At the age of seventeen, Kevin was Bury's youngest-ever first-team player. Adam invited Irene in to show her his Cambridge prospectus.

'This is where I might be going.'

'That looks nice.'

At the box on the Bolton road Adam dropped in his application form on which, he would discover later, he had forgotten to include his name. Irene talked to him as though she couldn't remember it either. Vicarious tension made her speak in machine-gun *non sequiturs*.

'I hope they win. I reckon Kevin'll score. He's dead nervous.'

'How do you know?'

'I went for a walk with him this morning.'

'Oh, I see.'

'Kev was going to call for you.'

'He didn't though.'

'We just got talking. And then his dad wanted him for something.'

'Oh right. Where is he now?'

'He went really early.'

Kevin was already in the Bury dressing room although he looked so young that the gatekeeper on the players' entrance had at first refused to let him in. Kevin had to call out to Mickey Bell to testify that he was a first-team midfielder rather than a spotty fan trying to get close to his heroes. Kevin had gone straight from Brangy Warriors to the Bury first team in five months. So, with still three hours before Bury kicked off against Leyton Orient, Kevin had been prowling around the dressing room, touching the silky kit, white shirt, blue shorts and white socks that hung on the pegs in numerical order.

Adam was glad to arrive at Gigg Lane where, settling in the Cemetery End, he and Irene had the football to provide a ready topic for conversation.

'Look. There's Kev in his kit.'

Adam looked up at the players going through their stretching exercises. He waved at Kevin, who broke away and came over to the terrace. Adam stepped forward to greet him but, before they said a word, Irene jumped in and wrapped her arms around Kevin's neck. Kevin felt like the primary school aristocrat all grown up, kissing a pretty girl in public on the day of his birth as a professional footballer. He peered over her shoulder at Adam.

'Hiya, mate. Good to see you. I was going to call for you but I got too nervous. I wanted to come down early.'

'It's all right. Have a good one. Imagine it's just Brangy Warriors.'

Kevin had missed the replay, at the behest of Mickey Bell, of the semi-final of the Lancashire Youth Cup. Without his inspiration the Warriors had been intimidated in Skelmersdale into a 4–1 defeat. Adam had kicked the ball on fewer occasions

103

than the full-back had kicked him and he had been substituted at half-time.

Leyton Orient began at a quicker pace than Kevin had ever known. For ten minutes the game revolved around him without him. Five minutes later and Leyton Orient took the lead, to the perverse delight of the Bury people who came to matches because they enjoyed having something to complain about. But then, gradually, Kevin found a rudder. Gradually he was able to orient himself and impart a direction from the centre of midfield. After half an hour of his debut, Kevin's first successful pass lifted him mentally into the company of professional footballers. Suddenly Kevin's comportment changed. He lifted his chin, began to look up rather than down, and assumed a swagger. Picking the ball up in his own half of the field, Kevin slalomed through tackles in an eventually fruitless diagonal that roused the crowd and loudly announced a lordly talent. Excited by the appreciative roar of his crowd, Kevin at once took on a leader's role, cajoling and encouraging his less blessed, more experienced colleagues. The Bury crowd tried a new name on their lips.

'That's right, McDermott. You tell 'em. Go on, son.'

The Bury supporters, like all football crowds, recognised the endeavour of one of their own. They appreciated talent but it was talent allied to effort that really won their hearts. It was obvious from the way that McDermott played that he cared as much as they did. McDermott was a fan in boots.

The rest of the team caught the contagion of Kevin's spirit and Bury came back to dominate the game after half-time. They scored a scrappy equaliser through their cumbersome centre forward who, at the age of thirty-three, was all set for the knacker, and then, with a minute on the clock, Kevin posted his application form to Bury's hall of fame. From a throw-in on the left, he simultaneously spun away from his opponent and took the ball as he extended into a stride. The Orient defence seemed to part to allow him through as Kevin practised the imperceptible deception available only to footballers of exceptional balance. As the goalkeeper approached, Kevin slid the ball calmly, almost gently, past him into the goal. Amidst the bemused celebration on the terraces Adam was trying to make it clear to people he didn't know that Kevin was his best friend, as if in hope that he too could shine in the reflection of Kevin's glory.

Kevin kept his place in the first team as Bury made their best start to a season for a century. After eight games, six victories and two draws, they sat on the top of the Fourth Division, already thinking of promotion. Kevin had added to his winner against Orient with vital goals at the expense of Hartlepool, Torquay United and Rochdale, in a fractious local derby. By now he was beginning to attract the attention of the local sports journalists. Kevin collected all the cuttings from the *Bury Times*, where he was the subject of a full-page profile. His picture was in the *Manchester Evening News* and the *Bolton Evening News* carried a glowing testimonial to Bury's new star. Bob Matthews came across the estate to read from a copy of *The Times*: 'The seventeen-year-old Kevin McDermott ended Rochdale's plucky comeback with an excellent late winner. We will hear more of this young man.'

'That's fierce.'

'I presume you mean that's good. When's your next game?'

'Next week. We're away v Cambridge United.'

'Our Adam's going down to Cambridge next week for an interview. You should have a word with him. He could come and watch if he's there at the same time. He'd like that. And it'd be nice to have a supporter. Make a change for Bury away from home.'

Adam had an interview that same Friday at Trinity College. He arranged to stay the night in a guesthouse and then go to the game at the Abbey Stadium the following afternoon. Kevin had persuaded Mickey Bell to badger Alan Whitehead, the first-team manager, to allow Adam to travel back on the players' coach. Even for a fair-weather fan such as Adam this was an exciting brush with celebrity.

As Adam sat with three other candidates in a draughty wooden hallway just above the porter's lodge, he reflected that he was no doubt the only one amongst them who was going to spend the next evening with a fourth division football team. That wasn't the only source of difference. As soon as he opened his mouth Adam felt distinctly regional. After brief introductions Adam said nothing more until he was called in to see Dr Geeta, who conducted a disinterested interview, barely listening to Adam's prepared, pedestrian received-wisdoms on Latin texts. After a quarter of an hour Dr Geeta took Adam through to see Mr Pittam's contact, Professor James.

Adam walked into unexpected darkness. At three o'clock in the afternoon all the curtains in the Professor's room were closed. Two scented candles threw out a little light from a coffee table in the far corner. From out of the gloom came a voice.

'Ah, it's young Mr No Name. Young Mr Anonymous. Do sit down, Mr Nobody.'

In the middle of the room Adam saw a deck chair, the sort his mum used to hire on the beach in Blackpool. Adam sat down, his head now emptied of prepared platitudes on A Level Latin. The voice spoke again and Adam noticed a small man twitching next to the curtains. Bizarrely, he was facing them, as if looking out of the window through the drawn cloth.

'So I take it you do have a name, even if you disdain to inform us what it is?'

Adam was so spooked he didn't realise he'd been asked a question. Professor James then spun round very suddenly and, caught in the candle-light, Adam was even more perturbed to note that he was the exact spitting image of Timothy Claypole from Rentaghost. 'You've got spooks and ghouls and freaks and fools at Rentaghost,' floated through Adam's head as Professor James clarified the question.

'Would you mind telling me what your name is, boy? I find it a useful tool for observing the conversational niceties.'

'It's Adam Matthews, sir. Sorry you didn't know it.'

'No, entirely your prerogative, young Matthews. Why should you give so much away so early in the day? If you give me your name I may never give it back. Lend me your ears. Certainly not; I'm still using them.'

Professor James exploded into hysterical laughter. Adam looked about him for help before joining in because he couldn't imagine what else to do. Just as suddenly, Professor James slammed on the laughter brakes and Adam's false chuckle bounced unaccompanied around the dark room.

'Now then, Mr Blank Space. You claim to have read the *Utopia* of Thomas More.'

'Yes, sir.'

'Let me tell you about More, young Master Empty Box. What does the word "utopia" mean?'

'It means . . .'

'Not at all; not at all. You're far too serious. It's a joke. A rather marvellous joke. Does he mean "outopia" with an "o", which is "No Place", or does he mean "eutopia" with an "e", which is "Good Place"? This is rather like you. This is your rather marvellous joke. Are you Mr No Name or are you Mr Good Name? Are you Mr No Man or are you Mr Good Man? Or, as they say on the *Brookside* television programme, are you Mr No Marks or are you Mr Good Marks?'

Adam said nothing. It seemed more like a speech than a question.

'Well? Which are you? Mr No Marks or Mr Good Marks?'

'Mr Good Marks, I suppose.'

'Glad to hear it. Pittam speaks well of you, Mr Good Marks. Very well indeed, I should say. Would you like to come here to study, Mr Good Marks?'

'Yes, sir', said Adam, though he was by now less than certain.

'Good. Well we shall be glad to have you, I'm sure. I've enjoyed our conversation. I trust I shall see you again in Michaelmas. Your interview was fine, I take it?'

'I hope so, sir,' replied Adam, who thought that the whole experience was all a bit too reminiscent of church. Trinity, candles and Michaelmas.

As Adam tried to lift himself out of the decaying deck chair he felt the wooden legs begin to give way. In order to avoid being snapped up as it closed he had to roll onto the floor on his side. This drew loud, appreciative merriment from Professor James, sounding suddenly like his namesake, Sid.

'Bravo. A fine show. You're the first young man who's not been eaten this morning. Yes, you'll be a fine addition to College. Good old Mr Good Marks.'

Adam got out as quickly as he could. He had once spent a week cowering in his bedroom because he thought Tez Satchel was going to beat him up. But Adam had never been as scared of a soul as he was of the Trinity College Classics tutor. He ran past the tall confident boys out into the light of the Great Court, through the wooden door and back into the world.

Adam did not venture out of his guesthouse that evening. The dark streets of Cambridge probably teemed with the cast of Rentaghost discussing the cabaret acts of classical literature.

In the morning, Adam had a late breakfast and walked up and down the Newmarket road for two hours, waiting for it to be time to go to the game. He was the first spectator to arrive at the Abbey Stadium and he sat in the cold, in the ramshackle stadium, contemplating what an odd situation to be expecting such a familiar face. After the extraordinary experience of the interview process, sitting entirely alone in the away end of the Cambridge football ground, Adam felt extremely sad. All of a sudden all his experiences were becoming unfamiliar. All at once he felt a time of certainty was drawing to a close and he was about to enter an unknown world lit only by candle-light.

Adam had been joined by seven other Bury fans by the time the game started. The rain began as soon as Cambridge kicked off and the standard of play declined in sympathy with the weather. As thick rain descended, the pitch became a bog which made any attempt to play the ball along the ground farcical. More than once a ball sat short of its target in a puddle, where-upon two reckless tacklers launched in to propel it onwards to the next lake of water. Though there was sport in this for the players it was a joyless spectacle from the terraces.

Kevin threw himself into the game with too great an abandon. A poorly timed lunge at the ball just after half-time earned him a booking. Adam tried out Professor James's joke on the man standing next to him.

'He's taken his name. I wonder if he'll give it back.'

'You what, son? What were you saying?'

'Nothing. Doesn't matter.'

After eighty minutes of featureless football, Cambridge United took the lead with a scrambled goal from a corner, conceded needlessly and mistakenly by Kevin.

As the game restarted Kevin tried to atone for his error by driving through two opponents in the centre circle. Sensing he was beaten, the second opponent hung out a trailing leg. Kevin cried out as if hurt, which he immediately belied by springing up in retaliation. Ten Cambridge players bristled in provocation at which Kevin butted his opponent squarely between the eyes. The two goalkeepers each ran fifty yards to join the universal mêlée, the upshot of which was that Kevin was dismissed. He trooped from the field to the abuse of the home fans above the players' tunnel, to whom Kevin directed a volley of insults and a two-fingered suggestion.

The Bury players had negotiated what they termed a 'late stay' which meant that the coach driver and the team stayed in Cambridge while the managerial staff went home in their cars. Adam met Kevin in the players' lounge and they shared a taxi with Andy Kelly, the goalkeeper, and Billy Kennedy, the left full-back and club prankster. As the taxi stopped at the round-about by Jesus College, Billy leant out of the window and shouted at a passing student on a bicycle: 'Get off and milk it, you cunt.'

Kevin and Andy laughed uncontrollably and Adam joined in dishonestly.

Billy had set the tone for the evening. As the drinks went down in a pub-crawl down King Street, the humour became more and more coarse and the violence less and less suppressed. Adam tried to stick close to Kevin because he felt uncomfortable with the other players and embarrassed at their loud singing.

'What time do we go?'

'Fuck knows. It's ace this though, isn't it?'

'It didn't go too well today, did it? You shouldn't have had a go at that bloke.'

'He deserved it, the twat. He'd been niggling me all game. Do you want another?'

'You're off your head. I thought you weren't meant to get pissed.'

'We can after matches.'

'He's like someone's fucking mum, your mate,' interjected Billy Kennedy.

'Better not have another drink, our Kevin. You might get fucking pissed,' added Andy Kelly.

'And then you might piss your keks and that would be a proper bastard.'

The Bury team roared at a private joke. Kevin saw that Adam found the laughter incomprehensible and felt suddenly protective.

'Anyway, mate, how did it go yesterday?'

'Totally weird. But I think I might get in.'

'Get in where?' asked Billy.

'The university. I've been down here for an interview.'

'Fucking hell, lads. We've got a right professor here. Kevin's mate goes to Cambridge University.'

'I don't yet . . .'

'You fucking clever posh bastard.'

Billy Kennedy was interrupted by the landlord tapping him on the shoulder.

'Excuse me, but would you mind your language please? Some of the customers have complained about your swearing.'

'You what? You having a fucking laugh or what?'

'Could you just tone it down a bit, please?'

'Who is it that's fucking moaning? Come on, who is it? Fucking students. Which posh bastard doesn't like a bit of normal talk? Who's the la-di-da Gunner Graham cunt here then, eh?'

'Just be quiet please or else I'll have to ask you to leave,' said the landlord, gently.

'Fuck off.'

110

'Right, that's it. I've been perfectly reasonable. Out you go and take your mates with you. Come on, the lot of you. Out you go.'

'I'm not fucking going anywhere.'

The landlord raised his hand to Billy Kennedy who immediately threw a punch. The landlady called the police at once as three men jumped over the bar to come to their landlord's aid and the other Bury players ran over to contribute. Kevin pushed Adam aside and landed a blow on one of the bar staff who, only five minutes before, had served him a round. The fracas settled down but the bloody noses of the pub staff and the word of the landlord were enough for the police to act on when they arrived twenty minutes later. Billy Kennedy and Kevin McDermott were singled out as the troublemakers and taken off, to the cheers of the team, to the Parkside police station. After delaying the team coach for two hours the Bury team, along with a very quiet Adam, eventually started on its long journey back to the North.

Kevin was called in to see Mr Whitehead as soon as he arrived for training the following Monday morning.

'I thought Mickey had spoken to you, lad. I thought he'd spelled it out. Do you know what I mean?'

'Yes, boss.'

'You'll piss it all up the wall if you're not careful. You've got a real talent, son, but you have to respect it.'

'Yes, boss.'

'Now Mickey tells me you've got a nice young lady. Why don't you spend some more time with her? A word to the wise, sunshine: You don't want to get too involved with some of the old lags in that dressing room. Take it from me, some of them won't be here long. If even half this team applied itself properly we could win this bloody league. Now get out and don't ever make me need to say this again.'

'Yes boss; thanks boss. You won't need to.'

Kevin trained hard and changed without joining in the repartee reliving Cambridge. Kevin wanted to put Cambridge behind

111

him. He left the ground, refused the offer of a drink and ran back home to the Harwood estate where he went straight round to see Irene Bradshaw who now worked at home, dressmaking with her mother.

'Come to the park.'

'Why? It's throwing it down.'

'Get your brolly then. Come on.'

Kevin dragged Irene to the park where he sat on a swing and scraped his feet on the gravel.

'So what's this all about? Do you want to chuck me?'

''Course I don't, stupid.'

'It's a good job. You can't now anyway.'

'Why not?'

'You just can't.'

Irene felt Kevin's cropped hair spring up when she pressed it down flat. Kevin rocked more vigorously on the high swing. He swung harder and harder until the swing turned over the top of the frame. As it rotated twenty feet in the air, he jumped off and landed perfectly on both feet with a dramatic plié for effect. Irene applauded and drew back her lips into a delightful smile.

'How old are you?'

Kevin and Irene were seventeen years of age and very much in love, with great expectations. They sang 'You Can't Hurry Love' together on the roundabout.

'Love don't come easy; it's a game of give and take.'

'You can't sing to save your life.'

'I used to be in a band, you know.'

'Yeah and you can't play the drums either.'

'You cheeky monkey.'

Kevin stretched out his arms and enveloped Irene in a long kiss. She was the smoothest thing he had ever felt.

'I love you, Kevin. Even though you can't sing.'

'Let's go and watch the bowls. I told Bob Matthews I might go and watch him play against The Marquis.'

'You're right romantic, you.'

'Come on. Race you.'

112

The game had begun when Kevin and Irene sat down on a bench at the side of the green.

'God, bowls is boring.'

'Irene? I want to ask you something.'

'Go on then.'

'It's important.'

Irene leant forward and twisted her body round so that she was directly in front of Kevin.

'What is it?'

Kevin looked beyond her.

'Do you love me?'

'You know I do.'

'But do you?'

'I told you before that I did. Why? What's up?'

'Nothing's up.'

'So what is it then?'

Kevin summoned all courage and sunk to his knees. Readjusting his position, he lifted one knee from the floor, took Irene's hand in his and spoke in a low monotone.

'If you love me will you prove it by marrying me?'

'You what?'

'You heard.'

'I know I did. But I don't know if I believe it. Say it again.'

'Irene, will you marry me?'

Irene pulled Kevin up from the floor and covered his face with grateful kisses as the jack came to rest three feet away and the bowls players scowled at their indecorous behaviour.

'Yes, yes. Yes. Yes.'

'I love you,' said Kevin, managing those three words for the first time in his life.

'Kev?'

'Yeah?'

'I've got something to tell you too.'

'What is it?'

'I'm pregnant.'

Kevin walked Irene back home and then headed down through the tunnels underneath the railway line. He found his best friend on the bridge over the River Irwell, coming home from a dose of double Latin at school.

'What you doing down here?'

'Looking for you. I thought you'd be on your way home so I thought I'd come and meet you.'

'Oh ta. I've not been met from school since infants.'

'I've got something to tell you.'

'What is it?'

Kevin led Adam on to the railway line. As soon as they stepped onto the bank their shoes sank in the stinking mud. Kevin clambered out with some ease but Adam was stuck. Kevin had continued thirty yards on the firmer grass before he realised that Adam was up to his calves in thick mud.

'Just lift your legs, you flid.'

'I can't. I'm stuck. Give us a hand, will you?'

Kevin pulled Adam out of the mire. They walked up the railway line and settled down in the overgrown bushes that now grew in the clearing that, six years before, had been their old den. Adam began to brush the drying mud off his grey school trousers.

Kevin cleared his throat to begin a speech.

'I want to ask you something.'

'What is it? Is everything all right?'

'Yeah, it's fine. Better than fine. I've asked Irene to marry me.'

'You've what?'

'I've asked her to marry me. And she's said yes.'

'Bloody hell. What's brought this on?'

'The boss has been on at me to settle down. Mickey Bell said it was a good idea.'

'You can't get married because Mickey Bell thinks it's a good idea.'

'I'm not. I like her.'

'Yeah, well, I like you but I'm not thinking of marrying you.'

'It's different though, isn't it?'

'Is it?'

'Yeah. Anyway, we're having a kid.'

114

'Bloody hell. Did you mean to?'

'Not really.'

'What do you mean, not really?'

'Well, no, not really. But I'm glad about it.'

'Is Irene going to have it?'

''Course.'

'Christ.'

Adam picked a crust of mud off his trousers.

'Aren't you pleased? Don't you think we should get married?'

'No, I do. I mean, I'm just surprised, that's all.'

'Well, I hope you're pleased because there's something else. Will you do something for me?'

'You know I will. Within reason. What is it?'

'Will you be my best man?'

Adam discovered a little grace, at last. 'Mate, I'd love to. I'd love to.'

Though Kevin was too embarrassed to proclaim that he loved Irene rather than merely liked her, he received Adam's hug manfully.

'Are you sure you want me? You don't want one of your uncles to do it?'

''Course I don't. You're my best man.'

Kevin McDermott and Adam Matthews were blood brothers, in their heads. For always.

part three: *A Disappointed Bridge*

Plight thee my Troth

As the Reverend Truman read out rhythmic sentences Irene fixed her attention on Kevin and Adam to ensure they did not laugh at Kevin's middle name.

'I, Kevin Baxter, take thee, Irene Susan, to be my wedded wife, to have and to hold . . .'

Kevin's voice echoed in St Thomas's Church as he repeated his vows after the Reverend Truman, ending up with a private joke between the groom and the best man.

'. . . and, thereto, I plight thee my troth.'

Adam's laughter escaped and set Kevin off. They had been speculating in rehearsal about what a troth might be and why they would plight it so readily. The idea of Kevin granting his virginity to the Reverend Truman was too much for Adam and it took a look of disgust from Irene to settle the two little boys.

Once he had composed himself, Kevin took the ring from Adam and slid it onto Irene's third finger. It was a cheap diamond substitute but this did not detract from the love that Kevin and Irene affirmed for each other nor the pride felt by their families. The noble feelings that attended the marriage of Kevin McDermott and Irene Bradshaw were as fine as at any society wedding. It was truly an honourable estate. When Irene looked Kevin in the eye and plighted her troth, the world that passed fleetingly through her mind was not their own. It was some imaginary utopia they could but dream of reaching.

Kevin looked handsome in the family suit which his father before him had graced at his own wedding twenty-three years before to the day. The suit had not been worn since. Wendy ran it through the mangle and, over a new cotton collar and a splash-design tie, it looked smart and respectable, even if Kevin did spoil the effect somewhat by putting a biro in the top outside pocket of his jacket. At Irene's insistence he wore after-shave which gave him an odour that was pleasant but unrecognis-able. By the end of the service Irene was trying to rub it off.

Irene herself looked divine in the dress that Dawn had made for her, cut low at the back with a trim of flower prints whose pallor set off the incongruous depth of her brown skin. Irene Bradshaw radiated young love. There was no wear and tear, no pain, no disappointment.

The Reverend Truman led the way through into the vestry for the signing of the register. He did not mention the scandal in the vestry which had led him originally to refuse to marry the happy couple. The Reverend had relented, on condition that Irene attend church to hear the banns, only when June Matthews vouched for her. June advised Irene to insist on the traditional wedding service and she even pulled the stepladders out of their hiding place and gave the sanctuary lamp its annual polish.

'Well done, everybody. That was very well done indeed. If you just want to sign your name there, Irene.'

'Thank you, vicar,' said Dawn, stiffly. 'Go on, love.'

'We don't see you in church very often these days, Kevin.'

'I'm banned; that's why.'

'Well, yes; there is that. I suppose we've lifted that ban now. Forgive and forget, eh? Well, forgive anyway. I believe you're doing very well for yourself these days.'

'Yeah, we should have gone up last year but half the team are boozers. We thrashed Scunny last week.'

'Yes, that's very good,' said the Reverend Truman who had no idea whether it was or not.

Irene looked tenderly at Kevin as he signed the wedding register illegibly and in the wrong place. With impeccable tim-ing, one-month-old Jason started to cry.

To the cheers of the McDermotts, the Powells and the Brad-shaws, Kevin and Irene stepped out of church into the rose garden. In a welcome of confetti Kevin clasped Irene to his chest and kissed her fully. He shook hands with the Reverend Truman and promised to come back. But Kevin would not set in foot in St Thomas's again for more than five years.

The congregation moved on to the Earl of Derby for a buffet and beer which was as far as Irene's dowry would go. Neither of the two families were extended which at least kept the cost down. Kevin's legion of aunts and uncles sent their apologies from Glasgow but illness, poverty and hatred kept them away. Sammy had fallen out with his parents over some trifle he could no longer recall. Though both his mother and his father were still alive Sammy had not spoken to either since his wedding day. The grandparents desperately wanted to know their grandchildren but they were too proud to make the first move, no doubt because they felt it would likely be rebuffed.

After a few drinks had gone down, the reception threatened to get out of hand. The McDermotts and Powells got hideously, unreasonably drunk and Uncle Bobby tried to paw Irene's mum. Wendy berated her husband through the bottom of a brandy glass for starting a row with Andy, recently married to their eldest, Irene, about her lost son Nathan. Tina also chose this occasion to remonstrate with Wendy and Sammy about the abortion she claimed they had coerced her into having. Her boyfriend, Paul Cornish, found out about the aborted child by overhearing Tina shouting at her mother. He didn't know that his twin brother Scott was the father. Maria tipped a pint of bitter over her husband of three months, Lee, whom she had caught trying to snog the bride. Meanwhile, the four Bradshaw aunts, Dawn's sisters, sat at their own table, moaning at what a common family their Irene seemed to have married into. Apart from the crowd, Bob and June Matthews had a quiet drink.

Kevin and Irene circled the room, pausing briefly with everyone and encouraging them to tuck into the buffet. Kevin sat down with Adam who was silently rehearsing his best man's speech to himself in the corner.

'You all right?'

'Yeah. You?'

121

'Great, thanks. I should get married more often.'

'You might yet.'

'I won't. Irene and me are for ever.'

'You're not blood brothers though.'

'I don't think she'd be on for that.'

'You never gave me the bloody choice. If I'd known there was a choice I might have chosen not to have my arm ripped apart with a blunt compass.'

'Tough. You can't choose your blood brothers can you?'

'No. You know, it's going to be weird when I go away.'

'Don't you want to go or something? I thought you wanted to.'

'No, I do. I've always wanted to go. But now I'm leaving it seems really weird.'

'It won't make any difference though, will it?'

'Tell you what . . .'

Adam reached into his pocket and took out a tiny plastic replica of the FA Cup.

'What's that?'

'This is my troth. Here you are. I plight thee my troth. It's the FA Cup trothy.'

'That's absolutely shit.'

'I know. It's the best I could think of though. 1900, 1903 and now 1985.'

'You really think Bury are going to win the FA Cup?'

'Well no, but it's a nice thought. Anyway, you've got your own now.'

Kevin took Adam in his arms and whispered, 'Thanks for everything.'

'I'm going to miss you, mate.'

'Come on; don't. I'm not meant to be miserable today. Let's get the speeches over and done with.'

'All right.'

Adam called for order by clapping his hands and inviting everyone to sit down. Uncle Greg restored chaos at once by standing up, uninvited, to give an awful speech about how the adept villainy of the family would ensure that Irene and Kevin never went without. He then upset Irene with an indiscreet litany of girls Kevin had once fancied. Sammy was next to take to the floor. He was no public speaker at the best of times but, half cut, he was boorish and puerile. The four aunts tutted as loud as they could but the virtue of their sister saved the day. The father of the bride was absent, whereabouts unknown, so Irene's beloved mother, Dawn, who had given her away, then offered a short and touching speech which showed the love was deeply reciprocated.

Then the best man spoke. Adam offered his thanks to all the right people and read out the two telegrams. There was a rude one from Kevin's team-mates at Bury and a straight message of good luck from Kevin's bosses, Alan Whitehead and Mickey Bell. Adam smiled at Kevin.

'Are you sitting comfortably?'

'Go on then; I'm ready.'

'Then I shall begin.'

Adam cleared his throat, theatrically.

'When Kevin asked me to be his best man I was very honoured but it did give me a problem. I started to wonder what I could say about him that you wouldn't know already. I didn't want to say how good he is at football, how he's just become the youngest-ever captain of a football league club . . .'

Bobby and Greg led a round of drunken cheers and applause.

'And I didn't want to mention how he's going to play for Manchester City and England one day, like his teddy bear, Colin.'

There were shouts of incomprehension.

'Oh, don't you know about Kevin's teddy bear? The best man's speech is supposed to be about Kevin's girlfriends. Now he might look to you like a strapping lad but, I'm telling you, before he hooked up with Irene, the only thing that shared Kevin's bed was Colin the teddy bear.'

'You bastard.'

'And I happen to know that Colin is still in Kevin's bed. So, Irene, you've got a fight on your hands because Kevin is very attached to that teddy bear. Colin does exactly as he's told and he lets Kevin do whatever he wants to him.'

123

'I'll twat you after this.'

'So I don't want to bother you with all that. We know Kevin's going to be a star. What I thought I'd talk about instead was dog shit.'

Kevin hid his head. He knew what was coming.

'I've got Maria to thank for this story. It's not so long ago, as you know, that the houses round here had outside toilets. And you might remember Brutus, Sammy and Wendy's dog. Now, Brutus wasn't exactly a pedigree breed . . .'

There was a roar of laughter. Brutus had been put down after he had attacked Tina in the back yard.

'Apart from being insane, Brutus did the smelliest dog farts you've ever smelt. After one especially heavy doggy meal Brutus had emptied his bowels on the flags in the yard just as Kevin came down in his pyjamas and Manchester City slippers to use the loo.'

'Manchester City?' accused Bob.

'He supported City then.'

'I still do.'

'Traitor. What's up with Bury?'

'After a satisfying piss . . .'

'How do you know it was satisfying?' interrupted Kevin, to interrupt the flow.

'All pisses are satisfying. Now shut up, this is my speech. You can batter me afterwards when I've finished. Anyway, after a satisfying piss, Kevin sleepwalked back through the yard and stood slap bang in the middle of a pile of Brutus muck. He went back inside the house and trailed brown footprints all across the kitchen, through the hall and up the stairs. When he got to the landing, instead of going into his own room, he took a wrong turn and got in between Sammy and Wendy. With his slippers on. Sammy woke up, kicked him out and went back to sleep. Then in the morning, Wendy and Sammy woke up and smelt what Kevin had left behind. Maria said all you heard was Sammy shouting at Wendy, "You smelly cow. Look what you've done in our bed."'

'She's always doing that when she's had a few.'

'Oh, thanks a lot. Bloody silvery-tongued bastard you are, Sammy McDermott.'

'There are also a few other things Kevin is very good at and I should mention some of them. It's not well known by the mums and dads of this area but Kevin was the finest knock-a-door-runner I have ever seen. Tony Greaves remembers one night, years ago, when the doorbell went every five minutes and there was never anyone there.'

'I bloody do and all.'

'I can now reveal that it was Kevin and he was hiding in the dustbin. And do you remember when a cricket ball went through the Cornishes' window nearly giving Old Ma Cornish a heart attack?'

'That was you, you bastard.'

'Well that was me. I thought I'd try and pin it on him.'

Adam poured more anecdotes into the brew. He paused to flick his bobbed hair from his eyes before the peroration.

'I just want to get serious for a minute now. Kevin's been a great friend to me down the years. My mum and dad didn't see fit to provide me with a brother and, for as long as I can remember, Kevin's been like a brother to me. I remember him once on the railway line, cutting my arm with a compass so we could be blood brothers. I want him to know that won't change just because I'm going away. We'll always be blood brothers and I can't tell you how proud I am of him. There have been times he's looked after me and I like to think that I'd do the same for him one day if he ever needs it. I'm sure he won't because he's got it all. He's got Irene and he wasn't the only one in the queue; I can promise you that. But, as he's bragged to me many times, she plighted him his troth. He's got a gorgeous little boy. And he's got a career in front of him. You could say that he's a very lucky man. But as he said himself once, it's not luck at all. It's skill. All those hours keeping a ball in the air in the back yard have paid off and Irene is the reward. Ladies and gentlemen, please raise your glasses to the bride and groom, to Kevin and Irene.'

'Kevin and Irene.'

Adam reached over to his blood brother. The dampness in their eyes said different things. Adam felt he had lost Kevin, who felt that he had found Irene.

Dawn stayed the night round the corner with Wendy, Sammy and Jason to give the newlyweds the run of the place where they were going to live. Dawn had decided she was going to follow her instincts and go to live with Peter, a lorry driver from Liverpool. For Dawn, it was like running away to join the fair all over again. As Dawn explained to Irene in a tearful conversation deep into the night, she had her own life to lead. Dawn's last kindness, before jumping into the lorry, was to agree not to inform the housing authorities that she was leaving, thus granting the house to Irene and Kevin.

Freed at last from the eyes of their public, Kevin carried his giggling wife over creaking floorboards, over the threshold of the house she had always lived in. Kevin and Irene were going to spend their wedding night in Irene's room in the same single bed she had slept in since she was ten years old, the bed in which their baby had been conceived. There was to be no honeymoon for the happy couple but it didn't matter. Kevin took Irene straight up to bed where he made love to her with more feeling than he had ever mustered. They drifted away to sleep cramped up in this single bed, in each other's arms, Irene's lashes matted with tears.

Please Release me

With a crack in his ankle that would reverberate in his head for years to come, Kevin hit the floor. There was a race, at full pelt, for a loose ball in the middle of the field, an innocuous ball on which nothing other than the pride of the two captains rested. Kevin reached it a fraction of a second before his opponent from Grimsby Town who was unable to pull up short as he gathered pace on the frosty grass. As his studs came down onto Kevin's abnormally contorted ankle, there was a sickening snap. Kevin's limbs whirled like a cat struggling against death after being hit by a car. The only static part of his body was his right ankle which lay in two motionless pieces. He screamed out in agony as he was shuffled to the side of the pitch to await an ambulance.

Kevin was in Bury General Hospital for a week. He underwent surgery on his ankle and on the snapped cruciate ligament in his knee. After four supine days he was permitted to wheel himself around the ward. Another fortnight later Kevin recovered to the level of crutches and, one week more, he was hobbling around the Harwood estate on a pair of sticks. Irene was irrepressibly, inspirationally attentive. She helped Kevin into his clothes, made all his meals and helped him into bed at night.

'Would you like to go away somewhere?'

'I can't go anywhere.'

'Yes you can, Hopalong. You can manage. Let's go to Blackpool for the weekend. We can have a late honeymoon.'

'We can't afford it.'

'My mum'll lend us the money. And she'll look after Jason for the weekend. Come on; let's go.'

Irene and Kevin had a wonderful weekend on the Golden Mile. The sun put its hat on as they stepped off the coach and didn't take it off until they had left for home. They spent the mornings on the beach where Kevin sculpted a car out of sand. He carefully manoeuvred the drying sand for the love of the job well done. Irene made him sit in the driving seat so she could preserve the memory with a cheap camera.

On Friday night Irene and Kevin went to the South Pier to see Freddie Starr. They walked out to the end of the pier where the old wooden structure drops like a disappointed bridge into the Irish Sea. As they held hands, looking out at the gentle waves, Irene soothed her husband.

'You'll be all right, Kev. Once you get off your crutches.'

'I know. I hate not being able to play though. It's boring.'

'Oh, thanks.'

'No, I didn't mean . . .'

'I know what you mean.'

Freddie Starr helped him forget with the old trick of rubbing the microphone on his genitals.

Irene and Kevin spent Saturday night at the penny arcade. Irene became the first person ever to grip a packet of Fruit Gums with the giant metal hand. Kevin pushed twelve two pence pieces over the edge of the step and down the waterfall. And Irene won a race, against the odds, by betting on the unfancied yellow horse. As they walked home gingerly, at Kevin's crutch pace, Irene pointed out an open carousel underneath Blackpool Tower. She laid Kevin's crutches down, helped him aboard and climbed up carefully herself. It was half-past eleven on a Saturday night in November and they were the only riders. As the fairground music began, they giggled and laughed, round and round, astride a fire engine and a contraption with a rudder that looked like a milk float, gazing out straight ahead to sea. All around, fireworks hit the night sky to remind them that it was Bommy night under Blackpool Tower.

Kevin and Irene came home to Bury where Jason filled in his

father's empty hours. Whenever the rain held off, Kevin packed Jason into the pram that had cost Dawn a month's solid embroidery and took him to feed the ducks. The park where Kevin and Adam had played as youngsters had a tiny pond in the middle. Irene and Kevin spent hours on the vandalised, rickety bridge staring into that murky pool, sometimes chatting together, sometimes in silence, but the silence of comfort, not the gap between hostile moments.

Irene and Kevin threw bread at the ducks, walked round the playground and made plans. They talked about how many children they would have and what they would call them and where they would move to. They would live in Greenmount in a house with a toilet downstairs as well as upstairs. That seemed the very acme of luxury. Kevin would travel all over the world with the England team but he would always look forward to his return. Irene would ensure that he came back to a family and a home. It was a dream and they dreamt with the best, did Irene and Kevin McDermott. They were great at marriage, Irene and Kevin. It was a hobble in the park.

Kevin's injury was mending slowly and his hobble was quickening. A week before Christmas he struggled on and off the bus down to Gigg Lane for his first session of physiotherapy at the club rather than the hospital.

'What you after?' said Tracey, the prickly receptionist who wore a scarf on her head because she suffered from alopecia.

'I've got an appointment with the physio. Is he ready?'

'How should I know?'

'Can you ask him?'

'Ask him yourself.'

'All right, all right. Keep your hair on.'

'You're a little bastard, you are.'

Kevin chuckled to himself and hobbled through to see Gerry Peers, the physiotherapist.

'Kevin, how's it feel?'

'Not so good really. It's still sore. Creases when I walk on it.'

'I hope you've been getting lots of rest. You shouldn't be

doing any walking at all. You have been keeping it still, haven't you?'

'Well, I went to Blackpool for the weekend but I didn't get up to much.'

'Kevin, what did I tell you? This is a very, very serious injury. Are you clear on that?'

'Yeah.'

'Kevin, I don't think you've got this into your head yet. This is a career-threatening injury. It's not easy to come back from a snapped cruciate, you know. You've absolutely got to do what you're told. You shouldn't do a bloody thing.'

'I won't.'

'It's touch and go, Kevin. I have to say that to you. I know it's hard to take in but it's best you know.'

'Right,' said Kevin, offhand, not really hearing a word.

'Kevin, I mean this. It's a very nasty injury you've got here and if you don't do exactly what I tell you then you've no chance. You've got to sit still for a bit. I know it's hard, but you've got to.'

This was exactly not what Kevin had wanted to hear. The worst aspect of his incapacity was the sheer amount of time there was to fill. With nothing to do, the fairground magic under Blackpool Tower had faded and Kevin had sunk into the dreary reality of his day. Starved of the routine of training leading to match day, ordinary life after the honeymoon had begun to seem interminable and Kevin was already conscious that he was trying the patience of his wife. He watched his team-mates struggle to a scoreless draw against Mansfield and then hobbled back home, thoroughly defiant.

When he arrived home Kevin did not even mention his conversation with Gerry Peers to Irene, who was getting ready for their weekly night out in the Greenhill Working Men's Club. Kevin pushed the Greenhill's steel door open with his crutch, saw his dad at the bar and motioned that he wanted a drink. They went over to Sammy and Wendy's usual table and grunted unaffectionate greetings. They stared at their drinks and Irene had only just cleared away the Christmas tinsel from the formica table before Kevin had drained his glass in two voluminous gulps.

'Does anyone want another?'

'Kevin, what you doing?'

'Just me, then.'

'Kevin.'

'I'm having a drink, that's all. I only have a drink once a week. It's not a crime is it?'

Irene, Maria and Tina came to join the party, dragging along their men, Andy, Lee and Paul. Kevin chatted amiably with Andy and Lee at the bar about football and cars but he had felt odd with Paul Cornish ever since he had stolen his globe at the age of eleven.

Kevin was buying his third pint in twenty minutes when he felt a familiar touch on his shoulder.

'Elizabeth, meet Bury's greatest living celebrity. After Victoria Wood of course. Don't let the crutches fool you. This is an athlete destined for fame and fortune.'

'Nice to meet you, Kevin. I've heard a lot about you.'

'Have you?'

'Yes, all good.'

'I should hope so.'

Adam ushered his glamorous, overdressed companion to the bar. He whispered to Kevin out of her earshot, 'That was a bit rude, mate. What's up with you?'

'Soz, I didn't mean to be. I'm just not in a great mood at the moment; that's all.'

'It must be shit being injured.'

'I hate it, mate. You don't know how shit it is. It's so boring.'

'You and Irene should come down to Cambridge next term.'

'All right, we will. I've nowt else to do.'

'It should cheer you up in here, anyway.'

'Oh yeah. Chinny.'

Kevin grinned at Elizabeth who stacked up another drink to go with the two he already had.

'What are you wearing, anyway? You look a right scruff.'

'These jumpers are really cool.'

131

'Are they 'eck. It's like something your dad'd wear. So how is it then? You've not been back much.'

'No, I've been a bit distracted.'

'I bet you have. The tits on . . .'

'Cut it.'

'Jesus . . .'

'No, really. She'll freak.'

'Why?'

'She just will. She's not that kind of bird. You can't even call her a bird.'

'Fucking hell. What kind of bird won't let you call her a bird?'

'If it's one who looks like that I'll call her Napoleon if she fucking wants . . . I hope the act's as good as usual,' said Adam as Elizabeth came back with the drinks.

'It'll be shit. It always is. Thanks, love,' said Kevin, to a grimace from Elizabeth.

It was the act that made the Greenhill Club precious. Every Friday, Saturday and Sunday a circuit cabaret singer strutted the tiny stage, systematically dismantling a series of once wonderful songs to the accompaniment of Graham on the organ, Alan on the drum and cymbal and a plinkety-plonkety backing tape. The audience's attitude to the act was always gently ironic. They were genuinely appreciative if someone was good. And many were very good. It shows how many people there are with some theatrical ability: far more than there are stars in the fame constellation. Hundreds of vocalists passed through the Green-hill Working Men's Club. Dealt different balls in the lottery, they might be making it in the musicals now rather than packing up the van for another night. Still, it's quite good money and free beer. They will survive.

The greatest joy, though, was when an act was awful. There were one or two of the regulars who couldn't tell the difference between Beethoven's Fifth and a fat bloke sucking a comb but they were the exceptions. Every superannuated Sinatra sound-nothing-a-like who groped for a top C and hit a middle H was confronted by sixty Brangy warriors straining desperately not to laugh.

Willie Jackson, the MC, appointed because he was the only committee member who didn't want the job, took up the microphone.

'Ladies and gentlemen, I know you'll give a very warm Greenhill welcome for tonight's act. Apparently he's a landscape gardener and she's a telephone operator. Put your hands together for two lovely people from Leigh, Ronnie and Gail.'

Ronnie and Gail burst out of the cupboard that doubled as a dressing room. Ronnie's hair was combed upwards from the neck and greased down so smoothly that it looked like he was wearing a skull cap. He wore an open-neck silk shirt and tight black trousers, with a white belt. Gail was sedately dressed in a trouser suit and a plain blouse. She bounced up to the microphone and grinned artificially while Ronnie set the backing tapes.

'Does anyone know Spandau Ballet or Duran Duran?'

'Who?'

'Let me try another on you then. This one was made famous by A Flock of Seagulls.'

'Not round here it wasn't.'

'Well, do you want Gloria Gaynor then instead?'

'Who's she when she's at home?'

'"Moon River"!' came a shout out of the dark.

After three songs the chatter began. Ronnie and Gail were worse than Teenage Kicks. They were Mid-Life Crisis Kicks.

But then the appearance of two pensioners on the dance floor gave Ronnie false encouragement. Every Saturday night Albert and his dancing girl took to the empty floor for the first dance. With the constricted movements of old-timers and no threshold for embarrassment they tripped the light alone. Aside from the lines furrowing his brow, the only thing that betrayed Albert's true age was the row of medals he wore proudly on his suit. As Albert whisked his dancing girl around the floor the committee members muttered under their invisible breath that he was making a fool of himself, cavorting with a younger woman. Albert was seventy years of age and his dancing girl was a slip of a lass of fifty-nine.

133

'Here. Stay on the floor. We'll do an older one just for you two,' said Ronnie, clutching at straws.

He rummaged around in his suitcase for a new tape while Gail cracked jokes to the sound of false teeth being clenched together.

'How did Bury go on today? Lost? I'm lost, I'm telling you. I've never been here before. We was on Bury Road tonight and Ronnie says what road are we on and I says we're on Bury Road. So we carried on and we ended up in Cheetham Hill. He says I thought you said this were the Bury Road. I said it is the other way. Oh we do have some fun. Right, what do you call a black fella in a suit? The accused. I love that, me.'

'Right, we're ready now. OK, here we go.'

Albert and his dancing girl gamely persisted to the end as Gail belted out 'The Windmills of my Mind' while Ronnie butchered the falsetto, at least an octave too high.

'Well, was that worth waiting for or what?' asked Bob.

'It's much better in here when the act's rubbish. Much better,' said June, speaking for everyone.

Ronnie and Gail gave way to Willie the M C.

'Let's hear it for Ronnie and Gail. Weren't they good?'

'They were a disgrace,' said Adam earnestly.

'They were all right. I've seen worse,' Kevin replied.

'They'll be back for another spot if you hang about,' Bob pointed out, smiling.

'Do I have to?'

'I bet they don't have this in Cambridge.'

'No. Exactly.'

'Now, the bingo will start in ten minutes so get your books from Betty in the corner. While you're doing that I'm pleased to say that Bill from the committee has agreed to do a turn.'

'Bloody hell.'

The committee members were always agreeing to do turns. There was usually a fight to grab the microphone and it never mattered who won. All the committee members sounded the same and they all, without variation, sang 'Please Release me.' Always. It was the still point of the turning world. Bob thought it a perfect song for the men in charge of an asylum, one tuneless Engelbert Humperdinck after another, in endless procession, forever.

'Thank you, Bill. I think you'll agree that was rather good. I think we'll let Bill on again. Now, if I can call on Walter to take his chair, get your pens at the ready and we'll start the bingo.'

Bingo cost a pound for a book, four little red lottery tickets with better odds but less remarkable prizes. The first book was played for a single line. The four-pound prize went to Alice who won every week. The second book was played for one on the top line, two on the second and three on the bottom. Wendy took the five pounds and recycled it straight through the bar. The third game was for a full house. Irene was quickly down to one outstanding number on her top box: Kelly's eye, number one.

'Number ten, Maggie's den,' said Willie instead and Mrs Cornish from the Harwood jumped up in delight to claim the five pounds.

There was a break in the bingo for the buffet which consisted of a sausage roll, a ham sandwich and a pork pie on a paper plate, all held in place by transparent foil. Adam and Elizabeth would sooner have eaten the plates. After the glasses had been replenished, the final game of bingo began in complete silence. This game, played for a full house, was known as the flyer and carried a substantial prize of thirty-five pounds. Kevin made an excellent start. He got off to a flyer.

'Blind ninety . . . two little ducks, quack, quack . . . seven and six, was she worth it?'

Kevin's numbers came thick and fast and he encircled them on the card with escalating excitement. He needed only two calls: all the fours, droopy drawers and legs eleven.

'Legs eleven.'

Willie's call was followed by wolf whistles, the tapping of glasses and long-buried memories. Useless numbers flashed by.

'Seven and eight, seventy-eight; snakes alive, all the fives; six and nine, any way up; on its own, number seven.'

Alice, the woman for whom bingo was an investment, scribbled down the numbers clinically, expectantly.

'All the fours, droopy drawers.'

'House.'

Kevin jumped up, holding his biro aloft. Alan from the committee took Kevin's card to read out the numbers. Walter checked on his ticker text that the victory was a fair one.

'Two fat ladies, eighty-eight,' demanded Alan with no recollection of any fat ladies apart from those who were actually playing.

Walter scoured his electronic box.

'We have no fat ladies.'

'False call,' declared Alan with unnecessary relish.

A bevy of cantankerous old women parked in the corner suddenly screeched into life with a volley of charges. Walter re-established order by resuming the game and, with an improbable streak, Alice came through to take the thirty-five pounds on the call of all the threes, thirty-three. Although in every other respect Alice was thoroughly blighted by the fates, she was lucky beyond the law of averages at bingo.

'She's a bloody fund manager, that Alice,' said Adam.

'Oooh, I know,' said Betty who didn't know what a fund manager was but felt sure that young Adam knew about these things.

'She cleans 'em out down at the Rank. They don't let her play any more,' said Betty's sister-in-law, also called Betty.

Kevin retreated to the bar to spend his own money on the grasping uncles who propped it up. When he sat down again, Irene stroked his hair, as though he were a child who had called 'house' out of sheer enthusiasm for the game.

'Never mind, love. It's only bingo.'

Irene took Kevin's hand and made his hair curl with her suggestive whisper. Gail from Leigh burst out of the cupboard dressing room in a skirt split, or rather ripped, to within an ace of indecency. Ronnie followed behind in a pair of white trousers and an electric blue satin shirt and asked if he looked at all like Marc Almond. Kevin made his excuses to Adam and let his wife lead him home to bed where they conceived their second child as the first slept in his cot beside them.

Mr No Marks

Irene gasped as she came into the twilight of Trinity College formal hall.

'God, that is gorgeous. Kev, look in here; it's amazing.'

'Yeah, amazing. It's only a room.'

Kevin had been in a rotten mood all day. It was a Saturday, which reminded him that he was not able to ply his trade. Kevin had a black mood like clockwork every week and it had not changed anything to be spending the weekend with Adam in Cambridge. He had endured Adam's tour of the university in unconcealed boredom shading into irritation at Irene's insistence that everything was so much prettier than Brandlesholme. Irene was even planning a transfer for Kevin to Cambridge United, not realising that it wouldn't be much of a promotion.

Adam had mugged up on the history of the university by talking to his parents. An illustrated history of Cambridge University had pride of place on Bob and June's bookshelf in the living room, strategically placed so that no guest could miss it. In relentless drizzle, Adam droned on about Isaac Newton's bridge at Queen's, the old Cavendish laboratory and the famous race around the cobbles of the Great Court. He laced his tour with legends about authors he would never read and of whom his guests had never heard. He showed Kevin where Wittgenstein had lived with only deck chairs for company, he described Lord Byron dragging a bear round on a lead and, back in his room, he read out the lines about Trinity's loquacious clock from Wordsworth's 'Prelude' which had been brought to his

139

attention on his first day by his new mentor, Professor James.

At the door of the hall Adam stepped into the black gown he was carrying. Kevin suddenly cheered up a little.

'It's like church this. Even the clothes are the same. Hey, I should give you a haircut. Come here. I'll give you a Bobby Charlton.'

Kevin punched Adam in the stomach and danced away, at which his knee reminded him that it was not ready to play just yet.

Adam and his two guests picked their way through the unnecessary gloom of the dinner hall. Professor James shouted out from the top table.

'Good Marks. Here you are. Up here.'

'Who's that?' muttered Kevin.

'That's Sid. He's my tutor. He's put us on the top table.'

Irene felt this made her impossibly important. She held her nose in the air as she tottered past gowned undergraduates on the lesser tables. There was a middle-class bellow, a noise recognisable to Kevin and yet oddly different, as Irene went by. Kevin stopped and stared at the Trinity College fourth fifteen. He stared at a large young man wearing a pair of donkey's ears who was drinking out of a rubber chicken.

'I'd watch it if I were you, mate, or I'll stick your chicken down your fucking neck and your ears up your arse.'

'Kevin, come on; don't start any trouble,' said Irene, ignoring the fact that one of the prop forwards was pinching her bottom.

Kevin sat next to Adam, opposite Professor James, with Irene on the end. At the head of the table sat a bespectacled lady of twenty-seven going on seventy, called Mary Maxwell. Adam's girlfriend, Elizabeth, sat opposite Irene, next to the Reverend Stuart, the college chaplain.

'Now then, Mr Good Marks, aren't you going to introduce everyone?'

Kevin leant over to Adam.

'Why's he call you that?'

'It's a joke.'

'It's a fucking shit one.'

Adam gave brief introductions and looked at his watch as the Master tapped a glass, rose to his feet and began to say grace in Latin. Kevin caught Irene's eye and the two of them giggled. When everyone had sat down again and the starters were arriving Adam tried to join in the levity.

'So now you know where Latin is.'

Kevin looked at him as though he had gone mad.

'I can't tell a fucking word you're on about half the time.'

Kevin turned to look at his prawn cocktail. He poked the pink lump in front of him and demanded loudly of everyone within earshot: 'What the fucking hell is that thing?'

'That's a very earthy request, young man. Is this your alter ego, Mr No Marks, Mr Good Marks?'

'Sid, it's nice to meet you,' said Kevin as Adam clasped his hand to his forehead.

'It's prawn cocktail, Kevin' said Irene, who had read the menu card. 'It's lovely. Just try it.'

'It's covered in sauce,' said Kevin, scraping the liquid off to discover two rather puny prawns underneath.

'The sauce is really nice,' offered Elizabeth, not realising she was making a categorical error.

'I like HP but apart from that I can't be doing with it. I hate things cooked in it . . .'

'Anyway, we've had a good day today, haven't we? said Adam, followed by mystified silence.

The party broke up into smaller conversations as a rubber chicken arrived, smeared in sauce. Irene impressed the delightful chaplain with the prejudices that she had borrowed from June Matthews about the Anglican service. The Reverend Stuart also showed such interest in Kevin's prospects that Irene was disappointed to get lost with Mary Maxwell whose interests did not seem to extend beyond the latest developments in industrial chemistry and who met every conversational sally about clothes or television programmes with a look of disapproval. Elizabeth rescued Irene by raising her eyes to the heavens as Mary started an exposition of the properties of magnesium.

'Is she boring you?'

'Just a bit.'

'Don't worry. She's well known for it. What's she talking about?'

'Magnesia or something. I thought that was diarrhoea potion.'

Mary overhead. 'No, it's magnesium. It's quite different.'

Adam came to the rescue. 'Kate's navel can't magnify all zinc ferrets. That's all you need to know about chemistry.'

'I'm sorry?' asked Mary.

'Ah, taught you something. It's true as well. Kate's navel just isn't up to the job. There's zinc ferrets wandering round totally unmagnified.'

'What's a zinc ferret?' asked Kevin.

'Exactly, Mr No Marks. A very good question,' said Professor James, who was finding the conversation right in the middle of his usual range.

Kevin's chicken in sauce was taken away untouched and was replaced by a stodge pudding in radioactive custard. Kevin took an enormous mouthful.

'Oh, so you like sauce on a pudding,' said Elizabeth.

'That's custard, not sauce. You don't have sauce on puddings.'

'What about white sauce or treacle sauce?'

'No, it's not sauce. It's custard.'

'You seem to be enjoying that,' said Irene, happy to see Kevin content again.

'Well I've eaten nowt else. It's bobbins the food in here, isn't it?'

Kevin drained his fifth glass of wine.

'You shouldn't drink so much, Kev.'

'Why not? It's free.'

'You'll get really unfit.'

Irene leant across Adam who was talking behind Kevin's back to his tutor.

'What's that old bloke like?'

'I don't know what he's on about. He's got funny names for everyone. He's nice about you, though. He reckons I should give those rugby players a right kicking.'

'Don't do anything of the sort. You should talk to the vicar fellow. He's really kind.'

'What's that woman like?'

'She's really boring. She just goes on and on about work. And I'm not sure if it is a woman anyway. She keeps going on about being a fella.'

'You what?'

'I asked what she does here and she said she's a fella.'

'It's fucking weird in here, isn't it? You don't really want to live here do you?'

'Not any more, no.'

Kevin grinned as Professor James passed him the port and a cigar. Ignoring Irene's admonishment he tucked into both.

Kevin was relieved to say goodbye to his dinner-table companions and limp by the Wren Library back to Adam's room. Adam took a bottle of white wine out of the fridge and opened it himself, to Kevin's surprise. After five minutes of jokes at the expense of boring Mary Maxwell and crazy Sid James there was a heavy bang on the door and the sound of drunken voices outside. A party had arrived. The man with the donkey's ears was at the back, shouting loudest. Adam put Stevie Wonder on and thirty-people bounced up and down on his floor, thoroughly annoying Mary Maxwell beneath as she was trying to read. To Kevin's acute boredom, a small squeeze of a party began to take off. He decided to carry on drinking in the hope that it would pass quicker that way.

As Irene danced with Elizabeth and Adam, Kevin was joined on the bed by an impossibly tall young man who introduced himself as Piers and who offered Kevin a smoke of something he referred to, in the poshest voice Kevin had ever heard, as 'waccy baccy'. Kevin commandeered a new bottle of wine which Piers opened and the two of them became engrossed in dope, alcohol and stories of great sports injuries they had known. In this respect, if in no other, Kevin was a natural student. Irene came over to remonstrate with Kevin for smoking roll-ups, which she claimed were even worse for him than proper cigarettes. Kevin and Piers just carried on laughing together. Kevin talked about football and Piers about rugby but neither of them seemed to mind or even notice.

In the opposite corner of the room, Irene was slumped in an armchair, laughing fetchingly. Next to her sat Barney, the large man whose donkey's ears now sat in his lap. Kevin was jolted out of his lethargy as the man's hand traced an arc through the air and alighted on Irene's knee. Without waiting to let Irene deal with the approach, Kevin leapt off the bed, crying out like an animal in pain, upsetting a bottle of wine and a nearly rolled joint as he did so. The party stopped at once. Like the soundtrack to Kevin's progress across the room, Billy Ocean played on.

'When the going gets tough, the tough get going.'

'Get off her, you cunt.'

Kevin grabbed the donkey's ears and slapped his rival across the face with them at which many of those in the static assembly laughed. Barney responded verbally in kind and, from a sitting position, kicked out and hit Kevin's knee with the sole of his Doctor Marten boot.

Kevin collapsed in agony on the floor and screamed so hard that Mary Maxwell came running up the stairs to find out who was being murdered. Kevin's evident pain ended the dispute at once and Elizabeth called an ambulance as Adam shut Billy Ocean up and showed everyone out.

By the time the ambulance arrived Kevin had stopped screaming and had started to breathe in sharp intakes that sounded like sobs. In tears, Irene smothered his head but Kevin broke angrily anyway, desperate for space to breathe. He was taken down the stairs on a stretcher wearing an oxygen mask, and driven away to Addenbroke's hospital with Irene. When they had gone Adam picked up the donkey's ears and put them in the bin.

Kevin could not move from his hospital bed for two days. Irene spent forty-eight hours on buses up and down the Trumpington road and sleeping on the floor, next to Adam's discarded underwear. Finally, four days later than planned, Adam helped Kevin out of a taxi at the station for him and Irene to start the long coach ride back to Manchester Chorlton Street.

Gerry Peers just shook his head when, three days after coming home, Kevin went in for a scheduled session of rehabilitation.

'What's up, Gerry? . . . say something.'

'I don't know, Kevin. I just don't know what to say sometimes.'

Kevin was put through a series of tests, shared between the Bury FC doctor and the specialist unit at Bury General Hospital. A week later he turned up at Gigg Lane for another of what had now become an interminable set of inconsequential meetings with doctors. As soon as he walked into reception, Tracey spat out at him, 'Mickey Bell wants to see you.'

'I've got to see Gerry in five minutes.'

'Look, I don't make the rules. I'm just telling you. He says you're to go straight in.'

Kevin limped down the corridor where the managers and the coaches lived. He found Mickey staring at the wall, staring at his cousin Colin. Kevin coughed and Mickey snapped out of his dream and swivelled round in his big chair.

'Hiya, Kevin. Sit down, lad.'

'Hey, it's good to be back.'

'Sit down, Kevin.'

'You all right, Mickey?'

'Just . . . sit down, Kevin. Please. Kevin, I need to talk to you seriously.'

'What is it?'

'We've had the report from the hospital. Our doctor's had a look at it.'

'What did he say?'

'It's not good news, I'm afraid.'

'What is it? What's up?'

'There's no easy way to say this, Kevin.'

'What?'

'I'm sorry, but the report from the hospital was very bad. The ligament's gone again. They're delicate things are ligaments and it's gone.'

'It'll be all right. It'll get better. It'll be OK once I get jogging again.'

'Kevin, you've got to listen to me and you've got to believe what I say.'

'No . . .'

'Kevin, your knee needs reconstructing. I don't think . . .'

Mickey caught his breath.

'No, Mickey. It's not that bad.'

'Kevin, I'm sure this is even harder to hear than it is to say. But I have to tell you. I'm afraid the hospital report was very clear. They've seen a lot of these injuries over the years. I'm sorry Kevin. Really I am. I'm very, very sorry.'

'Mickey, why are you saying this? Why? It can't be. It's not fair. It's not fair.'

'I know it's not, Kevin. I know.'

'Mickey . . . it's not definite, is it?'

'Kevin . . .'

'Is it, Mickey?'

Mickey Bell nodded sorrowfully.

'I hate this fucking job sometimes, Kevin.'

The Bury hall of fame looked down from their mounting on the wall as Kevin buried his head in Mickey Bell's midriff. He didn't want Mickey to see him crying even though Mickey was in tears himself. Kevin McDermott was eighteen years of age. Mr No Marks hobbled home to the Earl of Derby where he avoided the greetings of all acquaintants, speaking only to order pint after pint after pint.

After Football

Kevin woke Irene with his sobbing at twenty past three in the morning. Irene stroked his hair as he dry-retched face-down on the bed, choking back the tears. Irene held Kevin to her breast and he fell asleep without giving her any explanation. She woke first and risked his hangover because she knew that something terrible had happened. Irene received Kevin's news with a keen shot of despair.

'Oh, darling. Is it definite?'

'That's what they said. Mickey said they've seen loads of these injuries and people never come back from them.'

'I don't believe it.'

'That's what I said.'

Irene took a deep breath. She had already moved mentally on to practical matters. 'What are they going to do, Kevin?'

'What do you mean? Nothing, I don't think.'

'I mean about your contract. What did Mickey Bell say about that?'

'Nothing. Why? What about my contract? What do you mean?'

'Well, what did he say about your pay?'

'Nothing. He never mentioned it.'

'Didn't you ask?'

'No. I never thought about it.'

'Kevin, don't you realise what's happening here? If the physio has said you've got an injury and it won't get better they're not going to keep paying you forever, are they?'

'Irene, just leave it for now, will you?'

'Kev, you've got to think about it.'

'Just leave it, will you?

'Kevin . . .'

'For fuck's sake, Irene. Just leave it.'

'Oh Kevin, darling. Come here.'

Irene smiled thinly and opened her arms for her husband. For Irene, the quick chase to the practicalities was a disguise for the deepest despair. From the look of pain on Kevin's brow she knew that he felt it ten times over.

Only Jason could lift Kevin and even he only partially. Kevin unwrapped his son's Easter egg and then ate it joylessly himself. Kevin prevented Irene from opening the curtains but the outside world intruded when there was a knock on the door.

'Don't answer it.'

'Why not?'

'I don't want to see anyone.'

'It might be for me. And you've got to face people some time.'

'Just see who it is first.'

Irene peered through a gap in the curtains. 'It's Adam.'

'I'm not in.'

'Kevin . . .'

'I'm not in,' he snapped at an increased volume.

Irene lied on her husband's behalf and Adam went shopping in Manchester on his own.

Kevin avoided the world, and specifically his family and friends, for a week. Sammy and Wendy, Irene, Maria and Tina, Adam and Tez Satchel, all were met by Irene, the guard on the door who declared, with credibility wearing very thin, that Kevin was down at Gigg Lane, had popped out to the shops, was asleep in bed.

There was nothing after football for Kevin. He was suddenly inert, suddenly mute. Irene shook him out of his mood by letting Adam in, against Kevin's instructions. Irene made it clear by her tone that all was not well.

'You'd better come in. Kevin's upstairs.'

Adam knocked on the bedroom door and went in. Kevin sat up sharply underneath the bed clothes. The lights were off and the curtains were tightly closed.

'What you doing in bed, mate? Are you not well? I've been calling for you for days.'

Kevin opened his mouth but found that he was physically unable to speak. He had been eviscerated. All the expression had been extracted, all means of communication ripped away. Kevin could speak only through silence and through eloquent physical gesture. Adam repeated his question very softly in the resounding silence.

'What's up, mate?'

Kevin panted in loud, rapid breaths. He pulled the duvet away to reveal the ugly support he was wearing on his knee.

'Just . . .'

'What is it, Kev? You're not . . .'

'It's not fair.'

That was as much as Kevin could manage. As Adam wrapped his arms around his friend, Kevin's weeping was so loud that it brought Irene running up the stairs to check why he was screaming in pain which, at the deepest cut of all, he was.

Adam put Kevin back to bed and kissed him on the forehead like he was a precious little child. Irene filled in the Devil's details.

'They said he'd never play again properly. His knee's had it.'

'I'll absolutely have that idiot who kicked him when I get back.'

'He's in a bad way. I don't know what to do.'

'What's he going to do next?'

'I don't know. He won't talk about it. He's not said a word.'

Adam remembered that Kevin's other ambition had been to live as a tramp in the old mill on the bank of the River Irwell.

'Is he going to sign on?'

'He'll have to. We need the money. We've got another baby coming.'

'Have you?'

'Don't say anything. I haven't told Kevin yet. I don't know what he'll say.'

'Could you get some work?'

'Who'd look after Jason? Kev's hopeless with him.'

'We'll have to help him look for work.'

'I know. He just isn't interested though.'

'If there's anything I can do, just let me know.'

'I will. Thanks.'

Adam got up to leave.

'Look after him, won't you?'

'I will. I promise.'

Adam gave Irene a tender hug. It was the first time they had ever really talked.

With Irene's permission Adam imparted the news to all those who needed to know. Half an hour after he had left the house, Wendy and Sammy were knocking hysterically on the door, demanding to know what had happened to their son. Sammy brushed Irene's objection aside and attacked the stairs.

'What in fuck's name . . . ?'

Kevin, startled at the sudden commotion, sat up in bed and reached for the packet of cigarettes that were left on the bedside table next to Colin the teddy bear.

'I told you not to let anyone in,' he spat nastily at Irene as she whisked the packet out of reach.

'You can't not tell people forever, Kev.'

'If you can't tell your own mum, Kevin, who can you tell?' asked Wendy, with more hurt than Kevin had ever heard in her voice before.

'What happened? Tell me what happened,' demanded Sammy.

'It's fucked, Dad. My knee's fucked. That's all there is to it.'

'Let's have a look.'

Sammy pulled the duvet aside too violently and Wendy started to scream at him.

'Don't be such a stupid dick, Sammy. Can't you see the lad's in pain?'

'I'm sorry, fucking hell.'

'Let's have a look at it, Kevin.'

'There's nothing you can do, Mum. It needs rest but it'll never really heal strong enough.'

'What do you mean, never?'

'I mean never.'

Kevin swallowed his words, words he could not utter.

'The physio has told Kevin that he won't be able to play again,' said Irene calmly.

'No, they can't. They can't say that. Sammy . . .'

Kevin felt detached from his mother's hysteria. It was far, far too late for her reaction. He looked at her coldly.

'There's no point getting like that, Mum. It's finished and that's it.'

'You can't just say that. What are you going to do?'

Kevin took a swig from a can of warm beer. 'I'm not going to do anything. I'm going to lie here until I fucking die; that's what I'm going to do.'

'Don't start like that, Kevin. I don't want to hear another word like that.'

'I might as well. I've got nothing else.'

'Sammy?'

'How did this happen?'

'I had a bit of a scrap in Cambridge.'

'Kevin was looking after me when it happened. It was my fault really.'

'Don't be silly; it wasn't your fault. Some wanker started trying to feel Irene up so I had a pop at him.'

'Which twat was it? One of Adam's mates, was it?'

'Just some bloke. It's done now.'

'I'll fucking have him even if I have to go down there myself.'

'Leave it, Dad. I'll sort it out myself. Don't worry about that. When I see that twat again, and I will, I'll kick his fucking teeth down his throat.'

Irene led Wendy downstairs where they made tea and discussed their narrow options. Upstairs, Sammy was adding to the range.

'We can get a job up and running if you like.'

'Nah, you're all right.'

'You'll need some money coming in, lad.'

'I don't want to get into it, Dad.'

'What else are you going to do?'

'Dunno. Anyway, I'd be no use to you. I can't hardly walk.'

'Well, it's there if you want it. Now come on; I want you out of there. I want to see you come downstairs.'

'It's pointless. I can't be arsed.'

'Come on; do it for your mum.'

Sammy's hand felt unfamiliar on Kevin's shoulder as father led son in ginger steps down the stairway. Wendy greeted him at the bottom, linked arms and took him slowly through into the living room. As Sammy and Wendy were unable to offer any genuine consolation, not a word was spoken. After fifteen minutes artificially watching the fleeting celebrities of afternoon television, Sammy and Wendy excused themselves. As Irene showed them out she saw Wendy soften, physically. Kevin's parents walked home but the short trip round the corner was heavier and more onerous now.

Kevin received visits from all the family in turn and endured the same lack of anything to say with all of them. Three weeks drifted by unplanned. The weekend was announced more by the arrival of Adam's weekly mission from Cambridge than by any change in daily routine. Three weeks before his Part One exams, Adam brought up a birthday present for his friend and a bundle of application forms from the benefit office which Kevin declared he would probably fill in later. Irene had not yet found the right moment to tell Kevin but the pressure of her second pregnancy tested her patience with his predicament.

'Why won't you fill them in? We need the money.'

'It's too complicated. It takes ages.'

'Kevin, you've got to. Kevin, we've got another little one on the way.'

'You what?'

'I'm pregnant again.'

'Oh, congratulations.' said Adam, trying to sound surprised.

'Fucking hell; how long have you known that?'

152

Irene had been on the sofa for a month, ostensibly to avoid Kevin's knee but at least as much to avoid his temper.

'A while. I was waiting for the right moment to tell you.'

'And this is it, is it?'

'You've got to start applying for what you're entitled to, Kevin. You can see how we need that money.'

'I know we do. But have you seen how much you have to write? I don't know what I'm doing.'

'I'll do it if you want,' offered Adam.

'Would you?' said a grateful Irene.

' 'Course.'

'Have you been down the job centre this morning?'

'My knee was killing me.'

'Kevin, you promised.'

'You don't know what it's like. It was killing me when I woke up.'

'You'll never find a job if you don't look.'

'I don't want a fucking job. And I don't want to go down the fucking job centre. I shouldn't have to. I don't want to hang out with all the losers.'

'They're not all losers just because they're unemployed,' intervened Adam.

'I don't want a bloody shit job,' said Kevin.

'You have to do something, Kev.'

'I know I do. I want to play football like I've always done.'

'You can't.'

'I know I can't. You don't have to fucking spell it out. I know that. But I'm not going begging for a shit job with a load of other scrubbers. I'm not doing it.'

Kevin was as good as his word for another month. Adam at least managed to claim most of his eligible entitlement so Kevin and Irene's income was smooth even if it was meagre. Kevin disdained the job centre but he also refused the repeated bait from his father to exploit the poor pickings locked into the houses of the Harwood estate.

Irene, though, would not accept Kevin having given way. She bought the *Bury Times* every week and circled suitable jobs which

Kevin did not apply for. After six repetitions Irene responded on Kevin's behalf and her efforts were immediately rewarded with an interview at Tesco.

Kevin had no intention of getting the job and arrived at Bury precinct thirty minutes after the appointed hour. He was unshaven and unwashed. His clothes were creased and in need of running repairs. He was impolite and monosyllabic throughout the interview, greeting every question with an inarticulate grunt. Against all the platitudes of interview technique and much to his own chagrin, Kevin got the job. As British summertime rained on, Kevin began an unwanted new career.

On his first day he was told to stack the shelves full of tins, at which he was hopeless. When he wasn't stealing tins of beans, he was dropping them and putting large dents in the cans and when he wasn't doing that he was placing the peaches where the ravioli should be and the salted potatoes on the shelf reserved for luncheon meat. The supervisor grew increasingly exasperated at Kevin's inability to follow elementary shelf orienteering and his tendency to disappear for long stretches into the back room with his old school friend Terry Berry who was introducing him to types of sauce he would come to enjoy. After two weeks of incompetence, he was handed over to Barbara Kitchen and her till girls.

Barbara was a Tesco veteran of twelve years' standing. She was a formidable woman with a gigantic bosom into which young men had been known to disappear, never to return. Barbara adhered to the principle that it is better to be feared than loved and ruled the tills with a bosom of iron. She was a proud and self-styled tyrant, Atilla the Till.

Barbara was obsessed with punctuality, pathological about it, as though she had been abused in a former life by a clock. Every new recruit had to listen to a homily from Barbara on the importance of handing over to the next till girl at the correct time. Barbara liked to demonstrate her power, to show that she would brook no dissent. When one of her better employees, Julie Mawdsley, arrived a full eight minutes late, Barbara ordered her to report to the manager's office at the end of her shift. Julie endured a torrid three hours on the till, distracted and upset, before she was put into her misery by Barbara, who sacked her. From that day on all the girls aimed to arrive fifteen minutes early to allow for unforeseen delays. It was too great a disaster to be sacked because the bus broke down, like Julie Mawdsley.

Barbara was unpopular and misanthropic. But, for some reason that bewildered all the till girls, she had taken a liking to Kevin, had clasped him to her bosom, figuratively speaking. Barbara saw in Kevin the shadow of her own little boy who had committed suicide at the age of ten because he didn't think the girls liked him. She saw the same sense of despair and little boy loss that had driven her only son to his most tragic act. Barbara looked after Kevin because, like everyone else, she sometimes was able to throw off other people's perception of her.

Kevin repaid Barbara for her unsolicited affection by betraying her. He realised at once that goods did not need to be rung through the till if the customer gave him the correct money and he was soon earning an extra ten pounds a day on items priced in full denominations. He waved through kind donors to his personal fund, armed with a can of cheap peas and a tin of chicken broth. It never occurred to any customer that anything untoward was going on. They were there to buy peas and soup, not to catch robbers.

On his eighth day, Kevin got careless. He didn't notice that next in the queue was Lucy who worked on the till on Tuesdays and Thursdays. She had seen the previous transaction and realised exactly what Kevin had done. Lucy bought her shopping without a word and marched straight up to Barbara.

'He's got his grubby hands in the till.'

This wasn't quite true. Kevin was caught with his hand not in the till when it should have been. Barbara went to her boss to plead Kevin's case even though he didn't have one. Lucy and her colleagues were apoplectic that he was not sacked at once. Kevin spent the afternoon, head bowed, being insulted by a series of supervisors. It was just like being sent to see the headmaster at St Thomas's. He was finally allowed out with the parting words of the store manager ringing in his ears: 'Get your wages from the office, go home and I don't expect you back in the morning.'

Kevin could not tell Irene the truth of his fall from grace. Irene always occupied the moral high-ground in their disputes and Kevin could not admit his ignobility before her. It had been Irene's job in the first place and, as Kevin began his attempt at explanation, her swollen stomach chastised him. He told her instead that he had been laid off on the principle of last in, first out.

We Regret to Inform you

Kevin began to try. For the sake of his wife, his son and his child soon to be born, he began to try. He called in response to advertisements in the *Bury Times* and the *Bury Messenger* but received only application forms in return. Whenever an empty form arrived Kevin sent it to Adam who picked it up from a post office in Tel Aviv where he and Elizabeth were spending the summer. Adam sat in McDonald's with Elizabeth, applied for a job in Bury and sent the form back home to Kevin. By the time the application form had travelled to Israel and back the job had been taken.

Kevin's former grandeur counted for nothing. He was ruled infirm out of most physical work and he had no qualifications for desk work. A job for an unqualified man in Bury was a needle in a haystack. But, to complicate matters, the haystack had been thrown into the sea. Kevin walked into town every morning to check that the job centre still had nothing for him. If ever Kevin was suitable for the job then so was the rest of unemployed Bury. It was a race to take the white card out of the rack. First come, first employed, only employed.

Kevin never actually bothered with the cards in the racks. He asked the attendant if there were any good new jobs. On being told, again, that there was nothing new today, Kevin wandered to the King's Head, the terminus for sodden drunks, local mafioso and unemployed kids barely out of school. After a couple of pints and a few cadged cigarettes he excused himself, the only one who did, and headed home to Irene and Jason. In three months of genuine trying Kevin had two interviews, both of which ended in rejection. Slowly, gradually, failing to secure work sapped his spirit, eroding what vestige of esteem had survived a schooltime of academic humiliation.

The rejections also meant that the McDermott household did not have enough money coming in for even the gentlest kindness. Kevin spasmodically brightened Irene's day with presents. They were never lavish: flowers, earrings, chocolate, beer, a Manchester City pennant. On Irene and Kevin's budget, though, an extra pastie for Saturday dinner was profligate. Irene's mild disapproval at Kevin's improvidence easily gave way to tenderness, touched as she was by his unexpected largesse.

Kevin taught himself, by necessity and in defiance of his hopes, to be an expert in welfare. His moribund mind sprang into creativity as he invented his first fictional character. John White would cost nothing to feed, would require neither heat nor light and would pay his way with a monthly housing benefit cheque. The register of council tenants was too well maintained to allow fictional characters to be born into the public sector. Kevin needed to find a home owner so he had a word with Bob Matthews.

Bob's reaction was immediate and not for negotiation. He came round to see Kevin, to put him straight.

'I've never signed on the social in my life and I never will.'

'But I've got no work, Bob. You'd sign on if you had no work.'

'I wouldn't, I tell you. I don't want any hand-outs.'

'But we haven't got anything else, Mr Matthews,' said Irene.

'Well signing on's one thing but I'm damned if I'm going to start cheating the system.'

Bob, very proudly, told Irene and Kevin the tale of his own father, a tiny Brangy man, who had marched down to the welfare office every Tuesday to return his weekly entitlement. His argument had been that the money ought to go to poor people. According to every official measure Bob's father had lived below the poverty line but he had never once cashed a cheque. The Matthews family did not take hand-outs. To the Matthews family, all welfare was maundy money, silver mint handed out by an almoner to the destitute.

But not everyone who backed onto the Harwood estate took the same view. John White was soon alive and well and living as a lodger at the newsagents, the proceeds split between Roy the newspaper man and Kevin the author. The extra money did not stretch far. Kevin guarded his right to a few evening cans of lager and he smoked increasingly heavily, to Irene's moral and financial consternation. Irene's anxiety was stirred further by Kevin's occasional visits to the bookmakers with his father. For her part, Irene could not resist the lure of the catalogue and regularly ordered items that they could easily have done without.

Into the autumn of 1986 the letters of rejection kept hitting the doormat. At first, charged with false optimism, Irene and Kevin had opened the letters together. But the letters of rejection were always the same, always signed with an illegible squiggle, and Kevin came to recognise their pattern: 'We regret to inform you.' This was his cue. At this point he threw the letter away. Rejection letters should contain only these words. Everything else is superfluous and insincere. A large white piece of paper, no address, no telephone number, no date, no signature. Only, in capital letters, the judgement: 'We regret to inform you.'

Kevin soon tired of regrets. After two dozen identical letters he gave up. Kevin could not dismiss the thought of how unjust his impediment had been, how unfairly unlucky. He decided to save the squiggles the trouble of regretting to inform him. He could sit with his dad and moan. He could stay in bed and taste the smoke. He could call in on Terry Berry at Tesco to join him in the pleasures of his tea-break. He could watch TV deep into the afternoon and he could go out to the Greenhill Working Men's Club with his dad at night.

'How you doing for cash?'

'We're not doing so brilliant, to be honest.'

'Has the social coughed up yet?'

'The housing takes ages.'

'I know. The time they take, you'd think it was their fucking money.'

'It's a fucking nightmare, Dad.'

'There's always my offer, you know. It's always there if you need it.'

'I know. I'll be right.'

Kevin felt closer to his father than ever before. Irene began to worry that he was spending longer and longer watching late-night television with his father over tins of cheap beer. After four successive nights of arriving home after midnight the worse for cans of Kestrel, Irene objected. She had spent the evening nursing Jason through a fever.

'You never make time for me now.'

'Yeah I do.'

'You don't.'

'Well, I'm knackered half the time.'

'You don't do anything. The front door's needed mending for ages.'

'That's the council's job. Ring them.'

'You could do it. It's not a big job but you won't do anything at the moment.'

'I'm tired. The bloody baby keeps me awake half the night.'

'Don't talk about Jason like that.'

'Well, I wish he'd shut up for once.'

'He's not so well. Not that you care.'

'I do care. Don't say that.'

'You're always out boozing with your dad these days. I never see you. And you never come near me when I do.'

'I'm knackered, I told you. I've got to do something for fuck's sake. I sit around in here all day. It drives me mad enough as it is.'

'You'll have to stop boozing and smoking so much when the new baby arrives.'

'Oh stop nagging, will you? I've got to have something to look forward to. I've got nowt else, have I?'

'That's not true, Kevin.'

'It is. I've got nowt now. I might as well just get pissed up.'

160

'What about me? And Jason? Don't we count?'

'Fucking hell. I don't need this.'

'You'd rather sit in the Derby than look after us. Well how do you think that makes me feel?'

'Just put a sock in for once, will you? Haven't you got any washing to be doing?'

Kevin hobbled into the back room where, within sight of his own breath, he drank two miserable cans and smoked six miserable cigarettes. Irene sat sobbing in the kitchen for an hour, warming herself by opening the door of the oven. Irene curled up on the short sofa as soon as she heard Kevin go upstairs. He fell asleep face down on the bed and woke up an hour later raging to the sound of Jason's need.

With a second child imminent, income support was disappearing too readily into beer and cigarettes. As the leaves fell from the trees on the Harwood estate, Kevin was so inert that even his interior brooding had been cancelled. Kevin had become so lazy that he could not make it to the ashtray to flick away his fag end. He let it drop, instead, onto the brown carpet.

On the first day of November, when Irene was due, there was yet no sign of their second child, apart from the big bump it was making. Kevin avoided another conversation about the new baby by rousing himself to go to the off-licence. He came back in carrying six cans of cheap bitter.

'Don't think you're drinking those in here.'

'I'll do what I like in my own house.'

'It's my mum's house if everyone has their own.'

Kevin opened a can and took a provocatively large mouthful.

'Don't, Kev.'

'Well stop fucking nagging then.'

'I'm not nagging. We need to work out what we're going to do.'

Kevin reached over to the armchair where he had left his cigarettes.

'Have you shifted my fags?'

'Yes.'

'Where are they?'

'In the bin.'

'What have you chucked them for? There were loads left.'

'You're smoking too much. We can't afford it.'

'We can.'

'I hate you smoking.'

'So?'

'You never used to smoke when you were playing. You're getting a right fatso.'

'What have I got to stay fit for? I can hardly fucking walk straight.'

'That's because you're always drunk.'

Kevin struggled into the kitchen where he retrieved his cigarettes from the bin. Irene went to collect Jason from his grandparents and treated him to his tea in a café in Bury rather than risk going home. She came back to find Kevin snoring, mouth open, on the settee with the television blaring.

Jason was screaming with fatigue. Irene put him to bed, with tenderness and patience. She went downstairs hoping that the drink would have doused Kevin's fire and woke him by tousling his hair. Kevin snored more violently, so she poked him in the ribs. Irene made a drink while Kevin went to the bathroom to splash his face with water and flatten his hair.

'Where've you been?'

'I took Jason out for his tea. And I went for a think.'

'What about?'

'About us.'

'What do you mean by that?'

'I'm not going to carry on like this, Kevin.'

'What do you mean *like this*?'

'I mean I'm not going to stand by and watch you smoking and boozing your life away. You might not care about the children but I do.'

'Fucking hell. Here we go again.'

'You've got to stop feeling sorry for yourself.'

'Don't tell me to stop feeling sorry for myself. You don't know what it's like.'

'I do. I have to put up with you.'

'You don't have to put up with it if you don't like it.'

'I know. That's what I was thinking about.'

'What's that supposed to mean?'

'I mean I'm not having you behave like this. It's not fair.'

'Not fair. You're telling me what's not fair. So why is it fair that I've knackered my leg and my career's gone for a burton? Is that fucking fair?'

'It's more than a year now, Kevin. You've got to pull your finger out. If you carry on like you've been recently I'm going to go and stay with my mum for a bit.'

'That's right. First sign of trouble and off you go to the gyppo.'

'What did you say?'

'I said, you run straight back to gyppo land.'

The language that Kevin used in talking to Irene was despicable. In their grandparents' factories it would have been called industrial.

'Right, that's it. How dare you insult my mother. I'm not staying here to listen to that.'

'You can fucking stay with your mum if you want. Because I am bored fucking shitless with all your nagging. I'm not sticking it here.'

Kevin kicked the armchair, sending the ashtray high into the air and jarring his frayed ligaments.

'I've just about had it up to here with all this.'

'Well go on, walk out then if you're such a coward. Run away from your responsibilities, why don't you?'

'Shut your face.'

'Coward.'

'Shut it.'

Kevin hit Irene across the bridge of the nose and stormed out of the front door without even pausing to put his coat on. He walked with a long face down the hill into Bury town centre, past the statue of Sir Robert Peel. Kevin sat for twenty-three thoughtless minutes on the train as Besses o'th'Barn, Heaton Park and Crumpsall led into Manchester Victoria. Kevin was going nowhere, thinking about nothing.

At Victoria he had a drink in the grubby station bar. And

then another and another. After three hours of brooding he got on the train back to Bury, cold and cowed. As he clambered into the smoky carriage a girl's voice carried him back to classes in mental arithmetic.

'God, look who it is.'

Sandra McEwan beckoned Kevin to sit down next to her. He felt he could scarce refuse.

'Not seen you for ages. How you doing?'

'All right, I suppose.'

'God, your breath stinks of beer.'

'I've had a drink. It's not a crime is it?'

'Never said it was.'

'Sorry. I'm just used to being nagged, that's all.'

'You got married to Irene Bradshaw, didn't you?'

'Yes, worse luck.'

'Oh dear. That bad, is it?'

'She gets on at me sometimes. I can't handle it at the moment.'

'Are you going home now?'

'Don't know really. I've not got anywhere else to go.'

'Do you want to come to a party?'

'OK. Whose is it?'

'This lad called Scholesy. He lives on Chatham Park.'

'Yeah, all right.'

Kevin and Sandra took the train to Bury and, from there, the bus to Chatham Park where, for a reason lost in the mind of the borough's street name inventor, all the roads are named after towns in Kent. It lent a spuriously exotic air to a windswept estate next to the reservoir.

The party was in full swing to the tune of Berlin's 'Take My Breath Away' by the time Kevin and Sandra arrived. Tina was there, carrying a child in her stomach. Kevin averted his gaze from his sister necking with a man with a moustache, a glazier from Rochdale called Steve. Tina had obviously fallen out with Paul Cornish, though not before he had planted a seed inside her. Kevin accepted a small tablet from a boy he knew vaguely from long-forgotten football. He popped it down his throat and took hold of Sandra.

164

Within five minutes of arriving Kevin was in a bedroom with her with his pants down, struggling with the eternal riddle of a woman's bra strap. Tugging away as if he were pulling a bus in a strong man competition, Kevin forced the bra up painfully at the front to release Sandra's white breasts. To save time and eventual garrotting, Sandra reached round and released herself. The rest of their clothes followed quickly and in a boring order. There, with his head rocking against the loose wooden headboard and beneath the cheap coats of Bury's teenagers, Kevin McDermott was unfaithful to the vow and covenant he had with his wife. Downstairs, the crowd were bouncing up and down to 'The Final Countdown'.

'I've got to go.'

'Don't go.'

'I've got to. I shouldn't be here.'

Kevin dressed as he ran down the stairs. He sped out of the door, through the Kentish streets, round the reservoir and back to the Harwood. As he turned the key in the lock, the telephone was ringing.

'Hello?'

'Kevin. Thank God for that. Where the bloody hell have you been?'

'Out, why? What's up?'

'It's Irene. She's gone into labour. Your dad's gone with her up to Fairfield. They've been gone hours now.'

'Christ.'

'You'd better get up there. She had no idea where you were.'

'I was out.'

'It doesn't matter now. Just get yourself up to Fairfield.'

By the time the bus had chugged up the hill to Jericho, the tiny Susan Dawn had been born and named. Sammy had left and Irene was sitting bolt upright in bed, with moisture still enlightening her cheekbones.

'Oh, so you thought you'd put in an appearance, did you?'

'I'm sorry, love. I'm sorry.'

'You've really done it this time, Kev.'

'I'm so sorry, darling. I'm so sorry. I didn't know . . .'

165

'Kevin, things have got to change.'

'I know.'

'I mean it.'

'No, I know you do. I'm sorry, darling, I am. I just don't know what I'm doing half the time. I only want really . . . I don't know what to do. I just don't know . . .'

'Come here, love.'

'I'm sorry. I'm sorry.'

Kevin repeated the apology until Irene muffled his mouth with her soft hand. She led him to see Susan Dawn and as he gazed through her covered cot, Kevin's face cracked into tears.

'Oh darling, I wish . . .'

'I know. It's all right, baby. I know.'

Never Never

Kevin was at his wit's end as the bills piled up and as, every day, a new door was opened on Jason's advent calendar. Cigarettes and alcohol seemed the more alluring the less Kevin could really afford them. He was still going out too often with his father. Despite the paucity of his lifestyle he was living beyond his means. Irene was running a deficit on the Freeman's catalogue which had tempted her into purchases that she would never, never find the money for. Having given up on her husband, Irene went out to look for work herself. She got a few hours on the Tesco checkout that Kevin had stolen from, but any income she earned eroded her eligibility for benefits and Jason needed new clothes, new shoes. Jason always needed new things. Susan had to make do with little boy hand-me-downs.

The debts soon began to escalate. Rates, water, electricity, gas, telephone, TV licence, TV rental, the catalogue, the cassette player on HP, the dread of the postman bringing round more bad news in his little brown sack of doom. Every day was a red letter day for Irene and Kevin. The Gas Board were the first group of bureaucrats who determined to get them. The Gas Board wanted forty pounds and twenty-three pence and they were surprisingly demanding for the first red bill, threatening court action. Kevin didn't know that two red bills were lying under Tez Satchel's bed.

The post on the Harwood had suddenly become very unreliable and that was because Tez Satchel was hiding it under his bed. Up and down the Bolton road family rows had festered as relatives failed to send one another birthday cards, people didn't turn up for doctors' appointments and job interviews were missed. It was all junk mail to Tez Satchel, the lazy postman. He was sacked when his mother gave him up. She made him deliver all the lost mail anyway. Three months late, it came as a reminder of some lost world to its recipients. It didn't help that it was now all in the wrong order.

Kevin dared not ask his parents again. He had approached them in supplication too often lately and they didn't have forty pounds to spare anyway, certainly not in the run-up to Christmas. Sammy had another solution which Kevin still preferred to avoid. Kevin was due to answer for his poverty in court on the third Tuesday of the new year but he could prevent the action, which would idiotically add costs to the money he already didn't have, if he could come up with the money by last thing that Monday.

Irene pleaded with Kevin to let her approach Dawn who would stoically have endured the hardship forty pounds from her monthly budget would have caused.

'We can pay her back a bit a week.'

'No chance.'

'But at least we won't have to go to court.'

'We've got enough on the never-never. That's why we're in this fucking mess in the fucking first place.'

This was a direct and deliberate jibe at Irene who had, it was true, overspent in the alluring boutique of the catalogue.

'Well, if you'd get off your backside and get a job we wouldn't have to live like this.'

'There aren't any fucking jobs.'

'So how come everyone else has got one then?'

'Everyone else hasn't got one, you daft fucking cow.'

'Paul Cornish has got a job, your Greg's got one, Shaun Masters has got one in that new double-glazing company. Why can't you go down there and ask?'

'Ah, fuck off.'

'Kevin, you don't seem to get it. We'll be cut off if we don't find that money.'

168

'Just fuck off, Irene. You think I don't know all this bollocks.'

'You don't do anything about it.'

'Just fuck off, will you?'

'Do it yourself.'

'I fucking will before I belt you one.'

Kevin slammed the door so hard behind him that the whole house shook. Irene went upstairs to attend to Susan whose plaintive cries had gone unheeded throughout in the marital bedroom. As he walked aggressively through the estate Kevin had no specific plan except to return with forty pounds to prove to his Irene that he was worthy of her. He walked the streets for an hour to settle the noise in his head, stopping twice to chat, once with his uncle Greg and once with Bob and June Matthews who had been taking food from church to the old people of Castle Street.

As Kevin walked down Castle Street, an old woman was opening her door to bring in the milk. Mrs Smith wasn't as supple as she used to be and was clearly having trouble bending down to pick up the bottles.

'Shall I do that for you, love?'

'Oh, if you would, love.'

'Here you go. I'll bring em in for you.'

'No, it's OK, love.'

'Don't be a silly old moo; come on now.'

Kevin proceeded uninvited into the flat that smelt of incontinence and decay. A flat that smelt of an old lady on the threshold of death. Mrs Smith was seventy-four years of age and she had lived alone in Castle Street for forty-five years. Mr Smith had died in the war and there had never been another. Her three sons didn't get over often. It was early afternoon by now but Mrs Smith's timetable was irregular. She forgot what time old ladies are supposed to go to bed and what time they are meant to get up. She went to bed when she was tired and got up when she wasn't.

'Cup of tea, love?'

'I'll make it.'

Kevin pushed Mrs Smith out of the way in her own kitchen.

Kevin didn't quite know what he was doing. He decided to make a cup of tea and then leave. He brought the tea through into the living room, where Mrs Smith lived alone in unwashed underclothes and by the light of the gas fire.

'There's biscuits in the tin if you want, love.'

Kevin took three chocolate biscuits without offering them. Mrs Smith wasn't sure whether she knew Kevin or not. She assumed she must know him by the very fact that he was sitting in her living room, happily drinking a cup of tea and eating her chocolate biscuits.

'So how's your mum?'

Mrs Smith did not have the faintest idea who Kevin's mother was.

'She's fine.'

As they struggled for conversation Kevin noted an expensive carriage clock on the mantelpiece above the fireplace. He had the strong sense that he was prepared to do anything for Irene. Kevin got up from the chair whose odour was gently poisoning him and inspected the clock, ostensibly checking the time. It was no use to him. He needed hard cash. He pushed the clock aside to check for money secreted behind it. All he found were two letters written in the same hand. Mrs Smith had spent all the previous day trying to decipher why an old friend had written to apologise for her behaviour and then followed it up straight away with some very nasty accusations. It was probably her brain playing tricks with her again.

'Can I use the bog, love?'

Kevin held his nose with one hand and himself with the other. He left the toilet unflushed, thereby pretending to be in the bathroom still and sneaked, with practised softness, into Mrs Smith's bedroom to have a look around. Even as he patrolled the room on tip-toe Kevin did not want to be there. It was only forty pounds and she was so far gone she probably wouldn't even notice it was missing. There *had* to be money in the house. Kevin opened three drawers in the dressing table – bed linen, underwear, empty. On the table by the side of the bed sat a little box – incongruously luxurious, nicely carved with a discreet line

170

of ruby bubbles around its perimeter. Kevin pulled the top open harshly. Inside, amongst the hair clips and matches and single earrings there was a batch of notes, neatly folded and held together by a tightly bound elastic band. From the width of the notes Kevin surmised there must be a grand haul. He took the cash and snapped the box shut.

'What do you think you're doing, lad?'

Mrs Smith had given in to her curiosity.

'Give me that box.'

Kevin snatched it up from the bedside table, out of reach.

'Now just get out of the way.'

'Give me that box.'

'Get out of the way.'

Mrs Smith was blocking the door. As Kevin approached her she winced visibly but stood her ground.

'Give that to me. That doesn't belong to you. It's mine.'

Kevin attempted to push past but Mrs Smith hit out, catching him a blow across the eye. It was a feeble contact but a straggling broken nail caused a tiny breaking of the skin on Kevin's left cheek. Kevin caught Mrs Smith's next watery blow, pushed her gently out of the bedroom and made his way silently for the door, still carrying the box full of hair clips and the band of fivers in his pocket.

Mrs Smith was now hysterically defiant. She clawed at Kevin as he walked down the hallway and the pause he needed to open the chain lock on the front door was just sufficient for her to catch him a hefty blow on the back of the head. As he opened the door, Kevin could sense another strike which he pre-empted by jerking back his elbow, hard and true. He caught Mrs Smith a clean blow on the jaw which sent her careering backwards. She grasped despairingly for the ledge that ran along the wall as she hit the floor with a crack that was drowned out by the slam of the front door as Kevin made his escape.

Kevin already couldn't bear what he'd done as he ran down Castle Street with no thought for reducing suspicion. Kids were playing in the cobbled stone backs, old women were hanging out washing, the man from the next street was walking his dog, but none of them paid any attention to Kevin running rather manically down the street. Across the road, however, Bob Matthews asked June what she thought Kevin might have been doing. At the bottom of Castle Street there was a rubbish skip. Kevin paused momentarily and threw the beautiful wooden box in amongst the sodden earth and discarded bric-à-brac that even the jumble sales disdained. When he was safely away from Castle Street Kevin took the money out of his pocket. He was disappointed to discover that he had fallen victim to the folded paper illusion. There were only five notes. Twenty-five pounds.

Irene welcomed him back with a conciliatory kiss which he guiltily returned.

'What've you done to your cheek?'

Kevin dissembled, poorly but passably. 'I walked into a branch on the park.'

'Are you OK?'

'I'll live. You'll never guess where I've just been.'

'Where?'

'Dave down at the yard needs some stuff unloading and I said I'd give him a hand. Gave me twenty-five pounds as an advance.'

Dave was the owner of the sheet-metal yard at the foot of the hill. He had occasionally given Kevin an hour's work, loading and unloading the vans. The story was plausible and Irene was not sceptical. She was twenty-five pounds better off and there was no questioning good fortune when it paid a visit.

'Darling, that's brilliant. See, I knew you could do it.'

Irene kissed Kevin again, this time more lasciviously, simultaneously biting the mole on the left-hand side of her upper lip and blowing her fringe off her forehead in that fetching way she had. Kevin pulled away a little sharply, his duplicity punishing him.

'My mum'll lend us the rest.'

Dawn provided the deficit and the Gas Board's chase was called off. The cycle of bills turned blue again which meant that crisis point had been averted for another three months.

Kevin spent the next afternoon pretending to be at Dave's sheet-metal yard which gave Irene such hope that she asked daily if there would be any more work. She became so importunate on the issue that Kevin even went down to ask. Met with a sympathetic but definitive rebuff, he strolled home not exactly surprised but downcast all the same. As he left the yard behind him, a gentle drizzle began.

He took the short-cut home, past the old mill that the tramp lived in and the paper mill that was bought by a big American conglomerate. As he turned up the ginnel that led past a small private reservoir up to the tunnels where the bats flew, Kevin became aware that he was being followed. It is rare that anyone should be seen down here at dusk. The ground was marshy and waterlogged and the leaves were quickly trampled underfoot into a slippery sodden swamp. The steep sides of the railway bank blocked out the light and the playing fields which sat darkly on the other side gave the scene a shady, remote feel.

Kevin had spotted three men when he turned off the main road but he had paid them no heed. Preoccupied with how he might sugar the pill for Irene, he had ploughed on, heading home. Now, as he turned into the ginnel, black as night, his route retracted his steps sufficiently for him to catch three avenging angels silhouetted in the dark.

Kevin quickened his step. It was soggy underfoot and the putrid waters seeped over his shoes. There was a hole in Kevin's left shoe and he walked with his foot crumpled to dam the inflow of gruesome cold water. The act gave him a limp as he followed the enclosed side of the railway bank. He turned round to see that the three men had gained on him. Now there was no doubt. They were coming for him, no question. He started to run but his cramped foot impaired his movement. The ground gave softly beneath him and he was fatally slow in gathering speed. The three men rounded the corner sure-footed in the bog, magnetically attached to the shifting grass beneath. As he approached the railway line, Kevin stepped into a trot, to no avail. The quickest of the three was within a few feet of him when Kevin slipped on a clump of brown leaves that had lain in the path long enough only to gather a sheen of oily rain.

Kevin felt a surge of the most excruciating pain in his knee as his first assailant kicked him halfway up the railway bank. By now the two accomplices had caught up and were not to be denied their turn. The second kicked Kevin all the way back down the bank into the stagnant pool of the path's valley. The first blow had incapacitated Kevin. He was beyond fighting back, he was beyond self-defence. He abandoned himself to the assault.

One of the three assailants spoke as if there were a full stop after every word: 'You do not touch old women, sunshine. Do you hear?'

'Never. Never, do you hear? Against the fucking rules.'

'It's not on, isn't that. You know the score.'

With a final assortment of punches the three men disappeared into the tenebrous light of the tunnels, leaving Kevin writhing in agony on the stinking wet ground. He lay there all night, in unspeakable pain. Irene did not raise the alarm. Kevin had stayed out before when he had been drinking with a friend and hadn't made it home. He never rang. Nobody comes down through the dreadful tunnels at night and Kevin lay undiscovered until morning when the newspaper lad, on his way to deliver the *Financial Times* to the boardroom of the paper mill, heard his pathetic whimpering and ran off to call an ambulance.

Kevin spent two days in hospital recuperating. He was black and blue on the outside and repentant on the inside. His knee ligament had been torn again in the same place, putting paid to Irene's lingering hopes of defying the club doctor. Kevin was discharged into recriminations and tears from Irene. He was then laid up at home for a further week. Kevin tried again and again to explain to Irene that he did not know what had happened.

Kevin had just made it into the kitchen without help for the first time since the attack when there was a knock at the door. Irene was out at work, Jason and Susan were with their grandparents and Kevin wasn't expecting anyone. Before he could answer there was another knock, an urgent, irritated repetition.

'Are you Kevin McDermott?' said a uniformed officer who already knew the answer.

174

'Err . . . yes.'

'Could we come in, please?'

Kevin let the two policemen in, his heart sinking. They spoke in the circumlocutory way of people who are trying to sound official.

'We have reason to believe that you may have been in the vicinity of Castle Street on the evening of the fifteenth of December when a certain Mrs Smith was discovered injured in the act of attempting to avert a robbery.'

'Not me.'

'It has been brought to our attention that you were seen nearby a short period of time prior to the crime taking place.'

The police officers spoke a language that frightened and baffled Kevin. He stonewalled. He needed time to think, time to compose himself.

'It's a simple enough question, sir', the uniform droned on. 'Do you remember being in Castle Street on that afternoon? Because, if you do, you may have information pertinent to our inquiry.'

Kevin issued a perfunctory denial, buying time. The drone was ready for that and came back without pausing for breath: 'We have two signed witnesses to the fact that you were seen at 4.30pm approaching Castle Street from Lord Street and the same witnesses can attest to the fact that you were seen emerging from 34 Castle Street fifteen minutes later.'

'You must have the wrong person. It wasn't me.'

'You may be aware,' the other uniform interrupted, 'that a Mrs Smith of 34 Castle Street was discovered at 5pm precisely by our witness, conscious but unable to raise herself on the floor of her home. We believe she had been the victim of an unprovoked attack in the midst of a robbery.'

Kevin could feel the net closing around him.

'If you wouldn't mind accompanying us to the police station, Mr McDermott.'

'Why? I've done nowt.'

'So we can rule you out of our inquiries by checking your fingerprints.'

'What for? What do you want fingerprints for?'

'To ensure that they don't appear on a wooden box discovered near the scene which we have reason to believe was the property of Mrs Smith.'

By the time Irene had arrived home from work Kevin was in a police cell. As the duty officer shut the door of the cell, Kevin stopped him. 'Was she all right, the old girl?'

The policeman looked intently, judgementally, at Kevin then nodded.

'Just about.'

Kevin was asked if he wanted to make a call. He called Irene. She did not understand. She could not begin to understand why he had done what he had done. But then neither could Kevin. He tried to explain to her that he hadn't really been thinking *anything*.

'I just don't get it, Kevin. You don't hit an old lady by accident.'

'It *was* an accident. I was just holding her off and I caught her.'

'I thought you were better than that. To hit an old lady . . .'

'I *am* better than that. I didn't mean it.'

'You shouldn't have been there in the first place.'

'I know.'

'What were you doing?'

'We needed the money, remember? We were skint. *Are* skint.'

'But we'll not get it like that. No matter how desperate we get.'

The evening passed in frenetic panic. The whole McDermott clan, Sammy, Wendy, Greg and Bobby were drunk on indignation. Irene, confused and distraught, perplexed, let down, angry, but most of all as profoundly disappointed as if she had dropped into the sea when expecting dry land, spent the night and many nights thereafter in Liverpool with her mother.

Sammy and Wendy went over to the club for a drink. By now the news had spread. No visit by the police to the Harwood estate goes unnoticed and Sammy thought it best to face the neighbours at once. Besides, he was spoiling for a fight with

Bob Matthews. Bob was sitting in his usual spot, at the front by the stage, when Sammy charged into the large iron door, sending a bucket full of raffle tickets into orbit and startling Albert, who was cleaning one of his war medals, into pricking himself on the pin. Sammy made a straight line for the front but, before he could raise a fist, five Brangy men moved gracefully in unison and in silence to surround Bob. Sammy ploughed into the circle and was forcibly repulsed by the praetorian guard.

'You fucking put the pigs onto my boy. I'll fucking have you, Matthews. I'll have you.'

There were shrieks from Val and Ethel in row two as Sammy snarled. His arms and legs rotated as he was prevented from moving, sending him veering through farce before resting at tragedy. Sammy ranted on, implausibly blaming Bob for Kevin's injuries and repeating his threats to give Bob the same and more in return.

Tired of this ill-mannered interruption to his evening pint Bob Matthews emerged from his protective circle and took hold of Sammy. Bob was a small man but immensely strong when he was stirred. He held Sammy tight to bursting. He brought his face up to within an inch of Sammy McDermott's and waited for silence. Bob spoke in a controlled but forthright whisper: 'Your Kevin deserved every last kick in the bollocks. If that old dear had been mine I'd have fucking killed him. Now get out of here and don't come back till you've learnt how to behave.'

Sammy went straight home.

An Heroic Assumption

Adam was on his way home from a New Year reunion of old boys of Bury Grammar School. As the puddles on the dirt track had evaporated for once, he took the back route past the derelict mill. As he strolled by in the spring twilight, laughing to himself at the fuzzy beard and fisherman's sweater that Sacha Bland now wore, Adam noticed a prone figure propped against the wall of the mill. As he got closer he saw the figure twitch and, as he got closer still, he saw that it was Kevin.

'Oi, are you all right?'

There was no answer. Kevin looked like he was asleep. Adam lifted his head from his collarbone and recoiled as Kevin twitched violently. In the throes of a cataleptic fit, Kevin's eyelids were stuck, as though they were pink blinds that had been deliberately pulled down half-way. With every convulsion, a filmy soup escaped from his unnaturally still mouth.

Adam sprinted the quarter of a mile home as though the tramp in the mill were after him. He burst through the door and collapsed onto the telephone. 'Ambulance . . . My friend's having a fit . . . By the mill, next to the river.'

Adam burst into the living room where he found his father at the top of a stepladder, painting the ceiling in his stained overalls.

'Come to the mill, quick. It's Kevin.'

Adam and his dad ran down through the tunnels, Bob flagging as the gathering stitch in his stomach impeded his attempts to talk as they ran. Kevin's convulsions had worsened. Bob stood over him, panting to regain his breath.

'Oh God, Dad. What can we do?'

'Bloody idiot. There's nothing we can do other than wait.'

'What's wrong with him?'

'It's drugs.'

'Dad, we've got to look after him.'

The ambulance arrived and took Kevin, Adam and Bob up to Bury General. Kevin was taken straight through to see a doctor. Adam and Bob waited for two hours until the doctor came out to see them.

'Is anyone here for Kevin McDermott?'

'Yes, we are.'

'I'm afraid your son has had a fit induced by the drug heroin.'

'Oh, Jesus.'

'He's been very lucky in that the convulsions have now ceased.'

'Will he be OK?' asked Adam.

'Well, yes. Until next time.'

'There won't be a next time. We've got to look after him, Dad. He's in a bad way.'

'That is unfortunately true,' said the doctor, leaving them.

Kevin was kept in overnight and returned in the morning to slowly escalating hostilities with his wife. On his return from hospital, Irene made Kevin a cup of coffee and a crumpet and sat her husband down to talk.

'Now, Kevin, we have to sort this out. Just what is going on?'

'I had a bit too much to drink, that's all.'

'And you were kept in hospital because of it?'

'I had a bad pint,' said Kevin, sneering.

'Kevin, I'm not going to put up with this. You've really changed. First you're hitting old women and then you're found on the floor out of your brains on God knows what . . .'

'I was drunk.'

'What'll happen to Jason and Susan if you go to prison?'

'I won't got to prison.'

'What if you do?'

'I won't.'

'The health visitor's been. She's worried about Susan.'

'Why?'

'She's really tiny and underweight. She's given me a diet sheet. We've got to give her a proper diet or else she might be ill. We've got to give her more vegetables.'

'Where the fuck are we going to get vegetables from?'

'I might well ask you that, Kevin.'

'I'll ask my dad to do a job for us. I'm sure he can nick a few carrots if he puts his mind to it.'

'You don't even care, do you? You're so selfish. Just because you think your life is ruined you're not bothered about anyone else's.'

'I'm going out. I've had enough of this.'

'That's right. Run away as usual.'

'I'm going to see that old dear if you must know.'

'What for?'

'I'm going to say sorry so stick that in your pipe and smoke it.'

Kevin went round to collect Bob Matthews, who had called him to suggest that they visit Mrs Smith together. As soon as he entered he heard The Smiths upstairs which told him that Adam was home.

'I just wanted to say thanks for looking after me.'

'It's Adam you should be thanking. He was the one who found you. Why don't you go up and say hello. Then we'll go.'

Kevin found Adam lying back on the bed, reading.

'Hiya mate. What you reading?' he asked, awkwardly.

'It's called *Tom Jones*.'

'Any good?'

'Yeah, it's not bad. You can borrow it if you want.'

'You're all right. I just wanted to say thanks for looking after me the other day.'

'That's all right. You've got to get off that stuff, though. It's a killer.'

'It's all right. I've stopped.'

Adam changed the subject, clumsily.

'I heard . . .'

'Yeah.'

181

'What were you doing?'

'I don't know.'

'I couldn't believe it when my dad told me.'

'I know.'

'Fucking hell, mate. She's an old woman.'

'I know.'

'What were you doing?'

'I dunno.'

'You can't do that.'

'Adam, I know all this. I've just had my bollocks kicked in because of it. It was an accident. I never meant to hurt her. I just caught her by accident.'

'But what were you doing in there in the first place?'

'I needed the money. I don't know. I had a kid coming and everything. I don't know; it just happened.'

'But Kevin, if you needed . . .'

'You don't need to say anything. I'm not proud of it.'

'No. I was going to say that I'll lend you some money if you want.'

'It's OK.'

'Tell you what, let's go down to Gigg and I'll pay you in.'

'I don't know . . .'

'Go on, I'm going anyway. Come with us.'

'I've not been for ages.'

'You've got to get back on the bike eventually.'

Bob shouted that he was ready to leave.

'I've got to go. Your dad's taking me round to speak to that old woman.'

'I'll meet you outside the club at two, all right?'

'If I'm not there by ten past, you go.'

Mrs Smith kept the chain on as she spoke to the visitor she somehow recognised.

'What is it, young man?'

'I wanted to say sorry.'

'What for?'

'For coming into your house and for catching you. I didn't

mean to hurt you; it was an accident, I promise. I don't know what happened.'

Mrs Smith suddenly remembered who Kevin was and made to shut the door. Bob stepped from Kevin's side into her line of vision through the small crack of light.

'Hello there, Mrs Smith. Don't worry; he means it.'

Mrs Smith unhooked the chain and let Kevin in. Mrs Smith made the tea this time and offered round the biscuits.

'Now then, young man, what have you got to say for yourself?'

Kevin played with his hair and bit his fingernails.

'Kevin,' said Bob.

'I just wanted to say that I was sorry. There's no excuse for it and I haven't come here with one. I wanted to tell you that I'll never do anything like this again and I'm sorry I frightened you.'

'Have you made him say this, Bob Matthews?'

'I haven't. I was the one who got him into trouble with the police. But I know Kevin well enough to know he's not such a bad lad and I know if he says he's sorry, then he means it.'

'I do.'

'All right, young man. Like you said, there's no excuse. But I'm glad you've come to say sorry. There's plenty who wouldn't have.'

'I'm sorry.'

'Right, we've said what we came to say. We won't detain you any longer, Mrs Smith,' said Bob, gesturing to Kevin to leave his tea.

As Bob walked ahead down Castle Street, Kevin called him back.

'Bob?'

'What?'

'Thanks.'

'That's OK. Now, do something for me, will you? Go down to Gigg Lane with our Adam. He needs looking after.'

Bob smiled and suddenly all was almost right with the world.

Kevin met Adam and the two of them drifted down to Gigg Lane. Kevin had not been to Gigg Lane since his injury fifteen months before. As he walked through the big dark-blue gates to the turnstiles, Adam patted his back and felt the jelly of soft flesh.

'Bury against Grimsby on a wet Saturday. Brilliant.'

The look on Kevin's face reminded Adam that Bury against Grimsby on a wet Saturday had been the scene of the ending of his dreams.

'Let's go round to the players' bit. I'll get us into the directors' box.'

Kevin approached the man on the door to the restricted area.

'Passes, gents.'

'I've come to see Mickey Bell.'

'Can I see your passes, lads?'

'Come on, Kev. Let's go and get some tickets.'

'I used to play for Bury. I want to have a word with Mickey.'

'If I had a pound, sunshine, for everyone who reckons they used to play for Bury and who thinks there's a free ticket in it for 'em I'd have over hundred quid.'

'I'm Kevin McDermott.'

'Good for you, lad. I'm sure you're very famous in your own house but if you've not got a pass you can't come in.'

'I played last season.'

'Look, lad. I'm very sorry but you need a pass to get into the players' area.'

'He was captain last season.'

'I don't know the team. I wasn't here last season. I'm just told not to let anyone through without a pass and that's what I'm doing.'

'I assumed . . .'

'Well, you assumed wrong I'm afraid, sunshine. Now, the ticket barrier's over there. I suggest you go and get yourself a couple of tickets. You won't find the queue's too long.'

Kevin nearly went home at once. If Adam had not rushed off so quickly in the direction of the turnstiles he would have done so. As the pitch emerged out of the gap at the top of the stone steps, Kevin felt sick. The first sight of the impeccable green turf produced a lump in his throat the size of the balls he saw his old friends casually keeping in the air.

'This is weird. It's so weird.'

'Do you want to go?'

'No.'

Grimsby took an early lead as the rain came down in domestic pets. Kevin was terse, tense and uncomfortable. Adam nervously broke fifteen minutes of silence with unsuitable badinage.

'I reckon you'd still make the team. Even with a gammy leg.'

'Leachy was crap. I was always miles better than him.'

'You could beat this lot on crutches.'

'I could be out there now. I shouldn't be in the fucking stands.'

Grimsby scored again as Kevin spoke.

'If I ever meet that cunt who did my knee . . .'

'I know mate.'

'Do you? Like fuck you do.'

At half-time the spectacle improved. The grass looked very nice with no players getting in the way. Kevin tried, for Adam's sake.

'How's it going anyway down there?'

'It's OK.'

'What do you actually do? In your work, like?'

'It's like . . . You know . . . all sorts really . . . It's mostly about what sort of government you'd have if you could have anything.'

'Oh, right. What are you going to do when you've finished?'

'Don't know really. My tutor said he might try and get me into TV in London.'

'Jesus. You get all the fucking luck going, you do.' Kevin shook his head, angrily, almost in accusation. Adam secretly prayed for Bury and Grimsby to reappear. Kevin wanted to change the subject just as much and, less afflicted by embarrassment, did so easily, even at some cost to himself.

'Me and Irene are not so great at the moment. She's hardly talking to me. I don't suppose you can blame her.'

'You've got to show her you can get on. You need to start earning if you can.'

'Oh thanks, Mastermind. You're a fucking genius, you are.'

'Sorry. I was only saying.'

'It's OK.'

'I meant it before about borrowing some money, mate. If you need to . . .'

'I could do with some. I've got to pay a fine to the housing benefit.'

A careless signature had alerted an observant fraud detector. John White had been executed by the fraud office and Kevin, Sammy and the newsagent had to answer in court for the crime of writing fiction.

'Do you want a pie?'

'Yeah, go on.'

'Can you get them if I give you money? Get us a coffee as well, will you?'

Adam picked up a copy of the *Bury Times* that was on the unoccupied seat behind him. He flicked through the jobs pages while Kevin fetched the pies. An appeal for drivers caught his attention: 'Wheel of Fortune seeks responsible drivers. Call 764 3202.'

Kevin was balancing two pies on two cups of boiling chicory on his way back to Adam when he was stopped by his Elton Moor rival, Mark O'Reilly.

'Oi, Kev. Come into the bogs.'

'Fucking hell, Reilly. I didn't know you were an arse-bandit.'

'No, come on.'

'Blimey old Reilly. He's a fucking shit-stabber.'

Kevin let Mark take him into the toilet where he arched his foot against the liquid seeping up into his sole. Mark led him into a cubicle where he locked the door and took a small bag, full of white dust, out of his pocket.

'Have you tried this?'

'What is it?'

'It's called crack. Gets you right off your head.'

'How much?'

'Fifty quid.'

'I haven't got fifty quid.'

'Tough shit then.'

'Give us some.'

'No chance.'

'Oh come on, Reilly. I'll see you right.'

'No chance.'

'Forget it then.'

Kevin balanced the pies back to Adam with the price of crack ringing in his mind.

'Have you been growing that coffee?'

'Sorry. I saw someone I know.'

'There's an advert in the paper for drivers.'

'For what?'

'Chauffeurs.'

'How much do they get?'

'Doesn't say but they must be rich.'

'How come?'

'Look at the cars they drive.'

'I can't be a chauffeur, me.'

Kevin did not want to call. They turned to the second half and saw Bury concede two more goals in the endless drizzle. The final whistle brought immense relief to the Bury team and to the Bury fans but to nobody more than to Kevin.

On their way home Adam stopped off at a call box and spoke very quickly so that he could fit his conversation into a single ten pence piece.

'I've got some good news for you.'

'I could do with some.'

'That driving business wants you to go down for an interview.'

'Have you just rung them up?'

'I knew you wouldn't. But you'd be mad not to do it. You can drive, can't you? I never thought of that.'

'Yeah, Greg taught me ages ago.'

'You should do it. It'd be all right money. And you'll never guess whose business it is.'

'Whose?'

'Go on. Guess.'

'Joe Corrigan's.'

'No, but it is a goalie.'

'John Forrest.'

'Barry Mawdsley's.'

'God, is it? He can't drive. He's blind, that bastard.'

'And he's doing it with Shaun Masters.'

'Bloody hell. It's funny what happens to people, isn't it?'

Shaun Masters had devised a plan with a friend's father who was a hotel manager in Piccadilly Gardens, Manchester. He knew the exorbitant rates charged by car hire firms to take corporate freeloaders back to Manchester airport in the style they now impatiently expected. He also knew that there were no reliable companies providing this service. Shaun called his friend Barry Mawdsley who had given up keeping goal to run a garage. Barry had supplied Shaun with four Jaguars for a share in the business.

Kevin said goodbye to Adam as they took their separate paths on the Harwood estate. He felt more positive than at any point since Mickey Bell had crushed his spirit. But as soon as he entered his home Irene Bradshaw crushed him again.

While Kevin was at the football match, Irene had been a seeker after dust, poking in the cupboards in the marital bedroom. She had rummaged, for no particular reason, under the pile of Kevin's underpants and socks. It is in the places that gather dust, the hidden covens of their homes, that people hide their precious secrets. Amidst the decaying dried skin and the rotting insects that settled on Kevin's underpants and socks, Irene had discovered a big brown bag of white dust. She had taken the bag out, already distressingly aware of what it was. Irene had never actually seen any hard drugs. Yet confronted with a bag of heroin she just knew.

The rest of Irene's life shot through her head as she met the consequences of this discovery. There is no way back from an intuitive revelation like this. It is how all relationships end, with a flash in the mind of one party that it is over. Six tempestuous months had gone by since the squiggles had begun regretting to inform him. Then Irene saw the end flash by, compressed into a mental instant, into the fear that was contained in this bag full of dust.

As Kevin turned his key in the lock Irene sprung up from the brown settee. Kevin dropped his house keys on the shelf in the hallway and went through into the living room to find Irene standing, hard-eyed and silent in a dark room, with the brown curtains closed. She thrust his brown bag at him.

'I found this amongst your stuff.'

'You what?'

'You heard. I found this amongst your stuff.'

'What is it?'

'You tell me.'

'What were you doing rooting through my stuff anyway?'

'I was cleaning up. What is it?'

'I don't know.'

'What do you mean you don't know?'

'It's not mine.'

'So who's is it then?'

'I'm keeping it for a mate of mine.'

'Who?'

'This bloke I know. He gives me a few quid for looking after it because he still lives with his mum and dad and he doesn't want them to find out he's got it.'

'You bloody idiot. Do you know what would happen if this was found here?'

'I never thought.'

'No, you never bloody think. Get rid of it now.'

'How?'

'Flush it down the bog.'

'No, I can't.'

'You can. Flush it down the bog.'

'I can't.'

'Do it.'

'He'd go mad.'

'Who'd go mad, Kevin?'

'My mate.'

'Kevin, I don't believe you. It's yours, isn't it?'

'No, it's not. Honest.'

'Who's is it then?'

'It's Terry Berry's. He uses it all the time but he doesn't like to keep it at home.'

'I don't believe you.'

'It's not mine.'

'So get rid of it then.'

'I can't.'

'If you won't then I will.'

Irene moved towards the door.

'Give it here.'

Kevin followed.

'I said give it here.'

Kevin caught Irene's trailing foot as she climbed the stairs. She fell into a painful splits, cracking her pubic bone on the step. The white dust spilled out over the stairs and, screaming, Irene slapped at the heap of heroin, scattering it through the gap in the banister and onto the linoleum below.

'Stop it, you stupid cow. Stop it.'

Kevin grabbed Irene's wrist and yanked her away.

'Touch that again and I'll fucking kill you.'

Kevin fetched a spoon from the kitchen and scooped up as much as he could. There were irretrievable grains flecked into the carpet on the stairs, which only the hoover would pick up.

Irene staggered up to the bedroom where she shivered under the covers. When he had rehidden his brown bag, Kevin joined her, his anger at Irene's inquisitiveness mingling with remorse for his violent response.

'Get out.'

'It's not mine, I promise you. I'll be in for it when Bezza finds out that half of it's gone. He'll think I've had it.'

'Leave it, Kevin.'

'It's not mine. What would I want with that stuff?'

'I don't know, Kevin. You tell me.'

'It's not mine.'

The discussion went on for five hours with tears, cigarettes and cups of tea. Kevin argued himself into realising that Irene and the children were the only dream he had left. On three separate occasions Kevin felt he had convinced Irene that in the morning all her white dust troubles would disappear. But Irene knew this wasn't true. She wanted to believe Kevin. But it was too heroic an assumption. Irene knew.

They slept badly on the sofa, waking at a quarter to five to continue the discussion. By the time they had exhausted the argument, Jason and Susan were waking for the new day. Irene got up to attend to them while Kevin put his head down to sleep. At eight o'clock there was a sudden and vicious banging on the door. Irene opened it on Sandra McEwan.

'Is Kevin in?'

'He's asleep.'

'Can you get him up?'

'Why?'

'It's important.'

'What is it?'

'I need to talk to him.'

'Tell me and I'll tell him.'

'You don't want to know.'

'Yes I do.'

'You don't. I'm telling you.'

'Try me.'

'All right then. I'm pregnant.'

'So what? What's that got to do with Kevin?'

'He's the dad.'

'Don't be so stupid.'

'I'm not being stupid.'

'He can't be the dad.'

'He can. I should know. I was there.'

'Rubbish.'

'I will. When was it?'

'At Scholesy's party ages ago.'

'We didn't go to Scholesy's party.'

'Kevin did.'

191

Jason and Susan cried out for more breakfast in the background. Irene looked hard at Sandra, then broke out of the expression like an actress straightening her face after corpsing.

'I'll tell Kevin you came.'

Irene closed the door softly on Sandra. She dressed Jason and Susan and packed two small bags. As Irene slammed the door on her marriage the advent calendar fell off the wall onto the dirty brown floor. Irene, Jason and Susan had left the Harwood estate for Liverpool before Kevin had woken up.

Faithfully and Sincerely

Kevin flicked frantically through the address book he had never opened before. He found Dawn Bradshaw's number in Liverpool and called at once.

'Dawn, it's Kevin.'

'Kevin. Is everything all right?'

'Is Irene there?'

'No. Why? Should she be? Kevin, what's the matter?'

'She's gone. I went to sleep and she's taken all her stuff and left.'

'Oh my God. What happened?'

'She's just gone. I thought she'd come to you.'

'When did she leave?'

'This morning.'

'What time?'

'Don't know. It might have been about eightish.'

'She won't have got here then. She's probably on her way. I'll get her to call you as soon as she arrives.'

An hour later the telephone rang.

'Irene . . .'

'Kevin.'

'Where are you?'

'I'm at my mum's. Didn't you get my note?'

'No. I didn't see anything.'

'I left it on the table.'

'I didn't see it.'

'Well I left you one.'

'What did it say?'

'It's obvious isn't it, Kevin?'

'I'll stop. I promise. I'll get rid of all the drugs. I'll flush them down the bog now if you want.'

'It's not just that.'

'What else is it then? I'll get a job, I promise. I'll do anything. I'll ask Bob Matthews if he can get me in at Brown's.'

'And what are you going to do about Sandra McEwan?'

'What do you mean? What are you on about?'

'I know about Sandra, Kevin.'

'What about her?'

'There's no point playing dumb, Kevin. She came round and told me what you get up to when you go out in the evening.'

'What you on about?'

'Kevin, stop lying to me. I know what you've been up to.'

'I haven't been up to anything.'

'So Sandra McEwan must be the Virgin Mary then.'

'What?'

'So she's got pregnant by magic, has she then?'

'You what? She's not pregnant.'

'Go and ask her, Kevin. Go and ask her. And then you might as well move in with her because you've really done it with me.'

Kevin heard the final slam at the other end of the line.

He sat in a state of shock for an hour, quite unable to contemplate what had happened. Still not quite sure of what he was doing, he went round to see Adam. Kevin ignored Bob's puzzled look when he refused to come in and insisted instead that Adam come out.

'I need a word. Come for a walk, will you?'

'It's pissing it down. Can't we do it inside?'

'Nah, come on.'

Adam came out reluctantly only because Kevin's gravity, pulling him downwards, was written on his expression. Kevin did not soften the blow to himself.

'Irene's left.'

'Shit. How come?'

'Doesn't matter. Loads of things. She's just gone.'

'Where's she gone?'

'She's at her mum's in Liverpool. That's not the point.'

'What is the point?'

'How do I get her to come home?'

'It depends why she's left, doesn't it? Why has she gone?'

'She's been getting really pissed off that we don't have any cash and that I don't have a job. I think that's it, basically. She goes on about other stuff but it's about getting a job really.'

'In which case, mate, you've answered your own question. Why don't you give Shaun Masters a call?'

'I will. No, I will, this time. I will.'

Kevin saw a plan in bare outline. He saw the love that money could buy and he saw, in blurred form, the riches Mark O'Reilly had offered.

He called Shaun Masters who interviewed him on the telephone.

'Why should we give you the job?'

'Because you know me.'

'That's not a very good reason.'

''Course it is.'

'Imagine I'm a passenger. What would you say to me?'

'Nothing.'

'Why not?'

'People don't want the driver going on at them. They want some peace and quiet in the back. I know I would.'

'Fair enough. But what if I did want to talk?'

'Then I'd talk about football and how I used to be a footballer.'

'Yeah, OK. That sounds good. Have you got a clean licence?'

'Yeah.'

'OK then, seeing as we know you, you're in.'

Kevin put the telephone down and picked it straight up again to call Mark O'Reilly, inspired by the image of Irene and the children, in a verdant garden, surrounded by luxuriant flowers and the sweet smell of roses. The money Mark had alluded to teased and tormented Kevin.

First thing on Monday morning, Kevin put on the peaked cap and took up the wheel of fortune in Barry Mawdsley's Jaguar.

On his way back from his first trip to Manchester airport he parked in Rusholme and located the contact that Mark O'Reilly had made for him. Kevin paid for the goods and then passed them on down the line at an exorbitant price to the disaffected young men of the town centre pubs in Bury. Kevin found out how money begets money, like a list of descendants in the Bible. It was money for old rope, enough old rope to hang yourself with.

Kevin was an artless dodger in a big car. He made no attempt to throw a false trail over his activities and operated instead by ignoring the possibility of capture. Kevin dealt in The Old Mill, the entrepôt of all Bury's suppliers. Three police officers effortlessly infiltrated the drug groups, appropriately disguised in crusty clothing and accompanied by rancid, shaggy dogs on fraying strings. All three gentlemen of the law bought crack or heroin from Kevin, at prices which, the latter always boasted, could not be matched anywhere else in town.

Kevin was only a pawn. He had already led the police, unwittingly, to a far larger operation in Rusholme. Once his south Manchester supplier was safely locked away the police came back for Kevin. Late on a grey Tuesday in February, Kevin took a telephone call from an unidentified male voice. Kevin conducted the dialogue in a series of monosyllabic grunts.

'Is that Kevin McDermott?'

'Yeah. Who is it?'

'Bobby.'

'Yeah?'

'I've got two hundred pounds to spend.'

'Drink tomorrow?'

'OK.'

'Old Mill at eight.'

'No, not there. It's too obvious. There's pigs in there.'

'Where then?'

'Flying Shuttle. Rochdale Road. Next door to the Ritzy.'

'OK. See you at eight?'

Kevin arrived five minutes early and lit a cigarette, ready for a quick exchange. Exactly on time a tall, thin man with a grey pencil moustache walked into the pub and, looking around furtively, tried not to demonstrate that he knew exactly what Kevin looked like.

'Bobby?'

'Yes.'

'Not here. Come outside.'

Kevin followed into the car park.

'So what you got then?'

Kevin pulled out his wares from the back pocket of his jeans. He held it before Bobby who looked up, beyond Kevin, out over the Pennines. Kevin felt a hand rest on his shoulder, then another take his arm and bend it back, disabling him as he cried out in pain. Kevin tried to strike out but there were four of them, including Bobby. The arrest took place in an eerie silence. Only a single remark was passed as Bobby looked straight into Kevin's eyes and said, without feeling: 'We've got you now, you little bastard.'

Kevin had been nicked. And so very, very easily. Kevin was so unobservant that a statue of Sir Robert Peel himself could have caught him out. He was a statistic waiting to be recorded. Kevin had barely even been attempting to hide but the police were coming, ready or not. At no point in the game did anyone shout ally ally eeno.

After two Ireneless months on remand, Kevin was found guilty and sentenced to two years. He was taken from court to a police cell where he spent the evening before being transferred the short distance up Great Ducie Street to Strangeways. Incarceration intensified the anger and frustration that was the cause of Kevin's being there at all. Shorn of all distraction, he fell right down on his luck. Drugs were freely available inside, for the renunciation of privileges to the supplier, Lewis Satchel, so Kevin spent his days in a stupor, suspended between the present and the distant future at home with his children in the rose garden.

He was coerced into counselling with a well-meaning psychologist called Louisa who tried, usually in vain, to help vicious young men control their rising anger. Louisa began with a bio-

197

graphical inquiry in an attempt to trace the source of Kevin's pain. But Kevin was an unforthcoming interviewee. He had no interest in baring himself before a hippy in a flowery dress. Kevin wanted to be left alone. Meanwhile, his father and his wife did just that.

Adam was his first visitor. Kevin shuffled reluctantly, head down, into the bare room where the prisoners received their friends and relatives.

'Kev, how are you?'

'All right, I suppose.'

'Do you remember my song "The Prisoner"?'

'Yes, thanks. Shows how much you fucking knew, doesn't it?'

'Sorry.'

There was a lengthy silence. Ten seconds is an eternity to take out of a conversation.

'I don't really know what to say,' said Adam for want of anything better.

'Don't say anything then.'

'What happened, mate?'

'I got caught.'

'I know but . . .'

'There's no point going into it.'

'Isn't there anything else you can do?'

'If I fucking knew that, I'd be doing it, wouldn't I?'

There was another ten-second beat.

'Have you seen Irene?'

'No. Have you?'

'I saw her yesterday in town. Just by chance.'

'What did she say?'

'Not much, really.'

'Tell her I'm sorry if you see her. She won't talk to me. Just tell her I'm sorry.'

Kevin was in the penitentiary, sorry for his strange ways, but Irene was not there to tell. Adam found one useful suggestion in the awkward silences before he left, thoroughly downcast: 'Why don't you write to her and let her know what you're thinking?'

This was the only useful service Kevin's counsellor performed. She helped Kevin write a letter. Louisa typed as Kevin dictated. It was a simple, heartfelt letter, a statement of virtue written faithfully and sincerely, with corrections in grammar and diction by Louisa.

Kevin McDermott
Strangeways
Great Ducie Street
24 December 1987

Dear Irene,

How are you? How's Jason? How's Susan? I think about you all the time. It's horrible in here. Every day I get up and I hope that you'll come in and visit me. There are loads of things I want to say but I don't know if I'll say the right thing. My mum lets me know how you're getting on. She said you looked a bit lonely but you don't have to because I'm thinking about you all the time and I'll come and find you when I get out if you can wait for me. I'm truly sorry for what I've done. Things haven't gone right and I know I haven't always done what I should have. I know I've let you down but I never meant to. Happy Christmas darling.

Yours sincerely,

Kevin xxxxx

Kevin didn't know that Irene was contemplating moving in with her new boyfriend Ian and two toilets in Greenmount, a village underneath Peel Tower where posh people live. She had a new job now, as a receptionist at the paper mill by the railway bank and the beginnings of a new life. Every so often Irene passed on a non-committal message through Wendy who always embellished the greeting in relaying it to Kevin.

Hoping for a reply at least got Kevin out of bed every morning. He returned when the letter failed to appear once again. Finally, after a goading from Wendy that Kevin never knew anything about, Irene composed a short reply. Kevin's heartbeat accelerated when he recognised the curly girly handwriting of

199

his still beloved wife. He ripped open the yellow envelope and took out the embossed blue notepaper. Kevin asked Wendy to read out the following destructive words:

Dear Kevin,
Thank you for your letter and sorry I've not written back before now but I didn't know what to put. I can't keep waiting for you to come out of prison, Kevin. You could be down for a long time and you've let me down too often. I'm not carrying on with this . . .

'Mum, read it.'

I know things have gone wrong for you but that's no excuse for what you've done. We've all got our problems and you just have to cope. I've got Jason and Susan to think about and I need to make plans for their future. I know this is going to upset you and I wish it wasn't but I want to apply for a divorce. I don't know why you had to do what you did because I really loved you. It obviously wasn't good enough. I'm very sad about what has happened to us but I have to get on with my life now and I think you need to do the same. I'm sorry, Kevin.

Yours faithfully,

Irene Bradshaw.

'The bloody bitch, I'll give her what for when I see her . . .'
'Leave it, Mum. Don't touch her.'
'She can't treat you like that, the little madam. I'll . . .'
'You'll not. You'll do nowt.'

In two short paragraphs, in the only letter she ever wrote to him, Irene Bradshaw knocked Kevin over. He had once been a young man of distinction. Now he was not even Cock of his own cell and he was the only one in it.

Kevin did not become accustomed to his new routine so much as submit to it. He lived out eighteen months of his sentence, supine, lying down before misery. The enclosing walls of his cell mocked him with the nightly reminder that here there was no Irene. Her letter told him that there was no Irene on the outside either, as though he were condemned to carry those four walls around with him for good.

The tedium was lifted briefly and partially at visiting time, which meant Wendy and the sisters. Kevin said nothing during these visits. Instead he listened dutifully to the litany of nephews and nieces, to the latest cute saying of the newest born, of whom there now seemed to be a veritable legion. Tina had just had twins, one of whom, with cruel perversity, she had called Scott. Tina's little girl, Mary, had trouble breathing and required constant vigilance and consistent warmth which was rare in Tina's damp one-bedroom council flat. Maria's boys, Adam and Shane, were set to be joined by a baby daughter, Louise, courtesy of the new live-in boyfriend, Russ. Irene had three sons, Sammy, Graham and Simon and a new baby daughter, Angela, not to mention the unperson Nathan who was now in the top reading group at one of Bury's best primary schools.

Kevin heard the conversation but did not listen. Wendy talked on and on, insensitively declaring that Adam Matthews had passed his exams at university, that Bob and June had been to a service conducted in Latin and later that she had seen Adam last night on the television. On and on Wendy talked, fearful that any break in the monologue would reveal emotion better concealed. Wendy talked and Kevin's sisters talked, all so that nobody would ever have to *talk*.

Like Irene, Sammy never came. He sent his regards through Wendy but he was always indisposed on visiting days. Sammy had been inside in Scotland many years before and said, without elaboration, that prisons gave him 'the creeps'. Wendy's short, bitter reports conveyed exactly their stilted exchanges in which Kevin contributed barely a word.

Wendy noticed the change in his demeanour at once after Irene's letter. She had not elicited more than a grunt from him in six visits. After another pointless and frustrating hour of one-way traffic, Wendy took the matter into her own bucket hands and stormed uninvited into the prison governor's office.

'When are you lot going to fucking do something?'

Mr Prendergast, the prison governor, took a moment to recover his composure.

'Do you mind?'

'Listen to me. I've just been in to see my son and I'm telling you there's something up with him.'

'Yes, madam, I'm sure there is. He's in prison.'

This facile retort was too much for Wendy who vented her spleen on the spindly, officious Mr Prendergast. Grabbing him forcibly by his rutted throat and pressing him with a thud against the back wall of his overfurnished office, Wendy made her point in her own style. Her jowls hung down loosely like washing on a line and her scarlet cheeks blazed against the dyed ebony of her tightly permed hair.

'Do something, you bloody idiot.'

'There's nothing out of the ordinary in his behaviour, Mrs McDermott.'

'He hasn't said a bloody word for about a month or more.'

'Prison can often have that effect on the most vigorous characters.'

'There's more to it than that. Any fool can see that.'

Mr Prendergast did not tell Wendy that he too suspected there was more to Kevin than met the eye. He was concerned that Kevin had a supplier and that his aphasia was induced through large measures of illegal narcotics. Wendy shouted for five minutes before fizzling out. As she left the room she stopped, turned, and said with sudden and unmistakable softness, even with imploring sadness: 'Do something, will you? He's not himself, our Kevin.'

The day after Wendy beat up the prison governor, the warders on Kevin's block raided his cell and found a tiny bag of heroin. The stash was confiscated and Kevin brought to answer for his actions before the prison authorities. He was as monosyllabic in his own defence as he was in front of his voluble mother. Kevin was sent back to his cell.

That evening, Mr Owen was doing his nightly round. He peered through tiny windows at men perched miserably on the edge of hard beds. They call it doing time because time is all there is in prison. The last one, Kevin McDermott, was slumped forward, his head *in* his hands but not supported by them. There was a lifelessness about Kevin's posture that alarmed Mr Owen. He tapped impatiently on the metal door. There was no response. Mr Owen tapped again, this time more insistently.

'McDermott. You all right?'

McDermott did not stir. Hurriedly, Mr Owen fumbled for the huge bunch of keys that he carried attached to the thick belt that held up enormous trousers around his gargantuan belly. Mr Owen stumbled, as quickly as his bulk would allow, into Kevin's cell. Kevin's neck dropped as soon as Mr Owen tapped the supporting hand. The prison warder took one look at the insanity in his eyes and ran for help, leaving the door wide open.

Kevin spent four days in the detoxification unit. His stomach was pumped to relieve it of the sleeping pills that he had taken to deliberate excess. Louisa saw him every day after that, probing away at the injury that had ended Kevin's career. Met with a stone wall, Louisa persisted, at first to no avail. Then Kevin cracked open. He gave Louisa what he thought she wanted. She hungrily translated every blunt McDermott retort into the language of therapy, anaesthetising every bloody imprecation that issued from Kevin's deep well of anguish. Kevin had run out of reasons to continue serving out his time. His one remaining act of freedom, the only defiance he could muster against the pressing, intractable fates, was to put his interminable misery to an end, once and for all, by his own hand.

Kevin was allowed back to his cell but kept under strict supervision. He lay there, his face buried in the pillow, waiting for nothing. The endless expanse of Tuesday was broken when the duty warder banged on the door and informed Kevin that he had a visitor. Wendy and his sisters usually came on Thursdays. Still, Wendy could have changed her mind. Or perhaps, Kevin thought, he had the day wrong. He read no newspapers and followed no routine. Or rather, routine was all he had but it did not vary from day to day. Kevin's Wednesday was exactly the same as Kevin's Saturday. His only constant point was a visit from his mother which told him it must be Thursday. And now even that ritual was under threat.

The thought of explaining himself to his mother filled Kevin with inarticulate dread. He reluctantly pulled himself up and slouched through the open door as slowly as is consistent with not actually standing still. At no point did he lift his gaze from his dragging feet. Kevin was in a fit of fatigue. Even his hair looked tired. He proceeded sulkily to his usual seat and, as he looked up, his father spoke to him, in a tone of unrecognisable tenderness.

'Hello, son.'

Kevin looked straight at Sammy and Sammy looked straight back. Without any further words passing between them Kevin fell deep into his father's arms. There they stood, oblivious to the rest of the room, for a full two minutes, hanging on for dear life.

'You all right, you daft beggar?'

'Suppose so.'

'What's up, Kevin? What is it?'

Kevin could not say. There was far too much, all jumbled and unclassified and confused inside his head. Sammy broke the silence.

'I never meant you to end up in here.'

'It's not your fault.'

'No, Kevin. It is.'

Sammy lifted his chin deliberately, picked his face up off the floor, and looked directly into the wetted eyes of his son. Kevin had retained an uncritical admiration for his father throughout it all. Sammy breathed heavily, a waft of cigarettes and beer, straight at Kevin. Tears formed in Sammy's eyes as he began the speech of his life.

'I'm sorry, son. It is my . . .'

'No, Dad. It's not, it's not.'

'Listen, Kevin, and don't interrupt me. I've let you down, son. I've done my best but . . .'

Sammy paused, for breath and courage. He reached out to

take Kevin's hand in his own. Sammy's fingers coiled lovingly around his son's and he stroked Kevin's hand in a manner like never before.

'I've done my best . . .'

Sammy's voice broke. The episode was unbearably tense and difficult for Kevin, who had never seen his father like this before. For Sammy, an inarticulate man whose aggression belied his shyness and lack of confidence, it was the most challenging moment of his life. Sammy could steal from houses and Sammy could fight another man. But now he was out of his depth, drowning in streams of guilt.

'I've done my best, son. I'm sorry. I'm sorry, son . . .'

part four: *Pulling up Peel Tower*

With Honours

On a glorious day in June 1988 Bob and June Matthews found out where Latin was. It was in the Senate House in Cambridge watching their only son graduate, with honours, as Bob never failed to add, from the Classics Tripos. The sun streamed in through the windows and shone, as Bob and June saw it, right through Adam. The sacrifices they had made all came good on that day. It had been no hardship for being the rudder that kept their son on a straight path. As Adam received his degree Bob and June hugged each other like teenagers in a bus shelter tanked up on Woodpecker cider.

Adam dutifully had his picture taken in his gown and mortar board and he stood with his girlfriend, Elizabeth, whose parents were abroad, while June took photographs against the grandiose backdrop of fairytale Gothic architecture. Adam and his peer group posed for a keepsake picture on Trinity Bridge. Elizabeth, Piers, Arabella, Barney, Lucy and Adam. There were no Kevins and Irenes here. There were no Bobs and Junes and Wendys and Sammys here. The elite crew were there for the last time, drinking in privilege before making their way, fortified, into a world which was set up so hospitably to receive them.

Bob read from his programme, with perfect pronunciation, as they walked up the sheltered lane back to Trinity College.

'*Virtus vera nobilitas est.*'

June pushed open the large front door of the college and Bob said what he always said when he stepped into the Great Court.

'That's absolutely grand, is that. Fantastic.'

Elizabeth and Arabella sniggered at the sheer Northernness of Adam's parents. Although Adam had deliberately styled himself as the Stuart Sutcliffe of The Smiths, his accent had slowly melted into the educated hum of his new town. Bob and June's rich Lancastrian enthusiasm echoed into the Great Court. Bob's voice was not loud but it carried across the stone. It sounded so thoroughly unusual, to all of them. It was a special day that such a voice sounded out.

June and Bob skipped through to the Wren Library and out onto the perfect lawn for the champagne reception which Trinity College had laid on for its newly ennobled graduates. June talked to the other mothers, in a tone they all found unduly anxious, about whether their offspring had a job to go to and the importance of having some money coming in. She explained on three separate occasions that Bury was not in Suffolk. Bob informed anyone who would listen that his son had graduated with honours and, eventually, found himself taking lessons from the college groundsman on how to manicure a perfect lawn.

Meanwhile, by the river, Adam asked Elizabeth a question, fuelled by champagne.

'Shall we? . . . You know . . .'

'What about your mum and dad?'

'I won't invite them if you don't mind. Sweet of you to ask though.'

'Adam, you can't leave them down here on their own.'

''Course I can. Look at 'em. They've made more friends in half an hour than I have in three years.'

'That's because you, Adam Matthews, hate everyone.'

'Not quite everyone.'

Adam had met Elizabeth Mercer early in his first term, at a party in her room. At first sight he had written off all the other guests as cardboard but Elizabeth was something else. She was five-foot-four in her alluringly stockinged feet and she wore tiny plain black shoes laced with white ribbon. Her short, straight black dress had been simple and elegant and had defined her gentle curves. The low square cut of her dress had revealed an expanse of vulnerable flesh, made all the more attractive by the absence of jewellery. Elizabeth never wore a necklace. The short, tight sleeves had emphasised the flawless, untrodden snow of her skin as she had moved gracefully into the light provided by the lamp above. From Adam's vantage point in the corner of the room Elizabeth had been in front of a thick white pillar and she had appeared to him chipped out of stone by the hand of a genius. Elizabeth's pale beauty had been offset by her lips which were painted a lascivious red and by those astonishing eyes which had shone like the reflection on deep green pools. To her left the smoke from her cigarette had drifted upwards to the ceiling. Atop this portrait of desire the dancing Elizabeth wore a little black hat. It was a round hat, a womanly bowler, and Elizabeth wore it pushed back so that beneath it her carefully arranged whitewashed fringe poked out, giggling at its own impudence, like a child emerging from behind a curtain and shouting: 'Boo!'

During the jonquil-and-daffodil summer term of 1986 Elizabeth had taught Adam about classical music. He adored her too much to be able to say that he found it dull. In return, Adam had taught Elizabeth the lyrics to early 1980s pop music, information she would have been better-off without.

'You mean you've never even heard of Howard Jones?'

'Never. Have you heard of Shostakovich?'

'Yes, 'course,' Adam lied.

'Well, who is he then?'

'He plays up front for Red Star Belgrade. Educated left foot.'

Adam had endured his tutorials on classical music because he felt so sophisticated having a girlfriend who could play the piano. Then he would regularly surprise her by asking her to play Steiner's 'Crucifixion' or Bach's 'Jesu, Joy of Man's Desiring'. When they weren't breaking down musical barriers, Adam and Elizabeth had eyes only for each other and for the television. Nightly programmes were the starting point of a cabaret act, the inspiration for Adam's impromptu comic turns. He demolished Elizabeth's City boyfriend Will with a long routine about Just William in a fine Violet Elizabeth Bott voice. Adam created new worlds, a private Richmal Crompton inventing children's stories. He made up characters out of scenes private to them, with references so intimate that nobody else in the world could comprehend why they were funny. Elizabeth encouraged Adam to audition for the university comedy theatre but he descended the stairs to their rehearsal room with such overwhelming trepidation that he was too nervous to turn the handle of the door. But Adam didn't need the footlights at his feet when he had Elizabeth in his arms. Adam fell in love with Elizabeth in the summertime, in the wintertime, in the springtime and in the autumntime. He had cooked dinners with her, watched TV with her, let her spend hours alone in the bath and had driven to the all-night garage with her. They were crazy, the pair of them.

Elizabeth led Adam into the bedroom and they flopped contentedly onto his bed. On only this single occasion had Adam's love-making brought someone to tears. After accepting a degree and five glasses of champagne Adam made love to Elizabeth and she cried because she loved him dearly. There were no words to describe it, except to cry too, which is what Adam did.

He found the only words that seemed to suit.

'Will you marry me?'

In a theatrical flourish Adam took off the gold bangle that he wore around his girlish wrist and placed it, with deliberate ceremony, over Elizabeth's hand, which he held too long in his own. Elizabeth's smile lit up his world and her eyes, mesmeric eyes, shone like the reflection on deep green pools. Adam was looking up but there were no hills in view and there was no Peel Tower to guide him home. With every word she had ever uttered Elizabeth had taken him away from home. Elizabeth Mercer pulled up Peel Tower every time she opened her mouth.

Now she nodded and kissed him gently on the upper lip.

Adam and Elizabeth pulled on their clothes and rejoined the party on the lawn, where the food had been laid out on a long table by the river.

'Don't tell my mum and dad just yet. It'll be a bit much all on one day.'

They found Bob and June sitting on the grass, gazing over, in love, at a party on the adjacent lawn in front of the magnificently arrogant New Court. Elizabeth offered to queue for food while Adam sat with his parents.

'Eeee, I could live here,' said June. 'It's not exactly the Bolton road, is it?'

'It's all right. It's not as great as you think, though. There's some right chinless wonders here.'

'Don't be such a snob, Adam.'

'I'm not the snob. That's the point. It's the rest of them that are snobs.'

'You're an inverted snob. You shouldn't take against people just because of where they've been brought up. That's not their fault.'

'I read your thing the other day,' said Bob suddenly.

'What thing?'

'Your what's it called? The thing you wrote for your degree.'

'The thing about Cicero.'

June pronounced Cicero with two hard 'c's. It sounded like the Italian version of a trendy make of shoe and Adam couldn't help sniggering.

'What are you laughing at?'

'It's Cicero, Mum. With an "s".'

'It's all arse-about-tit in Latin. Anyway, I read it.'

'My dissertation.'

'That's the fella, your dissertation.'

'Did you like it?'

'I thought you were showing off half the time. There's no need to use long words when a short one'll do just as well. And I think you're daft about the Queen.'

'It's not really about the Queen.'

'Well, you're on about a republic . . .'

'Yeah, but it's the Roman republic.'

'I know it is. I know what you mean as well. Did you see that *Tom Jones* on telly the other night?'

'No, why?'

'It's the same things, isn't it, as you were on about in your dissertation?'

'Is it?'

'Yes. He's an orphan kid but we watched the last episode the other night and it turns out he's an aristocrat. That's basically the point of your thing.'

'Well, I suppose so, yes,' said Adam, failing to conceal his surprise.

Bob threw his son a hard look as if to say, 'Do not suppose I am stupid, young man. Do not.'

Elizabeth returned with her friend Arabella, from Hong Kong by way of Uckfield, carrying two plates each. Arabella insisted that the golden couple pose together. She fussed by their side for five more minutes, missing out on her life because she was too busy photographing it.

'Thanks, Arabee.'

'What's that young girl called?' asked June.

'Arabella.'

'Blimey, that's like something out of Sinbad the Sailor.'

'Everyone's called weird stuff here, Mum.'

'Your grandma had a friend called Isabella Bell. They don't come any weirder than that. They used to call her "Yes it is".'

Bob poked the unfamiliar food around his paper plate with a plastic fork.

'What the bloody hell's this, Adam?'

'It's teriyaki,' answered Elizabeth.

'We used to have a milkman called that.'

'No, Dad. That was Terry Mackie.'

'Same difference.'

'Do you like it?' asked Elizabeth, tentatively.

'No, it's bloody awful. Whoever it's named after.'

'Now what did I teach you? The universal law of sauce,' said Adam to Elizabeth who had forgotten the cardinal rule of Northern cuisine.

'They like sauce where I come from.'

'Where did you say your folks are from, Elizabeth?' asked Bob.

'Nowhere, really. My dad was in the foreign office so we moved around a lot when I was a child. We lived in Paris for a bit. Then Rome. And then Bogotá.'

'Blimey. So did you keep moving schools in all them places?'

214

'I came back to England to go to school.'

'She went to Elton Moor,' added Adam.

'I went to school near Brighton.'

'But where's your dad from?'

'I don't know, really. He was at school in Berkshire and his parents had a house near Windsor but my grandfather was a diplomat too.'

'They're very grand, the Mercers.'

'We're not really. We always had a big house but we didn't have much money.'

'So where would you say you're from then, out of all those?'

'I'm not sure. My parents keep a house in Hertfordshire but they're not there often. I'm not really from anywhere in particular, I suppose.'

'Well, you're always welcome in Bury.'

'Is that an offer or a threat, Dad?'

'As long as you kick the sauce habit.'

Adam went to find a bottle of white wine to wash down the inedible, unpronounceable food. He came back with the most expensive bottle June had ever seen.

'Very impressive,' said June, as Adam lifted the cork expertly from the neck of the bottle.

'That's what they teach you here. That's what I've learnt from Elizabeth.'

Elizabeth told the story of the first time Adam had tried to open a bottle of wine. Unsure whether to peel the top off the bottle first, uncertain how the steel spiral should be inserted into the cork, no idea what the funny rising handles were for, Adam had prevailed through sheer brute force and had triumphantly pushed the cork down into the cheap white wine.

'He just poured it out, in a zig-zag round the cork, as if that's how you're meant to do it. It was really sweet.'

'Well, I didn't know. The wine we had always had a screw top. We always had that fizzy stuff at Christmas. That's what I thought wine was.'

'We had that nice bottle when you passed your A levels. That had a cork in it,' said June, sharply.

215

'No, it didn't.'

'It did. I remember your dad getting the corkscrew out of the pantry.'

'It didn't. It had a screw top, Mum.'

'Does it really matter? We're not spoiling a great day by arguing about whether a bottle of wine had a screw top or a cork. Come on, son. Eat up your Terry Mackie, there's a good lad.'

'Dad, do I look like someone who likes sauce?'

'You bloody do these days. You're a right foreigner, you are. You'll not be coming back to Bury now you've gone over to the other side.'

'I might.'

'You won't, I tell you.'

'You never know. I might do.'

Bob cut off the jocular tone. 'Don't you dare. This is your world now. Look at it. Don't you dare come back home. I don't ever want to see you living at home again.'

'Oh, thanks.'

'You know exactly what I mean. You've got a job to go to and everything for you is down south now. So don't bloody bother about us or about Kevin or anyone. We'll be all right.'

'How is Kevin? Have you heard from him?'

'No, he's in for a while yet.'

'I've written to him but he never writes back.'

'He's not a letter-writer, isn't Kevin.'

'I know. But I wish he'd let me know how he's getting on.'

'You can't spend too long worrying about Kevin.'

'But he's my best . . .'

'He was.'

'No, he still is. I can't just abandon him.'

'You've got your own life to lead,' added June in support.

'If there's any looking after Kevin to be done, I'll take care of it,' said Bob, 'although the only one who can look after Kevin in the end is Kevin.'

There was a pause in which the four of them sipped the expensive wine and poked their food again. Bob exhaled heavily, portentously, and lifted himself off the grass to make an announcement.

'Now, Adam, I've got something to tell you and I want you to listen to this and to listen good.'

'What?'

'I can tell you now, your mum's right. It was a cork not a screw top. I remember going in the pantry.'

Adam pushed his dad over and tried to roll him down the riverbank but Bob was too strong and Adam had to promise never to come home to save himself from being dumped in the river Cam.

After another hour in the sun, the Matthews family was more drunk on still wine than ever before. Bob and June insisted on a final tour of Cambridge so Adam dragged them through King's College Chapel and onto the bridge at Clare where, at dusk, June took a photograph of her husband and son. Then they walked up between the Senate House and Gonville and Caius College. Just to prove that this time he knew how to pronounce it properly, Bob had taken to calling his door keys his 'Gonvilles'.

As the three of them entered the Market Square Adam noticed some workmen scuffling on the scaffolding that was holding up the jewellery store on the corner. Suddenly, in front of him, as if a film was unfolding in slow motion, a red-headed figure fell twenty feet from the wooden platform, over the metal barrier and, sideways on, crashed onto the pavement. The other men had already descended from the scaffolding by the time Adam got up close.

Adam took a single look at the prone figure and knew at once that he was dead. Under a curtain of bright red hair, his pale-blue eyes had given up all life and they seemed to recede into his sunken, ginger-freckled cheeks. Adam had a violent nauseous reaction and turned, instinctively, to his dad to do something. Bob hadn't approached. He had led June aside and they were standing aside under an empty market stall.

'Dad.'

'Come on, son.'

'Dad, he's . . .'

'Adam, come on. His mates'll take care of it. They've called an ambulance. There's nothing we can do.'

Adam walked with his parents back over Christ's Pieces and Jesus Green to their guest house on Chesterton Road. Bob and June tried to interest him in gossip from home.

'We've had all sorts of shenanigans at church.'

'Why? What's up?'

'We've got a new vicar. Alan Truman's got a new parish in Bolton. The new fella's one of them modern vicars. He's in the middle of what he calls "updating the service". He says the King James Version's old-fashioned. And now we've got guitars and all sorts. It'll be Lord of the bloody Dance next.'

'I like that one.'

'We're going on strike.'

'You're not going to go?'

'We'll go but nobody'll sing or say any new-fangled prayers. We're just going to sit there.'

'It's a revolution. Church is full of freedom fighters.'

'It's not funny, Adam. He wants to get rid of the Book of Remembrance as well. Says it's morbid.'

'Really?' said Adam, interested despite himself.

Adam left his parents at the bridge over the river Cam.

'Dad?'

'Yes, son.'

'Keep an eye out for Kevin, won't you?'

'I will. And Adam? Well done, lad. You've done us proud.'

'We've had a lovely day. Thanks, love.'

'OK Mum. Look after yourself. I'll give you a ring.'

Adam walked back to Trinity College for the last time. He was not sorry to be leaving. Adam had struggled here at first when the grandeur of the Great Court had only served to subdue him. He had seemed so small in it. He had felt out of place and assailed by the confidence of the people who seemed to have been bred to come here all their lives. He had never before known anything so utterly *posh*. Adam had lost himself in the gloom, the oak panels and the teak armchairs.

But he was found as well as lost in his new world. Adam had

gradually learnt to cope and now he was leaving with the girl. The vision of Kevin gave way to the vision of Elizabeth. He recalled their first meeting when, in a borrowed dinner jacket and a velcro bow-tie Adam had stared into the deep green pools of a beautiful young lady. Adam Matthews had never known such glamour and in the morning he was taking it away to Paris. Adam lingered, for one last look, on the threshold of the Trinity College at Cambridge that he had first seen in the glossy book in the school library.

The Sanctuary Lamp

Paris in the full bloom of summer. It was the best of times, it was the worst of times. Adam and Elizabeth stayed with family friends of her parents, which Adam found extraordinary. Elizabeth explained that because her father was a diplomat she had lived briefly in Paris. Adam added that his father had worked on a job in Bolton once but it hadn't come with a residence attached.

They stepped out into the summer night to wander the streets with their only aim to wander. They found a cheap fish restaurant by the Arc de Triomphe where Adam performed, for one night only, for his love.

'How come some things can be monged and not others?'

'I'm sorry?'

'Think about it. This fish has come from a fishmonger. But this pasta hasn't come from a pastamonger. Why not?'

'I don't know. What is monging anyway? What do mongers actually do?'

'They mong things. For instance, this fish and that chandelier have one thing in common which is that they've both been monged. Fish and iron are two of the three things that are most commonly monged.'

'What's the other one?'

'War.'

'You're mad.'

'Good mad or bad mad?'

'Good mad.'

Adam ordered a private joke: *fruits de mer avec linguine*. At their first dinner party, Adam had been dismayed to find pasta being served. Adam had seen pasta before but he had never eaten it, unless alphabetti spaghetti counted. He had been aghast to note how dextrously Elizabeth coiled it around her fork, how unobtrusively she piled beige lumps into her mouth. Adam had mimicked the act of wrapping spaghetti round a fork but very poorly. Elizabeth did not know whether to laugh or admonish him as Adam quoted himself by holding his fork high above his head and biting the strands off half way down.

After dinner Adam and Elizabeth walked arm in arm down the Champs-Elysées. As far as Adam was concerned that might as well be entered in the dictionary as a definition of romance. At two o'clock in the morning they were still walking. Elizabeth was dressed in a sleek black coat with fur trim and a black hat, the very picture of elegance. In the photographs she would look like Ingrid Bergman in *Casablanca*. Adam wore a jacket in dog-tooth check, a red and white paisley scarf, white jeans and brown loafers, looking like Jerry Dammers with nicer teeth. Adam was walking on blisters in the dimensions of a foot, hitting the sky in pain whenever he stepped on a crack in the pavement. But it didn't matter. For Adam the subject was Elizabeth and for Elizabeth the subject was Adam. Everything else was adventure.

Adam stopped in the Place de la Concorde.

'Look up.'

'Why?'

'Just look.'

Elizabeth looked up at the world above eye level where, amongst the architectural details never before remarked upon, the windows yielded untold stories, new narratives in another world. And beyond them, the stars. Elizabeth took a small box from her coat pocket. She took out a shining band of gold and asked Adam to put it on her finger. 'This is our family engagement ring. It was my grandmother's.'

Adam and Elizabeth walked to the Ile de la Cité, then ambled along the river bank to wait for dawn at the Eiffel Tower. At

222

Adam's insistence they strolled to and fro, crossing the Seine and back six times. Adam counted the bridges: Pont au Double, Petit Pont, Pont St Michel, Pont Neuf.

'It's Pont Quatre coming this way.'

And so on, until the Pont des Invalides and, *enfin*, the Pont de l'Alma. Adam and Elizabeth stood, holding hands, gazing up at the very symbol of Paris. To Adam and Elizabeth, Paris was the home of liberty and intellectual licence, city of romance, of Picasso, Hemingway and Anna Akhmatova, city of Bogie and Ingrid.

Elizabeth repeated an apocryphal story she had read: 'Apparently Maupassant had dinner in the restaurant every day because it was the only place that he could be certain he wouldn't see the Eiffel Tower.'

'Well, he was an idiot. It's fantastic.'

The Eiffel Tower felt like the Peel Tower of Adam's new world.

'I wonder what Kevin's doing now?'

'Don't think about it now.'

It was two-thirty on the morning of 1 July 1988. In the Champ de Mars, in front of the Tower looking now like the torch of liberty itself, there was a tiny deserted fairground. An Algerian stood in attendance, distracted, alone. Elizabeth asked if they could go in and Adam, throwing off embarrassment for once in his life, assented.

Two children on a carousel, for her the lion, for him the fox. Both up and down and round and round they go. If there was anyone else present they were invisible, immaterial. Adam leant over to kiss Elizabeth as the fox rose and the lion fell. He placed his lips on hers, nuzzled her nose and closed his eyes. It was the happiest moment of his whole life. As they walked away hand in hand from Gustave's great tower, wrapped up in a sleek black coat, dog-tooth check and in themselves, neither Adam nor Elizabeth took care to look back, where they would have seen a broad, beaming smile on the face of a lonely Algerian.

'Let's have a swing. Come on.'

Elizabeth giggled, with all girlish innocence, clambered onto a swing and turned herself round with practised art. By the time she implored Adam to join her she was already airborne. Adam jumped on beside her and ransacked his brain for long-dormant swinging technique. Elizabeth gave him a master class.

'Get on tip-toe and push off. Then straighten your legs at the top. Right, now tuck your legs in tight.'

Adam followed the rubric closely with his timing awry and, after three swings, Elizabeth was in the clouds and he was scraping the ground, his legs tucked in so far that his knees were creaking. Elizabeth was like Kevin McDermott who used to swing all the way over the top and then jump off. Elizabeth came down to Adam's level, pulled a face and soared away. Adam stretched out his legs, tucked them in and went nowhere. Elizabeth went into swing free-wheeling and slowly came back down to earth. She laughed again and set out for the sky. With this ascent she gave out an incomprehensible scream of joy. Meanwhile, Adam tucked his legs in and described a pathetic arc six feet above the floor. Still, it barely mattered when Elizabeth pulled up alongside him, leant over and placed the most enticing kiss on his lips that had ever featured in his wildest dream. For a brief moment Elizabeth was free. Elizabeth was never more securely in love with Adam than at this moment. The two of them there by the Champ de Mars, her on a lion and him on a fox, bobbing up and down on the swings of outrageous fortune.

It had been a long and beautiful day but, by the time they had arrived back in the eighth *arrondissement*, Adam had retreated. He went straight upstairs, more or less blanking his hosts, and he would not look at Elizabeth as they undressed in silence. He met her inquiries with an impenetrable wall.

'What's the matter?'

'Nothing.'

'Nothing' was the only answer which could not possibly be true. Two minutes of tense silence later, the exchange was repeated. And then once more. After five minutes of brooding Adam came out.

'Did you fancy that bloke?'

'Oh, so that's what's the matter with you.'

'Did you?'

'Which bloke?'

'The one at the fairground.'

'Which bloke at the fairground?'

'The one on the ride. You were flirting with him.'

'Don't be so silly.'

'Did you think he was good-looking?'

'Not really.'

'Yes you did.'

'I didn't fancy him though.'

'How can you not fancy him if you think he's good-looking?'

'It's easy. I just don't fancy him. Take Kevin's wife. Do you think she's good-looking?'

'No.'

'Don't be so obtuse.'

'What about Piers? Would you like to sleep with him?'

Adam's insecurity derived from the fact that he had parted Elizabeth from Just William. Adam was scared that Elizabeth might recast her life again, this time with him as victim. His jealousy had been bubbling and now it boiled. He started with the famous people. Carl Lewis was the latest in a long line of celebrity torturers. Before the pious priest of speed there had been a parade of dwarves. Like a bizarre circus act, Mel Gibson, Tom Cruise and Prince pranced before Adam, the subject of Elizabeth's inexplicable and painful lust. Before the three dwarves there had been Jim Morrison, in his absurdly self-important crucifixion pose that studded the desires of a million student girls. And before that, with a previous girlfriend, an extended period of trial by Simon Le Bon.

Adam moved woundingly through fantasy to reality. He knew Elizabeth had slept with eight men before him and he knew chapter and verse on each. Adam had so much detail he could have written a novel about it, though an excessively dull one. Every single detail was unbearable but horribly necessary. The details haunted him but he pushed harder, striving to force inconsistencies with previous accounts. After three hours of interrogation Elizabeth confessed to a new detail. She had once had a one-night stand with a man on holiday and Adam forced her to concede that he had been well-endowed. Adam wanted Elizabeth alone. He wanted her never to have been intimate with anyone, even before he met her. Adam knew this was stupid and outrageous. Elizabeth pointed this out, he knew it already, yet he felt it all the same.

'What was Will like in bed?'

Adam knew the answer to this but he was corroded by jealousy. He was rusting away from the inside. The unwelcome visions of Elizabeth's past had taken up permanent residence in his head. When it came to jealousy Othello wore a cassock and surplice. Adam capitalised jealousy, continuing his relentless quiz. He met every considered answer with nasty, caustic bitterness. Adam's denunciation of Elizabeth's past was vicious. His own history was beside the point as his esteem required that she be humiliated. As soon as Elizabeth began to cry Adam felt a little better, as though she had not really meant to do what she had done. But Adam had gone too far, further than he knew.

'So that's it, then? There are eight of them?'

Elizabeth said nothing.

'Well?'

Elizabeth said nothing still.

'Elizabeth? Are there any others?'

Nothing.

'Are there?'

This time tears broke the silence. As Elizabeth broke down she hid her face with her hands, like a child against a tree at hide-and-seek. She apologised, over and over.

'I'm sorry, sweetheart. I'm really sorry.'

'Why? What's the matter?'

'I wanted to tell you. I really did.'

'What? What is it? You've got to tell me now.'

'I've been trying to find the right time but I just never wanted to think about it.'

'Think about what? Who is it? It's Piers, isn't it?'

'Adam, don't . . . You don't understand.'

The tears welled up fetchingly before Elizabeth's emerald eyes. She spoke, faltering, unsure of Adam's capacity to understand. The equipoise that Elizabeth had planted inside him, he now gave back in return.

The words came reluctantly, from deep hiding. Elizabeth told Adam about the first time it had happened. She told him about a distinguished diplomatic gathering in a building near the Louvre and a trusted friend of the family, about her father's precarious professional standing and the searing guilt that *this is all your fault*. She recalled her ability to transport herself, as if levitating, so that she was absent every time it happened. She described her immediate immersion in the bath, scrubbing the skin until it was raw, to clean off the last dirty vestiges of invasion.

'I still see him. He's still a friend of my parents.'

'Evil bastard.'

'He's not evil really. He's pathetic. They're the most dangerous.'

Adam said something unprintable in response and, in the circumstances, the wisest thing possible. He said nothing. Confronted with the unspeakable, he had the wisdom to shut up. He blinked his eyes rapidly and cradled Elizabeth. After two minutes of silence he said the only thing he could think of to say.

'I love you.'

That was all, all that was needed.

Elizabeth asked if she could be left alone. She took a magazine from the rack, ran the bath and did what she always did when she was upset. She locked herself in the bathroom. Adam heard the door lock as a personal reproach but it was behind the locked door of the bathroom that Elizabeth found sanctuary. The bathroom was where she would go to ensure that nothing would get her, not even guilt. It was her den. She pulled the cord and lay alone in the bath, illuminated by the sanctuary lamp that never goes out.

227

Adam and Elizabeth spent the rest of the summer at Elizabeth's parents' empty house near Hertford. Adam went home to Bury for a fortnight when Elizabeth declared she needed some time alone. She said she needed to read up for her new job in banking and she could best do that without distraction. Apart from his obvious contempt for capitalism, Adam felt hurt and confused when Elizabeth told him that she did not want to get too close. Besides, his dad looked at him with increasing disapproval with every extra day he spent in Bury.

Adam went back as soon as he was given the all-clear and, for the rest of the holiday, Elizabeth read George Eliot while Adam learnt the London A–Z. They grew and cut their hair respectively into sensible colours and shapes. In September Elizabeth and Adam took the train to King's Cross to look for somewhere to live. Armed with a deposit courtesy of Mr Mercer and letters of reference from Goldman Sachs and the BBC, the two of them scoured *Loot*, the *Evening Standard* and the windows of letting agencies.

Elizabeth insisted that they started in west London, which was already full of her friends from school and the graduates who had preceded them from Cambridge. Adam dragged his feet through SWs 3, 6 and 10, not quite aware why he didn't like them, but very sure that he didn't. He had thought of the King's Road as the stage of the 1960s, the place to buy a mohair suit and bleached Levi's. It had been the site of Sex and the revolution that had introduced him to pop music. On his only trip to London, Adam had fallen in love with the pretty girls with straight teeth who glided through Sloane Square. He was horribly disappointed to find that it was so dreadful.

'Why's everyone dressed like they live in the countryside?'

'They're not.'

'Yes they are. Look at them. They've all got those crap green jackets on.'

'Barbours, do you mean?'

'Dunno. Probably. It's not very cool round here, is it?'

'Adam, this is the King's Road. You can't say it's not very cool.'

'I can. It's crap.'

'All right then, clever clogs, where do you want to live?'

'On the Eastenders map.'

'The East End's really grotty.'

'Even better. Come on, let's go and have a look. We can't afford it here anyway. Even if it wasn't crap. Which it is. 'They call her Natasha but she looks like Elsie. I don't want to go to Chelsea,' sang Adam in tuneless Teenage Kicks fashion.

Adam loved Whitechapel Road at once. He fell for the seedy glamour of streets he knew from Mayhew, alleys once terrorised by Jack the Ripper. He loved the cluster of curries on Brick Lane and the market stalls on Bethnal Green Road. He loved the Wren churches and the bells of Shoreditch. In the poorly lit streets and council blocks of Whitechapel, cheek-by-jowl with the dispossessed of London and its first-generation Bangladeshi immigrants, Adam felt instantly at home.

He found a large two-bedroom flat off Brick Lane for the same price as a shoebox with an SW postcode. Elizabeth did not understand Adam's desire to live on the set of a history of urban disrepute but she consented because it was a beautiful flat not very far from Fleet Street, where she was due to start work a week later. Besides, she loved Adam and wanted to be inside four walls with him, wherever they were.

Elizabeth had abandoned English literature. Although the loss was certainly Elizabeth's, Adam was concerned that she was plummeting into a world, business and finance, in which she had no interest. But she had followed the interview rubric sedulously, and after an hour's chat about the college that they had in common, a grinning investment banker had invited Elizabeth to join him selling European equities. Elizabeth had accepted gladly, though she didn't have the first idea what he was talking about. Her employer thought she was pretty and knew that the clients would enjoy flirting with her. Adam had decided, after three years of hard graft, that he would avoid work for a while. But work had not entirely avoided him. Professor James had recommended him to a friend, the Head of News and Current Affairs at the BBC, and before he could marshal the case for indolence, Adam had found himself at the BBC in White City, failing to decline a job as a researcher.

On the Sunday night before they both started their new lives in the morning, Elizabeth opened a celebratory bottle of Sauvignon Blanc. They went out for dinner and stared at each other and at Tower Bridge in the background. Adam felt like they had everything that anyone could ever want. They had a luxurious flat in Whitechapel, they would have more money than they needed, their feet firmly on the professional rung and they went to sleep every night with the backs of their heads touching on pillows bearing the legend of their initials. But Adam still found it hard to drink from the horn of plenty, for ancestral moral reasons. The example of his paternal grandparents ran deep inside him even though they had both died before he was old enough to experience events he would ever remember.

Barney

Half an hour after arriving at his new office in White City Adam had to go to the nurse with a throat full of phlegm. He had filled up as soon as he had picked up the telephone to ask a diary secretary if her junior Minister might be available to discuss the government's failing attempts to prevent publication of the *Spycatcher* book. Adam claimed he had been incubating a cold all week but the nurse kindly assured him that it was a common nervous reaction.

Adam sneaked back to his chair, frightened of the responsibility. He looked around the busy news room and, in an imitation of purposeful activity, walked three times between his desk and the coffee machine. He brought three cups of the wrong coffee back to his desk as he couldn't get the machine to work properly. Having drunk the three helpings of brown water Adam went to the toilet and back, three times. On his third return journey a young man on the international desk looked up and smiled. He spoke in an accent that was more Manchester than Johnny Marr deliberately putting on a Manchester accent.

'Found the loo then?'

'Yeah, it's over there.'

'That's all you're meant to do on your first day, isn't it? Find the loo and the coffee machine?'

'I've done both of those. Might as well go home now.'

'You've forgotten the photocopier.'

'You're right. I've still got things to learn.'

'It's always frantic in here. It seems weird at first but you'll get used to it. I'm Stephen by the way.'

'Hiya, I'm Adam. Nice to meet you. Where are you from?'

'Manchester.'

'Thought so. So am I.'

'You don't sound like it. Where in Manchester are you from?'

'Well, I'm from Bury, actually. Where are you from?'

'I'm from South Manchester. Near Wilmslow. You went to Trinity, didn't you?'

'Yeah. Did you go there?'

'Well I did actually, but in Oxford. It's very Oxbridge in here. It's a bit cliquey really but everyone's really nice. And they're all really bright. You'll fit in fine.'

'Do you think?'

'Do you need any help with anything? You do look a bit lost.'

Stephen introduced Adam to the cuttings file which, he said, would serve for most research purposes.

Adam pieced together the required material but was stymied by his computer which refused to work. Adam had never tried to turn a computer on and it was more complicated than it looked. A small card on his desk promised a helpline and, while he was waiting to be baled out of his technological *impasse*, Adam rang home.

'Mum.'

'Adam, is that you?'

'Yes.'

'Why are you whispering?'

'Everyone can hear. I'm at work. I'm not sure if I'm allowed to make personal calls.'

Stephen looked over at Adam and raised his thumbs.

'What are you up to?'

'I'm doing something on *Spycatcher*. It'll be on tonight.'

'Are you going to be on?'

'No, Mum, don't be daft; I'm only the researcher.'

'Oh, I see.'

June's tone was clear. She thought that Adam was more or less running the country, catching spies and all that.

'Do you want to talk to your dad?'

'Is he not at work?'

'No, he's not been so good. He's had the sweats. I made him stay off today.'

'Go on, then.'

'Bob, our Adam's on.'

'Did you ring him?'

'No, he rang us. Didn't you hear the phone? Honestly. Come on; he's at work.'

'Hiya, Adam.'

'All right, Dad?'

'I'm all right. Your mum's just fussing around me. How's your first day?'

'It's getting better. I'm doing a story for tonight about *Spycatcher*.'

'Will you be on?'

'No, I just do the research.'

'Your mum says you're going on holiday.'

'I'm going skiing with Elizabeth and some friends.'

'Val Doonican, your mum said.'

'It's Val d'Isère, Dad, as you well know.'

'I do not. I've never heard of it.'

'Oh, Dad, sorry. I've got to go. There's someone here to fix my computer.'

The mention of the word 'computer' sounded like *Tomorrow's World* to Bob.

The computer engineer turned the machine on and, as soon as he asked for a password, Adam diagnosed the problem and sent him away. Stephen told him that his password was 'Reith' but, after ten minutes of randomly pressing buttons, Adam had to recall the engineer. He didn't know how to turn this damned thing on, password or no password. The engineer pressed the relevant buttons at a speed which he thought was instructively slow but which Adam found incomprehensibly fast. When the engineer had gone Adam tried it for himself but, as soon as a screen came up that Adam was not expecting, he had to turn the machine off and start again.

Eventually he plucked up the courage to ask Stephen to show

him how to create a document and, a traumatic three hours after arriving, Adam began work in earnest. He carried on through lunch but by mid-afternoon it had become clear that the story was not going to run that night. At five-thirty Peter Bennett, the producer of the item, came over to speak to Adam. Peter's snappy temper sent a fearsome reputation before him but, as soon as he sat down, Adam was captivated by his hair. It was slicked and neat all over except for the front where he wore long strands, propelled by a labile cat flick across the full radius of his comically over-large face. The front strands were like two large, muscular, hairy arms enveloping his head, as though he were being cuddled by a gay clone. They were joined like non-identical Siamese twins to a neat, management haircut. Peter had two haircuts but only one head. He was a hydra-haired monster. Adam imagined that an alternative Peter lived inside his head. This *alter ego* sent out two strands of hair into the world to declare the idealist he might have remained. They belonged to the man he might have been in the rose garden, the Pete who had to concede as short-fuse Peter made his way through the organisation for the sake of his children. As they talked, Adam decided to keep his hair short forever.

'We're not going on air with the story but that's just the way it goes. It's died on us for today.'

'OK.'

'Are you going to MOMI?'

'Errr, yeah. I might do.'

Stephen came over as soon as Peter Bennett had gone. A visit from Peter always required a *post mortem*.

'What was Bennett saying to you?'

'Nothing much. He asked if I was going to moany.'

Stephen laughed in camp Mancunian.

'It's MOMI. The Museum of the Moving Image. We've got a load of tickets for the preview night.'

'Oh, right.'

Stephen pointed to a blinking red light on Adam's telephone.

'You've got a message.'

Adam had presumed his phone was broken. Stephen tapped

234

in the right numbers and held the receiver to Adam's ear. The last voice he expected came out of hiding down the line.

'Adam, hiya. It's Kevin.'

There was a long pause, as though Kevin had expected Adam to speak.

'I've just come out and I saw your dad. He gave me your number. Errr, I was just wanting to say hello really. And I was wondering whether you were coming up. Or if I could come down and stay. I could do with getting out of this shithole for a bit. Can you give us a ring? See you.'

Adam looked so disturbed as he replaced the receiver that Stephen squeezed the bangle on his wrist.

'Not bad news?'

'No, just a friend. It's just strange to hear his voice.'

Adam called Kevin straight away. Sammy picked up the telephone, sounding drunk. He shouted for Kevin without distancing the receiver from his bark and, at the other end, Adam rubbed his ear. Kevin answered, with a dying fall.

'All right.'

'How are you, stranger? It must be good to be a free man.'

'It's all right.'

'Do you want to come down, then?'

'Yeah, if you don't mind.'

'No, it's no problem. Come at the weekend.'

'Right. Ta.'

Adam had promised before he considered asking Elizabeth. Adam and Kevin continued in the same vein for five tricky minutes, at the end of which Kevin put the telephone down abruptly, before the conversation had concluded naturally. Adam collected his belongings and his thoughts and went to spot famous people on the South Bank.

He arrived back in Whitechapel to find Elizabeth having a drink with Piers, who was now a trainee barrister. Piers brought out the class Brangy warrior in Adam. Flicking through the dictionary, Adam had found a phrase to describe him. Piers was, he told Elizabeth, a poodle fakir, one that is overly given to tea parties and the society of ladies. Piers had played Romeo to

Elizabeth's Juliet at school. He was upper-class and good-looking so Adam cut him down by calling him Rah Rah Rasputin. But apart from sheer physical envy, Piers also annoyed Adam inexplicably, like someone walking at exactly the same pace on the pavement. Elizabeth pre-empted Adam by explaining what they had been talking about.

'We've decided to have a dinner party on Saturday. Piers'll cook if we host.'

'I've told Kevin he can come down on Saturday.'

'You've what?'

'That's all right. There's room for one more,' said Piers.

'You don't know Kevin,' replied Elizabeth.

'I do. I met him in your college that time. He's the footballer. Nice bloke.'

'Does it have to be this weekend, Adam?'

'Yes. He's just come out and he feels a bit lost.'

'Is he gay?' asked Piers, at the wrong end of the stick.

'Of prison,' clarified Adam.

'I'm not being horrible, Adam, but Kevin doesn't exactly fit in, does he? We were going to invite Barney.'

'It'll be OK. Anyway, I've invited him. I can't go back on it.'

Adam met Kevin off the three-thirty arrival from Manchester Piccadilly. He had the day planned. They would go up to Camden Market to look for second-hand records and then into Covent Garden for clothes. Kevin tore up the programme.

'Let's get a drink. I'm parched.'

Adam reluctantly took Kevin into a dingy Somers Town drinking house where Kevin settled in for the half-time scores on Grandstand and the promise of the teleprinter to come. After two hours of fractured chatting about football Adam revealed that Barney would be at the evening's dinner party. Kevin nodded and grunted that it was all a long time ago now. It took five pints before Adam could prise Kevin out of the pub. By this time, three in excess of his afternoon threshold, Adam was falling asleep.

An afternoon's preparation filled their nostrils as Adam and Kevin stepped into the flat. From the living room Adam heard the chatter of their guests: Arabella, Barney and Lucy. Adam rediscovered a strong accent.

'They're right posh bastards, this lot, I'm telling you.'

'Do you include me in that?' asked Elizabeth who had just come out of the toilet and was standing behind them.

This was a running sore. Adam deplored how often and how readily Elizabeth's friends claimed to love each other. Those three words had to be chiselled out of the Matthews family but Lucy and Arabella dropped them into every other sentence. He especially disapproved of Arabella, who had given up photography to work in her family's private client stockbroking firm. In private he referred to her as Hong Kong Phoney Number One Supergirl.

Adam greeted Elizabeth too precisely and kissed her too sloppily. Sensing he was in trouble, he took Kevin through into the living room and, to his friend's amazement, kissed the girls to say hello. Kevin hung back in the doorway. He had nothing to contribute to the conversation about why an abundance of choices can be a burden. He noted that Barney was turning over the pages of a lifestyle magazine in the far corner of the room. Barney's father had been a steelworker under Tinsley suspension bridge but Barney had left Sheffield behind to walk in a more lucrative land. Barney now earned a lot of money as a management consultant. It was a daily test of his character and he could not pass over a cliché in a magazine without wanting it.

Elizabeth asked that everyone take their seats and Lucy and Arabella jumped up, like a pair of grinning bookends at the heads of the table. Piers came in with a large dish of lamb korma which was met with an effusive round of 'that looks wonderfuls'. Almost unnoticed, Kevin slipped by Barney's side and the chitter-chatter was exploded by a sudden scream. Kevin stepped hard on Barney's foot and grabbed him by the throat.

'I am going to kick your fucking teeth down your neck. You ruined my fucking life, you cunt.'

237

Kevin jabbed Barney between the eyes. The party froze.

'I've been thinking all afternoon of what I was going to do to you when I got hold of you.'

'I didn't mean . . .'

'Shut it.'

'It was an . . .'

'Shut your face.'

Kevin increased the force. He pushed Barney up against the wall, knocking down a framed sepia picture of Elizabeth surrounded by girlfriends from a college drinking society.

'Do you know what I'm going to do?'

Nobody spoke.

'I might smash your knee to fuck like you did to mine.'

'Kevin . . .'

'Shut it, Adam. I've been waiting for this.'

'But that wouldn't ruin your career, would it? So I'll have to think of something else. What do you do for a living?'

Barney was too frightened to say anything and the others were too scared to intervene. Kevin repeated the question, inserting a swear word. Barney stammered a reply.

'I'm a management consultant.'

Kevin grabbed Barney's left hand.

'So you work with your hands then? Right then, you cunt.'

Kevin dug his nails into Barney's palm and the cry raised the level of Piers's courage. Wrestling Kevin from the back, he pulled him off which allowed Barney to escape from the wall. Before Kevin had fought Piers off Barney had fled out of the front door. Suddenly, the dinner party regained its morally outraged courage, led by Elizabeth.

'What the hell do you think you're doing? Get out of here. Now.'

'What?'

'I'm telling you to leave.'

Kevin looked at Adam.

'I wouldn't want to stay with all you tossers anyway.'

Kevin picked up his holdall, took his coat and went for the train back to Manchester.

As soon as the door had slammed behind Kevin, Elizabeth turned to Adam.

'Well, I hope you're satisfied now.'

'Barney's had it coming to him for ages. The highest ratio of salary to brains in London, that twat.'

'Adam, you cannot come to someone's house and do that. Have you lost all perspective on this? For God's sake stop apologising for Kevin.'

'Someone has to give him a chance. He's had a rough time. It's all right for you lot. You were born with silver spoons up your arse. You don't know what it's like to go without.'

'Oh and you do, I suppose.'

'I do more than you do. I can't stand it when you lot talk about Kevin like he's had every fucking chance that you've had in your lives. It's bollocks. You know where me and Kevin grew up. It's total bollocks that it's all his own fault.'

'Oh, poor little deprived Adam. Poor little wrong side of the tracks Adam.'

'It was harder for me than you. That's obviously true.'

'Maybe we should all go, Lizzie,' said Piers.

'Why don't you stay and listen to the violins. Adam clearly thinks his achievements are greater than ours.'

'You're fucking right I do. Because they are. There's no doubt about it. You've had it on a plate since you were in prep school. You haven't got any fucking idea.'

'Yes, that's right, Adam. I've had it really easy, haven't I? I've never come across a single problem in my life. I thought you of all people would have known that.'

'I'm going after him.'

'Don't you dare.'

'There's no knowing what he'll do in this sort of mood.'

'If you go after Kevin, Adam, you can forget about getting married.'

'Oh, be quiet.'

'I mean it, Adam.'

Adam ripped his coat down and shook the flat with the force of the door.

Adam got the tube to Euston where he found Kevin in the burger bar. He bought two coffees and tried to persuade Kevin to stay. Kevin refused.

'I don't know what I'm doing here in the first place.'

'You came to see me, I thought.'

'Yeah.'

'What are you going to do, Kev, when you get back?'

'I don't know. Nothing, probably.'

'Is there anything I can do?'

'I don't think so. Thanks, though.'

For a moment Adam and Kevin touched again. Then Adam let Kevin go and, as the train pulled out of the station, he waved goodbye. Adam was trapped in two minds, in two worlds. He went back to the burger bar and sat there on his own until they started sweeping around his feet. Then he rubbed his eyes and went home, where Elizabeth was already asleep. Adam pulled back the cover, stroked her soft skin and climbed into bed.

Lord of the Flies

Adam hung firmly on to Peter Bennett as the latter cut his way through the BBC. After six months in the newsroom, Adam had moved with Peter to make a documentary on the urban estates of Manchester. Adam had a bitter argument with Elizabeth about whether or not to hitch himself to Peter, whom Elizabeth thought to be a career opportunist longer on ambition than on talent. Adam upset her by remarking that she rarely spent long enough out of the bathroom to notice what he was up to. He decided, against Elizabeth's counsel, to move from making the news to researching *Breadline Britain*.

Adam made two visits to the Odsall estate in Salford. He felt like a visiting potentate as he dropped in for a cup of tea with the angry young recidivists in the community centre. Everywhere he went, Adam was introduced as 'the young man from the telly' and treated with exaggerated civility and respect. Everyone he met told Adam their story and every tale was just what he knew it would be: a losing struggle against circumstance. Each person had a winning way with words and leavened their tragic narrative, deliberately spiced it, with humour that mocked the fates and their whimsical victims. Adam recognised every one of them as Brangy warriors. He also knew that Peter would not want any of this. The people of Salford were far too wry and far, far too cheerful. Peter was looking for horror stories. His thesis demanded them. Peter had read about an estate in Rochdale where young boys had cut the head off a rabbit and scared pensioners by carrying it round on the end of a stick. Adam had been sent up North to find 'some *Lord of the Flies* stuff'.

He came back with a notebook full of worthy community action, boringly embittered teenagers and amusing stock characters who lived just on the black side of the market. At the first research meeting after he had returned from his fact-finding mission Adam was under pressure to describe a scene of urban desperation. He exaggerated the depravity of bored adolescents standing on street corners and affected affront at the illegal trading he had encountered. But, as he filled out the characters of the Odsall estate with contrivances worthy of melodrama, Adam knew that Peter had yet heard nothing that he would describe as 'filmic'. Adam had a litany of plausible individuals but, so far, no story to tell, nothing that dramatically revealed their characters.

'There's nothing really to get hold of.'

'There is. Some of these people will be great on camera. They're larger than life.'

'You'll be saying they're the salt of the earth next.'

'No, they are. You'll have to meet them.'

'Have you got anything else?'

Adam could feel the phlegm forming in his mouth. He panicked and a vivid story appeared in his head.

'There's this lad I met in North Manchester, not on the Odsall, on this pretty grim estate called the Harwood. It's near to where I was brought up. He's just come out of prison for drug-dealing.'

'And? . . .'

'And apparently . . .' said Adam, warming to the encouragement, '. . . he was a brilliant footballer when he was younger. He was the youngest-ever captain of a professional team and he was tipped to play for England but then he got a bad injury and he ended up back on the estate.'

'And what happened to him? Did it drag him down? Did he find work?'

'Sort of. He drifted in and out of crap jobs.'

'Is he married?'

'Yeah, he got married at eighteen.'

'Kids?'

242

'Two. Then he got made redundant and started getting into petty crime. His dad's a well-known criminal locally, apparently.'

'This is the one.'

'And then that led to getting into drugs.'

'Is he a user?'

'I think so. He started off using and he says that broke his marriage up. Then he got into dealing to try to win her back. Got caught and ended up in prison. Now he's out again but he's got a record so he's no chance of getting a job, even if there were any.'

'Will he talk to us?'

'He seemed quite keen.'

'And does he still play football? For a local team?'

'No, he can't. His knee got shattered. He hasn't kicked a ball for three years.'

'That's the one. That's the one.'

Three weeks later, Adam had still not spoken to Kevin but clearance had been obtained from Bury Metropolitan Borough Council to film on the streets of the Harwood estate. Adam persuaded Elizabeth to take a couple of days off work so that she could drive him north. Elizabeth had not been to Bury for a while. June often wondered aloud on the telephone, with a timbre of hurt that suggested she knew the answer, why Elizabeth had stopped coming with him. Adam could not admit, either to himself or to his mother, that his home town was full of people who were aliens to Elizabeth. Bury was full of Kevin McDermotts and Tez and Ray and Lewis and Jermaine Satchels.

Adam loved being driven north by Elizabeth. Having a girlfriend who had a car made him feel plutocratic and the open roads reminded him of their first trip to Bury, of the looks of admiration in the Greenhill Club and the madman who had sung 'The Windmills of my Mind' much, much too high. Then it had been the drive of their young lives. Adam had observed on the way that Elizabeth might have been to New York and Los Angeles and Prague and Budapest but she had never been to Bury. She had never even been to Manchester. She had concentrated on the road as he had risked their lives by planting soft kisses on her neck. Then, when Elizabeth had turned left at Leeds and headed west across the Pennines she had suddenly understood why Adam thought Cambridge was dull.

'You didn't tell me that it was beautiful,' she had said as they passed the farm in the central reservation of the M62.

Adam had looked at the bleak hills which disdained changes of season.

'I didn't know it was.'

On the way they stopped, as they always did, at the Watford Gap service station on the M1. Adam recalled, as he did every time, their first time here when his chicken and chips with barbecue sauce and her chips with thousand-island dressing were as fine a meal as either had ever tasted. They had followed up with a cappuccino. With chocolate on top, in a paper cup. A grubby service station on the M1. Chicken and chips, barbecue sauce, thousand-island dressing and two paper cups of cappuccino. Some kind of heaven. But this time they sat in a heavy silence broken only by the tell-tale clink of cutlery on crockery.

Elizabeth went shopping in Manchester while Adam went to work, interviewing the local Conservative MP and the Labour ward councillor, neither of whom was a regular on the estate. The visit of a film crew had much the same effect on the Harwood estate as a visit by the police. Curtains twitched and the bolder women, always the women who had less reason to distrust the authorities, came outside to investigate. But the artificial bustle that the presence of the film crew created was exactly the wrong backdrop for the story that Peter Bennett was trying to tell. He needed empty streets so the crew broke off to the local pub, the Earl of Derby, for lunch and came back when everyone had gone indoors. Adam did not join the team for lunch. He had still not spoken to Kevin, though Peter had been led to believe that the interview was set for that afternoon. Adam could not explain to himself, let alone to Peter, why he had been prevaricating so badly. In the back of his mind he hoped and trusted that his huckleberry friend would help him out.

Kevin sighed and picked himself lazily out of his armchair at the alarming ring of the door bell.

'Bloody Jesus, what are you doing here?'

'I need a favour. You've got to help me out. I've got myself into a right mess.'

'Why? What have you done?'

'Can we interview you for a programme we're doing?'

'You what?'

'I told my boss that you'd be on this programme we're doing. I couldn't find any interesting stories so when he asked me I just told him about you and he liked it so much that he asked if you'd do it and I just said yes. So will you?'

'Whoa, hang on. What is it?'

'Oh, it'll be all right. It's about what it's like to live round here.'

'So what do I have to do?'

'They want you to talk about yourself. Then they'll probably film you doing a few things around the estate. It shouldn't take too much.'

'I don't know. It seems a bit strange.'

'Go on, it'll be fine, I promise. Come on, blood brother.'

'I don't know.'

'I dare you. You've got to now.'

'I don't know what to say. I'm not brilliant at that sort of thing. I might make a right dick of myself.'

'You won't. We don't use stuff when you get it wrong. You can just say it again and anyway we can cut it up to make it sound good. Go on, please. I really need you to do this for me.'

'What do I get out of it?'

'You get to be on telly. I'll make you a star.'

'I meant from you.'

'I'll do whatever. Anything. I'll even walk down through the tunnels late at night.'

'You what?'

'Never mind. I'll do what you want. Just say you'll do it.'

'All right, then. It's a bit weird though.'

Adam sighed. He had half of what he needed.

'There's just one more thing.'

'What else?'

'You've got to pretend that you don't know me very well.'

'You what?'

'It's just . . . Well, it's a sort of rule that we're not supposed to know the people we have in the programme.'

'Why?'

'It just is. I don't know. So will you just pretend? When I'm there don't really talk to me.'

'That'll be easy. I never talk to you anyway. I'm not sure about this, you know.'

Adam looked beseechingly at Kevin who blew air into his puffed cheeks and exhaled.

'Thanks, mate. You've got me out of jail there.'

Later that afternoon Kevin walked, obviously going nowhere, back and forth in the park, followed by a camera man. Off set, a man with funny hair issued directions.

'Try to look a bit more natural. Just walk like you normally do.'

Kevin stepped onto the rickety bridge in the middle of the duck pond.

'Can you feed the ducks?'

'What with?'

'Have we got any bread?'

Not surprisingly none of the crew was carrying a loaf. Adam ran to the Co-op and bought a white sliced clunky metaphor. Peter crumbled a piece and asked Kevin to drop it into the water for the ducks. Kevin did as he was told for a boring hour. He found documentaries even duller to make than they were to watch.

He went on to the Greenhill Club for an interview. Peter positioned Kevin in front of the picture of the Queen that was pinned to the royal-blue curtains. As the lights went out and Peter began his prepared questions, Adam softly opened the iron door and sat in a plastic chair by the deserted bar. Kevin, by second nature, raised an arm to wave acknowledgement but remembered himself as Adam turned away abruptly.

246

Kevin answered all Peter's questions perfunctorily, slightly bemused that Peter should want everything to sound so dreadful and worried about divulging the detail of his benefit claims. At the end of the session Adam upset Kevin by refusing to talk to him properly. Whatever Adam might say, Kevin assumed that his barney in Whitechapel was the root cause of the silence. Adam packed up the equipment in the background and shuttled between the club, which looked so very odd to him empty in the dust of daylight, and Elizabeth's car which was ready to transport him back through the mean streets of Bury to the M62 and on to Elizabeth's house in Hertfordshire where they were going to spend the weekend.

When Peter was safely outside, Adam poked his head back around the door. Kevin was perched in front of the stage, on a low stool. Suddenly attacked by his layers of dishonesty, Adam did not linger. Instead, he grinned falsely and let out the coughing splutter of someone who is making himself laugh.

'Cheers, mate. I owe you one. I'll see you soon.'

The iron door clicked loudly behind Adam as he climbed into the car to take him back down roads sixty-two, six and one. Kevin did not move from the stool in the club for two minutes, then slothfully he made his way through the Harwood estate back home. Elizabeth and Adam moved smoothly towards the M62. Adam opened his mouth only to give basic road directions. Once they were on the motorway he grunted periodically as Elizabeth talked sceptically about the conceit behind *Breadline Britain*.

Research Adam Matthews

Bob and June Matthews sashayed into Broadcasting House as if they were turning up for the Oscars. Adam had invited them down to London for the preview of *Breadline Britain*. The small room was full of the half-life of celebrity and June's eyes flicked nervously from side to side so that no breakfast presenter should slip by unnoticed.

'Bob, is that whatsername?'

'Who?'

'She reads the news in the evening. That dark, good-looking woman. She's over there. Don't look like that; you'll show me up.'

'Clocked her. Yeah, that's her.'

The lights went down and *Breadline Britain* began. From the minor keys of the opening titles through to the silently rolling credits, the whole programme screamed tragedy. The metropolitan *cognoscenti* nodded at the picture of deprivation. Bob and June pointed out locations they recognised and June was admonished by someone familiar from the BBC for her exclamation when Kevin's rounded red features filled the screen. Although his face was four-feet tall on the big screen Kevin seemed somehow diminished by his sudden fame. He gave a thirty-second autobiography and the spectators nodded the more vigorously the greater the clarity of the tragedy.

'I used to play football for Bury but then I got injured. And there weren't any jobs round here.'

'Did you have a family, Kevin?'

'I've got a wife and two kids who needed looking after.'

'So what did you do?'

'I couldn't find work and then a mate of mine was getting into drugs and I got a bit desperate, like, because we didn't have any money coming in so I started doing a bit of dealing, and then I got caught.'

Kevin's face dissolved into an edited sequence of the old mill by the River Irwell and patches of barren urban land. Straining for sonority, Peter Bennett's voice took up the tale.

'Kevin's story is, in many ways, typical of these estates, in which a cycle of deprivation crushes even the most resourceful spirit. From misfortune to unemployment in the long term to a life on benefit, to petty crime or benefit fraud to more serious wrongdoing to imprisonment. As this cycle runs its course we are creating a generation of violent young men, embittered and angry, who feel they have no stake in a wider community.'

The accompanying montage cut from irrelevant footage of the Moss Side riots of 1981 to a routine Saturday night police chase through Rusholme. Slowly, the booming, incidental soundtrack faded out and the cops and robbers gave way to Kevin walking in the park, alone, throwing his piece of bread at the ducks. He gazed into the middle distance as the bread settled on the dirty water in the pond and the credits passed down his body. The words 'Research Adam Matthews' fell onto Kevin's head and dropped off the screen and into the water beneath Kevin's feet. The lights came up and the room was filled with spontaneous hearty applause.

Elizabeth slid her hands round Adam's neck and, to more applause, kissed him more lasciviously than he thought was decent in full view of his parents. Adam broke off the embrace to acknowledge his mum who was jumping up and down on the spot, trying to talk.

'What did you think?'

'Well done, love.'

'What did you think, Dad?'

'Yeah, it were good. Should we go and have a drink?'

'There's loads left here.'

'They've only got wine. I want a pint. I've been dying for a proper drink since we got here.'

Adam and Bob had been on the tip of an argument all day. As they had walked through St James's Park, their disagreement about the worth of the monarchy had gone, just about, unsaid. Slouching past Downing Street, a flowering row about Mrs Thatcher's responsibility for Kevin's plight had been discreetly nipped by June. Three coffees in a café by the Cenotaph had given Bob an opportunity to complain about the prices but a dispute over the genuine legacy of the Second World War had not been far from the surface.

Adam said goodbye to the rest of the team, to the faces that were now familiar to him personally. Bob led the way, at a pace that Adam found aggravatingly slow, down Regent Street. As Bob growled at every pedestrian who refused to clear his path Adam put his hands together to form a mouth which he then snapped shut. Elizabeth laughed guiltily at Adam's mime. He had suggested to her earlier that day that Crocodile Bury might be his second film for the BBC.

'Are we near Trafalgar Square here, Adam?' asked June, obliviously.

'Sort of. It's about twenty minutes walk. At your pace, anyway.'

'I'd like to see it before we go.'

Adam looked plaintively at Elizabeth who smiled indulgently.

'Come on, June, we'll go down there while the boys go for a drink.'

Adam and Bob went into a dirty pub north of Oxford Circus where, miraculously for a Friday night and to Adam's great relief, they found a tiny table and four stools. Bob sprinted to the bar where he had trouble making himself understood, so pure was his accent and so resolute was he in speaking at his own speed. Bob lived at the pace of his own choosing, slow or fast. He put two pints of lager on the table.

'It's daylight robbery, is this place. All but a fiver for two pints.'

'That's just how much it is. You don't notice after a bit.'

'It's bloody ridiculous.'

'Well there's nothing you can do about it, so there's no point in going on about it.'

Bob took a large mouthful to avoid getting into another row.

'What did you think then, Dad?'

'I've said. I thought it were good.'

'You don't sound very enthusiastic.'

'Well I didn't agree with most of it, I must say.'

'What do you mean?'

'All that stuff about how it's no one's fault. That's just not right. People do have a choice. When your grandma was alive they lived through far rougher times and you didn't see them going out robbing.'

'It's different . . .'

'It's not different. You made it sound like it has nothing to do with Kevin. Like it's not his fault if he turns out to be a bad 'un.'

'It's not his fault. It's not as simple as that. Kevin had his chance taken away.'

'I know he did and no one's more sympathetic than me.'

'Doesn't sound like it.'

'It's not doing him any good pretending that none of it's his own fault. Kevin's best hope is facing up to his responsibilities and doing right by his family. Believe me, son, I've been there. And your posh friends have got it all wrong if they think that it's someone else's fault. It's not. You have to look after your own. It's down to you in the end.'

'We said that as well but you can't deny that not having a job makes it more likely.'

'Just excuses.'

'There is a difference between an excuse and a reason, Dad.'

'They're bloody excuses and I'm sick and tired of this nonsense. I've heard it all before from Kevin's dad. Sammy could have made your film for you. You get all that from him about how it's not his fault; it's the social or the government or someone. It's always someone's fault but it's never Sammy McDermott's. Never got anything to do with him, oh no. And that's where you want to look if you want to find out why these lads turn out to be bad 'uns. Look at their fathers. It's no wonder Kevin's in a spot of bother. You know what Sammy's like as well as I do.'

'But Kevin's not like his dad.'

'He's heading that way.'

'That's because he can't get a job because he's got a record. It's not just because of his dad.'

'I don't know how you can do a big film with all that singing and dancing and not even mention that some of these lads come from rotten families.'

'Because we decided that wasn't the most important thing.'

'Well you must have your head screwed on wrong then because that's at the bottom of it all. You bloody Labourites are hopeless.'

'I just don't understand how you can be a Tory if you come from where we do. Have you ever met any Tories? It's ridiculous.'

'Don't tell me I'm ridiculous. I wouldn't be a Labourite if there was no one else. I still remember the grave-diggers going on strike. You were only a nipper then. It didn't affect you but there was no power half the time.'

'That's ancient history now, Dad. You can't keep dining out on 1978 forever.'

'It wouldn't be any different if you had them unions in power again.'

Bob argued Adam into a corner and Adam hit his way out with an excess of vocabulary and footnotes. They were both singing the same single note when Elizabeth and June arrived back from their trip to check that Nelson was still on top of his column. Elizabeth deftly managed the conversation through three more rounds.

Back home in Whitechapel Bob and June carried on drinking but Elizabeth went to bed, admitting defeat. Five minutes later Adam came into the bedroom and launched himself headlong at Elizabeth's pillow.

'Emergency. Help, emergency.'

'Come here, accident.'

'I bet your mum and dad never had pillows with their initials on.'

'What do you mean?'

'Think about it, slowcoach.'

'Don't be so disgusting. That's my mum and dad you're talking about.'

'You hated them a minute ago.'

'I don't. They're just hard work for a whole day. There's only so many blokes in funny hats at Buckingham Palace that a man can look at.'

'It wasn't that bad, was it?'

'And if I hear one more time how expensive a pint of beer is I'll shoot myself.'

'Don't be cruel; they're really nice.'

'They love you. It's me they don't like.'

'Don't be horrid; they love you to bits.'

'They treat you like you're their daughter.'

'I feel like that sometimes.'

'What do you mean by that?'

'Nothing.'

Adam rubbed himself closer to Elizabeth. She moved away.

'I want to kiss you.'

'I'm tired. Let's just cuddle.'

As imperceptibly as a child's growth, Adam and Elizabeth had started to live like brother and sister. They had been too wrapped up in new opportunities to notice but their days had become neatly choreographed. Early every morning, Adam took the mince out of the freezer and woke Elizabeth with a cup of herbal tea. She used the bathroom while he stayed in bed listening to the *Today* programme. Elizabeth left first, followed by Adam an hour later. They went to work and returned in the early evening. Whoever arrived home first fried the mince and onions. Mince and onions featured every day: they were the great constant in the life of Adam and Elizabeth. They enjoyed cooking, especially together, but they had a sadly limited culinary repertoire. Spaghetti Bolognese, chilli con carne and shepherd's pie. Mince and onions, Adam and Elizabeth on the plateau after the blaze of desire.

But in all their hours alone a cleavage was emerging. Elizabeth was spending longer in the bathroom, which annoyed Adam. He wanted to see her routinely naked, the nudity of both sex and love rather than just sex alone. Elizabeth tried to explain that she liked to be alone and that the need required no further explanation.

The absence of ardour frightened Adam. Adam had noticed Elizabeth brushing him aside more and more often. She had complained more than once that his touches were too soft, like an insect crawling over her skin. Adam had arrived back at where he came in. He was as frightened to touch Elizabeth as he had been when they had first met. But this was a dull, aching fear. His initial fear had been enchanting, magically encircled with the prospect of success. Now he wanted only to avoid irritating her. Adam once more felt inadequate but in a more permanent, insurmountable sense. He tried again but Elizabeth coiled up.

'I just can't, darling. It doesn't feel right.'

Adam saw a tear in the deep green pools of Elizabeth's eyes. She got up and wrapped the quilt around her, leaving Adam to cry out that he was cold. She left the bedroom and went to run a bath. An hour later, Bob went to use the toilet and was amazed by the oddity of Adam's girlfriend having a bath in the middle of the night.

A Journey Without End

A week later *Breadline Britain* was aired for the nation. Adam watched it for the umpteenth time, nervous because the morning's newspapers would begin the process of judging whether this was an important TV landmark like *Cathy Come Home* and *The World at War* or whether it was just another documentary. Peter Bennett certainly envisaged himself in the very highest company and he encouraged his protégé to think equally big. Adam and Elizabeth ate their mince and onions in front of the television, cuddled each other to sleep and woke up to start the whole process over again.

On his way to work, Adam received a critical response after the fashion of his father. After two paragraphs, Adam scanned the rest of the invective from the *Guardian*. The words 'patronising' and 'simplistic' looked like they were printed in capital letters a foot high. Adam arrived in White City to find Peter Bennett running his hand through his cat flick and twisting his hair around his index fingers, quite unable to believe what he had read. The *Guardian's* critic had been kind. *The Times* and the *Independent* had been a lot angrier and the man at the *Telegraph* was apoplectic. The executive producer came down to discuss their next move with Peter and Adam. The Birmingham and London episodes were already in the can and ready to be screened with a month's interval between. Adam listened to the conversation and tried not to turn into his father. At every repetition of the hand-wringing questions Adam wanted to supply Bob's answers but it was easier to take the junior's prerogative and say nothing.

After the most thoroughly dispiriting day of his short working life Adam sneaked out an hour early. He went to meet Elizabeth in the City but was irritated by Piers ordering a large bucket full of champagne, standing outside on the pavement on a cold Tuesday evening. At nine o'clock he excused himself and went home on his own.

He had been home for half an hour when there was a knock on the door. Adam and Elizabeth never had visitors they were not expecting. Adam was surprised to realise that he was frightened to open the door and utterly astonished to see the star of *Breadline Britain* on his doorstep.

'Jesus Christ, what the fuck are you doing here?'

'I've come to see you, haven't I?'

'I wasn't expecting you.'

'I know you weren't. I'm not dumb, you know.'

'No, I know. Come on; come in.'

Kevin sat down in the living room and declined a drink. He said nothing and, though it seemed ungracious to ask what he was doing there, Adam could not help but wonder.

'So how come . . . ?'

'I saw your programme last night.'

An overwhelming feeling of anxiety overcame Adam.

'What did you think?'

'I thought you were meant to be my mate.'

'I am.'

'You made me look a right fucking no-hoper. Is that what you think?'

'I didn't do the editing. Of course I don't think that.'

'You set it all up. I wouldn't have done it if you hadn't set it up. I thought it'd just be about there not being any jobs in Bury. That's what you said. But they made it seem like I was on the rob all the time and frauding the social and kicking people's heads in all the time. It's not like that. It's a lot more fucking boring than that. I wish there was a riot going on sometimes.'

'You didn't come over that bad . . .'

'You made me look a right twat and you know it.'

'I don't . . .'

'You made me look really stupid, Adam.'

'I didn't. I wouldn't do that.'

'Is that what you think?'

'No, it's not . . .'

'Come on; say it. You think I'm stupid, don't you?'

'No . . .'

'You've always thought that. Ever since I copied off you at Tommy's.'

'I don't think that.'

'Why not? It's true, isn't it? I had to leg it from Bury Grammar, didn't I?'

'The whole point was to show that you're nor stupid and that it's not really your fault that you get into trouble.'

'You've made a right stupid get out of me.'

'Oh Kevin, that wasn't the intention. You've got it all confused.'

'I don't give a shit. You've fucked it all up for me.'

'I haven't. You can't blame me. It's not my fault you're in a mess.'

'Who's fault is it then?'

'It's no one's in particular.'

'We can't all go off to university and get posh jobs you know.'

'I know. I don't think that.'

'I don't know why you bother with me any more. What's the fucking point?'

'You know why.'

'Do I?'

Adam was lost for argument.

'You don't have a clue what you've done, do you?'

'No.'

'First thing this morning Irene came round. She said she'd seen me on the telly and she was disgusted that I was robbing so much off the social. And I'm not. But you made it look like I was.'

'Kev, I'm sorry. I never meant in a million years . . .'

'It doesn't matter what you meant. It's what you've done.'

'I'm sorry; I really am.'

'It's too late for that. Damage is done. That's what I came down to tell you.'

'What?'

'That you've done it. That you shouldn't fucking expect me to bother with you after this. I wanted to tell you face to face.'

'Kevin, you don't mean that.'

'How do you know what I mean? Are you a fucking mind reader these days? Is that what you learn at university? How to read the fucking minds of people who used to be your mates?'

'Don't say that.'

'Why not? It's true.'

'It's not true.'

''Course it is.'

'It doesn't have to be.'

'Weren't you listening? I'm telling you it's true. We used to be mates and now we're not. I thought I was meant to be the stupid one.'

'Oh Kevin, don't be so obtuse.'

'Don't use your fancy big words on me.'

'I wasn't.'

'I'm not stupid, you know.'

'I know. What's the matter with you?'

'It's not the matter with me. It's the matter with you.'

'Kev, don't be like this. I've said I'm sorry.'

'You don't get it, do you? There's no point any more. Just forget it, will you?'

'I don't want to forget it.'

'Well you've no choice because I do.'

Kevin got up to leave.

'Where are you going?'

'Home.'

'You can't. It's too late.'

'Don't worry about me. I'll be all right.'

'Will you?'

'Yeah, I'll be fine.'

'Kev, please . . .'

'Forget it. I've said what I came to say and that's the end of it.'

Adam took hold of Kevin by the shoulders but he did not have the force to restrain him. He never had. Adam gripped Kevin who stared back at him. He did not move.

'Adam, get out of my way. I want to go.'

Adam moved aside.

'I'm sorry, mate.'

'Yeah.'

Adam went out in the rain to walk down Whitechapel Road. He had passed the Aldgate roundabout and was approaching Tower Bridge before he realised he didn't know where he was going. He carried on, with an empty head, over the bridge. He stopped and stared into the Thames, trying to think *something* at least. Suddenly everything seemed up for question. The more he thought about Kevin the more he worried about Elizabeth. He knew he should go home. Elizabeth would be home by now and he had promised to cook. It was going to be spaghetti Bolognese. But he did not want to talk about Kevin to Elizabeth. He was months away from understanding whether that was because he did not want to talk about Kevin or whether he did not want to talk about Kevin *to Elizabeth*. He carried on walking because it is the same thing as not making a decision. Adam could not work out what he was trying to make a decision *about* but he had a strong sense of reaching a pivotal moment.

Moving east, parallel with the river, for no good reason that he could imagine, Adam began to think about work. He liked work; he did not like work. He liked Stephen. He could probably call Stephen a friend. Although they fought about it, he had come to agree with Elizabeth about Peter. Kevin had confirmed this view but he hadn't planted it. Adam felt detached from work. He felt that there was nothing of him in it. He had convinced himself that the social policy series would unearth, under all the layers of confusion, the unutterable self that he thought he had brought with him from Bury. But if he had discovered anything, it didn't seem very likeable. Certainly Kevin did not like it and it didn't seem that Elizabeth liked it very much either. The thought-process of work had led back

261

straight away to Kevin and to Elizabeth and, for the life of him, Adam could not work out who or what he was really trying to think about.

He turned left and went up a dark alley to the riverside just east of Butler's Wharf. He sat down on a damp bench and sorted through the mess in his brain. As though he had no control over the matter Adam flitted between unconnected images from his distant and recent past. There was no narrative that they could be fitted into, not even a dominant mood. It was confusion in pictures. He sat still for a very long time. Not wearing a watch he did not know how long. Adam stood up and started a long trail back the way he had come along the south bank of the Thames.

In a conscious echo of Paris Adam crossed over bridges and back. But it didn't work like it had in Paris. He crossed Tower Bridge and then had to walk nearly a mile with no view of the river until London Bridge. He crissed-crossed his way west, over London Bridge one way, then Southwark Bridge the other. Finding the north bank of the river was difficult but it kept his mind focused on something trivial and that was his reason for walking. It facilitated the absence of thought. Now, as he approached Blackfriars, Adam had achieved confusion without pictures. On he went, deciding whether Hungerford Bridge should count. He decided it shouldn't and moved on to Waterloo where he had silly thoughts about Terry and Julie in the song. At Waterloo Bridge Adam stopped. He climbed the steps, stood in the middle of the bridge and gazed around. London looked staggering. Adam was reaching for epiphany but he set too much store by the fact of being able to see St Paul's Cathedral and the Palace of Westminster at the same time. He wondered about retracing the steps of the thrice mayor of London up to Highgate. He went through his comic routine about why Dick Whittington was going the wrong way given that he came from Bristol. It didn't seem very funny. He thought of a game to keep himself going. He tried to make his way round the Monopoly board, starting with the red ones. He tried to remember all the Monopoly pieces but he couldn't.

This was a journey with no end. Adam did not so much arrive at his destination as give up the desire to keep walking. At Smithfield he found an all-night café and went in to warm up. He noted from the clock on the wall that it was four o'clock. He had enough money to buy two coffees and made them last an hour and a half. He had the cruel thought that Elizabeth was probably in the bath. With his money and his thinking spent Adam started for home. In his meandering journey he had arrived at no conclusions, only senses, ill-conceived feelings that did not fit together. He loved Elizabeth very deeply but he worried she did not love him so in return. He sensed Kevin was right but wished him to be wrong. He loved the view from Waterloo Bridge but felt consumed by it. He wanted to go home and he didn't know where that was.

Single to Manchester

As he opened the door back in Whitechapel, the full acridity that heavy smoking brings to an interior rushed into Adam's nostrils. Adam knew at once that Elizabeth had started smoking again and that she meant her smoking as a deliberate act of defiance. Adam picked up the empty Marlboro packets that Elizabeth had left, ingenuously, on the dining table. There were remnants of tobacco leaves on the armchair, an abandoned packet of Rizlas on the floor and a lighter on the coffee table. He brushed away the tobacco that had rested on his shirt, dropped the useless fag packets in the bin and went into the bedroom to change.

Adam took one step into the bedroom and stood open-mouthed, apoplectic at what his darling had left for him on the windowsill, arranged with a pleasing horticultural delicacy. The mocking sheen of Elizabeth's engagement heirloom was flanked on one side by a full ashtray, one they had bought years before in Israel and which had been until then only ornamental. On the other side of the ring two condoms drooped under the weight of another man's semen. Like a pervert drawn pruriently to pore over the victims of a car crash, Adam picked up a cigarette butt in one hand and the tiny unrolled part of the condom in the other.

It wasn't the sheer depravity of leaving such things lying around, the literal *dirtiness*. It was the thoughtlessness, the brazen two-fingered salute of disrespect. All of this, the anger, the rational apprehension that this was a disgrace, insane behaviour, the last thing that anyone deserves, came much, much later. For the moment, in the midst of this vast insult to everything he loved, Adam crouched down. He doubled up as though he were being eviscerated. Three times he caught his breath before he let it come. The violent gulp, the animal yelp, then the sibilant anguish of his tears. Down there, with ash smeared on one hand and another man's ejaculation on the other, Adam wept as never before, without moving for two hours, until his namesake's lump felt like it would burst through his throat.

Adam called in sick and watched TV all day. He had just taken the mince out of the freezer when Elizabeth arrived home. Her first words were that she thought they should split. She looked at Adam with bloodless emerald eyes and instructed him to make love to her. For the last time. They said nothing as they went through the motions, in a baffling, passionless coupling. It was only afterwards that Adam asked.

'Who was it? It was Piers, wasn't it?'

Elizabeth pulled the face that children put on in the gap between pain and tears. Then the waterworks started and the incoherent apologies.

'I'm sorry; I'm so sorry. I'm sorry.'

'What? What is it?'

'I just don't feel right. I feel so guilty about it. I don't know why. I'm so sorry; it's not your fault.'

'What do you mean?'

'I'm too close to you. I just don't see you as a boyfriend any longer. I'm sorry.'

'I don't get it. What does that mean?'

'I see you as a big brother or something. I'm so sorry. It's not your fault. I just can't carry on. I'm sorry.'

'Why, though? I don't understand.'

'I know you don't.'

'I've tried.'

'I know. You've done more than anyone. That's the worst thing. I couldn't be doing this now without you. That's the tragedy. But you know it's not to do with you.'

'It must be. Or else if it isn't, then why can't we work it out?'

266

'We just can't. It's nothing to do with you. It was all set before I even met you.'

'We can work it through.'

'Adam, it's not working. You know that.'

'I don't know that. You're not trying. I've tried to tell you that you have to work at it, but you won't.'

Elizabeth had seen a counsellor, at Adam's instigation, to discuss the things she preferred not to think about. These protracted and dolorous sessions had left her exhausted and deflated. They were as painful as one can imagine, as painful as Adam could *only* imagine but never know. Adam blithely instructed Elizabeth that counselling was her only way but he knew nothing of what it was like *from the inside*. One day, two months after her counselling had begun, Elizabeth had declared she no longer needed it and no further word was ever said.

'I have tried, Adam. You know that.'

'But why?'

'You know why.'

'I don't know why.'

Adam was still desperate for explanations which he thought he deserved and, with equal fervour, thought he had not been given. Elizabeth agreed that Adam deserved an explanation but thought she had supplied one, as far as she ever could. Everything Adam said was a single question. *Why are you leaving me? Why?*

'I've told you so many times. I can't tell you any more than I've told you already. You were the most important thing in the world for me but we were too different. And I can't handle it.'

'You can if you try.'

'Too much has happened, Adam. I love you, I really do. But you know I can't do anything about it and you know why I can't.'

Elizabeth's argument was like a fly that zoomed its way around the room, irritating and persistent and indomitable. She explained at length that she had been unable to untangle the wires in her head. The wire that ought to lead from Adam to boyfriend had somehow become entangled, wound around the

267

wire that led to familiarity, comfort and support. The closer Adam came the more hemmed in she felt, the more compromised. When Elizabeth told Adam that she loved him she said it *de profundis* but she needed so much to be released. 'Please Release me' is her theme song, scratched and stuck on the soundtrack of her life.

'That's why I've wanted more time on my own.'

Elizabeth believed that being alone was an accomplishment. Adam thought of it as a sentence. But Elizabeth also wanted to be alone because there had been a time when she had wanted to be alone and she had been forcibly denied. Elizabeth had spent more and more time locked in the bathroom with the bubbles, *Marie Claire* and her thoughts. Her space in her head was hers and hers alone. Nobody was permitted access to that realm. It was permanently locked in the bathroom with the sanctuary lamp.

Adam did not understand. He did not need to be on his own physically, actually. He could be on his own while he was watching the football results. It made no difference that Elizabeth was in the same room reading *Bonfire of the Vanities*. Adam didn't believe in private space. He was a pull-yourself-together merchant. Intoxicated by his own rhetoric, Adam never for a moment stopped to consider *why* Elizabeth might need to be on her own.

'Why are you doing this? Why?'

'I need some space, Adam. I think we need some time apart.'

'But why?'

'I need to take stock, to think where my life is going. I just think we're actually quite different, Adam.'

'No we're not. That's not true.'

'I feel I'm constantly apologising for people in front of you.'

'I don't know what you mean.'

'I know you don't. That's part of the trouble. I just feel that I've lost my self.'

Still the valiant, indestructible fly would not die. One more time it buzzed off after the thwack of the newspaper should have dealt with it for good. Back it came for more, elusive and exasperating. Adam deployed all the charm he could muster, all the practised understanding, all the polished psychological insight, all the love in the world, to persuade Elizabeth that their lives could yet be salvaged. Adam refused to give up even though the sanctuary lamp had fallen down on his head. He tried to convince Elizabeth that great love is eating mince and onions, watching soap operas. Adam thought that relationships ended when love had declined. *Amo, amas, amat, amamus, amatis, amant.* He could not fathom that his love had not declined: it had exploded.

'Stay the night.'

'No, there's no point.'

'Please.'

Elizabeth, tired, desperately tired, tears sliding down her face like alabaster, yielded. In the morning she crept away.

Elizabeth did not come back for three days, during which Adam went outside only to buy packaged sandwiches. The rest of the time he prowled the flat, inert in contemplation. He rearranged his books twice, first collapsing all disciplines into a book alphabetti spaghetti, then putting them back as they were. He wondered whether the Bible was a book of essays or a work of fiction. He tried to decide which author it should be classified under. He analysed his clothes, his furniture, all the *things* that bore the blame for Elizabeth having left him. He decided he needed a sun-tan. Then, on his return, he would buy some new jeans and a white T-shirt. And then, and then. He called in sick on three consecutive days. He was past caring about urban decay.

On the Saturday morning Elizabeth rang to say that she was on her way round to collect some clothes. Adam turned the flat upside-down looking for the graduation day photograph on Trinity Bridge. He ripped it very carefully so that he was on one side and Elizabeth and her peers were on the other. Then he placed the two halves deliberately on their initialled pillows in the bed that was all of a sudden only his.

Time is always elastic and an afternoon spent waiting can be an eternity. With his trousers round his ankles and the debris of half-eaten fast food barely visible under a forest of tissue paper, Adam waited. Every twenty seconds he nervously fingered his whiskers as if confirming *I am a man still*. He matted his hair down to one side, glued by the gathering grease. A key turned in the lock and Elizabeth appeared in the doorway. The necklace she wore bounced on her bosom and glinted as it caught the light. She looked radiant even as she sucked on a rebellion lollipop. Adam looked away petulantly, dimly aware that he was scared of her.

'It's cold in here.'

As soon as Elizabeth had gone, Adam had turned down the controls on the radiators he only ever used for her benefit. Adam stumbled over inappropriate, rehearsed lines. Elizabeth strode around, picking out underwear and books, shoes and toiletries, mince and onions, the paraphernalia of everyday life.

Adam had been preparing his speech for days but Elizabeth refused to follow the script. As soon as he abandoned the book Adam was liberated. He spoke, suddenly, with impassioned *ex tempore* sincerity.

'Where are you staying?'

'With Arabee.'

'Will you stay here?'

'No, Adam.'

'Please, Elizabeth.'

Adam preferred humiliation to not getting what he wanted. The sight of Elizabeth heading for the door again was too much for him. He begged her to stay the night. She was adamant that she could not do so. They declined at once into the same old argument, always the same argument. Every conversation reduced to the same: pressure, compulsion, guilt.

'I feel guilty because I don't feel like I should.'

Adam screwed his face and scraped his teeth together in frustration. He ran his fingers down the cracked paintwork as if screeching on a blackboard.

'Just don't feel guilty. Just don't.'

'I do, though.'

270

When an argument reduces to this it is time to leave. This is the depth of the exchange, no further down to go. Instead, the argument went on and on, irritating like a telephone within earshot that nobody bothers to answer. Elizabeth had nothing more to say and made as if to leave. Adam had a thousand important lines to deliver, none of which he could think of and all of which amounted to *please don't go anywhere.*

Adam thought Elizabeth had lost her mind. He thought her unreasonable beyond words. He didn't recognise her. But Elizabeth was desperate for a way out. She thought the shorter and the sharper the blow the less shocking Adam would find it. She wanted to get out of the flat at once. She hated hearing Adam plead. It did neither of them any good.

With her arms full of dresses Elizabeth started for the door. Adam shouted at her not to go. She carried on. Their flat had a long hallway leading to the front door and Elizabeth was half-way towards freedom when Adam appeared in front of her like a bolt from a cannon. Elizabeth was startled into stopping, so for at least a minute she heard out the plaintiff.

'I'm sorry; I've got to go. I said I wouldn't be long.'

'Who to?'

Elizabeth looked down at the floor.

'Who to?'

'You know who to.'

The mention of Rah Rah Rasputin consumed the last of Adam's decaying reason. Elizabeth moved forward but Adam yielded no ground. He was shouting, incoherent, desperate, the declension of a man who is losing love. *Amo, amas, amat, amamus, amatis, amant.*

'Will you let me through, please?'

Elizabeth tried again to push her way through, this time more forcefully. She pushed Adam back, catching his finger with the gold bangle she wore round her wrist. Her momentum knocked Adam back against the door handle which pressed into the small of his back. In his pain and anger he struck out, hitting Elizabeth just beneath her eyes. In a mess of skirts on the floor, Elizabeth lay prostrate, sobbing, clutching her head. The Tez Satchel of his own domestic arrangements felt no immediate remorse because at least she had not left.

Adam reached down to pick Elizabeth up, to check she was not hurt. She slapped away his proffered hand. Adam had bought time with his display of cowardly machismo but he could not allow them to part on these terms. Elizabeth dragged herself up off the floor and sat down in the living room. Adam took some ice from the fridge and applied it to her face. He looked down at the tears forming in her beautiful eyes, at the water dropping slowly down her fair, childlike skin and he cried as a man who has lost his one most cherished thing. Elizabeth dragged imperiously on a cigarette, the forbidden tar. She pressed the brown tip to her lips and blew away seven seconds of her life.

Silence. Long, long silence.

Elizabeth stood up slowly and took a few wary steps towards the door. Adam made no attempt to prevent her going. He had done his worst.

'Can I come with you?'

There was such sorrow in this request, such love. Elizabeth bowed her head and nodded, almost imperceptibly. She still loved Adam too and it pained her immensely to have hurt him in this way. Relieved to be allowed out, she assented. Adam went into the bedroom to get his coat. He saw that Elizabeth had removed the torn picture from the bed.

Piers lived in Parson's Green, or Vicar's Snot as Adam called it. He had twenty-five minutes to put his case and fixed his eyes to the floor of the car all the way. If virtue is the willingness to do anything to uphold glory then Adam proved himself a man of complete virtue. He rose to the occasion. His tone was conciliatory, he spoke *sotto voce*, with patience and kindness. Adam pointed out that being with Piers was not the same as being on her own and, at each stage of his speech, was sure to gain Elizabeth's assent with a nod of approval. He managed, with heroic restraint, not to say Rah Rah Rasputin more than six times which Elizabeth did not find at all funny.

As they bounced over the hump of the bridge onto the New King's Road, Adam was prepared to say *anything*. He concluded with a statement of his abiding love and touched Elizabeth's heart. He was good, very good: Demosthenes with tears. But he wasn't quite good enough. As he finished his address Elizabeth smiled, said goodbye, and disappeared into the flat where Piers was waiting for her.

The negation of virtue is corruption. For six miles across London Adam had been wasting his breath. His arguments were neither true nor false: they were irrelevant. Adam, possessed of a too, too rational sensibility, collapsed into anger, manic and intensely despairing. He threw himself at the locked door, again and again, until the pain in his shoulder precluded any more. He shouted incoherent obscenities into an empty street, into an empty life. Twice they came to the window, her lover and she; twice he reasoned and pled. They closed the window and went to bed. The goddess had turned cold from his blandishments. Hard of heart, Elizabeth showed, *in extremis*, that she, too, was one of the Brangy warriors of life.

Adam tried to work on Monday but, as he looked through a window that gave out onto a railway bridge, he saw a train rolling by and the strength of his desire to be aboard, running away, made him consider resignation. He claimed he had phlegm in the throat and left for the day. He then spent most of the week staring at the telephone, avoiding increasingly frantic messages from hydra-haired Peter. After five days and four answerphone messages he fabricated an illness for his father to force Elizabeth to return his call. Adam never had any compunction about inventing illnesses for his father. Bob came down with a fever every time Adam was double-booked. Adam was tortured by the telephone's refusal to ring. If Elizabeth did not return his call there could be no rest. He could not concentrate on anything else until she called. Alone at night, Adam could see his own breath.

At eight-fifteen on the Friday morning the telephone rang. His coil released, Adam sprung up from the settee, raising the receiver before the first burst was complete.

'How's your dad?'

Elizabeth's genuine tenderness shamed him. Lies breed and

Adam gave birth to a family in order to cover his first. But he was consoled by the first syllable of Elizabeth's voice. He had begged of her that she should call and she had called. What was said was of no importance. The dreadful silence before the telephone rang was over. Adam stumbled over inappropriate, rehearsed lines as Elizabeth ran the conversation.

'I need to talk to you.'

'Go on then.'

'Not on the phone.'

'Sounds ominous.'

'I don't want to go into it now. What are you doing tonight?'

'Nothing much.'

'I'll come over. About eight.'

Adam spent the day trying to read *Middlemarch* but decided that George Eliot was boring. He started on the washing-up but realised it was trivial and pointless. He watched *Young Doctors* and got angry about haircuts. Their barbers were worse than his dad. Eventually, Elizabeth screeched up the street in a new BMW that Adam had not even heard about. She came unceremoniously to the point.

'I'm leaving.'

'I thought you'd left.'

'I'm going to Hong Kong.'

'What?'

'I'm going to Hong Kong with work. To live.'

'How?'

'They've been asking me for a bit and I didn't think I wanted to. But it seems like a good opportunity.'

Elizabeth picked up her coat. Adam said nothing. There was nothing more to be said. He was walking around the flat at random, in the zig-zag of a lunatic. He made an instant decision that he could not stay in London.

'I want a lift.'

'Where to?'

'Euston.'

'Where are you going?'

'Home.'

'What?'

'I want to go home.'

Elizabeth pulled into the underground car park at Euston station and turned the engine off. She reached over to kiss Adam goodbye but he moved out of reach. He did not even unbuckle his seat-belt. Instead he began to reminisce, to relive his last four years, without waiting for a response to any of his questions.

'Do you remember that little black hat you used to wear in Cambridge? You should dye your hair white again.'

Adam reached out to pull Elizabeth's hair. It was that haircut, that bleached crop, that Adam always saw poking out of Elizabeth's head. He knew it was still in there, engulfed by spreadsheets. It was the hair of Elizabeth as she once was. It came with a hat attached as though it were the nose and glasses that clowns wore.

'It's still there somewhere. Do you remember your thousand-island dressing at Watford Gap? Mince and onions? Terry Mackie? And what about your gold bangle? What about Paris? What about the lion and the fox? Where did they go, then?'

'Don't, Adam.'

It didn't seem much of a life when he listed it like that. But it was Adam's life and he had loved it, which is just another way of saying that he loved Elizabeth. Even at the last he thought that maybe the lion and the fox had the power to bring Elizabeth home. He laid his bid before Elizabeth, full of Violet Elizabeth Bott and Terry Mackie, but it didn't matter.

'I've got to go,' said Elizabeth.

Adam concluded suddenly that the great love of his life could now only be resolved in silence. He held her dear to his breast, kissed her tenderly and told her in a sorrowful whisper that they should never speak again. Finally, Adam got out. As Elizabeth pulled away she wound the window down.

'Goodbye, darling. Be strong. I still love you, you know.'

Elizabeth could barely see the traffic for the tears she shed for the love of a little boy she had left behind.

Adam ran home at once to Peel Tower.

'Single to Manchester.'

'We've got an hour's delay,' said the ticket vendor behind his thick glass window.

'How frequent are the trains?' asked Adam.

'Every hour,' said the man with no hint of a laugh.

'In which case, as long as I'm not catching the first train, which I'm not, it makes no difference whatever,' Adam pointed out.

'It does, sir. It's an hour late.'

Adam swore and asked again for a ticket although he had no reason to go to Bury. He was going there only so as not to be here. Adam sat down opposite an old lady in a fur hat. She smiled fondly and her wrinkly face exuded gentle kindness. Adam returned the compliment, like a little boy upset.

Thirty minutes passed without thinking. A caramel slice and a cappuccino in a paper cup had bought him half an hour. But there was no thousand-island dressing this time. The dull Hertfordshire plain flashed by as Adam slumped into the grubby seat. He stared blankly *at* the window rather than out of it. His unshaven, sunken face stared back at him, bottom lip protuberant and sullen, from the window's mirror. A pretty, self-assured young woman in her early twenties walked behind Adam and threw him a look of disapproval for his vanity.

At this precise moment Adam concocted the idea of never having been. To never have been would avoid pain to others. It would avoid the messy, practical business of suicide and it would put an end, once and for all, to the misery that he already knew would be interminable. He would just never have been, with no effect on anyone, like the burial wishes of the Mayor of Casterbridge. Please release me, let me go.

Adam was on a train to nowhere and, in full view of everyone in the carriage, began to sniffle. At first, intimidated in the presence of others, Adam blinked the tears back. Then he gave in. The blood came to his eyes and he rubbed hard. The sound of a man crying in full public view on a train is unmistakable. He spent the rest of the journey cuddled close to a dear old lady in a fur hat who knew the pain he wore on his face. As Adam sniffled his way down the line she whispered a soothing thought.

'We are now arriving at Manchester Piccadilly where this train will terminate. Will all passengers please detrain here.'

Adam lifted his head and extended his neck, proud of his red, raw eyes. He smiled his thanks to the old lady and wondered how detraining differed from getting off. His brain was racing ahead, angry at the world around him. As the train came to a standstill, the announcer repeated himself, as if anyone was going to remain on board just to defy him.

'We are now arriving at Manchester Piccadilly. This train will terminate here.'

Adam turned in exasperation to the kind old lady in the fur hat.

'No, it won't. The journey will terminate but it'll still be a train once it's stopped. It won't turn into an old woman in a fur hat.'

'I know dear, I know.'

Adam walked out of the station and down the ramp towards Piccadilly Gardens. Every few minutes he stopped to say something, to nobody, for all the world like a madman. He walked a hundred yards down the street, stopped and retraced his steps. He threw his arms up in the air and gulped in exasperation. Despair made him oblivious to the world. All the lunatics who gather in the streets to make noises are expressing their own particular despair. Every bus-nutter has a story to tell. Adam was on a night trip to madness, shouting in the street to nobody.

This love will terminate here.

part five: *Two Drifters*

In Loco Parentis

After he had concluded his business in London Kevin had come back home to his parents and had fallen straight into a routine. Every morning he climbed out from under the covers only for a very late breakfast, after which he repaired to his room to lie on the bed chain-smoking, waiting for the day to pass. The progress through treacle time in the long languor of the afternoon drove Kevin back to his cell. Time was his master and he served it faithfully. Going to the chemist for a stick of deodorant took Kevin five minutes but thinking about going took him five hours. As every day passed without sight or sound of Irene, Kevin wrapped his duvet around him as the wind rattled the never-mended window frame. Nobody called and Kevin received no visitors. Kevin was a lazy postman without any letters under his bed. He left the house once a day to walk around the estate. Twice a week he went as far as the bookies in Bury to pursue his only interest. Kevin no longer bothered with the job centre. There was nothing in there for an unskilled young man fresh from prison.

Nine months before, Kevin had been released from prison into his mother's arms. He had stepped out one blank Tuesday morning under a grey Manchester sky. Kevin and Wendy had taken the new tram back to Bury, after eighteen months away, back to the Harwood estate, back home, Irene having given up their house just the week before when she went to live with Ian in Greenmount. Kevin had glanced back up at the Strangeways tower. There are two roads that lead from Bury into Manchester.

From this day on Kevin only ever voluntarily took the top road, avoiding the entrance to the prison. The bottom road to Manchester he never again travelled.

Only Maria's two boys, Adam and Shane, had kept Kevin from sinking down into his duvet at once. Adam and Shane lived in the immediate present where the future holds no demons. After a game of indoor football with a sock, Kevin had retreated to his cell to look at his own breath. He had sat in there, motionless, for his first day of freedom and had no mind ever to come out.

The first person to bring him out of hiding was his wife. Her pretty face had creased up at the sight of Kevin's emaciated, worn features which looked like they had been finished off on a moon bed. Kevin had taken her through into the kitchen where, over a cup of tea, she had not spared him her news.

'Kev, I've got some bad news. The social services have been again about Susan.' Irene had muttered this sentence downwards, where she fixed her eyes on the dirty black-and-white floor tiles.

'What did they say?'

'Nothing really.'

'So what's up?'

'It's what they fucking did, Kevin. It's what they fucking did.'

'What? What have they done, Irene?'

'They've taken her. She's gone into a home for a bit.'

'What do you mean, for a bit?'

'I don't know. They said it's just to build her strength up and then I can have her back. It's only for a bit.'

'But why? What's happened?'

'They said she wasn't feeding properly.'

'What do you mean, not feeding properly?'

'I don't know, they did loads of tests, about vitamins and vegetables and stuff and they went on and on again about how you get iron and stuff like that.'

'But what happened?'

'They said she was too small for her age and that she wasn't being looked after properly, so . . .' Irene had choked on her words.

'That's not on . . . They can't fucking do that.'

'They've done it.'

'I'll sort it out. I'm not having the fucking social nicking my daughter. Why didn't anyone fucking tell me?'

'You were in prison. There was nothing you could have done.'

It had been left to Irene to fight on, quietly, determinedly. Irene never gave up. When she had cried herself through till morning that night it was because she felt she had failed.

'Does my dad know?'

'I think so. Your mum does. Not that she was any help.'

'Didn't he fucking do anything?'

'Not really. He wasn't there when they came.'

'Fucking social services. Interfering cunts; think they run your fucking life.'

Kevin had rung at once to offer a minute of gutter obscenity to the relevant department of the social services. But it was angry bravado. Kevin talked hard but played soft. He had replaced the receiver having agreed that it was better for Susan to spend a short period in care. Kevin had been intimidated by the posh woman on the other end of the line who kept saying *in loco parentis*. Kevin McDermott did not know Latin. He didn't even know where it was. Kevin had fallen apart before the good offices of the state, lost in ignorance and deference before a well-spoken woman fluent in a foreign language. While Kevin had been losing on the telephone Irene had been putting on her coat.

'Where are you going?'

'I'm not stopping, Kevin.'

'Why not?'

'Why do you think?'

'Don't go.'

'There's something else.'

'What?'

'Promise you won't go mad.'

'Depends what it is.'

'Promise.'

283

'I promise.'

'I've got a new boyfriend.'

Kevin went mad.

'You don't waste any fucking time, do you? Who is it?'

'You don't know him.'

'Who is he?'

'He's from Liverpool.'

'I fucking hate Scousers.'

'I've moved in with him.'

'What?'

'I might get Susan back that way.'

There was a sullen silence in which Irene had wondered how she could now excuse herself.

'Has he shagged you?'

'I'm going.'

'He's fucking shagged you, hasn't he? You fucking slag.'

Irene had turned her back and walked away. As she had swaggered through the hall, wiggling her bottom flirtatiously as she always did without realising it, Kevin had not let up with his anguished abuse.

'You fucking slag. He's fucking shagged you already.'

Kevin had made his point with the back of his hand. Before his time in prison the violence inside Kevin had been deeply hidden away beneath his palpable love for Irene and the children. But now he had a wounded, brooding aspect, like an animal that has been wronged and which lurks in its lair, waiting to pounce as soon as it is taunted. Dreams of glory had shone into Kevin like the rays of the sun and now he was suffering a reaction like angry skin as Irene left him to join her new boyfriend in the pursuit of the right vegetables.

The second person to bring Kevin out of hiding was his father. Every Saturday night Sammy insisted that Kevin join him for a drink in the Greenhill. The drinks were on Sammy. In fact, as Bob pointed out, the drinks were on the social which meant, in effect, that the drinks were on Bob. Sammy and Bob ran through this argument every week. Sammy relished it because he thought Bob was joking. Bob didn't, because he wasn't. Sammy, Wendy and their son sat at the same table every Saturday, next to the bingo caller. Every week Kevin sat silently, unamused, as a demented floozy choked the life out of 'I Will Survive'. He lifted his elbow robotically, at constant speed, and drained his bitter. He stood only to go to the bar to buy a drink or to go to the toilet to be rid of it.

This Saturday night, nine months after his return from Strangeways, Kevin found himself standing at a urinal next to Bob Matthews. The rules of urinals state categorically that a man should never stand next to another man if a spare urinal is available. Kevin was standing by the left-hand wall, leaving two urinals free. If Bob had been playing by the piss rules he would have stood by the right-hand wall when he entered to find Kevin already in full flight. But, in a daring breach of male etiquette, Bob took the middle urinal. Kevin was unnerved to find Bob's pale skin and round blue eyes so unnaturally close to his own. Kevin had just dried up and was about to enter the shakes when Bob broke the silence.

'What are you going to do with yourself then, son?'

This was not an innocent inquiry. It was not a request for information. It was palpably an accusation. It was a dare.

'Don't know.'

Bob had no truck with able-bodied young men who relied on maundy money. He thought they should be out looking for work. He did not spare Kevin in letting him know.

'Now look here, son. It's not my place to tell you this. It should be coming from your father but you'll never get any sense out of him. There's nowt down for lads moping about in their rooms when they should he out and about looking for work. You've got a wife and kids to support.'

Kevin was taken aback at Bob's directness. He shook himself inadequately and popped back into his trousers. As Bob continued his tirade of advice, inevitable droplets trickled down Kevin's leg.

'You've got to shake yourself,' said Bob, not knowing quite how true that was. 'I know it's not easy for a lad like you but you can't waste your life like this. You used to have something about you. Our Adam used to look up to you. I'd say to him: 'Would you jump off a bridge if Kevin McDermott did?' And I think he probably would have. But now look at you. The only thing stopping you jumping off a bridge is that you can't be bloody mithered.'

Kevin slumped against the wall.

'Look at me, lad. Lift your head up.'

Bob reached out to force Kevin's chin up. Kevin met his hand and pushed it away.

'Why should I fucking care? I couldn't get a fucking job before. What chance have I got now?'

'You've got to try. Someone will give you a go.'

'Oh, fuck off. There's no fucking point. I've never had any luck, me.'

'You make your own luck in this life, Kevin. And you've got three young children to support.'

'Jason lives with his mum.'

'It doesn't matter. He's your son. And so's the new little nipper, whatever you think of him. They're your responsibility. You brought them into the world and you bloody well ought to look after them. And if you do, they'll look after you one day. You're too pig-ignorant to realise that they're the only thing you have got and if you don't pull your finger out now you'll lose them for ever.'

Bob had hit the jugular. Kevin felt a singular love for his children, and Jason above all. Kevin's chin dropped onto his collarbone and the life seeped from his body. Bob had by now also finished at the urinal but neither of them moved towards the door.

'What happened to you, Kevin? What the bloody hell happened?'

The pinpricks darted at the back of Kevin's eyeballs. He held his stare open to stymie the tears which formed whole, magnifying his pale blue eyes. Kevin shook his head with tender sorrow and spoke, in a barely audible whisper.

'I don't know, Bob. I don't know.'

Bob Matthews stared, thoroughly impassive and unmoved by

Kevin's decline into tears. But Kevin was not reduced to tears. He was increased by tears.

'I'll tell you what happened, Kevin. You just followed the same old bloody path. You're just like your old man. He was always a bad 'un, was Sammy. From the moment he turned up round here. I remember it like it were yesterday, this great fat, big-headed brute thinking he owns the place, ordering folk about. Then at the first sight of a problem he's out robbing. He was a nasty piece of work from day one and you're no different. I thought you might have turned out different. I thought you might have been a civilised lad. You had something about you once. But now you're just like your bloody father.'

Kevin summoned a dispirited defence.

'I wouldn't talk about my dad like that.'

'Or else what, Kevin? What are you going to do about it? Beat me up? Would that help?'

'I'll see what my dad has to say about you slagging him off behind his back.'

'You do that, Kevin. I've said it a thousand times to his face and I'll say it again.'

Bob leant forward, to whisper conspiratorially, as if they were being listened to.

'You've got to realise, Kevin, that your old man is a bastard. Otherwise you've no chance.'

Bob Matthews' denunciation of Sammy McDermott was plain and brutal. Kevin wanted to dismiss it and go back to his pint but Bob was made of more noble mettle, the sort that did not tarnish on exposure to the open air. These were home truths that Kevin had never been able to see, cooped up in his room with his own breath.

Kevin walked straight out of the club without speaking to his parents. As he came out of the door he saw that Adam was coming in. Kevin averted his eyes and pushed past without speaking. Adam paused, unsure whether to speak but Kevin did not allow him the opportunity. Kevin shuffled home and Adam wandered into the club that, ever since he had left for Cambridge, he had found so unfathomably peculiar.

Adam came back to the Greenhill Working Men's Club like the prodigal returned. He had explained to Peter with the two haircuts that, for personal reasons, he had decided to leave down London and return to the town that still exercised such a strong hold over him. Peter understood that Adam had to work Elizabeth out of his system but failed to persuade his protégé that he was investing false hope in a nostalgic journey back to a place he had now left for good. Knowing Bury better, Adam disagreed. He argued that his world of minor celebrity was shifting and unreal. He wanted, in a tumult, to plant his feet deep into the rutted ground.

The celebrity of working for the television down London did not exempt Adam from the rules of the club. He was met with a sceptical stare from Bill on the door, who reasoned shrewdly from Adam's suspiciously expensive clothes.

'Are you a member, sunshine?'

'Errrr . . . no.'

'Has anyone signed you in?'

Adam had never been signed in before. He glanced up and saw his mother in her usual seat.

'My mum's a member.'

'I doubt that very much, cock robin,' said Bill, as superciliously as he could manage.

'No, she is. It's June Matthews.'

'I don't care if she's the Queen of Sheba. We have no women members.'

'Why not?'

'Because it's a working men's club.'

'Well, my dad's a member. He's on the committee, I think.'

'Who's your dad?'

'Terry Wogan, who do you think?'

'I don't know. I wouldn't ask if I knew, would I?'

'It's Bob Matthews.'

'Oh yes, you said, June's your mum. Right. Bob's not on the committee any more though. Hasn't been in a long while.'

'He is a man though. You can't deny that.'

Bob came over from the bar to intercede.

'Let the lad in, Bill.'

'Sorry about that but we get all sorts trying to get in here. That'll be a pound.'

'Daylight robbery,' said Adam, with ignored irony.

'It's the same for everyone. Even the members have to pay.'

Adam immediately felt out of place in his Yves Saint Laurent shirt, his leather jacket and his moleskin trousers. They seemed suddenly too tailored and fine. He went straight to the toilet to hide away. Sitting glumly in the cubicle Adam noticed a warrior's braggadocio in bold black felt tip: 'Brangy born and bread'.

Adam went to the bar, trying to hide his trousers, which is a hellish difficult thing to do when you're wearing them. He ordered a round and was corrected by Steve the barman for getting it slightly wrong. Bob Matthews drank McEwans, not just any old lager. As he turned to deliver the drinks a man at the bar spoke with a sneer of hostility and suspicion.

'You not from round here, lad?'

'Yeah. I live just round the corner. Backing onto the Harwood.'

'Where's your posh voice come from then?'

'I lived away for a bit. But I'm back now.'

Adam sat down next to his mother and fielded the procession of Bettys who asked him, in turn, about down London and told him why they wouldn't like to live there. He knew the steps to this conversation and they couldn't see his trousers.

'Are you up for Christmas, love?'

'No, I've come home now, Betty.'

'Oooh, I knew you would. I knew you wouldn't stop down London. It's right dirty, isn't it?'

'Not like Bury, eh? You could eat your dinner off the pavement in Bury. There's not a speck of dirt to be seen anywhere.'

'Oooh, you're a cheeky devil, you are, Adam Matthews.'

And then the dance steps changed.

'Where's that lovely young lady of yours? Is she staying down London?'

'Yeah, she's staying down there.'

Three Bettys had completed their dance steps when MC Willie, the man on the microphone, asked for everyone's attention. Old men looked up uninterestedly from their dominoes, old women abated their gossip and a hush fell on the club.

'I'm afraid we've got some bad news. Dorothy, the turn, can't make it this evening.'

'That'll serve us right for hiring anyone from Bolton,' said Bob, mixing parochialism with irrelevance.

'The committee will go into a huddle to decide what the evening's entertainment will be. If you could talk amongst yourselves we'll be with you as soon as we've reached a decision.'

Adam was delighted to hear that Dorothy had not left Bolton. Strangely enough, she had been the turn on the last occasion that he had been in the Greenhill. Dorothy began in the register of raucous and ascended rapidly to a shriek but even at the top of her range she was upstaged by her own sequins. There wasn't a middle-of-the-road classic that Dorothy hadn't taken outside and strangled. Adam was positively delighted by the gruesome alternatives to the absent cantatrix. He envisaged a procession of committee members begging tunelessly to be released.

The committee members went into an emergency session for half an hour, negotiating feverishly to salvage the evening. The fragile egos involved made this a parlous task. The bruises were still showing from last week when Bill and Willie had come to blows over whose turn it was to switch the lights off. Hence it was no minor triumph when Willie took up the microphone and announced a revolution.

'The buffet will be brought forward to eight-thirty. After that, I know you'll be delighted to know that one of the regulars has agreed to do a full turn accompanied by Graham on the organ and Alan on the drum and cymbal.'

An hour later and more full of pork pies than he was accustomed to, Adam laughed at his mother's suggestion that some of the regulars were really very good. He began practising the art of uproarious internal laughter with quivering but straight face muscles. Willie lifted the microphone from its stand.

'I hope you've enjoyed the buffet which I think was marvel-

290

lous. Thanks to Gladys and her team, as usual. Now I'd like to invite our turn for the evening to take the stage.'

A short, fat man made his way from the back of the club, through the tables and chairs. He took the microphone from Willie, held up his hand to arrest the polite applause and asked if anyone knew 'Moon River'. Graham and Alan clunked through the introduction that would serve them for every song and Sammy McDermott enunciated the title in a deep, rich baritone voice. Wendy beamed as Sammy entered another realm. Anyone who can sing like that knows about beauty, deep down. Sammy McDermott carried beauty inside and here it was, let out to fly.

Two drifters, off to see the world, there's such a lot of
    world to see.
And they're both after the same rainbow's end, waiting
    round the bend,
My huckleberry friend, Moon River and me.

Sammy's regal control, his lightness of touch, his phrasing and texture, his mellowness, was shocking and humbling. In the hands of Graham and Alan and the mouth of Sammy, Henry Mancini's music came alive. It shocked Adam to discover that talent often lies buried underneath a misanthropic surface. But Sammy brought tears to his eyes. This hulking, vicious man, standing before him, bringing a shiver to his spine with a voice of distinction deep and pure.

Happy Mondays

The other drifter was off, not to see the world, but to see the man at the dole office. Kevin had arranged a meeting with a careers advisor, encouraged by Bob Matthews, by the imaginary pressure of Jason and Susan McDermott and by the dreamy vision of Irene Bradshaw.

The air in the dole office was heavy with cigarette smoke. The unforgiving light focused the pasty complexions of the morose men who sat in a long queue of plastic chairs, waiting impatiently for money or advice. The staff sat behind reinforced glass as though they were expecting a drive-by shooting. Another disappointed hopeful emerged from the back office as twelve clicked to thirteen. Each man held a numbered slip in his hand and so the next futile interview commenced. For an hour and twenty minutes Kevin waited his turn. Across the desk a name badge declared 'Andrew Smith: Careers Advice'. Andrew Smith had a thankless task. He had to talk about work to young men who were not equipped for jobs, in a town that wasn't creating any. Andrew Smith was trained to break bad news sweetly. Andrew Smith regretted to inform you for a living.

Kevin was a novice at interviews and made the mistake of telling the truth. Another twenty-two-year-old once-upon-a-time footballer with no qualifications, an aborted job in a super-market, a term in prison and the dole in between times. It was the *curriculum vitae* of the left behind. All Kevin had taken from school were the free dinners. By the time of his exams Kevin had become renowned at Elton Moor only for wagging school.

It had been his best subject. Five years of school reports had told this tale but Sammy and Wendy had taken no interest in school reports. Andrew Smith put on his most caring face but Kevin didn't need to be a genius to work out his chances. He wasn't a genius and he worked them out straight away.

Kevin walked home slowly and dispiritedly. He had pulled himself part-way up. For an optimistic moment, he had entertained the hope that 'Andrew Smith: Careers Advice' might help him remain upright. But now, as he came out of the subway into the drizzle, Kevin looked up at Peel Tower and felt again one of the benighted Brangy warriors of life.

He flicked on a confessional talk show as soon as he arrived home. He had been watching without interest for a quarter of an hour when he heard the click of the broken gate as it was lifted. The hope of Irene jumped into his head. Kevin opened the door instead on Bob Matthews, making the quantum leap over his fence to the Harwood estate. He was carrying a new pair of navy blue overalls, still in their cellophane wrapping.

'Is this a bad time?'

'No, come in. But my dad's not in.'

'I haven't come to see your dad. I've come to see you.'

'What for?'

'What you like with your hands?'

'Don't know. All right, I suppose.'

'Tomorrow morning, get yourself down to Brown's for nine.'

'What for?'

'Mr Brown wants a word with you. He's looking for a lad.'

'Did you tell him about me?'

Bob stared blankly at Kevin and ignored the question.

'So I'll see you there at nine, then.'

'Yeah, I'll see you there.'

'Don't be late.'

'I won't.'

'And err . . . you can cut out the smoke and all. He won't have it.'

Bob dropped the overalls onto the sofa and saw himself out, leaving Kevin so flabbergasted that he forgot to say thank you.

He took the overalls out of their cellophane and turned the sleeves and trousers up to make them fit.

Bob returned to the other side of the fence for a Matthews family meeting over dinner. Bob thought Adam had been foolish to resign. He thought that coming back to Bury was sentimental and pointless, the more so as Adam was now unemployed and at the mercy of the maundy money. Five years before, when Bob had waved Adam off to Cambridge, he had hoped they were saying goodbye for ever. Adam tried to explain to his father that his resignation was not about the BBC, it was about Elizabeth. He tried to explain why there is no solace in professional success if it comes with packaged sandwiches from the all-night garage. There was more to life, he said, than money and a good job.

'But what will you do?' asked June.

'I don't know. I've lost all my motivation.'

'But you were doing ever so well, too.'

'I know but I don't care.'

'Why not?'

'You know why.'

'You can't just bloody well give up like that.'

Bob had the last word. He stared at Adam, disappointment etched so very visibly on his brow, which he clutched in exasperation as his headache took over. Bob left the room, with nothing more to say. Adam, also in silence, went up to his old room to reacquaint himself with his own breath.

He did not stay long in the cold bedroom. After a week of oppressive silence Adam found a small flat overlooking the reservoir where he and Kevin had once gone fishing. Alone in his new flat, depleting his meagre BBC savings, Adam began to sink down into the duvet. He gave up on music which suddenly seemed to have forgotten to include words. Cookery was the major casualty of solitude. Cooking for two is an adventure but cooking for one is a chore. Washing the pots made Adam realise that, alone, he was eating purely to reproduce himself. He couldn't bring himself even to peel any onions or fry any mince. It was easier to live on take-aways and packaged sandwiches from the all-night garage. Adam found no romantic charge in the dirty forecourt, standing unshaven in the queue with the other transients buying petrol so they could drive away.

At the end of his first week Adam arrived back from the garage, armed with a ham salad on white, to open his door onto a disreputable mess. He did not wipe his feet on entering. He was loathe to do any cleaning at all. The rotting insects and decaying skin soon stuck to grubby surfaces but, clean or dirty, nobody else saw the place and Adam didn't care either way. He took the salad out of his sandwich, put it in the bin and sat down to watch football matches on teletext when there was a knock at the door.

'Can I come in, then?' asked his father.

'It's a bit of a mess.'

Bob grimaced at the smell of a week's unattended washing-up and the sweaty clothes that Adam had dropped carelessly onto the floor. Bob went through into the living room, where he encountered a wardrobe lying sideways on the floor, the door facing inward to the wall.

'What's that doing on the floor?'

'The previous tenants left it. They used the living room as a second bedroom.'

'Why don't you shift it?'

'I can't be bothered.'

'But there's no room in here.'

'You get used to it.'

'You're bone bloody idle, you are.'

The wardrobe took up most of the floor space. Adam found it dull, wooden and obstructive. He expected it, any moment, to leave to take up a career in business. But the time required to move it was disproportionate to any single instance of being annoyed by its presence. Adam adapted to the wardrobe and lived around it.

'Have you done anything about a job yet?'

'Not really. I was going to have a look next week. I was going to head down to the BBC on Oxford Road or go down to Granada. I know a few people there.'

'There's a job going in the office at Crompton's.'

Crompton's was the mill at the bottom of the tunnels, at the foot of the hill. Though the mill had long since been bought by an American conglomerate, local people still gave it the original Lancastrian name of Mr Crompton who, in 1779, had invented the mule designed for fine spinning.

'It's not really my kind of thing, Dad.'

'No, I know that but you need something to take your mind off things. It'll tide you over until you get back on the rails. I said you'd go down Monday to have a word.'

Adam went to Crompton's on Monday morning to placate his father. He didn't really intend to take a job. The quickest route took him along the railway line and down through the tunnels but the rain had not relented throughout the first week of June and Adam preferred to walk half a mile further down the main road than ruin his suede shoes. As Adam emerged onto the Bolton road from the ginnel behind the all-night garage, Kevin McDermott was walking in the same direction, thirty yards behind, heading for his first day at Brown's Plumbers and Joiners. The two of them proceeded down opposite sides of the road at a constant distance, maintained deliberately by Kevin, of thirty yards. Adam stopped between Jimmy's barbers and the funny shop that sold only batteries. As the lights turned red he began to cross the road. Thirty yards behind, waiting round the bend, Kevin ducked behind a lamp-post, his brand-new over-sized blue overalls peeking out on each side. Kevin made himself thin as Adam disappeared into the cobbled cul-de-sac which led to Madison's paper mill.

Adam swaggered into reception, breaking into a walking dance to The Happy Mondays on Piccadilly Radio. He was greeted by a beautiful young woman with black ringlets, which she blew up fetchingly from her face as he announced that he had an appointment with Mr Littlewood, the managing director. This was the first time that Adam had seen Irene Bradshaw, as he still thought of her, for more than two years. Irene showed Adam through to Mr Littlewood's office where he decided he would, after all, take a temporary job as a clerk until the philosophical capital of the world could produce a job in TV production. Adam started at once and immediately impressed Mr Littlewood by staying late. His boss didn't realise that Adam was a man with a wardrobe on his floor who stayed at work because there was a ghost waiting for him at home.

Satisfied that Adam was out of sight, Kevin followed up the cobbled path to Brown's. He walked in on six men sitting at a small wooden table, drinking strong tea and reading the tabloids. Kevin asked for Mr Brown's office and one of the men pointed sullenly to his left. Joey Brown was a colossal, muscular man with a large handlebar moustache, a hairless head and sideburns which were like long arrows, pointing out his baldness. He looked like a stereotype of a gay man though he would have pointed out his wife, mistress and six children of various addresses as proof that there was nothing light on the loafers about Joey Brown. Kevin entered Mr Brown's office very sheepishly, ten minutes early.

'Mr Brown?'

'Aye.'

'I'm Kevin McDermott. Bob Matthews said to come.'

'Oh.'

Joey Brown spoke only in vowels. During this monosyllabic interview Joey never once let it slip that he didn't really want any relation of Sammy McDermott anywhere near his business. He'd agreed to see Kevin only because Bob Matthews had vouched for the younger McDermott. Kevin began that morning and his first job, repeated every day for a week, was to fetch pasties from the pie shop over the bridge.

Unadulterated

A month later Kevin had graduated from the pie shop to the back of the van. Early every morning he was thrown from side to side as his team drove up through the hills, over to Rossendale. The other three members, the senior partners of the gang, were Dave, Andy and Gerry. Dave was the company foreman, the right-hand man and trusted confidante of Joey Brown. Dave was thirty-eight years of age and had two children by Justine, his second wife. Dave's first wife, Helen, had lost her mind and tried to kill him but Dave did not welcome comments on his history. Dave was a no-frills, honest-to-goodness joiner who worked hard and liked a few beers. Dave taught Kevin the rules of the game. Any spare nuts and bolts and screws were perks. But the real hardware of the job was Joey Brown's property. This immediately put paid to Kevin's hope of meeting his sister Tina's request that he bring home some radiators to deliver her children from the cold.

The main perk of the job was a free fried breakfast. Every morning Dave pulled up at Rosemary's Kaf and the crew disembarked. Next to Dave, on the two available seats, sat Andy and Gerry, both thirty-three years of age and both married with two children. Both Andy and Gerry had black curly hair and both wore gold curtain-rail earrings in their right ears. The only way to tell Andy and Gerry were different people at all were that they were always together and that one answered to the name Andy and the other to the name Gerry. Dave bought Kevin breakfast every morning. The three of them read their tabloids, enjoyed the tits and the football, scooped up their tomato juice onto buttered white bread, discussed the rumours that Joey Brown was going bust and flirted with Rosemary before beginning their day's graft an hour later than usual.

Kevin was a bag carrier, the man who climbed up and down the scaffolding, the man who fetched the dinner, who made the brew. He sat in the back of the van amongst the equipment, providing sport for Dave who deliberately took corners far too sharply. Every morning, at the Ramsbottom roundabout with a view of Peel Tower, Kevin shot across the floor of the van, smashing his head into an open tool box. Oh, how they laughed, Andy and Gerry, Gerry and Andy, Gerryandy.

Dave, Gerry and Andy took a while to accept Kevin and he was very quiet with them at first. Kevin was preceded by his reputation as a bad 'un and he had to prove why he should be so deserving of Joey Brown's largesse when plenty of honest lads were looking for work. But after a month of fried breakfasts and smashing his head into a tool box Kevin felt at ease with Dave, Andy and Gerry and started to participate in their gentle mockery of each other. Kevin bore the abuse with equanimity and good humour and, in time, was permitted to answer back. He was also, tentatively, winning the battle against himself, renouncing the drugs he had come to rely on in prison.

Kevin was handy at his work, pinning a joint here, firing a pot-rivet gun there while, in the background, DJs from central casting begged for their ticket to London on Piccadilly Radio. When Gerry proved that he was distinct from Andy by being ill, Kevin showed how skilled he could be with his hands. Dave ceased fretting about leaving Kevin unsupervised and gave him advanced work to do. It was good to have a lad who was more than a passenger, more than a pinball for the van. Dave's verdict that the 'job's a good 'un' was always fine praise.

The banter and the repartee, the football and the tits, Kevin enjoyed them all, in reverse order. But, best of all he enjoyed the money. Every Thursday evening the Rossendale four called back in at the office to pick up their pay packets. They were paid in cash, in a brown envelope, on a weekly basis: wages not salaries. Kevin was paid three pounds an hour before tax for his fetching and carrying, plus time-and-a-half for overtime. Another perk of working out of the office was fiddling the hours. Dave prepared the time sheets and ensured that the starting and finishing times always included the entire journey home. Working away meant more coffee and cigarette breaks, less work, more pay and free breakfast. The week that the four of them spent in London fitting an investment bank on Fenchurch Street was a riot of bogus expenses. Kevin earned a hundred pounds a week which was all beer money except for the twenty pounds he gave Wendy for lodging. Against the advice of his father, who counselled profitable indolence, Kevin relented on his refusal to help Sandra and Darren.

His wage, and the respectability it conferred, meant that Kevin felt suddenly fortified in his relations with his wife. Irene had wrenched Jason off the Harwood estate into a three-bedroom semi-detached with a garden and a swing where he could learn to go over the top. Irene brought Jason back to the Harwood to see his father whenever Ian permitted.

'Can I take Jason out for the day next Saturday?'

'How are you going to manage that?'

Kevin was surprised but heartened that Irene did not know. With the swelling of huge pride he did not at all regret to inform her.

'Actually, I'm working.'

'You're what?'

'I'm working.'

'Where?'

'At Brown's. I'm learning to be a joiner.'

This was an exaggeration because Kevin was only really learning how to eat a fried breakfast and carry a tool box. But it was his moment of triumph. And with that Irene smiled at him. She smiled and, from behind the creases that age and indigence had lined into her face, the stunning young girl peeped out, the daughter of the rampaging gypsy with the wild hair and dark, delicious eyes. Kevin turned, without speaking, and walked, with his head held up and his back arched. Irene stood, tight-lipped and watched him go. She watched him go, dear Kevin McDermott whom she still loved, in some buried fibre of her being.

The following Saturday Kevin stood outside McDonald's to wait for his son. A low-slung red sports car pulled up sharply, travelling far too quickly for the busy town centre street, with a perturbed looking four-year-old on Irene's knee. As Irene contorted herself out of the passenger door she blew her fringe into the air. Irene set Jason down on the pavement and he ran, as fast as his legs would carry him, into the outstretched arms of his father. Kevin swept Jason up into the air five times, on each occasion exulting with joy. Irene rudely interrupted the theatrical display by saying without feeling: 'Make sure you look after him.'

'I will.'

'We'll pick him up here at six.'

Kevin found a tenderness in his voice that he did not know he was capable of.

'Thank you.'

Irene recognised that there was no anger in Kevin's speech. She responded gingerly: 'It's all right. And Kevin?'

'What?'

'I think I might get Susan back.'

'Good.'

Kevin spoke almost inaudibly, ashamed that Susan was permitted back into Flash Ian's life but not his own. Irene dropped her head and climbed into the car which sped her back to the semi with the garden. On the way to Greenmount from Bury they passed through Brandlesholme. From the top of the hill, the peak of the green mount, Irene and Flash Ian looked down on the Brangy warriors of life.

Down in the valley, father and son walked the fifteen yards into McDonald's where Kevin indulged Jason with a far too Big Mac and a huge carton of Coke. Jason was delighted to be with his dad for the day. He bragged about being Cock of Greenmount Nursery School as they stood in the queue with the silent weekend-dads, picking up their plastic food as a bribe in declining relationships.

Kevin tried to explain to Jason that Darren was his new brother even though he had a different mummy. The explanation failed but Kevin's esteem did not suffer in the eyes of his son. Jason was still young enough to have no criticism of his father. Jason McDermott was the only person on earth who thought Kevin the finest man alive. He was proud to have Kevin McDermott as his dad. Jason had a complete, childlike, unadulterated love for his father. Kevin knew lots of words that, strung together in the right order, would announce the fine feeling that lived inside him. He had no way of pulling these words together. Jason was a boy of very few words and yet thoroughly articulate. As father and son sat down to eat from plastic trays Jason looked straight at Kevin, put his arms around him and said, with a child's eloquence: 'Dad. It's great, this.'

Jason was doing his job, doing it well. He was being the person who thinks Kevin McDermott is the best. Not the best at anything in particular; just the best. He was exciting the finer feelings for which Kevin had no words. Kevin swallowed hard to prevent himself from breaking into tears in McDonald's surrounded by emotionally vacant weekend-dads and their bored offspring. With a single hug and four words from a four-year-old child Kevin was cut apart, increased by tears.

Tom Jones in Italics

To his great surprise Adam began to enjoy his work. He found an odd pleasure in reconciling columns of figures and great satisfaction in the fearful symmetry of balance sheets. Adam scored twenty-four out of twenty-four every day. At dinnertime he enjoyed the games of football that took place on the patch of waterlogged grass on the other side of the railway bank. Just occasionally he managed a whole morning without Elizabeth or Peter's cat-flick attacking his brain.

And then there was Irene. Adam's office was next to the reception where Irene sat blowing her hair up off her face. As soon as he had completed his sums for the day Adam lingered in reception, reading the newspaper, singing along to 'Where the Streets Have no Name (I Can't Take my Eyes off you)', drinking coffee out of paper cups and regaling Irene with some-one else's autobiography. Adam told tales from the pen of another Crompton of Bury, doing funny voices for Just William and Violet Elizabeth Bott. He composed poems at his desk but even Adam knew they were too evidently risible. They were full of words that Irene would never use and of sentiments she would never believe. Adam's poems were a very long-winded and pretentious way of saying: 'Attention, attention; I'm a sensitive idiot.' Adam had a hole cut in his life in the shape of Elizabeth. He cut Irene out of cardboard and slotted her into it.

On his first Friday Irene introduced Adam to his new colleagues over bitter in the Earl of Derby. He was immediately trapped at the bar with Phil from the post room. Adam was finding Phil insufferably dull until he mentioned that he had recently married Maria McDermott. As soon as it was no longer rude to do so, Adam extricated himself from Phil, to the latter's complete relief.

'Bloody hell, he's not much fun is he?' said Phil, restarting what had lately become a fertile topic of conversation in Madison's post room.

Adam sidled over to Irene who was talking to Gary, one of the company's salesmen. Gary was a caricature hairdresser. Not a hirsute barber, like Jimmy, but a hairdresser. Gary was tall, with sunbed-drenched skin and blonde tints in his hair. Gary wore well-pressed black slacks and a silk shirt open three buttons down to demonstrate his gymnasium pectorals.

'Hiya,' said Gary in an accent as Bury as black puddings and Peel Tower.

'Hello. Nice to meet you.'

'Oh bloody hell, we've got a right posh 'un here. Where you from?'

'I'm from round here but I've been livin' away.' Adam left the 'g' off deliberately.

'Where've you been then?'

'First in Cambridge; then in London. But I came back recently.'

'Oh right.'

'Do you know London?'

'Yes.' Gary said 'yes' in the sense of 'yes, I have heard of it'.

'Have you ever been down?'

'I don't think so.'

'*I don't think so*,' thought Adam, who found himself drawn irresistibly into idiocy.

'It's about two hundred miles away.' As though that cleared it up. As though Gary would now suddenly remember London. The London that's two hundred miles away as opposed to the one just off the Bolton bypass.

'Did you, like, buy house down there?'

'No, we just rented.'

306

'I've just got this new house up Holcombe Brook. Could you not get house down there, like?'

'Everyone lives in flats really.'

'I wouldn't fancy that. I wouldn't want to share my bog with people I don't know and all that sort of stuff, like.'

'We had a little studio of our own.'

'I've got a semi,' said Gary, with complete triumph. 'Excuse me,' he added and shuffled off to the toilet.

'I wouldn't want to share our bog and that sort of stuff, like,' wittered Adam with cruel mockery.

'Oh, don't be so horrible,' said Irene with an indulgent laugh.

'Well his voice is ridiculous.'

'It's not that bad. Everyone talks like that really.'

'I don't.'

'That's just because you, Adam Matthews, are a Bury Grammar Cambridge University posh snob, and you know it.'

'Just because you've lived somewhere other than Bury, it doesn't make you a posh snob, you know.'

'Yes it does.'

This was Adam's cue to embark on a selective autobiography, the version in which he appeared as a windswept, interesting and, at times, slightly tragic hero. The culmination of his disquisition was a comparison of his own picaresque with that of Tom Jones.

'Oooh, me mum likes him.'

'Who?'

'Tom Jones.'

Storing this exchange away as an anecdote, Adam knew already that Irene and he were doomed, damned by a single phrase. Adam belonged with the Northern diaspora, lost for all time in the metropolis. He took his place in the long line of glory boys who walked southward with their spotted hankies down motorways sixty-two, six and one. A vision of Elizabeth flashed through his head.

Irene looked at her watch and got up very suddenly to leave.

'I've got to go.'

'Do you have to?'

'Yes. See you tomorrow.'

'Hang on a minute.'

Irene's mood had altered so quickly that Adam was intrigued to know more.

'Can't you have just one more?'

'No, I'm late already. Ian doesn't like it if I'm late.'

'Can't you ring him? It's only eight.'

'I'd better go.'

As Irene made once more to leave Adam placed his hand on her shoulder with insufficient force to prevent her from going but with enough feeling to mark a change in their relationship immediately evident to both of them.

'Just one more. I'm sure Ian will understand.'

'I don't think he will.'

'What kind of tyrant is he?'

'What?'

'What kind of person is he if he won't let you have a drink after work?'

'He gets really angry about that sort of thing.'

'You can't let him tell you what to do like that. Do you want another?'

'I want one but . . .'

'Then I'm going to get you one.'

Adam skipped to the bar before Irene could change her mind. When he returned with two bottles of lager he found Irene sobbing into her glass.

'Irene! Irene, what is it? What's up?'

There were no tears, only a physical jerk forcing Irene's bosom and nostrils up and down in a strange dance of the sobs. She took a long, shallow breath and looked hard at Adam, who wondered, not for the first time, at how sexy she was.

'He gets so angry if I'm late. But I don't mean anything by it.'

'You can't let him get away with that.'

'He just loses control. It's really scary.'

'Does he ever hit you?'

'Well no, not really.'

'What do you mean, not really?'

308

Irene did not answer. She dropped her head slowly.

'Do you mean yes?'

'Only once or twice.'

Adam put his hand under Irene's chin to lift her head. He stroked her cheekbone and planted a soft kiss on her forehead.

'You can't put up with that.'

'It's not that simple.'

'It is that simple.'

'It isn't. I've got kids to think about. Jason's at school and I'm getting Susan back.'

'You can't bring her back into a house where you're getting knocked about.'

'But Ian's done a lot for us. He's got us a nice house and he's just having it done up. He's fitted double glazing and he's turned the cubby hole under the stairs into a new loo. It's a good place for the kids.'

'What, the loo?'

'No, you idiot. The house.'

'And is it a good place for you?'

'That's not the point.'

'It is the point, sweetheart. If you're unhappy there do you think Jason doesn't know? Children are not stupid, you know.'

'I don't think he does.'

'Don't kid yourself. 'Course he knows. Sweetheart, you can't stay in a house where some bastard is beating you up.'

'It's not that bad.'

'Stop making excuses for him.'

Adam took Irene's hand from around her glass and clenched it, very tight, as if to fortify her for the counsel he was about to give.

'Irene, you've got to get out. You must. For the children.'

'You're a right bossy one, you are.'

Irene thought that if she told him he was known in the office as Saddam Matthews that it might change the subject. It didn't.

'I mean it. You've got to get out.'

'I've thought about it. But where would I go?'

'I don't know. What about your mum?'

309

'She's got no room. And anyway, she's in Liverpool and our Jason's settled at school.'

'You could stay with me.'

'You haven't got any spare rooms.'

'I know. I've got a wardrobe you could sleep in.'

'You what?'

'Nothing. What about Kevin? Could you not stay there for a bit?'

'At his mum's?'

'It's better than a beating.'

Irene bit her bottom lip with her top teeth but said nothing.

'Isn't it?'

'Kevin had another baby and he didn't even mention it to me.'

Before the dance of the sobs could begin again Adam had extended both arms around Irene's neck and let his lips rest on hers. As she responded to his advance, he gently opened his mouth and, through a display of such mastery, negated all his attendant virtue.

After four more bottles each Adam and Irene took a taxi up to Greenmount. They were both delighted to find that the absent Ian had not applied the curfew to himself. Irene collected enough clothes for a week and set out to join Jason who was staying the night with his father and his grandparents.

And so for Kevin the goddess Fortuna arrived at the eleventh hour as he lay sleeping. He was woken by Sammy, in his vest and pants, shaking him awake with urgent news.

'Come downstairs, lad.'

'What for?'

Sammy left the room without further explanation, his pants pulled down to reveal a sightly portion of bottom cleavage, like a legendary builder. Kevin yawned and, without any particular curiosity, struggled to his feet. Sammy's cigarette coughs were visible in the air in front as Kevin followed down the creaking stairs. Kevin stumbled into the living room, curiosity still not overwhelming fatigue. A fair sight met his sore eyes.

'Make us all some coffee, Sam,' said Wendy. Jason's plaintive cries could be heard from the landing so Wendy headed upstairs to take him back to bed. Irene felt bloated. She looked pale and nervous and she had a splitting headache.

'What's up?' said Kevin, more ungraciously than he meant.

'Can I stay here tonight?'

'Why?'

'I've left Ian.'

'Why?'

'I just have.'

'So what happened?'

'Can we talk about this in the morning, Kevin? I need to sleep.'

Sammy wandered in with four cups of coffee that nobody wanted. He drank one and Kevin drank another, to while away the time as Irene went upstairs to check on Jason.

Irene walked into Kevin's bedroom where the two of them had made love under the covers in the early days. She found Wendy perched on the end of the bed, smiling to herself, with Jason's index finger twirled around her own. Jason looked a clown in Kevin's pyjamas with the sleeves and the legs comically turned up.

'Is he asleep, the little bugger?'

'Not so little now. He's on the way.'

'OK, I'll see you in the morning, Wendy.'

'Irene, stay up a minute. Sit down, love.'

Irene sat down next to Wendy, whose rotund face seemed suddenly lifted. Wendy placed a hand affectionately on the dark skin of Irene's arm. It was a newly tender gesture from a woman who had never before shown Irene anything other than suspicion.

'Is Susan going to be all right, Irene love?'

'I think so. I think as long as she's feeding properly it should be all right.'

'If you need anything, love, you've only got to ask.'

'I will.'

'It must be hard not having your mum here.'

'It is.'

'Look, love, I'm sorry I wasn't more help when they took

311

Susan away. Our Kevin was going through a bad patch and I was worried about him.'

'You are his mum.'

'I know but I didn't think about you or the little one. Me and Sam weren't much help.'

'I don't know if you could have done anything.'

'We could have. This time we've all got to pull together more. We've got to make sure that Susan gets all she needs. When she comes out we can't have her being taken off you again. You're a good mother, a lot better than I've ever been.'

Wendy's face had an aspect that Irene had not seen before. She looked crestfallen, consumed by sorrow, an overweight, ugly woman who, suddenly displaying emotional tenderness it did not seem was within her, cast herself in a loveable beauty. With one hand clasped to Irene's arm and her index finger curled around Jason's, Wendy unburdened herself of a pain she had not mentioned in more than thirty years.

'If I tell you something, love, do you promise not to breathe a word of it? Not to Kevin; not to anyone.'

'Promise.'

'When I was a kid, I had a baby, long before I met Sam and we had our Irene. It was a young lad. He was a lovely little thing. I called him Darren. I got pregnant by a lad who used to live round here but he's been gone thirty years now, I don't know where. Well, it were quite a scandal still in them days and my dad said I had to get rid of the kid. I said he couldn't make me and I wanted it. You see, love, I wanted a little baby so I could look after it and be like my mum. My dad was never there and when he was he used to drink a lot and hit us and when we'd gone to bed he'd hit our mum. My mum was on my side but when I had the baby my dad put his foot down and he made me give Darren up for adoption. They took him away and I've never seen him since. He'll be in his thirties now.'

'Do you still think about him much?'

'I think about him all the time, especially now the other kids are grown up and left home. I imagine that he lives down London and he's got a right good posh job like Adam Matthews got. And I think that one day he'll come into the club in posh clothes looking for his mum and then we'll . . .'

Wendy's voice broke off as her fantasy proved too much.

'So dear, whatever else happens, when we get little Susan back we can't let her go again. So like I say, love, anything we can do, just ask. I'm always here.'

Irene hugged her mother-in-law and implored her to smile which she managed, weakly. The door creaked open and Sammy peeped his head round.

'All right, ladies?' he said with inapposite gaiety.

'We're just coming, Sam. We'll be down.'

Sammy made more unwanted coffees which all four drank this time, small-talking. Conversation between Irene and Kevin did not come easily but Sammy did a passable job of filling in the gaps. After ten minutes of lethargic chat, Kevin took command.

'So what happened?'

'Nothing much.'

'So what are you doing here, then?'

Irene stared down at swirling patterns which seemed to revolve in increasing, unfocused circles the longer she gazed. The brown and muddy yellow of the gruesome carpet swayed like the movement of a wave and Irene sat in silent sickness, unwilling to involve Kevin in her private affair but aware that she had nowhere else to go.

'I just had to get out of there.'

'I thought you liked all that flash bollocks, fitted carpets and two bogs.'

'It's nothing to do with that.'

'I thought you loved the flash bastard. That's what you told me, anyway.'

'I was wrong about him. We all make mistakes. Like you must of.'

'And that's it? You've suddenly realised that you don't like him when it's not five minutes ago that you were talking about divorce.'

'I couldn't stay there any more, Kev.'

Irene's tone had changed. It had lost its defensiveness and turned into a plea.

'What's he done to you?'

'Nothing.'

'I don't believe you. Tell me. What's he done? I know he's done something. He's been slapping you about, hasn't he?'

Irene's silence was all the confirmation that Kevin required.

'The fucking cunt. I'll fucking have him.'

Kevin, assistant to the Cock of Bury, Kevin writhing on the muddy floor with Terry Berry, was rising to the surface. He leapt up from the sofa to fetch his coat. Irene asked a redundant question.

'Where are you going?'

'I'm going to teach that flash twat a lesson I should have taught him yonks ago.'

'No Kevin.'

Kevin ignored Irene's call and headed for the door with fire in his eyes. Irene could not let him go. She tugged at his coat sleeves, at first imploringly, then hysterically. Irene screamed as she never had since childhood, since the time she ran round the Harwood estate shouting ally ally eeno. The game was over, there had been a breach of the rules and ally ally eeno is never called in jest. For once Kevin yielded to Irene. He came back inside where the pair of them spent the night on the sofa, bolt upright, in each other's arms, on a fire engine and a milk float. Kevin slept not a wink. It was his best night for three years.

Honest

Adam's enthusiasm for his temporary work lasted three weeks. The satisfaction of balancing sheets of figures wore off and Adam simply stopped. He sat there, occupying the space, as if his chair had developed a lump in the shape of his body. And occupying the space, sitting useless, unproductive and immobile was somehow, just about, all right. If Adam had wandered the nearby streets, investing wrongly remembered lines of poetry with untenable personal meaning, that would have been a dereliction of duty. But Adam got away with occupying a seat. It had become his occupation.

He sought solace in the Monday jobs pages of the *Guardian* and in flirting with Irene. The first day of every new week promised him a return behind the looking-glass of the television screen. Every other day promised a dinnertime walk with Irene, through the pretty yellow weeds which emerged every May, up to the pastie shop at the bridge over the Irwell. Adam bragged away to demonstrate that, along with his promiscuous confidence, he had brought sophistication with him up motorways one, six and sixty-two. By mutual silence, they ignored the kiss they had shared, for which they competed in guilt. Adam tortured his logic by dreaming of Irene providing the affection that he had recently been denied. But of all her attributes, the only ones he did not mangle in his head were physical.

Irene told Adam instead that she thought about running away but her mother had no room for three semi-permanent house-guests. Irene now depended on the generosity of her estranged husband and Dawn was trapped in her own home, a prisoner of another enraged member of the male species. Dawn would have loved to offer a home to Irene, Jason and Susan but she was so submerged under her new man that she dared not even ask. So, Irene made the best of it in the McDermott house. Jason and Susan had the three sisters' old room. When one of the girls was at home, which was often, given the fraught nature of their relationships, a camp-bed was hastily assembled and everyone moved up.

Maria had left Bury when her husband Phil left the mill for a factory in Bacup. She had broken off all contact with her parents after her husband and her father came to drunken blows in the Greenhill Club over the right way to bring up children. It barely pained Maria never to return to Bury but Adam, Shane and Louise missed their grandparents. Irene's children, Sammy, Graham, Simon and Angela, were the most frequent visitors as Andy and Irene lived on the Harwood estate. The Howarth lads had established themselves as the high pugilists of the next generation, feted every bit as much as their uncle Kevin, one-time Cock of St Thomas's primary school.

There was one other grandchild who *never* visited. Nathan had just told his mother that he had got into Elton Moor, by now the best comprehensive in Bury and that he wanted to go to university in Manchester one day. Irene received this news with a proud tear in her eye because the word 'university' sounded so far away and so magical.

Tina turned up one night, her face as orange as her hair, with tears streaming through her freckles. She had split up from Steve because he was no help with their daughter Mary who was plainly very ill with whooping cough. Scott and Mary moved in to join the unhappy hoards looking at their own breath. Kevin decided to decorate the bedroom to cheer his youngest sister and even got as far as stripping the walls. As the soggy paper fell to the floor the damp seeped out. Tina called the council and a voice said they would come.

Amid this moving cast of thousands in one bedroom, Irene moved back reluctantly into the marital bed. Kevin did not understand why she would withhold sexual favours but, after a couple of essays in gentle coercion, he at least stopped trying.

Kevin was, at least, making an effort now. He had graduated to the third seat in the van after Andy proved once and for all that he was distinct from his twin Gerry by moving to the Wirral to live with a woman he met in a Birkenhead club after the Bury versus Tranmere match. Andy left with the claim that Joey Brown's would be closing down soon, 'any road up', as he put it himself.

The third seat in the van brought with it no extra money but it was a prestigious seat, a seat of learning. Kevin enjoyed work. It was better than plummeting down the road never again travelled back to Strangeways. Joey Brown's wasn't quite a horn of plenty but it was a horn of a little more than usual. Kevin's new junior was his old adversary Terry Berry, finding his first work for five years to support two wives, three mothers and four children. Terry now insisted on being called Terence, having finally realised that his name was ridiculous otherwise.

Kevin loved having Irene back, even on platonic terms. He tip-toed over eggshells in sudden chivalry. Kevin was now bringing in enough money to buy the scorned vegetables that would keep Susan at home. Sometimes there was enough left over for a treat. Sandra McEwan was touched to receive a first birthday present for Darren from Kevin. Irene had relented on her initial demand that Kevin ignore Darren when she saw Sandra opening the door onto a cold dark flat on the Harwood estate.

The greatest treat, for Kevin anyway, was the chance to take Jason to his first football match. Jason sat in a blue plastic seat at Gigg Lane for the first game of the season, while Kevin recounted the great Bury sides of the past.

'I thought you liked City, Dad.'

'I do but Bury are my second team. I used to play for them.'

'But Bury are rubbish.'

'No, they're not. They've won the FA Cup twice.

'Was that last season?'

'No, it was 1903.'

This seemed such a very long time ago to Jason that he

decided there and then to support Manchester United. The spectacle before them was turgid and third division and Kevin spent the ninety minutes trying to make Jason see that Manchester City could be better than Manchester United even though they clearly *weren't* better than them.

He woke up the next morning to find that he was looking forward to going to work. Getting up suddenly seemed like a good idea. Kevin had a routine day but, as he was packing up the van to leave the site, a red Porsche flashed onto the car park. Kevin was aroused by a shiver of recognition. A toothy salesman bounced out and swaggered towards the administration office of the factory. Flash Ian was twenty yards away from Kevin who, staring at him, salvaged the memory that ally ally eeno is never called in jest and let him go.

It was an ordinary day's graft but, on the way home, Kevin remembered that he had left his coat behind and so asked Dave to drop him off at work. By the time they arrived everyone had left for the evening so Dave lent Kevin his keys. As he was collecting his coat, the telephone rang. It was Joey Brown.

'Is Bob still there, lad?'

'No, I don't think he were in today. He's not been so good.'

'What about Dave?'

'No, there's only me here. Dave's gone home.'

'OK, I'll ring him there.'

Kevin arrived home to find an ambulance waiting outside the house. Tina ran out shrieking. She and her mum went in the ambulance up to Bury General Hospital, where in the dead of night, Mary McDermott stopped coughing once and for all. She was the same age as Wendy's grandmother's lost little sister Mary who died of the same affliction in 1900.

Sammy announced the news to the family at breakfast. Kevin could not begin to think what to say. He slipped out as soon as he could get away. As soon as he arrived at work, he was summoned to see Joey Brown.

'You're not even clever, are you?'

'What?'

'It's no wonder you get nicked so easy.'

'What do you mean?'

'Don't come the bloody innocent with me, you little bastard. I fucking knew we shouldn't have bothered with a fucking jailbird. There's plenty of lads who'll do a honest day's toil without robbing owt from you.'

'What are you on about? I haven't robbed owt.'

'So radiators get up and walk, do they? We had six brand-new radiators delivered yesterday, sitting over yonder. I gets in this morning and they've fucking scarpered. Got up in the middle of the fucking night and legged it? I *don't* fucking think. I was the last to leave the office and they were still there. And then you turned up and, like a fucking idiot, in the middle of robbing the bastards you answered the fucking phone. You couldn't make it up, you really fucking couldn't.'

'It wasn't me. I don't know anything about it, I don't. Honest.'

'Honest. You don't know the meaning of the fucking word. I should have known that any son of that bastard wouldn't last five minutes without nicking something. It's in your fucking blood, you lot. Do you think we can do with having stuff nicked like that? We're not doing fucking brilliant as it is. Didn't you even think you might be fucking things up for good just so you can flog six fucking radiators?'

'No, no. It wasn't me. I swear it. I don't know what you're on about.'

Joey snapped like a shot of a gun. He was a large and fearsome man and even a former Cock of his school such as Kevin recoiled in fear. He did not need to say any more. Kevin was finished. Even now, on the verge of an assault from Joey, Kevin's only thought was that he had let Bob Matthews and Irene down.

Kevin did not sink into depression so much as drop into it in a single movement. Sammy reacted typically by skulking down to have it out with Joey Brown and received a black eye for his trouble. Joey Brown could really look after himself. He was the Tez Satchel of the dads. Kevin went into immediate hibernation, barely appearing in the open air, so frightened was he of seeing Bob Matthews. He sat in his room alone, communicating with nobody. Even with the need to console

Tina, Wendy watched Kevin like a spy as he sank deeper and deeper into his mattress.

He rose from his sloth on the Saturday night, at Wendy's behest, to accompany his father in pouring benefit down his throat. As Kevin approached the door of the Greenhill he saw through the window that Bob and June were in their usual seats. He also noticed that Adam was with them. Kevin put his arm gently across his father and without an explanation, pointed to a table in the far corner, away from the eyes of the man with no respect for the rules of urinals and his finely tailored son.

Adam had seen Sammy and Kevin come in. He was relieved when they settled out of his line of vision. When Adam's round came he checked that Kevin was not at the bar. He did not visit the toilet all night, to his leg-shaking discomfort, and surprised his mother by being delighted when the bingo began. Alice's bingo fund continued its impressive performance, defying the laws of averages, mathematics and natural justice.

The turn did a first set, then there was the buffet and, full of the only pork pies he had eaten since his last visit to the club, Adam chatted to Tony Greaves who was the foreman at a ducting company in Whitefield. Tony managed to look like both Ron Atkinson and John Craven at the same time. He was the middle man in the photograph fade series from one to the other.

'How's work, squire?' Adam inquired.

'It's a job.'

'Is it going all right?'

'It's a job.'

Tony would not pretend he enjoyed it. He had a job though.

Adam checked that Kevin was still seated and bought another round of drinks. The turn was ready to resume with her dance section as Adam leapt back and forth, between their table and the bar. As he was leaving the bar a man asked Adam if he was interested in radiators.

'What, in the abstract, as a field of study?' he thought but did not say.

Adam was thinking about Elizabeth. He was not interested

in radiators and did not wish to buy any, even though they did sound impossibly cheap. And, after an unfeasibly large mouthful, it looked like Kevin might need to head for the bar. Adam thought nothing of the strange offer as he retreated to the sanctuary of his seat.

'This place gets weirder every time I come. Some bloke just tried to sell me a radiator.'

'Which bloke?' asked Bob, suddenly animated.

'That one.'

Adam pointed to the man he had spoken to at the bar and was amazed by his father's response.

'Fucking hell. The bastard.'

Brangy Warriors Once Again

The low dirge of the parlour's music accompanied the funeral gait of the McDermott family as they made their way into the blank, grey room in which the ashes of little Mary were waiting behind a scarlet curtain. Tina sobbed quietly, comforted by Wendy. Irene and Maria thanked the grace by which they had been spared this fate and muttered reassuring platitudes to their sister. Kevin said nothing. He was deeply touched but unable to find the words. He held his wife's hand so tight that he was hurting her. In the background, Tina McDermott was now declaiming hysterically to Steve that she would never go back to the freezing flat they had shared and which she blamed for exacerbating Mary's condition. She ignored Bob and June Matthews who approached her to sympathise and who moved on instead to Kevin.

'We're sorry, Kevin,' said June.

'Yeah.' Bob looked at Kevin through cigarette smoke, disconcertingly straight between the eyes. 'I knew it wasn't you.'

Kevin was confused and even a little frightened by Bob's sudden change of direction. This was the first time Kevin had seen Bob Matthews since the radiator scandal a week ago. Kevin was scared of being arraigned as a scoundrel before the court of a good man.

'What wasn't me?'

'The radiators. I knew it wasn't you.'

'It wasn't me, Bob. It wasn't me.'

Kevin finally opened up and his sorrow burst forth. Wendy,

Sammy and the girls assumed Kevin was crying for Mary. Bob stood, impassive, as Kevin delivered an emotional broadside consisting of only eight words, repeated again and again: 'I didn't do it, Bob. It wasn't me.'

Bob waited for Kevin's passion to burn out and said simply: 'I know what happened. I know who it was.'

'Who?'

'Never mind.'

There would be no vigilantes this time. The culprit would be dealt with properly and it would be enough of a personal tragedy for Dave, the thirty-eight-year-old foreman with two children to support in a precarious second marriage.

'Come to Brown's tomorrow at ten.'

'What for?'

'For your job back. Joey's a fair man. When he knows it wasn't you who nicked the radiators he'll give you another go.'

Kevin was too wounded to allow this.

'He can fuck off. He can stick his fucking job. He fucking accused me and I told him it wasn't me.'

'I know but you can hardly blame him, can you? It did look bad.'

'But he had no proof and he fucking kicked me out. Whenever anything goes missing it'll always be my fucking fault.'

'Yes, Kevin, it will, but you made your own bed, sunshine. There's nothing you can do about that now, but feeling sorry for yourself won't do any good. You've done well with the drugs but you can't stop now. You've got to swallow your pride and get down to work. It's the only way. Now think on.'

Bob looked intently at Kevin and took a long brown envelope from his coat pocket.

'I've never shown this to anyone before. I want you to read it. And as I said, think on.'

Kevin opened the envelope Bob had given him. It contained a piece of paper with lots of handwriting in boxes. Kevin looked at it briefly and then folded the paper back up and replaced it in the brown envelope.

Irene picked up where Bob had left off.

'If they know it wasn't you, you can go back in.'

'Why should I? They sacked me without even listening.'

'But Kevin, we need the money.'

'So what?'

'So what? The kids need new shoes. That's so what.' Joey Brown knows you didn't do it. What more do you want?'

'I'm not going, Irene. Why should I? He accused me.'

'Kevin . . .'

'Irene, I'm not going.'

'But Kev . . .'

'I don't want to talk about it.'

Irene decided it would be better to reconvene the following day.

'Why don't you come down to Crompton's tomorrow? I can ask around for you and we can go and get some dinner.'

'Don't know.'

'Oh, go on. Isn't seeing me better than lying here?'

Irene put a consoling arm around her husband. Irene knew already that Crompton's had nothing for Kevin. Crompton's too was learning how to decline. But Irene knew that a pastie and some chips from the pie shop meant that, briefly, Kevin would once again be walking upright down the road with his gaze fixed in the world above eye level.

Kevin arrived at twelve-fifteen the next day and was met by a kaleidoscope of sports kit. The men of the mill were trooping through the carpeted lobby in their mud-caked training shoes on the way over the railway bank. At the back of the group, ostentatiously juggling the ball, Kevin noted Adam. Irene reached for her handbag but before she could get any further the captain of the footballers greeted Kevin as a long-lost old friend.

'Hey Kev, how you doing?'

'All right.'

'Good to see you.'

Kevin had not seen Tez Satchel, the Cock of his once glorious world, since he had disappeared into Strangeways. But here was

Tez, the leader, as ever, of a weekly kick-about on long wet grass in the sunken bog of the railway bank.

'Do you still play?'

'Not really.'

'Fancy a kick about?'

'I haven't got any stuff.'

'You're hardly in your Sunday best. Those trainers'll do.'

Kevin looked at Irene who smiled, indulging him.

'Go on then.'

Adam and Kevin avoided one another studiously as the group climbed up the railway bank and down the other side. Kevin caught up with Tez Satchel. Adam juggled the ball and said nothing. But when Tez picked Kevin and Adam to be on the same team they could avoid each other no longer. Adam hit the ball to Kevin who looked up at him. They stopped, struggling for words, fiddling with the gearing mechanism of their time apart. There was a long silence, the silence of the difference of their years.

'How are you?' asked Kevin.

'OK.'

'I heard.'

'About?'

'You know. Your bird.'

'What have you been up to?' Adam evaded.

'Not much, you know.'

'Should be a good game, this. You be Blackie Gray and I'll be Roy Race.'

'I'm Tubby Morton these days.'

'You said it.'

What *was* Tubby Morton doing in Kevin's head after all these years? The two of them stood in the soggy grass, enduring a second extended silence, a silence more eloquent than anything they could muster to say.

There was only one subject that Kevin and Adam still had in common. Unable to speak to one another after their break, suddenly the passage of time and their disparate experiences in worlds pulled apart by a gear stick produced a great divide.

Adam and Kevin regressed to childhood, which was where they only ever really existed together. Kevin and Adam could ride bikes together, make dens together, find tramps together, walk on the wrong side of bridges together, crush tunes together or they would do nothing at all. Their common language was football and it was to the undisguised relief of both that Tez arranged the coats on the floor, kicked the ball into the makeshift goal and declared that his team were winning 1–0. And so, after a seven-year hitch, Kevin and Adam came to be playing football together, like Brangy Warriors once again, overlooking the reservoir where once they went fishing.

Kevin hadn't kicked a ball in anger since his injury. Kevin had always been a thick-set child but the natural musculature of youth had dropped away, leaving unexercised flab hanging on a small frame. With his pale complexion and his red hair now too long Kevin was the very picture of ill-health. He looked like Shaggy from *Scooby Doo* fed on pork pies from the Greenhill rather than tall sandwiches. His extra weight counted straight away and he was too slow to get into the game. After five minutes of strenuous effort the cigarettes were taking their toll as Kevin wheezed his way round the field, struggling to catch his breath. He was reduced to a strangely quick hobble, like the athletes in the ten-kilometre walk who have deliberately handicapped themselves by refusing to run. If there were a version of football that were played at a walk, then Kevin was playing it. Adam, no less of a stick insect, was charging around as if he were still an eleven-year-old kid.

And then a moment that makes the heart ache for all the lost souls whose talent explodes before their very eyes. Adam won the ball over on his favoured left side. He looked up and saw Kevin in space, bent over with his hands on his knees. Adam hit the ball hard, far too hard, at Kevin. It was a poor pass, over-hit, misjudged. Kevin took a lazy pace to his right, virtually caught the flying ball on his instep and dropped it right in front where three opposing Brangy warriors were snapping at his feet. With a swivel of Kevin's hips not visible to the untrained human eye, three hopeless fools fell over, leaving Kevin to walk through unhindered. He repeated the trick on the goalkeeper who oblig-ingly rolled over and let Kevin slide the ball effortlessly between Tez Satchel's coat and his own.

That touch. It was still there. The touch you never lose. A hypertrophied Kevin McDermott will one day be on the threshold of death and someone will throw a ball at him which he will bring to rest perfectly by his right foot. He will flick the ball up and juggle it for hours. He was champion of the North-West under-sixteen age group at juggling a football though no one would have known it from the chips-and-gravy figure he had become. But a majestic swivel of Kevin McDerm-ott's hips and whole teams used to fall over. He could have made it, could Kevin McDermott. He really could have made it.

His display of raw talent lifted Kevin and the next morning he got out of bed before nine for the first time since he was sacked. He washed and shaved in cold water, got dressed and walked down the boring road, past the boring shops to Brown's Plumbers and Joiners. The first person he saw was Gerry who had that minute resigned to start his own business as a carpenter. Gerry wished Kevin all the best and gave him a small wooden box, carved exquisitely and delicately by his own hand.

Kevin walked into Joey Brown's office without knocking. Joey, who didn't like interruptions, stood up from his desk and offered his enormous hand. Kevin shook it.

'I'm glad you've come. I want you to take the van. We've a job on in Burnley.'

Kevin lifted his chin, stared hard at the world above eye level and took up the wheel in the van.

Lord of the Dance

Adam's first application came good. An executive producer at Granada TV in Manchester was delighted to find a local boy with some experience. Adam was appointed co-assistant producer on a new cookery series that was set for national distribution. Adam began to instruct the bourgeoisie in the preparation of linguine with gorgonzola, pancetta and wilted rocket. It was a far cry from chips and gravy.

On Christmas Eve Adam had to say two goodbyes. It was easy to say goodbye to Mr Littlewood who, although sorry to lose someone with such arithmetical facility, realised that Adam would be trouble as soon as he was bored. It was more difficult to say goodbye to Irene. During the dinner break on what he knew would be his last day, Adam asked Irene if she would go for a walk around the reservoir.

To his great discomfort Irene was annoyed and asked him what he had thought he wanted from her. Adam went into a prolix and inappropriate discussion of his deeper feelings, the intractable, irrepressible longing he still felt for Elizabeth.

'So what were you doing coming on to me?'

'It was a mistake.'

'Oh thanks a lot. It's really nice to know that I was a mistake.'

'No, I don't mean it like that. You know what I mean.'

Adam felt wretched at his behaviour. There was a momentary silence which seemed to last a geological era. Adam waded in with nonsense. Armed with too much poetry and too little understanding he drowned Irene in words. When Irene asked him again, bluntly, what he had hoped for he was forced to confess that he had no idea. He had even less idea what she might have wanted. Adam was incapable of recognising her sorrow, lost as he was in his own.

'So is that it then?'

'I think that's best, don't you?'

'I don't know.'

Irene looked sadly at Adam through her fringe which drooped over her eyes.

'You've got Kevin to go back to. I've got no one.'

'Don't bloody tell me what I've got to go back to. What do you know about it? You've not lived round here for years. You've no idea what goes on. You think because you come back for ten minutes that you can mess about with people, don't you?'

'I don't think that.'

'You do. You think I'm not good enough for you. As soon as you get back into your posh telly job I'm not good enough all of a sudden. You'll want someone who's been to university and who's read all them books. So off you go with some university woman, see if I care. But don't come telling me what I've got to go back to. You have no idea what it's like.'

'I do. I'm from round here too, you know. I was born here.'

'You might as well not have been. What's it like then to try and feed two young kids when neither of you have got a job? Come on, tell me, Mr Clever Clogs Cambridge University. How does it feel to lose your daughter because you can't afford the right vegetables? How does that feel? Tell me, come on.'

'I don't know.'

'No, you don't know. You might as well come from the moon. You haven't got a clue what goes on here any more. You haven't a bloody clue.'

'I'm sorry, Irene. I didn't mean it to be like this.'

Adam was talking for himself. He was saying that he had lost his capacity to walk on the wrong side of bridges. He was saying that Elizabeth would live in his head for a very, very long time.

The dinner hour was almost through. Irene and Adam, now

in silence, walked back through the railway tunnels and down the muddy ginnel back to the mill. Adam stopped Irene outside the reception and took her in his arms. He leant forward and, ashamed of himself, planted a valedictory kiss on her red lips.

'I know you're right. Sorry, sweetheart.'

As Irene mounted the steps into the reception and Adam turned to the left to take the back entrance, neither of them noticed a man holding a long brown envelope and a carved wooden box, a hundred yards away on the bank of the River Irwell. Kevin stopped in amazement at what he saw before turning away and retracing his steps from whence he had come, his head filling with the law of retaliation.

Kevin walked back and forth over the bridge, feverishly angered by the tramp who worked in the mill. He crossed the bridge and back six, seven times, staring down into the effluent of the Irwell. On his final crossing Kevin paused and threw down the crafted box that he had been bringing as a present for his wife. All his calculations, plans and dreams were floating away, sunk to the bed of the broth underneath the familiar bridge.

Kevin had clocked in that morning and sat down at the communal table for his morning tea, cigarettes and tits. He was still on his only page when Joey Brown came out of his office and told Kevin he wanted to see him straight away. Kevin feared the worst. The order book had not been full lately. All the men seemed to spend longer these days at the table in the office consuming tea and tabloid pornography. Kevin was not privy to any of the firm's senior negotiations but there had been rumours for weeks now that they were in trouble.

'Sit down, lad.'

Kevin sat down.

'How's tricks?' asked Joey, prolonging the agony.

'Not bad, I suppose.'

'How are things going?'

'Yeah, all right.'

'Only all right?'

'No, good.'

Kevin was irritated by Joey's gnomic questioning. He preferred to cut to the quick.

'Why don't you just come out with it and stop all this bollocks?'

Joey smiled good-naturedly.

'OK then, sunshine, I will.'

Joey stood up and walked from behind his formica desk over to the metal safe in the far corner of the office. He twiddled the knob three times, some secret number known only to himself and to Bob Matthews, and pulled out a brown envelope which he threw down onto the table in front of Kevin.

'There you go. It's in there.'

Kevin opened the envelope distractedly and pulled out one hundred pounds in brand-new ten pound notes.

'It's your Christmas box.'

Kevin did not know what to say. He sat there with a hundred pounds in his hand, breathing heavily and saying nothing.

'You've grafted well since you joined us. That's your Christmas present from the firm. Happy Christmas, Kevin.'

'Thanks, Mr Brown. Thanks a lot.'

It was the proudest moment of Kevin McDermott's life since he had signed on at Bury FC. He felt like the hat-trick hero of Brangy Warriors. As Kevin got up to leave the room, bursting with self-esteem, Joey spoke again, in an uncharacteristic whisper.

'Oh and Kevin, I'm sorry about that misunderstanding we had. Are we quits now?'

'Quits.'

Kevin had occupied himself by sitting still all morning. At dinnertime he had decided to surprise his wife with a hundred pounds and a lovely wooden box, crafted by an artistically gifted man who had spent most of his adult life eating fried breakfasts and fitting ducting. Now the box was floating away towards Manchester and Kevin was heading for the door of reception.

He burst through, his muddied boots leaving a trail on the pristine carpet. Irene was not in her usual seat. The only person there, lazily slumped into one of the armchairs for waiting guests, was Tez Satchel. Tez looked up from his newspaper and saw, with one glance at Kevin's face, that the kindred spirit they had once shared was alive and well.

'What's up?' asked Tez without need of any preliminaries.

'Seen Irene?'

'She went out a minute ago. She was upset about something. Why, what's going on?'

'Adam Matthews around?'

'He's in the office. He's leaving. Why?'

'He's what's up. That cunt.'

'He's all right. What's he done?'

'He's fucking shagging my wife. That's what he's fucking done.'

'Fucking hell.'

'I'm going to fucking twat him, I'm telling you.'

'Come here.'

Tez abandoned his temporary stewardship of reception to lead Kevin through the back door which gave out onto the car park. This was the door nearest to Adam's office, the door he usually left by, when he wasn't at the front flirting with Irene. The lazy postman, after an adult lifetime of temporary employment, suddenly rediscovered his element.

Tez was mastermind of the project. Kevin supplied the animus but Tez supplied the brains. Tez had noticed that the mill car park was obscured by the railway bank on one side and a wrought iron fence on the other. Kevin had once lain in agony all night twenty yards away, the victim of retribution. Unless someone in the management office happened to be looking out of the window at the time, entrants to the car park were invisible. Tez and Kevin leant against the back wall of the factory, saying nothing. Kevin was already late but he was not going back until this business was sorted out. Then the door opened slowly and Adam came out, carrying a sports bag in which he was carrying his life back to the world beyond the television screen. Kevin and Tez were standing to one side of the door, invisible to anyone leaving the building.

'Sneaking out the back, are you?'

Adam recognised the voice at once. He dropped the bag and looked at Kevin. Neither spoke. For a moment it seemed that nothing would happen. Then Tez took over. He grabbed Adam by the lapels and dragged him across the car park onto the railway bank. Adam struggled but he was no match for Tez Handbag; he never had been. Tez dumped him down in the sodden valley of the old railway line and the cold, muddy water irreparably damaged his tan jacket and white shirt. As soon as Adam's back hit the ground Kevin waded in with a torrent of vicious punches to the face, to the stomach, to the lower abdomen.

'That's for touching my wife, you posh fucking cunt.'

That much was the law of revenge. But that is as far as the law goes. Tez, finally revealing why he had been for a long time the Cock of all Bury, knew no bounds. Amongst the clutter of the disused Bolton-to-Heywood railway line Tez spotted a discarded petrol can. As Kevin continued his tirade at the prostrate Adam, Tez ran down the line to pick up his treasure. He shook the can to find it was half full. He handed it to Kevin.

'Go on. Teach the fucker a real lesson.'

Adam was too frightened to resist. But now he whimpered a plea: 'Please release me, let me go.'

Now unwilling to lose face in front of intimidating, out-of-control Tez, Kevin drenched Adam with the contents of the can. Adam's fear reinvigorated his dervish attempts to release himself from Tez's practised grip. Kevin took the matches from the pocket of his jeans. He lit a match and held it up to the sky. The whirling limbs of Adam's struggle gave him an idea.

'Dance, you bastard. Go on, dance.'

With each repetition of the word 'dance', Kevin dummied to throw the match, sending Adam into ever more frenetic gymnastics, interspersed with cries of pain, as Kevin sank his foot into Adam's choir-boy smile. As the blood sped down Adam's chin, Kevin dummied a final time to drop the match and Adam gave out a piercing scream. That was enough for Kevin. He had wanted Adam at his feet begging for mercy and now he had it. He blew the match out and instructed Tez to let him go. After ten minutes on the wet ground Adam struggled to his feet, collected his bag of belongings and staggered home to wash off the stagnant water which had been poured all over him from an old petrol can.

A Stain on your Overalls

Kevin did not return for his afternoon shift. He gave up the wheel of fortune without explanation and walked the wet streets of Bury town centre instead. He caught a glimpse of his father at the pool table in the Roach Fold Inn but decided not to join him. Kevin walked, back and forth across the river, tortured by the loss of Irene.

After the *revanche* mission had been accomplished, after the cuckold had been unceremoniously dumped on the railway marsh, remorse crept stealthily upon Kevin. He knew that the received response was to throw Irene out of the house. But he didn't want to lose her. And he didn't want to lose Jason, the only person on earth who thought he was the best. From out of the fog enveloping his head Kevin drew no conclusions. He walked, as a substitute for resolution, in concentric circles of decreasing diameter, around the pile of crumbling bricks which once formed the house of the tramp who lived at the top of the tower. Wet and confused, Kevin crossed the river a final time. He crossed over the railway bank and crept through a vandal's gap in the fence into work.

The office appeared to be empty despite the unlocked door. Kevin took off his overalls and washed his hands. He threw his work clothes untidily into his locker and snapped the metal door shut. As he lifted the latch of the front door Kevin noticed that it too was not locked. Before he could leave, Bob Matthews came out of Joey Brown's office. Kevin noticed that Bob was grimacing in pain as he spoke.

'Where've you been?'

'Out.'

'Kevin, have you been crying?'

'You what?'

'Your eyes are red.'

'No, I'm all right. Have you hurt your arm?'

'It's nothing. I've got a bit of pain in my joints. It comes and goes. You have been crying, haven't you?'

'No, honest. I'm all right.'

Bob walked towards Kevin, who did not move. Bob clenched Kevin's head tight, holding him with his powerful hand, fixing on the neck just below his ears. Kevin's jaw shook with the effort of controlling his emotions.

'Tell me.'

'It's nowt.'

'It's not that. If you don't want to discuss it that's fair enough. But it's obvious there's something up.'

Bob strengthened his grip on Kevin's head then let his arms fall to his side. He scratched his bald head, furrowed his brow very deliberately and strode towards the door.

'Make sure you lock up. You know where the keys are. Do the back as well.'

'Bob?'

'Yes, lad?'

'Can I talk to you?'

'You know that. What's happened now? Is it work?'

'No.'

'So home then?'

'Yes.'

'The kids?'

'No.'

'Irene?'

'Yes.'

'Well?'

Kevin swallowed and stared down at the floor.

'Are you splitting up?'

'I don't know.'

338

'So Irene's not leaving then?'

'I don't know.'

'So what is it?'

'She's got someone else.'

'But has she said she's leaving?'

'No.'

'Have you talked to her about it?'

'No, not yet.'

'Well you must.'

'I will.'

'What are you going to do?'

'Chuck her out, I suppose.'

'Are you sure?'

'Suppose.'

Bob paused to take a deep breath.

'You don't have to leave her.'

'Why not? What else can I do?'

'You could do nothing.'

'How do you mean?'

'I don't know the details, Kevin. It sounds like you don't know much either so it's hard to comment. But you've got to talk to her. You've got to find out if it's serious or if it's just a stupid thing. We've all done stupid things, you know, and maybe it's just one of those. You've done stupid things in your time and so have I. If my wife had taken the same attitude as you're taking I probably wouldn't be here today and our Adam certainly wouldn't.'

'Why not?'

'I don't need to spell it out, Kevin. It was a long time ago and it's best forgotten. Or at least, it's best forgiven. If you can. Can you forgive Irene, Kevin?'

'I don't know. Should I?'

'It's not about whether you should. It's about whether you can.'

'I don't know. After what she's done.'

'Look Kevin. Think about it like this. It's like a stain on your overalls. Now they're all but brand-new and you dive out of the

339

way of the dirt so you don't get mess on them. But then you get a stain on them and you hate it because it ruins your brand-new overalls. But a year from now the stain will have faded. You wash it a bit and it'll fade away and then ten years from now you'll barely see it. If you look closely you'll still be able to see it. If you want to see it you can. But you don't have to look that hard, you see, Kevin. You don't have to look. It's up to you.'

There was a long silence.

'Thanks, Bob.'

As Kevin closed the door behind him Bob called him back.

'Who was it, lad?'

Kevin looked straight at Bob. He paused and then, when he began to speak, stuttered.

'I . . . It . . . I . . . It doesn't matter. Forget it. It's been dealt with.'

Irene knew nothing of any of this. She did not know that Kevin had seen her exchange a final kiss with Adam. She did not know that her husband and his childhood mentor had made their disapproval plain to Adam on the railway bank. Irene had spent the afternoon filing, answering the telephone and asking visitors to sit in reception. She was annoyed with Adam but not unduly upset. Fey sensitivity of the down-London kind had the power to turn Irene's head for a single kiss but she knew anguish greater than this. Irene Bradshaw knew anguish by its first name.

Irene was already at home with Wendy, Sammy, Jason and Susan when Kevin arrived. He ignored his mother's greeting and addressed Irene directly.

'I need to talk to you.'

'Well go on then.'

'On your own.'

'Why? What is it?'

Kevin did not want an audience.

'Upstairs.'

Back in the cold bedroom, with the foul wind rattling the loose window frames, Kevin fought to save his marriage through visible gasps of his own nervous breath. His voice fell strangely

340

at the end of the sentence, as though he were asking a question.

'I know about you and Adam.'

'There's nothing to know.'

Irene moved away from Kevin, marginally, instinctively. Irene had known violence from the four hands of two lovers. Instead of approaching her, Kevin withdrew. He leant back against the door, almost nonchalant, and waited for an explanation, which did not come. He prompted.

'Aren't you going to say anything?'

'There's nothing to say.'

'I saw you.'

'You've got it wrong. It's nothing.'

'Is it?'

'Yes, I promise. It is. Really. It was nothing and it's finished.'

Kevin paused, to remind himself how much he was in debt to Irene. His question surprised her.

'What are you going to do?'

'Nothing, I don't think. What are *you* going to do?'

'This.'

Kevin moved athletically towards Irene who recoiled. She ran back four steps until she hit her back hard against the wall, at which she gave out a quiet cry of fright. Kevin advanced upon her, raised his hand to her face, and stroked it gently. Kevin pulled Irene to him, pawed her hair in his hands and kissed her trembling lips.

'Don't do that again. Don't. Promise. I love you. I do. Don't do it.'

'I won't. I won't. Promise. I promise.'

Kevin declared the issue dead. But there was always a stain on his overalls, always a stain.

Peace and Quiet

That same evening Adam had arranged to accompany his parents to church. It was a frosty night, teasing with the illusion that the morning might bring a white Christmas to conform with the card industry. Every Christmas Eve when he was a small boy Adam had gone to midnight mass. He hadn't been now for ten years.

To a young boy, St Thomas's Church had seemed preternaturally dark. The candles carried in by the choir had lent it a magical look. As Adam had squinted through the dark to the pews, St Thomas's had always been full to the rafters. Even better, the music was transformed from the year-round dirge into a fantastic sing-along: 'Hark the Herald Angels Sing', 'Once in Royal David's City', 'O Come All ye Faithful' and, Adam's favourite, 'In the Bleak Midwinter'. Half-way through the midnight mass the Reverend Truman had declared that it was now Christmas and the choirboys had exploded with excitement led by the head chorister, Adam Matthews.

Adam was still intact after his beating but parts of his face were changing colour. He decided to ascribe his injuries to an especially violent game of football. There was no prospect he could let his mother down by not attending the midnight service and he was due to spend Christmas Day back at home anyway, as he had done every year of his life without exception.

Adam was late setting off and met his mother, looking anxiously at her watch, in the church porch. Bob had already gone through into the vestry to get into his cassock and surplice.

June and Adam slipped into the back row which afforded a view across the sparse congregation. Church seemed so much *lighter* than it once had. Adam could have sworn that, back in his day, it was pitch-black. Suddenly St Thomas's Church seemed so much smaller, so much less imposing and the congregation, still the same faces, looked old and weary. Maybe the pews had never really been bursting with Brangy warriors as Adam had squinted through the darkness years before. St Thomas's Church *had* declined in the interval between Adam's day in the choir and his return this Christmas Eve. The congregation had aged, as people do, but the dear departed had not been replaced by a younger generation. The songs were every bit as good, though, and Adam sang as lustily as ever.

'Snow had fallen, snow on snow, snow on snow. In the bleak midwinter, long ago.'

The new-fangled Reverend Newbold declared that it was now Christmas. Adam just felt sad. Of all the ghosts conjured up by the decline of St Thomas's the most vivid was that of Elizabeth, who had never been there.

Adam had never known how to approach Communion. He felt hypocritical going up for the sheer joy of a sip of sherry. But he did not want to offend his parents, so he usually let his theological objections pass. As he walked through the chancel Adam looked over to smile at his father in the choir stalls. Illuminated by the light of the sanctuary lamp, the dark shades made by Kevin's fists stood out on the skin beneath Adam's eyes.

After the service was over Adam lingered in the porch with his mother who was hugging the whole congregation, wishing it Happy Christmas. He wasn't sure if some of the older people still knew who he was. They did, of course. But Adam stood off, shy at being close to people he had left behind a very long time before. After a couple of minutes standing like a spare part in the church porch, Adam felt a hand on his shoulder. It was the Reverend Truman, back from exile in Bolton for the night after taking an early retirement.

'I hear you've done very well for yourself, young man. We always knew you'd make something of yourself. Yes, we always knew you'd get on. Can I introduce you to David Newbold?'

After a sticky start the Reverend Newbold had slowly gained the trust of the St Thomas's congregation. He had abandoned his early plans to abolish the Mothers' Union, the young wives' club and the amateur dramatics group. The Reverend Newbold had become a thoroughly conventional vicar which was exactly what the votaries of St Thomas's had wanted in the first place.

'Happy Christmas,' said Adam, avoiding the compliment and the introduction.

The congregation gradually dispersed. June went back into church to kneel in the back pew. So lost was she in contemplation that she did not notice Adam's arm draped comfortingly around her shoulder. Adam smiled and, again, had the wisdom to say nothing. June and Adam sat for five minutes in silence, all alone in their church, in the presence of the ghosts of their lives. Adam liked to be surrounded by noise. Silence made him think about Elizabeth. June rose to go but Adam held out his hand to indicate that he had something to say.

'Mum, I love you. Happy Christmas.'

'Happy Christmas, love. What have you done to your face?'

'I got it playing football.'

'Let's have a look. Oh, it's proper bruised. Who did that to you?'

'It's nothing.'

'It doesn't look like nothing.'

'Oh Mum, stop being so soft.'

'Have you had the doctor out?'

'I'll go down to Peel when I get a chance.'

The vestry door opened and the choir came out from the mince pies and sherry reception that always took place after midnight mass. Bob looked hard at his boy and asked him, in a tone that brooked no lies, what had happened to his face.

'I got it playing football earlier.'

'How?'

'It was a clash of heads when we went up for a header.'

Bob said nothing until the three of them arrived home. June poured the drinks and heated the mince pies.

'Happy Christmas, love.'

'Happy Christmas. Happy Christmas, son. Now come on, let's hear about that shiner of yours. Who's been battering you?'

'It was just a clash of heads with one of the blokes I worked with. It was an accident.'

'I don't believe you.'

'Oh leave it for now, Bob. It's Christmas Day.'

'That's no excuse for lying.'

'I'm not lying.'

'You don't get that sort of black eye from banging heads. Someone's given you a bloody good whack, haven't they?'

'No, there was nothing . . .'

'Adam, I wasn't born yesterday, you know. Now come on, stop lying.'

'Look, don't get too excited but I got jumped earlier on as I was coming home.'

'Oh, Adam, love.'

'Who by?'

'I don't know. I didn't see them.'

'Them?'

'There were two of them.'

'And you didn't even get a glimpse of them?'

'It all happened really quickly. It's a bit of a blur. And they got me from behind so I didn't see them coming.'

'Come off it, Adam.'

'I didn't see them at all.'

'It was Kevin, wasn't it?'

'What?'

'Wasn't it?'

Adam's silence betrayed him. Exposed before his parents, Adam was again a boy being called in early from hide-and-seek.

'It was Kevin, wasn't it?'

'Adam. Was it Kevin who did this?'

'Yes, Mum. It was Kevin. And his mate. They jumped me down by the mill as I was leaving.'

'Have you told the police yet?' asked Bob, with stress on the final word.

'No, not yet.'

'But you are going to?'

'I don't know.'

'You must. You absolutely must. It's beyond the pale, is that.'

Bob stared at his son with a hardness that Adam had not seen since he was a young boy.

'We'll ring the police first thing in the morning.'

'You can't do that on Christmas Day, Bob,' June interrupted.

'I can and I will.'

'Can't you leave it?'

'No.'

'Why did he have to go and do that anyway, Adam?'

Adam could not bring himself to tell his mother. He hoped his silence would speak for itself.

'Why, Adam? What's the matter with you and Kevin?'

'Because of how friendly he's been getting with young Irene.'

'Is that it, Adam?'

June repeated her question.

'Adam? Is that it?'

Adam could not reply.

'Adam. I can't believe you'd do that. I thought we'd brought you up better than that.'

'I'm sorry; I was just confused. And anyway, it was nothing.'

'That's not good enough. It's pathetic.'

'Well, Dad, I felt pathetic. I needed to do something to get Elizabeth out of my head.'

'But how's getting friendly with young Irene going to help that?'

'I don't know. It's not like I've been sleeping with her.'

'That's not how Kevin sees it. Adam, you've got to start dealing with this properly.'

'It's easy for you to say that.'

'You won't say a word about it. Why don't you talk to me or your mum?'

'I've got nothing to say about it. I was in love and she left me and now I feel like I might as well die.'

'Don't get so stupid.'

'It's not stupid. How do you know what it's like?'

'You can't mope about Elizabeth all your life, son.'

'I'm not moping.'

'You are. Leaving your job at the first sign of trouble. You've a lot of growing up to do yet, son.'

'I didn't want to stay there. It didn't feel right there.'

'You're not even trying to pull yourself out of it. You can't let Elizabeth ruin your career.'

'You just didn't like her.'

'That's got nothing to do with it.'

'Oh, so you didn't then?'

'It's irrelevant.'

'No, come on; you might as well tell me what you thought.'

'Don't, Adam,' said his mother.

'No come on, Dad; I want to hear it. What does Bury wisdom say about Elizabeth, then, eh?'

'You know I thought she was a bit of a fly-by-night.'

'Meaning what, exactly?'

'She was a bit flighty. Never one for settling.'

'You don't know what you're talking about.'

'I do. I'd seen her sort before.'

'Dad. You don't know what you're talking about.'

'I bloody well do. I've seen all sorts and I've seen her kind.'

'Oh, shut up will you?'

'Do not tell me to shut up in my own house. You keep a civil tongue in your head.'

'Oh, shut the fuck up, will you? Just fucking shut up. You don't know what the fucking hell you're on about but you carry on like you're the fount of all fucking wisdom.'

'I won't have this. We'll have some peace and quiet around here.'

And after this last word Bob stormed from the room, slamming the door behind him as he all but ran for the stairs. Bob had climbed three steps when he was attacked. With his right hand clutching his forehead in vain Bob toppled back down from whence he had come and hit the bottom step with an unmistakable and mortal thud. June gave out a terrified exhalation, immediately certain. Adam sprang from his chair and was the first of the two to reach him, now motionless on the floor of the hall. Frantically, Adam lifted his father's head and felt the life remaining. And then, without ever regaining consciousness enough to utter a word, Bob Matthews passed away, on the cold stairs in the arms of his only son.

The Brangy Aristocracy

After the ambulance had taken Bob's stone body to its dignity, Adam and his mum sat through the early Christmas morning in the unheated cold of the kitchen, June chain-smoking and the both of them chain-tea-drinking.

'Shall I put the radiator on, Mum?'

'No, love. I'm not mithered.'

It seemed fitting that the radiators should be left off. It was what Bob would have wanted. As dawn peeked through the dark, the lights came on over the Harwood estate as young children ripped through the paltry presents that had been left in stockings on their beds by Father Christmas. June locked the doors and took the telephone off the hook. She cooked the turkey that she had bought for the three of them. At dinnertime June turned the screw on their annual bottle of sparkling white wine. Adam and his mum sat, staring into space, to the unheard accompaniment of Christmas television shows.

The funeral was set for New Year's Eve at 2pm. It would be held, of course, at St Thomas's and it would be conducted by the Reverend Truman. June could not face the arrangements so Adam took to the telephone. It was a massive task, as he only discovered when he began. Every call led to another. Every person Adam spoke to told him not to forget old so-and-so who would also want to pay his last respects. The Brangy warriors were kind and understanding and very generous in their appreciation of Adam's father. It took Adam three days to make it through the list his mother had prepared and the subsidiary list he had engendered himself.

Adam and June arrived in the church last, at June's request. The Brangy nobility was packed into pews as Adam linked arms with his mother, suddenly so small and frail, suddenly her brown hair flecked with grey, suddenly an old woman. Adam led his mother down the aisle to the unaccustomed position of the front pew. As he turned to go back outside to be an urn bearer, the phalanx of hard-faced men in their black Sunday best hit him right behind the eyes. St Thomas's was full of Brangy aristocrats. The only one who could remember the last time he had set foot in church had once been expelled for revealing himself in the vestry.

Adam swallowed hard, lifted his head into the world above eye level, and walked proudly back down the aisle. As he did so, one man after another stepped silently out of the pews to shake him by the hand. It was already clear that Bob Matthews was worth so much more than the three thousand pounds and thirty-three pence fortune he left to his wife. Only in death did Adam realise his father's true standing. The name of Bob Matthews would be entered in the Book of Remembrance and would not be forgotten. The congregation rose, men, women and children blinking hard, as Adam followed the Reverend Truman towards the altar, carrying a small urn in which he held the ashes of his deceased father.

The service flew past. Adam gripped tightly onto his mother's hand as the tears streamed down her face. The soaring voices of St Thomas's raised the roof with 'Cwm Rhondda' in memory of the man who so loved this uplifting tune. With the dying fall of the last note June looked at Adam and whispered: 'He knew, you know. He didn't know I knew too. But the doctor told me.'

Adam held onto his composure, for his mother's sake. He endured a lump pressing right through the taut skin of his throat but he came through with dry eyes. The euphonious words of the service made him wistful about Elizabeth but he held on. It was an exhibition of mastery.

And then as Adam and his mother walked back through the knave, following the urn out of the church, following the ashes of his father which were about to be sprinkled in the rose garden, he saw Kevin sitting apart from his family and weeping proudly. Adam swallowed hard to no avail. By the time the procession was outside his face was awash with tears and contorted by pain. Adam held his jaw firm as the mourners gathered in the rose garden to see Sir Robert Matthews committed to his grave.

The congregation trooped in Shaun Masters's cars up the Bolton road to the Greenhill Working Men's Club for the wake. June and Adam were welcomed at the door by Bill, newly anointed as head of the committee after Albert had passed away peacefully with his dancing girl by his side. The parade of cheap black cotton brought the whole event to June who sat at the front surrounded by sausage rolls and cheese straws, with a constantly replenished glass of whisky. Adam walked the room, thanking everyone for coming. In the corner, talking distractedly to his parents and clinging very firmly to the hand of his wife, Kevin watched Adam closely.

Adam's tour of the club produced a fund of anecdotes. He was surprised, but oddly pleased, to learn that Bob had been a tearaway in his youth, that he had almost gone into care because his parents had neither the money nor the energy to handle such a boisterous child, especially when Adam's grandfather lost his job sewing Egyptian cotton on the banks of the River Irwell. There were tales of Bob's brother Tommy who died in infancy, of Bob at football matches, of Bob sneaking away from June for a secret Newcastle Brown or ten, of Bob winning a few quid on the horses and not mentioning it to his wife.

The most telling story came from Mrs Rudd, Adam and Kevin's old primary school teacher, who had taught them about the Romans and times tables. Mrs Rudd recalled Bob marching in to confront her on why Adam had stopped getting twenty-four out of twenty-four *every* time. She remembered Adam's trail of stars across the night sky. But, as she took a seat two tables away, Mrs Rudd was unable to disinter the specific memory of Kevin McDermott, buried as it was alongside so many others of its kind.

Everyone sought for the story that captured Bob and everyone told tales of a man that Adam did not recognise. To Adam, Bob was his dad who went to work, who painted the house, who planted flowers, who sang in the choir and who sat in the garden shed. Adam indulged the stories, feigning amusement. Brangy warriors draped in black ate pork pies and drank mild in memory of one of their own. Adam joined his mother, alone at the table with her whisky. June's sorrow was too deep for Adam to connect.

'Do you mind if I go for a walk, Mum? I need some fresh air.'

'No, you go on, love.'

Adam set off across the Harwood estate for the path down to the tunnels and the mill by the river. As he crossed the Bolton road he did not notice that Kevin, who had been watching him for the past ten minutes, was following on behind.

Adam walked down through the tunnels where the bats were hanging, past the site of his old den, towards the mill where the tramp lives. Suddenly the gradual and fractional changes that the five years had visited on the topography of his home town appeared before him, speeded up as in a wildlife film. The infant school that he had gone to before St Thomas's was being knocked down to make way for luxury housing. The physical world of Adam's childhood had disappeared in his absence. He found himself echoing his father by thinking how recently all this used to be fields. This was the sign of ageing and extirpation. Adam saw with great clarity that he was one of the long line of glory boys who packed up the spotted hankie and set off down roads sixty-two, six and one.

The past was now irretrievably lost. Adam had no photographs of his life. He had torn up the hopes captured on Trinity Bridge. He had no photographs of himself as a child and none of his mother and father. He had no photographs of Elizabeth. She had kept the few they ever took, the record of Paris. Adam had no photographs of himself at all. He had a higher opinion of himself than cameras did. The only prompt Adam had to recall the whole of his life was the faulty record of his own memory.

Adam stood on the disused railway line and looked out over the Pennines. For the second time in his life Adam noticed that

Bury is framed by hills. Of course he knew it was framed by hills but he had never really *noticed*. Somewhere in his mental journey he had acquired the capacity to lift his eyes up from the road. Turning to the left, he was struck by a sense of unusual space. The huge factory that had always sat at the bottom of the hill had gone, replaced by a DIY store with a garish fascia, advertising itself to the cars that flashed by on the newly widened and revamped traffic interchange that ran by the old bridge over the River Irwell. Further on, snuggling up to the horizon, the skyline, which used to be divertingly jagged, cut into crenellated pieces by the rough edges of the metal factory and the paper company fortress, had been flattened into a retail park. Adam wondered what had become of the men who had clocked into the factory day after day, fathers of his generation, trained only in the skills the world left behind.

Adam picked out Brown's Plumbers and Joiners in the trough in the valley where the Peel family had once lived. His father had spent the last fifteen years of his working life in this little yard. Adam lifted his eyes towards Jericho to look at the old mill, to discover, with audible shock, that the bulldozers were moving in to sweep it away. All that remained of the old mill where the tramp lived was a pile of crumbled bricks and mortar on the useless, worthless, rutted ground by the side of the fetid river. In the absence of photographs the old mill now exists only in Adam's mental picture, sepia-tinted, saturated with the excitement of discovering the tramp but tempered by the weary adult knowledge that there never was any tramp.

As Adam stood, thinking of the tramp and of his father, he was startled by a voice he recognised at once.

'Adam?'

Adam turned to find Kevin on the other side of the railway bank, biting his top lip and staring down at the flattened grass. Adam froze as Kevin approached. Kevin kept coming until their faces were barely a foot apart and they were staring right into each other's eyes.

'I want to tell you summat.'

'What is it?'

Kevin stumbled. Words failed him, briefly.

'If it's Irene, I don't . . .'

'It's not.'

'So what is it then?'

'I just wanted to say that . . .'

Kevin stopped. He looked beyond Adam, to collect himself.

'He was a good 'un, was your dad. He was a fucking good 'un. He got me working, did you know that?'

Adam replied in a whisper.

'Yes, I know.'

'He did more for me than anyone did. He was the only one who fucking cared.'

'I cared.'

'No, you didn't. Once you'd got off out of here you didn't really give a fuck any more. No reason why you should. I wish I could fuck off sometimes. But your old man looked out for me. He was there. Always. When I needed help, he was there.'

Adam, for too long consumed by his own problems, did not realise that Kevin did not have to leave Bury to go on a journey. When Adam had left Bury to seek his fortune, Kevin had stayed to be denied his. Kevin had learnt how to decline while Adam had learnt how to decline a verb. Kevin reached inside his wedding suit jacket and offered Adam a brown envelope.

'Your dad gave me this.'

'What is it?'

'A school report.'

'What's it say?'

'I don't know.'

'Why not?'

Kevin looked down, away from Adam, down at the floor.

'I just don't.'

Adam suddenly realised that Kevin could not read properly. He recalled all the occasions that he had read aloud from *Roy of the Rovers*. Kevin could not read the lesson that Bob, his strength and shield, had left for him.

Adam took the envelope from Kevin and opened it. He found an old school report from 1943 for a young pupil called Robert

Matthews. The paper was yellowed but well preserved, as though it had barely been opened in half a century. The paper was marked with florid handwriting in dark-blue ink.

'Read it for us, will you?'

Adam cleared his throat and read out the prognosis of his father's life from when he had been a little boy of eight years.

Robert Matthews, Class 4. Robert has made a very poor effort this term. He shows very little appetite for work and struggles to keep up in Arithmetic and English. At his current rate of progress I very much fear for Robert's future prospects. Robert is very boisterous and very easily distracted. He needs to apply himself more. As a child who is not naturally the most gifted Robert is likely to face severe problems when he leaves St Thomas's. Grade E. Signed Mr Goldthorpe, Headmaster, June 1943.

Adam looked up at Kevin whose face was crumbling with grief. Adam and Kevin both understood the gearing mechanism of their lives. Adam had been born in the same Jericho hospital, a month and six days before Kevin. They had lived in back-to-back houses in which they could see their own breath. The touch on the gear stick had been all but imperceptible but its effect on their futures had been profound. Different gears, different paths, four hundred yards apart. The journey had been a lesson for the pair of them, a lesson in coming to terms, in finding a language in which the past made sense. This love, this intimacy will terminate here.

Kevin stared into Adam's eyes and held out his hand. Both of them breathed deeply, visibly in the biting cold. Suddenly taken aback, Adam was lost in Kevin's bear-hug, Kevin's flood of apologies, Kevin's love for Bob. Adam recalled the lost memory of the smell of Kevin's bright red hair. Adam held on tight to his oldest friend and resolved that, the memory of his father notwithstanding, he would let his bruises fade without the help of the police. It was no more, no less than telling a fib to Mrs Rudd.

'Blood brothers.'

'Yeah.'

Adam's reply was distant. He was away again, back down motorways sixty-two, six and one. Kevin broke away, hanging onto Adam's arm with both hands. Adam had once been Kevin's best man, his huckleberry friend. He had once been Kevin's second. It seemed a very long time ago. The pair of them began to walk together, dragging their feet over the stones. It seemed unusually quiet to them both. Perhaps it always was this quiet to adult ears. Perhaps they needed the sensitive ears of a child to hear the cacophony that they now only dimly recalled. Memory made a carnival of undistinguished streets. A child, in too high a gear, pedalled furiously by on the pavement.

The Harwood estate seemed smaller and less threatening, just empty, windswept and unkempt. Heavy trellis doors that would never be repaired rattled in the wind. The dustbins were out in force for collection day. Debris escaped from the bins and the rubbish blew away. A middle aged man walked slothfully by. A young girl, with her hair tied violently off her face in a style like a pineapple, pushed a pram along the pavement, stopping every few paces to swear at the naughty child she dragged along with her free hand. Something that looked like a squashed rat from a distance turned out to be a folded glove.

These streets had frightened Adam Matthews as a boy. Had he not been friends with Kevin McDermott he would have been scared to set foot on the Harwood. Today it looked what, in fact, it always was: an ugly but honourable estate for people buried in poverty. As Adam and Kevin looked at each other with tears in their eyes and apologies in their hearts, it was so difficult to see themselves in the two eleven-year-old boys who ran across them down the tunnel, two little drifters off to see the world, of which they were, so fleetingly, the undisputed Cocks.